PRAISE FOR VANESSA DEL FABBRO

"Del Fabbro, who was born and raised in South Africa, offers a fascinating window into the stark beauty and random violence that characterize the 'Rainbow Nation,' where racial hatred still threatens the fragile peace that has been won. Through dynamic characters and an unflinchingly honest perspective on human weakness, Del Fabbro concocts a winning story of the triumphant power of female friendship."
—*Publishers Weekly* on *The Road to Home*

"*The Road to Home* is a journey you won't want to miss. Its plot is ingenious. You'll peer into the lives of four patients who would never have met under any other circumstances. Hopefully, Ms. [Del] Fabbro's characters will stir the conscience of her readers and help them realize we are all children of God."
—*Rendezvous*

"Intricate, vivid and lyrical, a story that transposes the dark era of South African racial struggles with the healing brilliance of two women who risk everything to reach for each other, *The Road to Home* is an amazing first novel."
—Deborah Bedford, *USA TODAY* bestselling author of *When You Believe*

"I was deeply touched by Vanessa Del Fabbro's poignant account of an unlikely friendship in a brutal land. With lyrical prose, this gifted author illustrates Christ's great teachings about the true meaning of love. *The Road to Home* is both powerful and heartbreaking."
—Catherine Palmer, Christy® Award-winning author of *Leaves of Hope*

D0972211

Vanessa Del Fabbro

Sandpiper Drift

Steeple
Hill®

Published by Steeple Hill Books™

STEEPLE HILL BOOKS

Steeple
Hill®

ISBN-13: 978-0-373-78565-0
ISBN-10:   0-373-78565-8

SANDPIPER DRIFT

Copyright © 2006 by Vanessa Del Fabbro

For my mother, with love

Acknowledgments

I am so grateful to my wonderful agent, Helen Breitwieser, for her enthusiastic support, and my editors, Joan Marlow Golan and Melissa Endlich, for their smart direction and vision. I want to thank Joyce Zulu for sharing with me her knowledge of Zulu customs. As always, I thank my husband for being in my corner and my daughter for being the sweetest little piglet I ever could have wished for.

A Note from the Author

After my first book, *A Road to Home,* was published, many American readers commented that they would have appreciated a foreword giving some background on South Africa, where I grew up and where *A Road to Home* and this sequel are set.

A Road to Home was set in 1998, and *Sandpiper Drift* takes place two years later, in 2000, six years after the first democratic elections in South Africa that swept the African National Congress (ANC) into power.

In the early 1990s, following a long period of resistance by various antiapartheid movements, most notably the ANC, the white National Party government began to negotiate itself out of power, lifting the ban on the ANC and releasing its leader, Nelson Mandela, from prison after twenty-seven years. When South Africans of all races went to the polls in April 1994, apartheid was finally laid to rest after an infamous rule of forty-six years.

In the new South Africa, all people are free to live where they want, work in any field, marry whomever they want, say what they want and vote for any party. The majority of the country's people were not granted any of these basic rights under white rule.

In 2000, the fledgling democracy has seen more changes, most conspicuously in the highest office in the country. South Africa's beloved President Nelson Mandela has been succeeded by Thabo Mbeki. The shoes President Mbeki must fill are big, since just about all South Africans, black and white, credit Nelson Mandela with the wonder of a peaceful transition from apartheid to democracy.

The government continues its program of building new houses and bringing electricity and clean drinking water to the country's poor. New medical clinics have been opened, especially in rural areas where they are desperately needed. Life has improved for millions, but more than half the population still lives below the official poverty level of $53 U.S. a month, and around forty percent of black Africans are unemployed.

After decades of iniquity, change cannot come overnight, and the ANC aims to halve unemployment and poverty by 2014. If anything can sabotage this impressive goal, it is the monumental AIDS crisis facing the country. In 2000, the year in which *Sandpiper Drift* is set, South Africa held the dubious distinction of having more HIV-positive citizens than any country in the world, with nearly 10 percent of the population infected. But unlike other African countries, such as Uganda, where the combination of AIDS education and antiretroviral drugs was proving successful, in 2000 President Mbeki was publicly questioning the link between HIV and AIDS, as well as the value of these drugs, and he refused to provide them to infected pregnant women, when to do so would halve the rate of transmission of the disease to their babies or even reduce it by two thirds. While he deliberated, thousands of babies were needlessly born with HIV.

The high level of crime, especially violent crime, continues to cause outrage among all South Africans. In most countries the leading cause of nonnatural death is automobile accidents, but in South Africa in 2000 it is murder. Many well-off South Africans choose to emigrate to escape the crime. Some of those who stay behind take the law into their own hands.

The advantage of reading a novel that's set a few years back is that we know how these issues progress and whether the problems are resolved or not. For those of you who will be touched by the characters in this book as they face these issues on a personal level in their everyday lives, I urge you to turn to South African newspapers on the Internet as well as other Web sites, such as www.int.iol.co.za, www.mg.co.za and www.southafrica.net, to learn more about the country. There is one thing I can promise you—South Africa is not only beautiful, it is also fascinating.

❧ *Chapter One* ❧

Koppies, muted brown and dusty, fell off in gentle folds on both sides of the steep road they'd just ascended. Even with her sunglasses, Monica found the warm summer daylight achingly bright as she climbed out of the rental car and hopped onto a large boulder for a better view.

"Henry, you have to see this!" she called to the cameraman shooting the footage for the story she hoped would be her entrée into television journalism. Henry was asleep on the back seat.

Below lay a small town that was almost hidden from view by great swathes of colorful flowers.

"Bougainvillea!" exclaimed Henry, joining her on the boulder. "Like I've never seen them before."

Cerise, burnt orange, brilliant pink and sunshine yellow, they billowed over fences, walls and gates, weighed down veranda roofs, scaled tree trunks to take up residence in the branches and crept along telephone lines. What appeared to be a main street was lined with palm trees, as well as the persistent bougainvillea. With the sun reflecting off the green, blue and deep red tin roofs, the whole town had a bright glow, almost like a halo.

"I feel as though I'm in a glass-bottomed boat looking at a coral reef," said Monica, and Henry murmured in assent.

The sight was unexpected, especially as, since leaving Cape Town, they'd spent an hour and a half passing stubby clumps of reeds with small brown florets and shrubs with thin, leathery leaves. "Fynbos," Henry had explained, reading aloud from Monica's guidebook. It literally meant "fine bush" in the Afrikaans language.

On the western edge of the town a pile of rocks signaled the end of land and the beginning of the Atlantic. Large, jagged and precariously balanced, they were a sign that the ocean was not always this placid. Before Henry had fallen asleep he'd told her that less than a few hundred yards off the coast many wrecks lay covered in seaweed—breeding grounds for tuna, snoek and the great white shark.

On the northern edge of the town a lagoon stretched inland in the shape of a giant horizontal question mark. The tide was out and the mudflats surrounding it glistened in the sun.

Monica and Henry got back into the car, and as they began the descent past limestone outcrops, Monica opened her window just an inch to breathe in a grassy, lemony scent that was unfamiliar but quite pleasant. More than two years ago she'd been attacked by a carjacker, shot and left for dead. Like a stubborn stain, she could not erase from her mind the vision of those mirrored sunglasses and the drops of sweat sliding down the man's shaved head. The limp she had been left with in her right leg was a constant reminder. He had not been captured and she'd given up all hope that he ever would be. Her anxiety seemed silly in this bucolic place—after all, she'd been carjacked in Soweto, a sprawling dormitory town adjacent to Johannesburg, the largest city in South Africa—but it was almost involuntary, like her heart pumping blood.

The main street of the town was flanked with open ditches carrying streams of fast-running, clear water. Storefronts faced outward, their display windows shaded by tin roofs that covered the entire sidewalk. Potted pink and orange geraniums stood sentinel at uniform intervals. Outside the Lady Helen General Store, two white-haired men lounged on a bench, reading newspapers, a scruffy dog at their feet. A little farther along, a woman sat straight-legged on a blanket, rows of beaded jewelry and hair ornaments spread out in front of her. An infant lay cradled in her lap, nursing under a light, crocheted shawl.

"That's strange," said Henry, shaking his head. "There's no litter."

He was right—not even a single cigarette butt. The town gleamed like a much-loved home.

It seemed to Monica that many of the stores housed art galleries. Watercolor renderings of the local landscape dominated the displays, but there were also vivid abstract works, folk art, curvaceous stone sculptures and black-and-white photographs.

In Mama Dlamini's Eating Establishment people hunched shoulder to shoulder around a counter.

"Let's stop," said Henry.

"Dr. Niemand's expecting us," said Monica, trying to ignore the aroma of strong coffee.

Niemand. What a strange name. In Afrikaans it meant nobody.

Then she saw a sign for the hospital and concentrated on maneuvering her car around a donkey cart piled high with firewood. The driver tipped his faded black fedora at her, shook the reins and whistled at the donkey. The beast cocked its head as though it understood and then resumed its slow steady clip-clop.

The main street ended in a park that ran along the beachfront for about a quarter of a mile, palm trees forming a natural break between the neatly mowed lawn and the white sand. In the middle was a gently sloping grass amphitheater with a stage at the lowest level, and behind it a rock garden of poker-red aloes, dusty-pink pincushion proteas and delicate red African heather.

Monica slowed down as she passed the cemetery, as much to look at it as to give Henry time to finish combing his hair. There were few tombstones; instead, most graves were marked only with a pile of rocks. A wrought-iron fence of curlicues and ornate shields ran all the way around the perimeter, ending in an arched double gate topped with a row of fierce-looking spears.

Monica thought it strange that no expense had been spared on the gate and fence and yet there were so few tombstones. Could the cemetery have historical significance? In any case, she found it disconcerting that the cemetery was next door to the hospital.

The Lady Helen Hospital was an old farmhouse that had a wide covered veranda with a polished green concrete floor, a heavy wooden front door with a stained-glass inlay and a large brass knocker. A ginger cat lay sleeping on a canvas cushion atop a riempie bench whose crisscrossed leather straps sagged from years of use. As Henry stretched, groaning loudly, the cat opened one eye, then went back to sleep.

Monica lifted the brass knocker and let it fall. A minute went by and nobody came to the door. Inside they could hear loud, urgent voices.

"Give it another go," said Henry.

She did. Still nothing. Henry opened the door and put his head in.

"Hello."

"Take a seat on the left. I'll be with you in a minute," called a woman's voice.

Monica closed the door behind them. From the outside it may have looked like a farmhouse, but inside the smell was undeniably hospital, and immediately Monica thought of her own time in one. When she'd awakened in that crowded ward, she didn't think she'd be able to stand the pungent hospital smells. But the odor wasn't the only reason she'd wanted to be transferred: the hospital her taxi-driver rescuer had taken her to was in Soweto, and she'd been the only white patient in it.

A small boy shot past them, threw open the door and bounded across the veranda. From an office off the waiting room a nurse appeared and watched him disappear down the road.

"He'll never make it," she muttered before closing the front door.

Monica wished they'd gone into the café so they would have arrived after this crisis had played itself out.

"Excuse me," she said. "I'm looking for Dr. Niemand."

"We have an emergency," said the nurse. "You'll have to wait."

"No problem," said Henry, selecting a typist's chair from the motley assortment that lined the walls.

Monica chose a hard-backed kitchen chair and laid the bag with the mike, cables and recording paraphernalia at her feet.

The piece she was about to do for the newsmagazine program *In-Depth* needed to be her tour de force; the reporter Monica was filling in for had decided not to come back from maternity leave, and the editors were looking for a permanent replacement. If Monica was chosen, she'd have to resign from the reporting job she loved at the radio station, but for as long as she could remember her dream had been to work in television—and now, especially, the bigger salary would be welcome, because of her two adopted boys. Sipho and Mandla: her boys. She hadn't ever called them her sons and probably never would; they would always be Ella's sons. The dear friend Monica had made while in the hospital in Soweto had been gone a year, but not a day had passed in which she had not thought of Ella and her brave fight against the disease her husband had passed on to her.

Monica had wanted to do a story on crocodiles being airlifted out of Lake Saint Lucia because of the ongoing drought, but, after casually mentioning it to a cameraman, one of her colleagues was suddenly booking a ticket to Durban and arranging a four-by-four transfer to the Nibela Peninsula. Then a letter had arrived at the office, addressed to

Monica, with an invitation to see the new burn unit at a rural hospital in Lady Helen, an hour and a half's drive north of Cape Town. Monica had been touched by Dr. Niemand's frank admission that through television exposure he hoped to attract the funding needed to keep the unit going.

The nurse approached Monica. "Can I talk to you later, when this emergency is over and you're finished with Dr. Niemand?"

Monica nodded. "Of course."

"Hey, this would make a great dolly shot," called Henry, wheeling himself across the floor with the camera balanced on his shoulder.

The nurse stared at him as though he were an unruly student. Soon it became clear that she hadn't had much experience with anyone who didn't shrivel under her scrutiny, because she merely pulled her face in disgust and left the room.

The front door opened again and the little boy was back, wild-eyed, breathing hard and pulling on the hand of a woman who wore a man's shirt over her nightgown. She stumbled as they made their way across the room, but the boy did not slow down.

Ten minutes later a man wearing green scrubs appeared and stuck out his hand. "Monica Brunetti, I presume," he said. "I'm Zak Niemand."

Monica stood up to take his hand. "Pleased to meet you." She turned to Henry, who was drumming on the windowsill with two pens. "This is Henry Radebe, our cameraman."

The doctor was tall, about six foot three, with dark hair cut so short he could pass for a military man. He took off his small, rectangular glasses and rubbed his eyes. They were red-rimmed.

"I'm sorry, I don't have much time this morning. We just lost a patient. He was tending to a sick ram and reached into his bag to get out a medicine dropper when a snake bit him. Must have crawled in to get some shade. From the boy's description, we think it was a black mamba." The doctor shook his head. "The little fellow got his mother here just in time to say good-bye. Anyway, Sister Adelaide will show you the new burn unit—I have to speak to the family, make the arrangements."

A child had just lost its father, a woman her husband; what did a news story matter? Impressed at the way the doctor was prepared to give up the limelight, Monica shook his hand and thanked him for the invitation to Lady Helen.

Sister Adelaide was in her late thirties, of medium height and rather stout. Her white dress looked overly snug, suggesting a recent weight gain, but if she was at all uncomfortable, Sister Adelaide showed no outward sign of it. Quite the contrary, her movements were fluid and graceful and she seemed to glide across the room as she led them out the back door, across a patchy lawn and into the first of a jumble of prefabricated structures.

Sister Adelaide waved her hands as she talked, and the numerous silver bracelets she wore rode up and down her arm. Henry was mesmerized, and Monica had to remind him to set up his camera so they could begin filming. She quickly saw the advantage in using charming Sister Adelaide on camera. With her long braided hair and demure smile, she would be far more photogenic than the obviously exhausted Dr. Niemand.

After the interview they would film a few of the patients and then wrap up with a couple of exterior shots of the hospital. It seemed straightforward, but when Sister Adelaide led her to the first patient, Monica was shocked; she hadn't expected to see children in the ward. Why on earth hadn't she asked Dr. Niemand all the relevant questions in their preliminary telephone interview? And why had she assumed all the patients would be adults? Of course there would be children in a burn unit.

The little girl appeared to be watching her, but when Monica approached, she lowered her eyes as a sign of respect.

"This is Zukisa," said Sister Adelaide. "Her name means 'be patient.' She has third-degree burns from her chest down to her knees. The little angel hasn't shed a single tear since coming here."

Monica put out her hand to stroke the girl's forehead, but the fear in Zukisa's eyes made her withdraw it.

"Boiling water," said Sister Adelaide, anticipating Monica's question. "She was making the family's pap for the evening meal and tripped over a dish towel."

Monica looked at the small figure swaddled in gauze and thought of the children hanging upside down on the jungle gym at the park near her house, their smooth, pink bellies peeking out from under bright T-shirts.

"Where was her mother?" asked Monica, and then, realizing how accusatory that sounded, she made a mental note to edit it from the footage.

Sister Adelaide shook her head sadly. "Collecting mussels to sell to the restaurant at the golf course resort just north of here. They serve them in a white-wine sauce and charge eighty rand." She shook her head. "Imagine paying eighty rand for a plate of food! I can get a week's groceries for that. Zukisa's father works for a pilchard-canning company in Cape Town. He comes home on weekends, which is more often than when he worked on the mines in Johannesburg. Then he lived in a compound with hundreds of men from all over the country."

"You must know the family well," said Monica.

Sister Adelaide looked surprised. "Lady Helen is not a big place. You'll see." She stroked the child's arm as she spoke. "The skin grafts have taken amazingly well. Zukisa will be scarred, but she will have full body movement and be able to live a normal life."

She turned to the child and said something in Xhosa. Her words must have been encouraging because the girl smiled.

"I just told her we're having liver and onions for dinner," Sister Adelaide explained. "It's her favorite."

"Cut," said Monica, and Henry lowered his camera.

She did not want to leave Zukisa. She felt an urge to give the child something, but what?

Ever since she'd become an instant mother, Monica found herself crying pitifully when the news showed Red Cross volunteers in Angola and Mozambique weighing skeletal babies whose mothers had trekked miles on foot after their milk dried up. She found herself dropping coins into tiny upturned palms at every traffic intersection, whereas in the past she would have kept her window closed, resigned to the fact that there would never be enough to feed the millions of hungry mouths in Africa. She smiled in commiseration with red-faced mothers wrestling their screaming toddlers in the mall. Mandla had gone through that stage, too. Instead of the irritated stare she'd once reserved for those who brought their children to restaurants and movies, she now nodded in acknowledgment, as though they were all members of a sorority. "Welcome to the other side," a friend with three children had told her when she'd adopted the boys.

They interviewed one other patient, a boy who'd burned his face playing with fireworks. When they left, Dr. Niemand was delivering twins and Sister Adelaide said it was best not to wait; if there were no emergencies, he liked to wash and dress the new babies himself.

Monica pictured the tall doctor fitting tiny diapers onto the newborns, his big hands easing little undershirts over their newly washed bodies. The doctors she had come across in the hospital in Soweto never had the time for such tender involvement with their patients, even if they'd had the inclination—and she didn't believe many of them had. Dr. Niemand was clearly in need of sleep and yet here he was doing a nurse's job. She sensed that although his caring attitude seemed special to her, it was actually typical for Lady Helen, where every patient or customer or person waiting in line behind you was someone you knew and would meet again tomorrow or the next day. It would be wonderful for children to grow up in this close-knit community where people knew your name and cared about you. But it was only a daydream. Television reporters for national programs drew inspiration from the relentless beat of the city; they got their material by digging around in the muck, watching for the sparks from the friction of millions of people living in close proximity to each other. If this story on the Lady Helen

Hospital earned Monica a permanent place on the *In-Depth* team as she hoped it would, then Johannesburg was the only place for her.

As the airplane began its descent into Johannesburg International Airport the next morning, Monica looked out at the tangle of glass-and-steel skyscrapers in the distance and found her thoughts drifting back to the little town with the bougainvillea and palm trees. Nobody would think of planting geraniums—or any flowers, for that matter—in planters on the sidewalk in Johannesburg. They wouldn't be there the next morning. How sad it was, she thought, that the residents of Johannesburg and, indeed, the entire country, had lost the capacity to trust others with even the tiniest of God's creations.

❧ Chapter Two ❧

A thunderstorm had just blown through when Monica arrived home from the airport shortly before noon, but not a drop of rain had fallen. In her neighborhood north of the city, gardeners were out in force raking up lilac jacaranda blossoms on the sidewalks. They didn't have much else to do because the lawns, by now usually thick and green from regular summer rain, were a papery yellow from the drought. Mowers were brought out, only to be wheeled back in again in disgrace for the cloud of dust they created.

Yet another of her neighbors had topped his wall with electric fencing. She knew her mother would approve; it was more discreet than the broken glass used by one or two homeowners. Every house bore a sign announcing the name of a security company. Within minutes of being alerted, the armed men from these firms would screech up in their compact Korean cars. With the police stretched thin, a few hun-

dred rands a month was a small price to pay for peace of
mind. Of course, you could be carjacked at an entrance to
a highway, as Monica had been, or even getting out to open
your gate, as had happened to a couple two streets down a
few months ago.

Atop the perimeter wall the cerise bougainvillea Monica's
mother had planted almost fifteen years ago looked faded
and tattered. Thanks to the emergency water restrictions, it
was a shadow of its former glorious self. Monica didn't have
the heart to tell her mother that her garden was dying and
studiously avoided all mention of the weather in her letters
to her parents in Italy. She knew her mother wouldn't learn
about the drought from the media; a drought in Southern
Africa didn't feature prominently on world news agendas.
Maybe the rest of the world thought that because Africans
were used to droughts, they could cope. But why an African
might be better at surviving on less water than anyone else
she did not know.

Her father had settled in comfortably in the now exten-
sively renovated house of his birth in a little town on the
northwest coast of Italy. Although her mother never said as
much, Monica sensed that she had not. It had always been
her father's dream to take his family back to live in his home-
town, but the only way he had been able to accomplish it
was without his son and daughter.

Ella had said that the Brunettis' house reminded her of a
Greek island postcard. Together as a family, they'd designed
the white, flat-roofed building with its floor-to-ceiling windows, angles and interesting shadows, but Monica's brother,
Luca, had never seen it completed.

When Luca had finished high school, it was compulsory for all young white males to complete two years of military service. After his basic training, Luca was sent to the southern Angola-Namibia border, where South Africa was based for its interventions into Anglola's civil war.

From his letters it was clear that his troop wasn't doing much except waiting for orders. During the long, dusty days, the boys—for boys they were—amused themselves as best they could. The last thing Luca did in his nineteen-year-old life was run into the bush to catch a Frisbee. The land mine he stepped on had escaped his troop's reconnaissance.

The automatic garage door closed behind Monica, and she switched off her car. It was actually her mother's car; hers had been recovered after the carjacking but not before it was used in an armed robbery of a supermarket. Her father sold it because it was riddled with bullet holes.

As Monica lifted her suitcase out of the trunk, Mandla banged open the kitchen door and ran toward her, yelling, "You're back, you're back!"

She scooped him into her arms. "Did you miss me?"

The three-year-old nodded. "Francina made me eat tomatoes."

Monica smiled, taking in the cowboy hat, cape and rain boots. So the tomato plants were bearing fruit. Francina, the longtime family housekeeper, had purposefully planted them in pots so they wouldn't be affected by the ban on the watering of gardens.

"Tomatoes are good for you," Monica told the boy.

He looked at her skeptically.

"Where's Sipho?"

Mandla sighed the exaggerated sigh of a long-suffering spouse. "Reading."

As Monica carried Mandla into the kitchen, Francina turned from the stove to greet her. "How was it?" she asked, wiping her hands on her apron.

Monica put Mandla down and lifted the lid of one of the pots. "Excellent. I'll bring the tape home as soon as it's finished. Is this what I think it is?"

Francina edged her out of the way to continue stirring. "Yes, polenta." She shook her head. "We blacks have been eating it for hundreds of years and calling it pap. Now you whites give it a foreign name and think it's fancy."

Monica laughed, deciding not to point out that her father's ancestors had been eating the grain in Italy for hundreds of years, too. And polenta was made with yellow maize whereas pap was white.

"You better get Sipho's nose out of that book before he goes squint," said Francina. "I wish he'd play outside sometimes. Now this one—" she picked up Mandla and squeezed his chubby cheeks till he squealed "—he'd be happy if he never had to come inside."

As Ella had lain dying in Monica's bedroom, she'd given Monica final instructions. "Don't let Mandla tire you out," she'd said. "He's a firebrand…a bit like…I used to be. And Sipho…sometimes he's too serious. Get him to laugh."

Not long after Monica had promised her she would, Ella's tight, painful breaths subsided, and silence filled Monica's old pink bedroom again.

It was not a memory Monica shied away from. On the contrary, every day was a renewal of her promise to look after the boys for her friend. This was her purpose in life. For a brief while, when Ella's ex-husband had wanted them back even though he himself was dying of AIDS, she thought that she might have misread God's will for her. But then she'd gone to see Themba in the hospital, and he'd given her permission to adopt his sons because he knew it was what Ella had wanted.

Francina clapped her hands. "Okay, you two, dinner's ready. Wash up and ask Sipho if he'd care to join us."

"Francina?" said Monica, moving closer. "That's a pretty bracelet."

Francina fingered the row of tiny bronze elephants that encircled her wrist, trunk to tail.

"It's new, isn't it?" persisted Monica.

Francina never wore jewelry except for a pair of tiny gold studs in her ears. She followed something of a personal dress code: homemade dresses with no waist and high necklines, men's lace-up shoes and a scarf around her head. On Sundays she went to church in her red-and-black choir uniform.

With her prominent cheekbones, aquiline nose and flawless complexion, the housekeeper looked almost regal, but there was something strange about the way her left eye stared without blinking. Only her family and the people of her village knew that her ex-husband, Winston, had once beaten her so violently that the doctors had to remove her eye and replace it with a glass one. It happened during her first job in Johannesburg. Winston had accused her of flirting with the gardener, but he was drunk and seeing things where there were none. After that Francina vowed never to let another man get close to her, and she believed that if she looked good, they would only be tempted to try.

"Never mind about my bracelet. This polenta's going to be dried concrete if you don't get ready for dinner."

Monica let it go and found Sipho in the living room curled up on the sofa with a wildlife magazine.

"What are you reading there, sweetheart?" she asked, bending to kiss him on the cheek.

He flipped the magazine over to show her a picture of a shark. "These scientists say it's bad to feed sharks. It makes them associate people with food."

Associate. It was a big word for a ten-year-old, but Sipho's teacher had said that he was way ahead of his class and more than likely gifted. Understandably, nobody had tested him because the school system didn't have money for that. Back in the dark days of apartheid, when there were separate education departments for black and white children, aptitude tests were given to white children, but black children were lucky if they had a desk. Now, with one education department, a large proportion of government funding went to support those children whose parents could not afford school fees. Monica knew she'd have to do something to keep Sipho from getting bored.

After dinner Francina washed the dishes and went to her room earlier than usual. Monica presumed she had an outfit to finish. Her mother had given Francina her old sewing machine, and she was always making tent dresses for herself or outfits for her friends. She was scornful of the quality of store-bought clothes and their prices. "Those people have to make a living, too," Monica told her, but try as she might, Francina could not appreciate the workings of the free market system.

The water restrictions were the cause of much embarrassment to Sipho, who had not bathed with his brother for years but now had to to avoid a fine. Monica was banished from the bathroom but hovered outside the door listening as he instructed Mandla to stay still while he washed the food from his hair.

"You shouldn't get so dirty," she heard him say in exasperation as Mandla protested at the rough scrubbing.

After tucking them into their bunk beds, she picked up a few cars Mandla had left lying around and put them in the toy chest. The only sign that this room had once been her brother's was the squadron of model fighter jets suspended with fishing gut from the ceiling, their colors subdued like the bushveld, little South African Defense Force emblems peeling from their tails. She'd thought of moving them to the garage, but Mandla liked looking up at them when he awoke in the morning. They were a memorial of sorts—an ironic one, considering that Luca had died while fulfilling his military obligation to the country.

Monica would never forget the peach fuzz on the lip of the military policeman who came to their door to tell them. Her father had just put out the milk bottles for the next morning and was wearing his pajamas when he listened to the teenager tell him that they were trying to recover all the bits of Luca's body. He took the army's form letter thanking him for his son's service, put a match to it and ignored his wife as she ran at him, scratching, kicking and biting.

* * *

Francina took the letter out of the chocolate tin and read it for the sixth time. She considered herself a wise woman—not in the way Monica might be considered clever with her degree, as Francina had only attended primary school for four years—but in a more natural and, as far as she was concerned, useful way. She only had one eye, but she could tell just by looking at someone if they were lying. Before a vendor on the street gave her change, she could tell if he was going to cheat her, she knew when people were talking about her eye. A dog that is kicked by a stranger lets go of its fear and suspicion over time; a dog that is kicked by its owner goes to its grave trusting no one.

The sentences were plain. There were no descriptions, no words of exaggeration like *very* and *extremely,* no extra words at all. Upon a whim she counted them. Exactly one hundred. Had her correspondent set himself a limit? Francina could not help but admire the way he had crammed all that information into one hundred words.

There was no mention of feelings or emotion in the letter, and for this she was grateful; men did not share these unless they wanted one thing. It was such a formal letter, he might well have been writing to a great-aunt, and Francina would not have had it any other way. One mention of the word *heart* and she would have tossed the letter away without reading to the end.

She hadn't thought to ask him what he did for a living when they'd met at the church-choir competition in Ermelo. If she hadn't been in the bathroom when her group left the hostel for the church hall, she probably wouldn't have spoken to him at all, but with nobody else around, she'd accepted his offer of a ride. He'd gone back to the hostel because he'd forgotten his retractable baton and never conducted his choir without it.

She folded the letter and returned it to the chocolate tin where she kept her bank book, a picture of the Crucifixion, her identity book, which allowed her to vote, and a beaded necklace her mother had sent her when Winston had convinced the village—and her father—that he'd beaten her because she was seeing another man. It was patterned with little shields that symbolized protection from attack, and it had been her mother's way of telling her that she didn't believe Winston and that she hoped her daughter would be safe alone in a far-off city.

She turned on the television—the one Monica had kept in her flat before she moved back to her parents' home—to watch the news. This TV was much bigger than Francina's old portable, and it was color, too. In the two years since Monica had returned from the hospital, things had changed. It had started with the questions. Did Francina have a husband? Where was she from? Why didn't she have any children? At first Francina was annoyed. She'd worked for the Brunettis since Monica was nine, and if Monica hadn't needed this information for more than twenty years, then she could certainly live without it for another twenty. But Monica was persistent, and so Francina told her what she wanted to know. There on the wall was the magazine article Monica had written about her, right above the dresser where Francina kept her plates, knives and forks in the top drawer, her food in the middle one and her stockings and socks in the bottom.

A girl working at the grocery store had recognized her from her picture in the magazine and told her that she, too, came from the Valley of a Thousand Hills, but it was from a village far from Francina's and she did not know the girl's people. Francina had not been angry with Monica for including what she'd said about the Zulus needing an independent homeland. This was South Africa, since 1994 the land of freedom, and people could say what they wanted here. She was proud that the country was not like so many others in Africa where a person could be locked up or just disappear for expressing an opinion about the government.

The television news was full of the African Nations Cup. She hoped *he* was not sports mad like other men. Even the men at church could talk of nothing but soccer. That they could be singing their hearts out one minute and discussing goals the very next made her uneasy. He'd talked of his mother when he'd come over to her in the dining hall after the competition. His mother was going to be disappointed, he'd said, that his choir had not won the competition again this year. Francina had permitted him to join her at the table, partly because she was in the safe company of three of her choir sisters, and partly because a man who talked of his mother was not to be treated badly. Why she agreed to go for a walk with him that afternoon before departing for home she could not tell, but she was glad she did and felt silly that she'd asked one of her friends to shadow them. He'd asked her where she was from, where she lived now, whether she liked it, and not once did she catch him looking at her eye the way most polite people did.

There would not be another letter unless he heard from

her. Of that she was sure. He was not a man who would chase a woman merely for the thrill of it. Francina wondered if she should ask Monica to compose her reply, thanking him for the bracelet. No, she would do it herself, and if she never heard from him again because he found her grammar simple and her spelling laughable, then she would be better off not knowing him at all.

That reminded her—she hadn't told Monica about Sipho's test. Francina had signed it for him when Monica was away doing her story, but the teacher had accused him of signing it himself. What a silly woman. Why would a boy with an A-plus need to forge his parent's signature? She had also meant to tell Monica what Mandla had said about his mother. He was holding the bag of pegs as she hung out the washing when out of the blue he said he'd seen his mother. "Where?" she'd asked, trying to sound nonchalant. "In the clouds when we were on the airplane coming home from Italy," he replied, and then, looking puzzled, he said that she was a lot fatter than in the picture he had of her in his room. Francina had merely nodded and told him that nobody was sick in heaven.

Monica could not concentrate on her story. They'd only been back from visiting her parents in Italy for three days when she'd had to leave for Lady Helen, and she hadn't had time to catch up on her sleep. It had been an overnight flight from Milan. Sipho had slept the entire eleven hours, but she'd had to pace the aisles with Mandla.

She'd been nervous about the boys meeting her father. He'd envisioned grandchildren in his future, but certainly not black ones, and for this reason he had not accompanied his wife on her first visit home. It grieved him that his daughter had chosen to remain in Africa where it was clear to him whites were not wanted. The French, Belgians, English, Italians and Portuguese had left, and so, too, should white South Africans. But what Monica could not get through to him was that, unlike those settlers, most South Africans were not holders of a European passport, or even entitled to one.

"Where would Mom go if she were not married to you, an Italian?" she'd asked.

He'd merely grunted. Africans had killed his son, shot his daughter, and he wanted no part of the cursed continent. That Monica would choose to remain was something he would never understand.

Sipho and Mandla adored her father, and Monica felt guilty for ever having worried about how he would treat them. He had his shortcomings, but he would never be unkind to children, especially not orphans who'd watched their mother die. He took pleasure in cooking for them—pasta, gnocchi, polenta and sausages—and beamed with joy if they accepted a second helping. She watched with satisfaction, knowing that to an Italian there was no better way of expressing love.

She closed her notebook to sift through the growing pile of unopened mail and found a letter from Sipho's school. She tore it open. The principal wanted to see her. It was a matter of urgency, she said, but gave no details. Sipho could not be in trouble. Maybe they were concerned because he wasn't as sociable as most other children. Maybe they wanted to move him ahead one year. She put the letter in her diary and turned out the light. Without sleep she would be of no use to anyone.

It was stressful being a parent, but with Francina around, Monica didn't consider herself a single parent. A more unlikely pair would be hard to find, but they worked well together. Francina was bossy, just as Ella had been. Although Francina had never fully accepted Ella in the house because she was one of "those ANC people" and because she had the dreaded "thinning disease," she'd always loved the boys fiercely, and Monica did not know what she would do without her.

If she had tried three years ago to imagine her life now, she would have been entirely wrong. God had led her down a road she hadn't even known existed, but like so many alternate routes on a journey it was turning out to be more rewarding than the one planned.

Chapter Three

A large framed photograph of the African bushveld at sunset hung outside the principal's office, its warm amber tones a stark contrast to the shiny gray tiles, artificial plants and black vinyl chairs of the waiting room. Monica imagined children staring longingly at the fish eagle, wishing they could soar away with him over the umbrella-shaped acacia trees on the grassy plain.

The principal's office was in a single-story administrative building that adjoined the Great Hall—so named for its size and not for any aesthetic touches. At Friday assembly, students sat cross-legged on the cold tiled floor as they listened to the assigned class lead the school in prayer and a Bible reading. Poetry would follow, or a play, acted out by students in home-made costumes, and the parents of the children involved would sit upstairs in the gallery on hard wooden benches.

A bell sounded for morning break, and Monica could see the exterior corridors and stairwells of the adjacent three-story brick building filling with students, their squeals and shouts filtering through the closed windows of the waiting room. She stood up to afford herself a better view as the crowd fanned out across the athletics field. Boys in gray shorts, white shirts and blue ties wolfed down the contents of their lunch boxes so they could begin their games in earnest, games that seemed to involve large groups and running. Girls in blue tunics and white shirts sat together in circles on the grass or in pairs on the concrete-terraced seating. As far as Monica could tell, there seemed to be no segregation of the black and the white children. Unable to spot Sipho, she wondered if he was among the boys chasing one another up the embankment in the far corner of the field.

"Mrs. Pringle will see you now," said a voice behind her, and Monica turned from the window to follow the principal's young secretary to the office at the end.

The woman who rose to greet Monica as she entered was in her mid-fifties, heavyset, with shoulder-length gray hair. She wore a navy suit, thick makeup and simple pearl earrings.

The secretary pulled the door closed behind her, and Monica took the armchair she was offered, while the principal sat down on the sofa opposite.

"Tea, Miss Brunetti? You've come just in time."

"Thanks," said Monica.

The principal poured her a cup and handed it to her. "I know you have to get to work, so I'll get right to it."

"If it's about the test," interrupted Monica, "Sipho didn't sign it himself. I was away on business, so Francina, the housekeeper, signed it."

The principal stirred her tea and said, "I see." She took a

sip. "That's not why I wanted to see you, but we could be onto something here. You say you left your boys overnight with the maid?"

"Yes, but it's perfectly all right. She's a grown woman." Monica cringed at her defensive tone.

"I see," said the principal again, before taking another sip of tea. Then she put her cup down and said, "You might want to reconsider this arrangement when I tell you what Sipho has been doing."

Monica felt the anger rising in her and prayed quickly for God to give her patience. If there was a problem that involved Sipho, she had to hear this woman out and not get into what could easily degenerate into a nasty argument.

"Sipho has been disappearing," said the principal, taking a bite of a large macaroon.

"What do you mean?"

The principal waved her hand in front of her mouth to indicate that it was full.

"What does that mean?" persisted Monica.

The principal wiped her mouth. "Children have been playing truant since the beginning of time. Please calm down."

"A boy alone on the streets is not safe here," said Monica. "Why didn't you call me when he went missing the first time?"

This woman was critical of her for leaving the boys with Francina because she feared for their safety, yet she'd allowed Sipho to go missing who knows how many times before acting.

Sipho had not turned up for class on six occasions, usually after the morning break, but because he would reappear after the second break the principal had waited before contacting Monica. "I thought he might be having problems at home," she explained. "I know the poor little thing lost his mother and that his new living arrangement is, should we say, unconventional."

Monica could not believe what she was hearing. Did this woman expect her to believe that she had Sipho's best interests at heart when she'd compromised his safety? For the first time Monica wished that she had a husband to take control. No, she could not think that way; the principal was trying to make her feel as though she were an inadequate parent. The most important thing to do was to speak to Sipho and find out what was going on.

Francina sat down at the kitchen table with a cheese sandwich and cup of tea. She'd vacuumed and dusted, the bathrooms smelled like bleach, every surface in the kitchen shone, and the washing on the line was almost dry. In fifteen minutes she'd wake Mandla and they'd walk to school to collect Sipho. That gave her plenty of time to read the letter. He must have replied to hers immediately, as only a week had passed since she'd sent it. Dundee was a mere three hours away, but it still had to be a record for the postal service. Prevent HIV said the postmark. She cut open the letter with a pair of kitchen scissors, taking care to preserve the stamp for Sipho. Had he found her letter simple and childlike?

When she'd finished reading, she took a big gulp of tea and fanned her face, for it felt suddenly warm. He wanted to meet her at the next choir competition and take her out to a place of her choosing. Definitely not, she thought. A friendship through the mail was fine, but going out with him alone was impossible. She'd write and tell him that she was not the sort of woman to go running around town. But his feelings would be hurt, and that would probably be the end of their relationship—if you could call it that. Maybe she should ask Monica for advice. Monica, still single at thirty-one, was no expert on men, but she had been clever enough to get rid of Anton. Francina had never had a good feeling about Monica's former boyfriend. He had often talked of important, personal things within earshot of Francina, as though she were a potted plant or a family pet.

The best time to talk to Sipho, Monica had decided, would be after they'd watched her segment on *In-Depth,* and she'd arranged with Francina to stay a little later than usual in order to put Mandla to bed. That way she and Sipho would have complete privacy. Francina wanted Monica to move Sipho to another school, but it was not so simple, as this was his zoned school.

Everybody gathered round the television, Sipho a few feet away from the screen on a chair he always brought from the kitchen for important viewing events, Mandla on Francina's knee, and Monica on the sofa with Ebony, her fifteen-year-old cat that spent most of her time lying in the sunlight in the kitchen. Mandla jumped up and down all over Francina as the show's urgent electronic music ushered in an aerial shot of the Johannesburg skyline at night, while an imaginary typewriter clattered out the words *In-Depth* in block letters at the bottom of the screen.

Thandi, a beautiful girl with long braids, explained the lineup for the show in a British accent, and Francina made her usual comment about never seeing Zulus on television, only ANC people.

The first story was the one about the airlifting of crocodiles out of Lake Saint Lucia. It was heartbreaking, because in some places they were mired in a foot of mud, yet it was thrilling, too, to watch from the helicopter as the creatures were raised up into the hold. Monica had known it would make for riveting viewing, and so as she watched Sipho hold his breath, she struggled not to resent her colleague for taking her idea.

Her story was next. The hospital seemed smaller than she remembered, despite the jumble of prefabricated additions that sprouted like mushrooms behind it. Sister Adelaide had an almost luminous quality on-screen, and for once Francina had nothing to say, because even she could not take her eyes away.

"What's that little girl's prognosis?" asked Sipho. Another big word for a ten-year-old, but one he'd known ever since he'd decided, when his mother was ill, that he was going to be a doctor when he grew up.

"The nursing sister is about to tell us," replied Monica.

Sipho listened as Adelaide explained that Zukisa's burns would heal completely. He gave a satisfied smile.

Henry had taken some brilliant atmospheric shots of the sun riding low above muted blue-green koppies and the palm trees and bougainvillea receding into the distance as they'd retreated over the hills. With the warm yellow light on the tin roofs and purple shadows on the ground, Lady Helen looked more like a painting in pastel crayons than a real town.

Francina, Sipho and Mandla clapped after Monica had

signed off, and she grinned with pleasure at this affirmation from her most important critics. Their praise was not automatic; her previous story on street children had met with silence, and after the boys had gone to bed Francina had asked, "How could you let the boys see that?" This was the one aspect of child rearing over which she and Francina clashed. Monica believed that it was important for the boys to be aware of inequities in the world if they were to develop a social conscience. When she was a child, the dark side of her country's character had been hidden from her, and she had grown up to become a naive, insular and sometimes self-ish young woman. It had taken a long stay in a mostly black hospital and Ella's gracious friendship for Monica to be able to see herself as others did.

"Stay with me a minute," she said as Sipho kissed her goodnight. She waited until Francina had disappeared with Mandla before speaking again. "You're doing very well in school. Francina tells me you just got an A-plus on a math test."

"Yes, but it was an easy one," he said, ever modest.

"Do you miss your mom, sweetheart?"

He nodded solemnly.

She opened her arms to him, and the little boy who thought he was too big to be hugged came to her.

"I miss her, too. Do you remember what Pastor Wessels told you?"

He nodded again. Pastor Wessels had been a regular visitor ever since Monica adopted the boys. His visits often involved horseplay on the floor with Mandla and an earnest discussion about astronomy or wildlife with Sipho, but he had also explained at length to them both about salvation.

Apart from the physical-education teacher, he was the only man in the boys' lives, and Monica was grateful for his interest in their family.

"Sweetheart, is there something on your mind that you wish you could tell your mother?"

His eyes filled with tears.

"Do you think you could tell me? I'll try my best to listen as well as she always did."

He thought about this for a while, and then it all came out, how the children called him "little professor" because he always had his hand up with the correct answer and got straight A's on his tests, how they taunted him in the playground because he was always the first to be caught when they played catches. One of the other black children had called him a "klonkie," a derogatory term for a person of mixed race, because his new mother was a white woman. He'd started going down to the bottom of the playground with a book in order to get as far away from the other children as he could. Then he'd spied a hole in the fence and had wriggled through it to sit in the grove of wattle trees until he heard the bell ring for the end of break. When nobody noticed his absences, he started extending them through the midmorning classes until the end of the second break. Because he saw his homeroom teacher for only the first and last hour of the day, she was unaware of what he was doing, and none of the other teachers said a word to him.

"I always read my encyclopedia or a wildlife magazine," he explained, as though it was a perfectly reasonable swap for the classroom material he missed.

He probably did learn more on his own than he would in

class, Monica realized, but the law said he had to go to school, and, besides that, she worried what might have happened to him. People who came to the area looking for work often slept under the bushes on the koppie behind the school—you'd see the flicker of their cooking fires at night. Pushing the horrible possibilities from her mind, she made Sipho promise never to do it again.

"I'll speak to your teacher about those children."

"No, no, please don't," he protested. "They'll say I'm a baby, too."

"Do you remember what Jesus said about turning the other cheek? Can you do that when they call you names?"

"I'll try."

She gave him a big squeeze. "Good boy. And please tell me the next time you have something on your mind. Your mother would be happy if you shared your worries." She felt him squeeze her in return.

After tucking him in bed and kissing Mandla, who was already asleep, she found Francina in the living room watching television.

"Everything okay?" asked Francina as she switched off the game show.

"Yes, I don't think he'll do it again. But it doesn't really solve the problem."

"Mmm."

"Is everything okay with *you*?" asked Monica.

"Yes. Actually, no. Can I ask you something?"

"Of course," replied Monica, happy that Francina felt comfortable enough to confide in her.

As she listened to Francina tell her about the man and

his letters, Monica could think of only one thing: *She's going to leave me.*

"What should I do?" asked Francina nervously.

God forgive me for my selfishness, prayed Monica. Francina is an extraordinary woman and deserves some appreciation. She forced a smile. "You should go out with him."

"But? I can see you're holding back a but."

Monica laughed nervously. "I just don't know what I'm going to do without you."

Francina put her palms to her forehead. "Talk about eating the pap before it's cooked."

"I know, I know," said Monica.

She wanted to remind Francina that everyone had left: Anton, her parents, Ella, but she didn't—it was the sort of manipulative technique her mother would have used.

Francina thanked her for the advice but seemed lost in thought, and Monica regretted having said so much.

Waiting on Monica's desk the next morning was a telephone message to see the managing editor of *In-Depth* as soon as she had a minute.

"Well done. Good piece last night," said Aidan, one of the announcers, on his way to the recording studio.

"Thanks," she replied.

"Hey, Brunetti," called Vusi from across the warren of partitioned cubicles. "Great work. You have all the fun, while we're stuck here like hamsters."

She looked around the room, at the shelves overflowing with tapes, at the notice board filled with cynical cartoons, classified advertisements and union rules, and with a feeling of nostalgia, she realized that a chapter of her career was closing. She would miss this job and her colleagues, but working full-time for television had always been her dream. Half an hour till lunch. Her story on Danish aid for a literacy campaign among rural women in KwaZulu-Natal was finished. She'd take an early lunch break to be sure to catch Jan, the managing editor, before he left for his daily visit to the sandwich bar down the street.

Jan looked at his watch and reached behind him for the navy blazer that hung over the back of his chair. Monica stood up.

"Can we shake on it?" He stuck out his hand.

It felt damp, she thought.

"Don't forget what I said about the future," he said, steering her out of his office.

She nodded.

He opened the door to the stairwell. Jan never took the elevator. "Bye, Monica," he said and let the door slam behind him.

As she rode down the eleven floors, she looked at herself in the mirrored walls. Her face was pale. An alternate when they were short-staffed? That was not what she had expected. He had not liked her story on the hospital at Lady Helen. None of the editors and producers had, he'd said. Why hadn't she interviewed the doctor in charge? The story had come off feeling lightweight. Where were the comparisons to other burn units and the mandatory mention of the state of the nation's health-care system? "Focus on the specific and then move out to the general," he'd told her. Those were the rules for *In-Depth*. The only reason they'd aired it was that they didn't have anything in their filler pantry at the time. "We don't do PR here," he'd said.

They'd hired someone from outside for the permanent position Monica had wanted, a woman who worked for an advertising agency and had been educated in London. Although Monica did not know her, she'd recognized the last name as that of a prominent political family, and Francina's words had echoed in her mind. It was obvious that Jan had seen the light of recognition in Monica's eyes because he'd quickly added that, unlike Monica, Nomsa would not turn down an assignment should the location be a little less than safe.

Coming from a father of three who never left his office, it was a cheap shot, but Monica did not blame Jan—he was only trying to preserve his job. He might have been honest with her though, instead of insulting her work. But maybe he *was* being honest. Had she been swayed by her desire to help Dr. Niemand win funding for his little hospital? It was not the worst journalistic transgression one could make, but it was a transgression nevertheless.

Somehow she managed to drag herself back to the radio office when all she wanted to do was go home and bury her face against Mandla's soft skin. He would take her presence as a sign that they were going out. He loved being in the fresh air, but they could only allow him out during the day and kept him close to the house. It was a shame that his entire childhood and teenage years would be spent cloistered behind the high perimeter wall of their house. What was it Ella had said? "What sort of freedom have we won when we cannot let our children play in the park alone, when we have to look over our shoulders as we walk to the store in broad daylight, when we cannot answer a knock on the door after the sun has gone down?"

Monica called the school and Sipho, thank goodness, had stuck to his word not to disappear again. It was a positive step, but this was merely a symptom of the problem and she still had to find a cure.

As she went through the motions of editing filler material for the impending "silly season," the month when everybody went on holiday and nothing happened, she could not push aside the thought that Francina might leave her, now that she seemed to have overcome her dislike of men. Or she might leave to be closer to her elderly parents. What would Monica do alone?

In the two years since surviving her attack she'd learned that faith in the Lord would see her through difficult times. It had been a slow and often painful lesson, but those were the ones that stuck, so she prayed for God to guide her as she tried to do the best she could for her family.

❧ Chapter Four ❧

A chorus of harmonized hallelujahs filled the minibus taxi as the flat, yellow land of mine dumps and smokestacks gave way to hills, at first gentle, and then undulating like a heavy sea. Without a pause, the choir went straight into another joyous hymn of praise, sung in English in preparation for the competition they were about to attend in Pongola, a small sugarcane town near the Swaziland border.

The town they were passing through now had once been the cultural center of a wealthy Afrikaans farming community, but on this day it was difficult to spot a white person anywhere. Where had they all disappeared to? Francina wondered.

"I will give myself to Thee," sang the choir, shifting to another hymn in the marathon they would keep up until the minibus had delivered them safely to the dormitory where they would stay for the competition. These taxis were always bursting tires or colliding with trucks as they raced to pass on single-lane country roads. You'd see it on television: cardboard suitcases and boxes spread across the asphalt, tins of food, packets of cookies, new children's shoes scattered to the wind. Francina always thought about the children waiting anxiously at their villages for the mother or father who would never arrive.

The hills should have been green at this time of year, but because of the drought they were a lightly baked brown. Cattle and goats grazed so close to the edge of the road Francina could see their ribs. The driver slowed down as they neared a village. School had just ended for the day and the sand roads and footpaths that crisscrossed the hills like a spiderweb were filled with children going home. The girls wore white shirts and black tunics, the boys white shirts and short black pants if they were in primary school, long ones if they were in high school. The younger boys chased each other barefoot over the stones and hard ground. The older boys with their lace-up shoes and earnest intentions of impressing the girls took a more leisurely pace. Outside an adobe trading store, men sat on upturned cooking-oil tins listening to a radio and watching the high-school girls walk by.

Francina thought of the man she was about to see again at the choir competition. Why was he interested in her when there were so many young girls around? Did he think she had money? Ha, that would be a mistake. A tiny part of her had wanted to sew something special for their date tonight—something with a waistline—but she'd decided upon the black skirt and red jacket of her choir uniform instead because she didn't want him getting any ideas. Men got them so easily. With all the pictures of half-naked girls on bus stops, magazine covers and television, you'd think men would get tired of their ideas, but no, it only made them think of more.

Why they couldn't turn their active imaginations to more useful pursuits, she did not know. The country had enough problems for all of them to work on. Like that right there—another minibus taxi had passed them on a corner, forcing the oncoming car to leave the road. Thankfully, there had not been any children or livestock in its way. Her choir began another hymn with renewed energy.

When the choir competition was over, Francina planned to go to her village, a four-hour drive away through the rural interior of the province of KwaZulu-Natal. It had taken her five years to brave a visit back home after Winston had convinced the village he'd beaten her because she was unfaithful. Under normal circumstances her husband would have taken her home, and then the two families would have met to discuss a solution to the marital crisis, or, the terms of the separation.

In Zulu culture, if the divorce is the man's fault he decides whether or not he gives his wife and children anything; in some rural areas men considered one cow a reasonable settlement. If a husband was mean, he'd give his family nothing and make his wife find a new husband to take care of them. If the split was the wife's fault, the families would divide the lebola, or dowry, that the husband had paid; some would be returned to the husband and the remainder would stay with the wife's parents to support any children that had resulted from the marriage. But the end of Francina and Winston's traditional marriage had not come in the traditional way; instead of being present when the two families had decided that it was best they divorce, she was alone in a hospital bed with a thick bandage wrapped around her head.

Her father was not able to reject her in the flesh when she finally went back, but she knew that he would never try to clear her name. To do so would have been stupid. Winston had become the new chief of the village after his father passed away, and her father would only be evicted from his land, beaten or worse.

For twenty-three years she'd ignored the whispers. For twenty-three years she'd hidden whenever His Majesty the chief was nearby. No more. The incident was ancient history, but her people seemed to have a talent for hanging on to it like a mangy mutt with a bone. What if she had to go back to her village permanently? At one time her father told people he didn't have a daughter, but *she* would return to take care of him if he needed her. In Zulu culture it was the youngest son's duty to take care of his parents, and Dingane and his wife, Nokuthula, were doing a good job, but if they needed help, Francina would be there. Old gossips would say she was doing it to try and get a piece of the inheritance, which, according to custom, went to the youngest son, but she wouldn't take a cent.

The dormitory was down a side street, next to the primary school where the competition was to be held the following day. A crowd of children gathered to watch the driver pass their suitcases down from the roof of the minibus. Francina fished out some of the sweets she'd brought for her nephews and, as was the custom, the children clapped twice in a sign of gratitude before receiving them in both hands.

There were ten beds in each room, and Francina took the one closest to the door so that she wouldn't disturb any of the other women if she were late returning from her date. They hung their uniforms on the hooks next to their beds, and then, as it was past lunchtime, went out together to eat.

Later that afternoon, one of Francina's fellow choir members came out of a stall in the bathroom to find her checking her black headscarf in the mirror.

"Have you gone crazy?" she asked. "The competition is tomorrow."

Francina liked it that the women looked out for each other, but just this once she wished it were not so. There was nothing she could do now except tell her that a man would be arriving soon to escort her to dinner.

Within minutes they were all crowding the bathroom, wanting to know if it was that quiet man she'd gone for a walk with after the last competition. When she told them that it was, the older women nodded in approval, but the younger ones looked disappointed and began discussing going to the chicken place down the road for a milk shake. Why should Francina be the only one to go out?

Francina did not want to wait for her gentleman caller outside for fear of seeming too eager, but the fear of having to introduce him to everyone was greater. He was ten minutes late. African time was fine for some, but not for a lady waiting alone outside a dormitory in a strange town, even if it was just past six o'clock and still as light as midday. This was not a good sign. He only had to walk three blocks from the dormitory where his group was staying behind the post office. She decided to give him five more minutes, and then she would go back inside.

Just as she was beginning to give up on him, she saw him running down the street toward her. He was wearing a suit, and all of a sudden she wished that she were standing there in a dress created especially for the evening.

"I'm sorry, Francina," he said when he reached her. "Some of the men thought it amusing to hide my suit."

So he, too, had been teased.

"I should have anticipated such antics. The men become like excitable children on these trips."

Her heart sank as it dawned on her that it would not be necessary to ask him what he did for a living. He spoke like a schoolteacher, and surely he would find her dull. She had intelligence, of that she was sure, but she could not wrap it up like a gift in fancy words.

"Have you decided upon a place to eat?"

She wondered if the tiny restaurant she had seen on her walkabout would interest him. They served only two or three dishes a night, and she'd been thinking of the beef curry all afternoon.

The young waitress took one look at Francina's uniform and directed them to a table alongside a boisterous group that was discussing the competition in loud voices.

"Could we have that one instead?" Francina's escort asked, pointing to a more private table at the back of the restaurant.

The girl shrugged and moved their silverware.

The beef curry was just as Francina had imagined it: thick and rich with just enough spice to give it bite. She'd tried some at an Indian shopping center in Johannesburg and it had made her sweat, but this was perfect. Would the Zulu woman in the kitchen be willing to share her recipe? Sipho, Mandla and Monica would love it. Maybe it wasn't a good idea—the waitress wasn't too helpful, and Francina didn't need any fuss tonight. She was relieved to see that the man was eating well. Those thin cheeks had worried her, but a man with an appetite was not sick.

"Let me hear you say my name, Francina."

She hadn't ever addressed him by name because she seemed always to be answering his questions or responding to what he had told her. Smiling, she thought of Monica, who knew of him only as "the man."

"You find it amusing?" He looked crushed.

"No, no, I don't, er, Hercules."

He put down his knife and fork and wiped his mouth on the roller towel. "Having this name has been a Herculean struggle."

He seemed to be waiting for her to respond, but she did not know how because she had no idea what he was talking about.

Sensing her discomfort, he tried to put her at ease. "My father was a cook at a private boarding school, and he used to come home with all sorts of information he'd gleaned from the masters in the dining room. I suppose you can say I'm the product of a classical education."

Francina had no idea why he was laughing, but she joined in because she'd looked up his name in Sipho's encyclopedia and thought it funny that this tall, pointy man with no meat on his bones could be named after a Greek who looked like a white version of a Zulu warrior.

"Tell me about your employer," he said when they'd run out of laughter. "You seem fond of her."

Francina nodded. "Monica was the moodiest nine-year-old I'd ever met when I first came to work for the family. But she's come a long way."

"Have you ever thought of leaving?"

Francina wondered if he was getting ideas. No, he hadn't even touched her, nor stared into her eyes as though looking for something he'd lost. The men on her favorite soap operas always did that when they wanted something from a woman. And the women fell for it every time.

"My parents are getting old. If they need me, I will go to them."

He nodded. "My mother lives with me." He withdrew a photograph from his wallet and offered it to her. "This is my wife," he said.

Francina pushed her chair back and stood up.

"My *late* wife," he said. "I'm sorry. Please sit down."

She did as she was asked but couldn't help thinking that nothing good could come of this.

His wife had died of malaria fifteen years ago, he told her, and he hadn't gone out with a woman since. Francina studied the photograph. The woman was leaning against a tree and not looking directly into the camera because the sun was in her eyes. She had dimples and a shy smile.

Anything Francina said now would show Hercules whether or not she was interested in him. She wished she could go back to her dormitory to think, but that would look like a rejection, and she was not ready for that yet. *Decide quickly, Francina,* she told herself. *Let's see if you're as clever as you think.* Was it a good thing he hadn't gone out with a woman for fifteen years or was it strange? Hadn't she herself stayed away from men for twenty three? But men were different; they couldn't do without women. Could he be a special type of man? After all, he hadn't even held her hand yet. If she said goodbye now, she might miss out on the one man she could learn to trust. And why should he not still love his wife? Francina reasoned. We don't stop loving a mother, father or grandparent when they die, so why should he stop loving his wife? The question was whether he had any love left over.

"Francina," he said. "Do you want to leave?" It was almost as though he'd seen her thoughts.

Suddenly, she felt uncomfortably warm.

He leaned closer, waiting for her answer, and for the first time she felt brave enough to look into his eyes. They were dark and kind and so full of worry that she wanted to pat his hand. "No," she said. "There are fresh mangoes with ice cream for dessert."

The next morning in the primary-school hall, whispers ran up and down the row where Francina and her choir were waiting their turn.

"That's him…Francina's boyfriend. A nice serious man," said one of the older ladies.

There were murmurs of agreement.

"Looks like a giraffe," said one of the younger girls, causing a chorus of muted giggles.

Hercules extended his retractable baton and raised his arms in anticipation of the first note from the ancient organ.

Is he my boyfriend? wondered Francina. At what point do you call someone your boyfriend? After a date and a promise to meet up again after the competition? Then I suppose he is my boyfriend, she decided, and she put her hand over her mouth to hide the little smile that would not stop.

At the end of the day, when Hercules walked onto the stage to accept the certificate for first place, Francina turned to the younger girls in her choir and nodded. This time not one of them had a single clever thing to say.

❧ *Chapter Five* ❧

"Watch over this vehicle, please God," Francina prayed the next day as she stepped into the minibus taxi that would take her to her parents' village.

The rest of her choir had departed straight after the Sunday-morning church service, but Hercules had waited with her until he had to leave with his group at noon. They had not been able to spend any time alone together the evening before, since there had been a celebratory dinner for all the choirs after the competition.

After dessert had been served, the director of the choir that had come in second had climbed onto the stage and started everybody singing. The sound of all the voices at once was so loud that Francina wondered if the neighbors might call the police. But a person would have to have a stone in their chest instead of a heart not to appreciate the stirring beauty of this passionate singing. Halfway through the second song she looked across to where Hercules was sitting with his choir and their eyes met. He smiled warmly at her and she did the same. And then, without any shyness, they'd both continued singing.

She squeezed herself into the minibus's only available seat in the middle row and watched to make sure that the driver remembered to load her suitcase onto the roof. The rest of the passengers were asleep, some leaning against the windows, others with their heads resting on the bags in their laps. A loud whispered greeting startled her. Francina had not realized that the old lady in the back was awake behind her dark glasses.

The minibus bumped along the dirt road, passing the outdoor curio market where she and Hercules had strolled along the aisles after church. She reached up to the collar of her dress and touched the beaded-chameleon brooch he'd bought for her. "A reminder of our time together," he'd said, to which she'd replied that she would never forget it, chameleon or no chameleon. Now, as the minibus rejoined the tar road, she hoped that Hercules wasn't a chameleon himself. No, he couldn't be. She was too good a judge of character to fall for a trickster. More than likely he was exactly as he appeared: a kind, earnest man with great sorrow in his past.

The driver kept yawning, and Francina wondered if she should sing a hymn. Looking around at the sleeping faces, she decided against it. They might throw her off the vehicle and then she'd be stuck at the side of the road for who knew how many hours. Monica had taken leave from work to watch Sipho and Mandla, and Francina had promised to be back on Tuesday night. I wonder how my boys are? she thought, smiling to herself.

As they turned onto the road that would take them to the northern tip of the Valley of a Thousand Hills, Francina handed the driver a stick of chewing gum in the hope that it would keep him awake. He looked at her in the rearview mirror and smiled broadly. Typical, thought Francina. She stared out the window at thin cows nosing around in the dirt, looking for grass. A herd boy waved at her and then went back to throwing stones at a tin can. He looked no older than Sipho.

At the next village the driver stopped outside a trading store and yelled, "Gentlemen out!" Everybody woke with a start. The man sitting behind Francina asked politely if she would climb down so he and his two brothers could get past her, and as she obliged, she noticed an old woman craning her neck to see into the minibus.

"Is he one of these, Mama?" called the driver.

After a long pause the old woman shook her head, and then, leaning heavily on a stick, shuffled off in the direction of the small brick houses.

"She's waiting for her dead husband," explained the driver, and there was a chorus of "Ah, shame" from the women.

The driver handed the men their baggage, wished them luck finding a new job now that their factory in Middelburg had closed down, and the rest of the passengers rearranged themselves to take advantage of the extra space.

With all the men except for the driver gone and the end of the journey approaching, the talk became lively. The elderly woman at the back was going home after an operation to remove cataracts from her eyes; there was a domestic servant returning home for a long paid holiday because her em-

ployers had gone to England for a sabbatical. Francina did
not know what the word meant, but she was not going to
ask the woman, who seemed to think she was high society
just because she cleaned house for a professor. It's not as
though knowledge rubs off like floor polish, she wanted to
tell her. There was also a young girl who didn't say a word,
even when addressed directly. Francina thought she was
very rude, but what could you expect from a girl with bright
red nail polish and platform sandals? The rest of the women
were all related and returning from a visit to their daughter
and niece, who was about to marry a boy from Johannesburg.

"She's not bringing him home for the wedding," whispered the girl's aunt to Francina. "They'll probably have a
quick ceremony in front of a judge. Girls nowadays think
they can forget the ways of our people." She shook her head.
"How can we be sure he'll be good to her if we don't know
his people?"

Francina wanted to tell her that the man could be from the
same village, he could be the son of the chief, and he'd still
use his fists on you if he wanted to, but she didn't wish to scare
the woman, who looked as though she was about to cry.

Plump hills rose up around them, one upon the next, like
bread rolls baking in the oven. The road climbed upward,
and when they reached the highest point Francina looked
out across the valley at the contours of God's land and
thought, as she always did when coming home, that this was
surely one of His masterpieces. From the way the other passengers all fell silent, she realized that she was not the only
one who felt this way.

Fluffy clouds floated lazily across the blue sky and a gentle breeze sent a shiver through the dried blond grass. Francina slid the window open and took a deep breath. Her village, Jabulani, which means happiness in the Zulu language, was spread over a hill across the first valley: little square brick houses mixed with traditional round adobe huts and kraals made of tree branches to keep the livestock in. On lines stretched between umphafa trees, clean clothes fluttered like the flags of a faraway kingdom. She thought she could see a wisp of smoke coming from her parents' compound on the farthest side of the village. That would be her mother preparing food for her homecoming.

It was a miracle that her village had escaped the violence that had swept through the province in the early nineties. Watching the television news alone in her room in Johannesburg, Francina had shed enough tears to fill three buckets. Burnt huts and bodies, wailing women, men with fear in their eyes: these black-and-white pictures would forever be in her head. There was still tension between the supporters of the mainly Zulu Inkatha Freedom Party and the ANC, but no more massacres in the middle of the night.

As they descended into the first valley everybody started talking at once—everybody, that is, except the young girl with the bright red nail polish, who sat staring out the window as though she were on her way to prison. Francina asked her which village she was from but the girl did not answer. She wasn't deaf, that was clear, because she'd jumped like the rest of them when they'd heard a loud bang earlier on and thought it was a tire bursting. Luckily, it was only a tractor backfiring.

The Valley of a Thousand Hills had changed since Francina first left at the age of sixteen. It used to feel like the far end of the world. When someone arrived in the village, it was because he had come to see his family, not because he'd taken a wrong turn looking for a bed-and-breakfast. Over the past few years artists' colonies, tea shops and guesthouses had appeared, and the locals now had to pull over to make room for tour buses filled with foreigners trying to get the perfect picture of pretty little huts and waving children.

Francina thought it strange that you never saw them touring the ugly squatter camps in Johannesburg; these, too, were the real Africa. It was as though tourists wanted the Africa they'd seen in the movies: never-ending bushveld, animals at every turn, wide-verandaed hotels, cocktails at sunset served by smiling natives. You could get all this and more at private game lodges where most South Africans wouldn't be able to afford to stay even a single night.

However much she moaned, Francina did not really mind the changes in the Valley of a Thousand Hills. Her elders wouldn't be laughing so loudly if *they'd* thought of the idea to build Zulu cultural centers to show tourists the workings of a traditional village—not with the thirty-rand entrance fee being charged. The centers provided jobs, too, which meant fewer fathers had to seek work in the cities.

As the minibus bumped along the dirt track that led to Francina's village, she began to feel the familiar snake in her stomach that couldn't get comfortable. This was her land, these were her people, but it seemed that Winston had changed that forever with a mouthful of poisonous lies.

There was her mother, standing a short distance away from the trading store with an umbrella open for shade. A year had passed since Francina last saw her, but she had not changed, not even, it seemed, the outfit she'd worn to see Francina off. It was the elegant pleated skirt and long jacket Francina had sewed for her to wear on special occasions, such as a visit to town. She smiled to herself. Her mother never went to town. Her mother had never even been to a doctor or dentist. A government nurse came to the village once a year, and her mother's four babies had all been delivered by local women.

Despite years of bending over a hoe in the family field, her tiny, delicate mother had the posture of a queen. Francina had inherited her high cheekbones and thin, straight nose, but not her mouth, which remained zipped unless she was addressed directly. No one ever heard her complain that she was tired, or that her feet hurt, or that she missed her firstborn who had died in a mine accident in Johannesburg when Francina was only nine. Sometimes you wouldn't even know she was home, except that the dirt yard was neatly swept and there was a curl of smoke coming from the lapa, the reed enclosure where she cooked.

Francina wished the group of ladies luck with their daughter's coming marriage and then regretted mentioning it when the mother started to wail. While the group attended to her, Francina told the girl with the red nail polish that she was wise to go home because the city was too harsh for a young girl on her own. The girl looked at her for the first time and gave a nervous smile.

Francina and her mother waved at the minibus as it sped off to the next village.

"Something has changed in you, my daughter," said her mother.

Francina was glad she'd remembered to take the chameleon brooch off her lapel and stuff it into her pocket. Her mother would have known immediately that she'd met a man.

Township jazz blared from a radio on the veranda of the trading store. Maize Gives Strength, said a rusted sign on the adobe wall. A group of men sat on upturned wooden crates in the shade of the tin overhang. Ignoring their stares, Francina picked up her suitcase and took her mother's arm.

"No, Mama," she said as her mother headed toward the path that would lead through a grove of umunga trees before circling the village. "From now on I will walk through the center of the village like everyone else."

Her father was sitting on his favorite old lawn chair outside the door of his sleeping hut when they arrived. Francina put down her suitcase and took his outstretched hands.

"Welcome, Daughter," he said warmly, but from the troubled look on his face she knew that word of her route through the village had reached him before she had.

Her father was seventy years old. He had brought four children into the world, built up a herd of cattle from the single cow he'd inherited from his father, and he planned to spend the rest of his days on this land where his ancestors had lived for hundreds of years. If she were to confront Winston, it would have to be done in such a way that her father and his livelihood would not be affected.

The family compound consisted of three traditional round huts with thatched roofs: one for Francina's parents, one for her youngest brother and his wife and one for their teenage sons. A three-room brick building in the center of the dirt yard housed a living room, bathroom and kitchen. Three years ago they had been connected to the local power grid yet Francina's mother still insisted on cooking outdoors, so the kitchen was used only for the preparation of food. Down the end of a well-worn path was a little wooden lean-to: the long-drop toilet. Her mother had made up a bed for her in the living room and told her that nobody would enter in the morning until she had come out.

A short while later Francina's brother and his wife drove up in an SUV. For twenty years Dingane had worked as a tracker at a luxury game lodge thirty miles away. Before his employers allowed him use of their vehicle to and from work, he'd lived in a little gatehouse with the rest of the staff, and had only come home on his day off. The new arrangement suited his wife, Nokuthula, much better, as she got a ride home from her cleaning job at a guesthouse and no longer had to spend sleepless nights worrying about all those single girls who worked at the lodge as maids. Her name might mean peace in Zulu, but she got none when he slept away from home.

"*Sawubona,* Sister," said Dingane in greeting as he unloaded two plastic bags from the back of the vehicle. "Leftover roast beef from the lodge, Mama." He held the bags aloft as though he were a hunter returning with his kill.

"*Sawubona,* Mama, *sawubona,* Baba," said Nokuthula, bowing her head as she greeted her parents-in-law. "It's good to see you again, Sister." She kissed Francina on the cheek. "I'll wash my hands and then help you serve the meal, Mama." She picked up one of the ten-liter bottles of water that she'd filled the previous evening and went into the house.

The entire village had watched in silence the day the government workers installed the faucet outside the elders' meeting hall a little over a year ago. After the workers had left, the men argued over who would test the water, and finally Winston chose his cousin, whom he'd once accused of cheating him over the price of a portable television. Before the appearance of the faucet the women had collected water from a nearby river, and at times like these, when it was nothing more than a trickle, tempers had flared and the whole village had lived on edge wondering if the government would send in the water truck. Now there was talk that each home in the village would have running water within two years.

Dingane emerged from the house, having placed the meat in the small refrigerator he'd bought from the lodge after one of its regular renovations.

"I worry about you, Sister," he said, taking another lawn chair and sitting down next to his father to await the evening meal.

He, too, had heard about her walk through the center of the village.

"It is something I have thought and prayed about," said Francina.

Her brother nodded. Theirs was one of thirty families that had left the traditional church to join the Methodist one in the next village. A local man had gone to Pietermaritzburg to study engineering so he could build roads but had come back an ordained minister and built a church instead. Winston and Francina had been married there, but when Winston returned from Johannesburg to become chief he asked the villagers to reject what he called the white man's religion and go back to the beliefs of their ancestors. For a time it had seemed that the village would split in two, but Winston did not like the idea of being chief of only half a village, and so he instructed his men to stop intimidating the Christians and let them go to church in peace. He never set foot in the church again.

"I will have to trust you then," said her brother. "All I ask is that you honor our parents."

Her father remained silent.

"I will," she promised. Sometimes she thought that her family was so used to seeing her with a glass eye that they'd forgotten why it was there.

As she prepared for bed, Francina took the chameleon out of her pocket and ran a finger along its beady spine. What would her family say if she told them about Hercules? Her brother in Durban wouldn't be shocked. After four years as a bricklayer in the province's biggest city, Sigidi fancied himself a man of the world.

Francina pulled the quilt up to her chin. The smell of her mother's pumpkin fritters still hung in the air. She'd never seen teenage boys with such an appetite. Her nephews had returned from putting the cattle in the kraal with the hunger of lions. They were growing into strong young men. Next time she would bring them tinned pilchards, not sweets.

A cricket chirped outside her window, but that was the only noise in the otherwise silent night. There were no shrieking car alarms, no security patrols cruising up and down the street, no automatic pool cleaners sucking in air.

The light of the full moon fell through the lace curtains and onto the geometric design of the basket she'd woven as a gift for Winston on their wedding day. Her mother had found it behind his compound, covered in compost. The number of points of the design signified how many cows Winston had paid her father in lebola. Twelve was a good price and he had not asked for any to be returned. Was that not proof of her innocence?

As yet she had no plan of action for the next day. "Please, God, show me what to do," she prayed. "And let it be over quickly, because I must get back to my boys."

In the morning her mother was waiting for her with a bowl of pap and some fried liver.

"You need your strength," she told her daughter.

Her brother and sister-in-law had left for work more than an hour ago, after washing outside so that they wouldn't disturb her. The boys had just sprinted off to school before the principal locked the door. Across the veld she could see her father mending one of the fences that kept his cattle from eating the family's maize, tomato, potato and pumpkin plants.

She finished eating and went inside to brush her teeth. When she came out, she noticed that her mother had put on her shoes.

"This is something I must do alone," said Francina.

Her mother shook her head. "You have been forced to do too much alone, my daughter."

Francina smiled at her mother and they set off toward the village. Women hunched over in the fields straightened and stared as they passed; a group outside the elders' meeting hall stopped beading to whisper to each other; men arguing loudly over how they would feed the cattle when the remaining grass had gone went silent.

As they approached the one-room building that served as a post office, her mother made a wide arc off the main path. Three months ago a tribunal composed of Winston and his indunas, or councilors, had found a man guilty of stealing two cows, and he was hanged from the tree that provided shade to people waiting for their mail.

Like most family compounds in the village, Winston's was enclosed by a low adobe wall, but his had a tall wooden gate. Francina and her mother stared at the carved bull's head as they waited for someone to become aware of their presence. It was not more than two minutes before a bare-chested man appeared.

"Yes?" he barked, opening the gate.

Francina stepped forward. "Please tell Winston that his ex-wife is here to see him."

The man closed the gate again, and Francina shook her head impatiently as though they'd been told to wait for another bus because this one was full. But it was only a brave show for her mother's sake, because inside, her blood felt like ice.

Fifteen minutes went by before the man came back.

"Follow me," he said.

Francina turned to her mother and kissed her on the cheek. "You stay here," she instructed her. "If it wasn't for you, my legs would not have carried me this far. Thank you, Mama."

Her mother bowed her head, and Francina knew that she would be praying every minute she was inside.

There were seven traditional round huts with thatched

roofs in the compound: one for Winston, one for each of the three wives he'd taken since reverting to his tribal beliefs after his divorce from Francina, one that was used as a kitchen, one for storage, and one for his guards. Together, Winston and his wives had twelve children: seven sons and five daughters.

Winston was sitting outside his hut on a wooden chair with a high straight back and wide armrests carved in the shape of crocodiles. He watched her walk across the neatly swept yard.

"You look old," he said when she stood before him.

"I have forty years," she said, "and I do not look old. I look young because I have not had to care for you."

"It's a good thing I did not waste my time with you, because you're a barren woman. I can see it in your eyes."

Francina felt like taking out her glass eye and throwing it at him.

"Do you know that your beating cost me an eye?" she asked.

He shrugged. "I know what I saw."

"You were drunk. What you saw was me giving the gardener some tea."

"I don't drink," he shouted at her, and his bare-chested guard, who had been squatting in the shade of a banana tree, started toward them. Winston waved him back.

"Maybe you don't now, but you'd just won money and were celebrating."

"You accuse me of gambling, too?" he thundered, and this time the guard came to stand at Winston's right hand. "My people know that I do not engage in these vices, and I expect them to be just as righteous."

The guard nodded. "You are the most righteous, Chief," he said.

Francina glared at him. "Can you ask him to go away, please? Surely you don't need protection against a woman."

Winston frowned but told the guard to leave anyway. She knew then that she had made progress.

"I know you won't apologize because you aren't sorry, but I want my honor back," she told him. "I don't care how you do it, but if you don't, I will tell everyone about your drunkenness and gambling in Johannesburg. And if you do anything to make my parents' lives difficult, I will have you arrested for assault. It's not too late. I checked with a policeman."

He stared at her for a long time. "Go," he said finally. Then he got up and disappeared into the darkness of his hut.

The guard was waiting outside the compound.

"Don't touch me," Francina told him as he grabbed her arm. There must have been something in her voice, because he let go immediately.

❧ Chapter Six ❧

The day after Francina's return from the Valley of a Thousand Hills, Mandla lay in front of the fan holding an ice cube above his stomach and watching the drops collect in his belly button. The boys had both taken a cool shower earlier in the evening, and he had refused to put on his pajama top. Monica couldn't blame him; it had been the hottest day they'd had this summer. All afternoon, storm clouds had massed on the horizon, but apart from a few rolls of thunder and a gusty wind, it had been yet another pathetic display that left nothing but a layer of dust on the furniture and a slight breeze that rustled the dead leaves of a tree fern outside the living-room window.

In the dry months of winter, veld fires were common, but just last week one had blackened the koppie behind Sipho's school. It was only a matter of time before the same thing happened to the vacant land between the highway and the entrance to their suburb, where hawkers sold everything from reconditioned mufflers to hand-carved wooden giraffes.

At the first electronic beat of the signal tune for *In-Depth*, Mandla threw down his ice cube.

"Monica's gonna be on TV," he called to Sipho, who was going through a geography workbook with Monica at the dining-room table.

"No, she's not," replied his big brother.

Mandla looked at Monica, and she shook her head.

"No, sweetie, I'm not going to be on TV anymore. It's another lady's turn." She asked Sipho, "Do you want to watch?"

He shook his head.

"That's fine, but I must. I'll help you with the rest of this in a little while."

She sat down next to Mandla on the sofa.

"No, no, leave me," he said as she tried to lift him onto her lap.

"That one is full of fireworks," said Francina, coming into the living room with a basket of clean laundry. "Okay, let's see this girl with the important daddy."

Nomsa was on first, with a story about the government's new equitable social pension scheme and how it had changed the lives of those used to receiving far less than whites under the apartheid government. In rural areas especially, grandmothers had become the main breadwinners in many homes. Her accent was upper-crust English, her delivery faultless, if a little flat, and she had a pretty face and shiny, straight hair that she kept tucking over her ears.

"Extensions," said Francina, reaching for another pair of socks to roll into a ball.

Monica felt too depressed to say anything. If the woman was horrible, she might have consoled herself with the knowledge that she'd been hired solely because of whom she knew. But the woman was not horrible. What did that say about her own capabilities? She felt as though someone had shown her another view of herself and it was not very pleasing. Maybe she wasn't such a good reporter after all.

A cup of hot chocolate and a long bath was what she really wanted, but she'd promised to help Sipho with the rest of his work, and the dear boy would not go to bed unless he'd finished the chapter. He loved the workbooks she'd ordered on the recommendation of a professor in the education department at her old university. Of course they would only put him even further ahead of his classmates, but his teacher had agreed to let him work on them whenever he finished in class, so he would always be occupied.

"No," protested Mandla as she turned off the television. "I want to see you."

"I'm not going to be on," she told him, but he would not budge from the sofa.

She turned the television on again, and while she went back to helping Sipho and Francina went off to her room, he sat glued to the screen for the rest of the show.

After kissing the boys good-night, Monica lay down fully dressed on her bed. It had been a difficult day even before watching her replacement on television. The union representatives were talking about a wage strike, and she didn't know how they'd survive if that happened. With hundreds of unemployed graduates who wouldn't think twice about crossing a picket line, a strike could go on long enough for the union to run out of money. And what if the company stopped their health insurance during the strike? She might have to sell the stocks her father had left her when exchange controls prevented him from taking all his money out the country. They'd plummeted in value and she was hoping to let them increase over time, but now it appeared that she might not have any. In the old days she would have taken an extra job waitressing, but now she needed to be at home to look after the children.

A mosquito danced dangerously close to the lamp next to her bed. She rolled over and stared at the black-and-white photograph of her parents on her nightstand. It was taken on their wedding day, and they wore broad smiles, as though confident the life that lay ahead of them would be easy just so long as they had each other. They'd tried their best and still things had gone wrong, so how was she to cope on her own? Moving to her parents' bedroom did not make her a parent; every day she made a mistake or had a new worry. When she first joined the radio station, she'd felt like a clumsy fool who couldn't get anything right, but now she knew what she was doing. With parenting it would never be that way; as soon as she got the hang of things, the boys would grow and change and she'd be facing new situations. How could she ever be a good parent if she never felt sure of her abilities?

Dear God, she prayed, please give me direction, because I seem to be losing my way.

Sighing, she sat up and began sifting through the pile of mail she'd brought with her to the bedroom. There were bills that had to be paid tomorrow; flyers advertising housepainting and new gated communities; a postcard from her parents who were visiting Rome; and a letter postmarked Lady Helen. She tore it open. It was from Dr. Niemand at the hospital. He wanted to thank her because donations had poured in after her story aired. With her prestigious and rewarding job he knew she wouldn't be interested in the advertisement he'd enclosed, but he wondered if she wouldn't mind passing it along to any friends who might be. It was a tiny snippet from the *Lady Helen Herald*. The paper's editor—and sole reporter—was retiring and looking for a successor.

Monica read it. Then she read it over and over until she was sure.

"Thank you, Lord," she whispered, "for answering my prayer."

She got up and paced the room, thinking furiously. Mandla would have more freedom to run around outdoors; Sipho would be in a smaller class and get more attention; the school principal might even push him ahead a year. *In-Depth* had probably been her only chance to work on television and that had been taken away from her. Why not work for a newspaper? Lady Helen was enchanting—how could they not be happy there? She stopped pacing. But what about Francina? How could Monica ask her to move that far away, especially now that she had a boyfriend? Sipho and Mandla had lost their mother; they could not lose Francina, too.

Francina snipped the thread with a pair of scissors and held up the finished garment to admire her handiwork. A week had passed since her visit home and the sense of satisfaction she felt when recalling the look of defeat on Winston's face had grown so that she could no longer contain her merriment. The chuckle she had allowed herself had become a full-throated roar of laughter.

The single lightbulb that hung from the ceiling was naked, yet it was bright enough to hatch chickens, or allow a one-eyed seamstress to spot a crooked seam, uneven darts or lumpy facings. It was another of the thoughtful changes Monica had begun carrying out after she came home from the hospital.

The lady at the Indian store had sold Francina the fabric at half price because it was stained, but one gentle rub with washing powder, three successive late nights at the sewing machine, and Francina had a beautiful flowing dress with a dainty Oriental collar, three-quarter-length sleeves, and most importantly, a waistline. She slipped the dress onto a padded hanger and hung it on the hook on the back of her door. Deep mauve was not a color she had ever worn before, but she'd searched through the rolls of navy and brown fabric and they were all flawless.

"It is time for you to find happiness," her mother had told her when they were saying goodbye.

Francina had never thought of that word in relation to herself. When Winston had chosen her to be his bride she'd called herself "the luckiest girl in the village," but she had never called herself happy. What is happiness anyway? she wondered. Isn't it the feeling you get when a child falls asleep in your arms, or when your house smells of polish, or when you flop into bed after an afternoon digging in the vegetable patch with an inquisitive young child at your side, or when you spend an evening shining a child's school shoes and listening to him practice the poem he'll recite at assembly? She pitied those for whom this wasn't enough. White smiles on white ski slopes were not life. They were an advertisement. If this was what you were seeking, disappointment would be your lifelong companion. Highs and lows were for teenagers, and as soon as people realized this and stopped trying to recapture these feelings there would be far less mischief out of wedlock, people would concentrate more on their families and their jobs, and the world would be a more contented place.

Had her mother given her this advice because she'd found the chameleon? No, her mother would never search through her things. Francina could not think how she had found out, but she felt suddenly sure that her mother knew she had a boyfriend. Was this what it meant to be a real mother—that you could live far away from your daughter and still know her heart? Francina would never be a real mother. She wished she could rub *that* reality away with a little washing powder.

Surely Hercules's mother was heartbroken that her only child wanted to bring home a woman who had passed her time. Francina had put him off for now with the excuse that she couldn't leave Monica and the boys again so soon, but she would have to go sometime. He seemed to be in a hurry for her to meet his mother. If she had her way, they would continue at the same pace for a couple of years—maybe forever. Her own mother worried about what would happen to her in old age with no children, but her nephews wouldn't let her starve. And Monica had once told her that she would give her a pension. No, never again would she rely on a man—not for money or security. Hercules would just have to understand.

Monica opened the workbook and Sipho began to read. "Most of South Africa sits at a high elevation, which means that temperatures are generally lower than other places at a similar latitude. The me...mete...what's this word, Monica?"

Monica was looking out the kitchen window. It was almost six-thirty and Francina would be coming in the back door to serve dinner any minute.

"What was that, sweetie?" She turned back to the page but had no idea where he was reading.

"This word," he said, pointing.

"Meteorological. It means to do with the atmosphere and weather conditions."

She could not put off telling Francina about the job in Lady Helen, not with her uncanny knack of knowing when something was brewing. It was a shame; in the week since her return from KwaZulu-Natal, Francina had been unusually cheerful.

As Sipho continued reading, the kitchen door opened and Francina entered carrying a dress that was covered with a dry-cleaning bag. When she saw that Monica and Sipho were busy, she hung it over the back of a chair and began dishing up the pasta.

Monica had faxed her résumé to the newspaper, and the outgoing editor wished to interview her immediately. Pastor Wessels thought it a wonderful idea, even if it meant losing his two favorite little friends. He'd had the good fortune, he told her, of spending a family weekend in Lady Helen after his son graduated from the University of Cape Town, and his wife had not wanted to leave.

"Sipho," Monica said. "I have to speak to Francina for a minute. Can you carry on without me?"

He nodded, rather too vigorously, she thought. She hadn't been much help to him this evening.

Francina grated Parmesan cheese while Monica pleaded her case.

"Lady who?" she wanted to know when Monica was finished.

"Helen."

Francina shook her head. "Never heard of it. Why isn't it called Sir something—or whatever you call the husband of a lady?"

Monica had not expected this. "She ran away from him and started the town with a group of slaves she'd freed."

Francina had grated enough cheese to accompany the meal but she continued. With her cheeks puffed out, she exhaled slowly, just as Sipho did when he was working on a particularly difficult math problem.

"It's a tiny place, but there's a sense of space there," added Monica. "The houses aren't enclosed behind high walls like they are here."

"Hercules wants me to meet his mother."

It was a simple statement, but it changed everything.

"I see," said Monica, trying not to show disappointment.

"I told him I couldn't take any more days off and that it would have to be in a few months' time."

The editor wanted to meet Monica this weekend. She'd take Friday off from work and the boys would accompany her. There was no need to postpone the inevitable.

"You can go on Friday if you want," said Monica.

Francina covered her forehead with her palms. "Ah, so soon?"

"You have your dress ready. I presume that's it on the chair."

Francina slipped it out of the plastic covering.

"It's gorgeous," said Monica, touching the fabric. Then she noticed the waistline. "And very feminine."

Francina hid her face behind the dress.

"Don't be shy," Monica told her. "You're a beautiful woman. But he knows that already, doesn't he?"

Francina left to take the dress back to her room before Mandla got his hands on it. As Monica sat down at the dinner table with the boys, she had a sinking feeling that Francina was about to disappear from their lives, as well.

"What's wrong?" asked Sipho.

"Nothing, sweetheart."

She was ashamed of her selfish thoughts. Francina was going to lead a comfortable life as the wife of a schoolteacher. She should be happy for her, not worrying about how she was going to cope alone.

"Would you like to go on an airplane again?" she asked.

"Yes, yes, yes," shouted Mandla.

Sipho's eyes widened. "To see Nonna and Nonno?"

She rubbed his back. "No, to have a look at a new place." She decided that it was not wise to tell him the real reason they were going when it might all come to naught anyway. Sipho had had enough disappointment in his short life.

"Will I have to miss school?"

She nodded, and it pained her to see how relieved he was. The editor had to offer her the job; they needed Lady Helen.

⚘ *Chapter Seven* ⚘

"Where do dogs sleep on a boat?" asked Mandla, kicking the back of Monica's seat.

Sipho sighed and rolled his eyes. At his insistence, Monica was relating the story of Lady Helen's beginning and she had just told them how Lord Charles Gray, British magistrate and collector of hunting dogs, had come to the Cape in 1806 to prepare for the formal cession of the colony from the Dutch to the British.

Sipho knew about slavery, but the next part of the story went over Mandla's head and Monica thought that she would wait a few years before explaining it to him.

Although slavery was common at that time, his wife, Lady Helen was horrified to be greeted at the wharf by a British commander bearing a gift of fifteen men and women to work in her kitchen and garden. A few of them had been imported from Asia, and the remainder had been captured in

Angola, Mozambique and Madagascar, because the Dutch East India Company, which started the Cape colony in 1652, had decreed that indigenous people were not to be enslaved.

"Lady Helen set up a secret school to teach the slaves how to read and write," continued Monica after passing a coloring book and crayons to Mandla. He hated to be still for any length of time. "But her husband discovered the school and ordered her to shut it down or go back to England."

"Why?" asked Sipho.

"It's easier to control people when they are ignorant. That means—"

"When they know as much as farm animals," said Sipho.

"That's right," said Monica. "So that same night she stole away with fifty slaves, all her husband's horses and four supply wagons, and traveled up the West Coast past the colony's outermost settlement of Saldanha Bay."

"Did he find her?" asked Sipho.

"They lived in peace for eight months before Lord Charles's search party found them. The slaves were whipped and marched back to Cape Town in chains, and those that survived the journey without food and water had their right Achilles tendon cut to prevent them from running away again."

Of the many history books Sipho had read, most related brutal events, but Monica still searched his face in the rearview mirror to make sure that he wasn't upset. He wasn't, and seemed to be lost in thought.

"What about Lady Helen?" he asked.

"Nobody knows. Some say she was shot and buried on the spot, others say she was taken back to Cape Town and imprisoned in her husband's wine cellar for the rest of her life."

As Monica turned off the main road toward the town of Lady Helen, Mandla's coloring book and crayons slid to the floor and Sipho leaned over and placed a light blanket over his sleeping brother.

"I think I see the ocean," he whispered excitedly.

"You're right. You win the prize for being the first to spot the Atlantic."

He'd seen the Mediterranean in Italy, yet this was the first time he'd seen the ocean in his own country.

"The reflection is so strong," he remarked, shielding his eyes.

In Italy, the humidity had softened the light, but here it was another of those endlessly blue, crackling dry West Coast days.

Sipho opened the window to sniff the air, and Monica decided to abandon the history lesson and let him enjoy the experience instead.

What she left unsaid was that the rudimentary town Lady Helen had started had been deserted for almost a century before a group of Afrikaans farmers moved in to form an ostrich-farming cooperative. The feathers fetched good prices in overseas markets, where they were highly prized in women's fashions, but before long, the co-op found that it could not compete with the slick operation in Oudtshoorn, a small town southeast of Lady Helen, and eventually it disbanded and the farmers turned to the ocean instead.

For almost sixty years Lady Helen was a thriving fishing port. But when deepwater trawlers started appearing on the horizon, the local fishermen were forced to abandon their homes and seek work in Cape Town, often with the very fishing corporations that had killed off their livelihood.

The town might have withered away in the sun had the celebrated artist S. W. Greeff not happened upon it on one of his walkabouts and fallen in love with the overgrown bougainvillea, run-down fishermen's cottages and clear bright light. Other artists followed, and soon the town had developed a reputation as a serious art center.

When a Malaysian businessman built a luxury golfing resort just north of town, farmers and merchants moved in, hoping to supply it with fresh produce, meat, milk, bread and cleaning equipment. This never happened. Save for the abalone that local women scraped off the rocks, everything was trucked in from Cape Town. And, to make matters worse, the guests didn't venture out of the resort grounds. Some said golfers just weren't art lovers, but there was more to Lady Helen than art galleries. Only one man from the town had been given employment at the resort. He washed dishes, and acted as the town's spy. He was the one who reported that the developer and owner, Mr. Yang, was telling his guests that it was unsafe to leave the resort's premises. This, of course, was untrue, but as most of the guests were foreigners, they did not know enough about the area to suspect otherwise.

The farmers and merchants were disheartened, but as luck would have it, they did not have to pack up and leave. Lured by accounts of the clean water, clear light and peace, people began arriving in Lady Helen by the carload from places as far afield as Zimbabwe, and it was not long before the artists' colony was a proper little town with a school, a hospital and a mayor. The most recent addition to Lady Helen's economy was a collection of scuba operations that specialized in wreck diving. Lady Helen was healthier than it had ever been.

Mandla woke up when Monica stopped on top of the koppie so that Sipho could take a look at the town down below.

"Is that a playground?" he asked sleepily as she picked him up out of his car seat.

Remembering how her first sight of Lady Helen had made her think of a coral reef, Monica smiled. Sipho was more interested in the ocean than the town.

"If you were on a boat and headed west you'd reach South America," he explained, but Mandla had picked up stones and was enjoying the sound they made as he threw them one by one onto a giant boulder twenty feet below.

Main Street was closed to traffic for the town's summer art festival, an event that drew visitors from all over the country, and by the time Monica entered the pasture that had been fenced off as a parking lot for the weekend, it was almost full. If the editor hadn't reserved them a room at a bed-and-breakfast owned by one of his friends, they would be driving back to Cape Town tonight.

"I'm hungry," announced Mandla, spying a display of pastries in the window of the café Monica remembered from her first trip.

It had been four hours since their early lunch at the airport.

"Let's go in then," she said.

Mandla charged ahead into Mama Dlamini's Eating Establishment. People moved aside when they saw who was poking their legs.

"Don't do that," Monica told him, apologizing to everyone as they made their way through. But nobody minded.

They all exclaimed how adorable he was, and one woman in an elegant black-and-cream caftan even pinched his cheeks. Mandla gave her an angelic smile, and she hurriedly wrapped up her half-eaten Chelsea bun, took a long swig of coffee and offered them her table.

"No, please finish," said Monica. "We'll find another one."

"No, you won't, lovey," said the woman, standing up. "Not this weekend. None of us artists like this hullabaloo, but it's what enables us to stay here." She wore a ceramic butterfly barrette in her afro and around her neck a string of asymmetrical brown ceramic beads.

Mandla had already climbed onto her chair and was looking at the picture on the front of the menu. Sometimes Monica could not believe how like his mother he was.

"Well, then, thanks," said Monica.

Suddenly, the woman pointed straight at her. "It's you! You're the girl from television, the one Max is interviewing for his position."

Monica reached for Sipho's hand, but he moved away from her.

"Once you've discovered Lady Helen, you always come back," continued the woman, oblivious of the awkwardness she'd caused between Monica and Sipho. "All these people come back year after year. Only the lucky ones like us get to stay." She touched Monica on the shoulder. "Max is going to love you, I can tell."

After she'd gone, Sipho picked up a menu and studied it in silence.

"I didn't tell you because I wasn't sure if it would work out," said Monica. She reached for his hand again, and this time he let her take it. "And I wanted to see if you liked the place, too. Please, sweetheart, don't be cross."

"Okaaay," he said, drawing out the word. Then he clapped his hands sharply, and Mandla immediately put down the jug of maple syrup he had been about to pour into the sugar bowl.

They ordered chicken wraps, and Mandla devoured his as though he hadn't eaten for days. Sipho, who was normally not fussy, picked out the chicken and complained that the dressing was too salty.

Mama Dlamini was doing her rounds to check that her patrons were satisfied with their meals. Mandla watched her squeeze her large shape between the tables and was about to deliver a loud comment, when Monica held her finger to her lips to shush him. Mama Dlamini's laugh was a series of yaps, like a little dog, and it seemed to be brought on by everything: a greeting, a compliment on the food, a request for more coffee. Monica looked around her. People seemed to be chewing slower so that their host would get to them before they had finished their meal.

"Do you like your chicken wraps?" she asked when it was their turn to receive her at their table.

"They're just wonderful," said Monica. She knew that Sipho would not contradict her.

Mama Dlamini put her hand on Mandla's head. "This one is a firebrand," she said.

Monica felt as though her heart had skipped a beat. It was the exact word Ella had used on her deathbed to refer to her youngest son.

"I hope I see you again, young man," she told Sipho, resting her hand between his shoulder blades.

Sipho smiled, but he was not comfortable being touched.

After they'd wiped ketchup from Mandla's hair, hands and eyelashes, visited the bathroom and paid the bill, they left Mama Dlamini's and immediately found themselves in the midst of a crowd. A sign in front of the large gallery next door announced that S. W. Greeff would be talking about "The Artist as Instrument of Social Change" at four o'clock.

"Can we wait?" asked Sipho.

Monica was surprised. "Do you know who he is?"

"He painted *The Little Girl and the Whale*. It was on the cover of one of my nature magazines. The whale had beached itself and died, and the little girl was standing staring into one of its huge eyes."

"That's so sad."

"It's nature. Some say an ear infection can affect their navigation, some say they swim into bays with narrow openings and panic when they think they're trapped."

He's growing up, thought Monica. Not long ago an image of a dead animal or an animal killing another for food would have brought tears.

A teenage girl in ripped jeans and a white cotton tunic appeared at the door and announced that there was no more space in the gallery. The crowd outside groaned.

"Sorry, sweetheart," said Monica.

"I don't think *he* would have sat still anyway," said Sipho, tipping his head in his little brother's direction.

"Oh no," said Monica, rushing to disentangle Mandla's fingers from the shimmering fringe of a lady's poncho.

She apologized profusely, but the lady said how could she

mind when her little stalker had such a darling face. Mandla's charm had worked again, but Monica thought it wise to get him to an open space before he landed in real trouble.

Remembering the park that ran along the beachfront, she took Mandla's hand and led the boys down Main Street. The distance was longer than she recalled, but Mandla kept up with her steady, limping pace and Sipho did not complain.

A stiff breeze gusting off the ocean made Mandla catch his breath, and sent him down the lawn, flapping his arms like a baby albatross learning to fly. Even Sipho smiled.

A group of string musicians was setting up its instruments on the amphitheater stage, and soon Mandla was singing at the top of his voice to the amusement of everyone within earshot. When the group opened with an upbeat folksy number he began to dance, and before long he'd gathered a small audience. People even started leaving their picnic blankets and lawn chairs in the amphitheater to see what was going on up top.

"Give a bow," Monica told him, hoping to put an end to his performance.

His fans clapped as he swept his hand low to the ground.

"Let's go see the ocean, my little star," she said.

It probably wasn't wise as the breeze had picked up, but it was the only way she could get him away. What would he have done next? Climbed onstage with the musicians?

The narrow strip of beach between the palm trees and ocean was a white haze of blowing sand. Just offshore, a large pile of rocks was being pounded by the incoming tide. While

Sipho and Monica watched from the grass, Mandla ran along the beach squealing. Sand clung to his clothes, his hair, and even his eyelashes when he returned. Monica dusted him off and said that they'd better go and find Abalone House before the owner gave their room away.

With the concert in full swing the park had filled up, so Monica led the boys behind the stage toward the rock garden, where they came upon a man welding a wrought-iron fence that enclosed a statue.

"I want to see," Mandla said, trying to escape her grip.

"No, it's dangerous," she explained, but this only made him struggle harder.

The man switched off his torch and lifted his welder's helmet. "Sorry, Mam," he said. "I wouldn't normally do this with people around, but someone has stolen one of the globes off the top of this gate and a little kid could get hurt if I left it like this." He shook his head. "How they cut it off I don't know."

"Why would someone do that?" asked Monica.

The man shrugged. "Bored teenagers dragged here by their parents? Who knows? Kids nowadays aren't interested in building anything new, just tearing down the old."

The statue was of a woman dressed in a long skirt, fitted jacket and frilly bonnet. A plaque underneath identified her as Lady Helen Gray.

Mandla finally managed to wriggle free and touched the tattoo on the man's forearm.

"Come here," said Monica, embarrassed.

"That's all right. You think I've drawn on myself, don't you, little fellow?"

Mandla grinned and looked at Monica as though to say, "See, I'm not the only one who does things like this."

"That's what you do when you're young and have been cooped up on a ship for three months."

Mandla nodded vigorously, as though he understood.

The man's face was lined, his hair almost completely gray, but under his faded checked shirt his arms and shoulders were muscular, his back broad.

"Have you found anything you want to buy?" he asked.

Monica shook her head. "We're not here for the festival. I have a job interview."

"Ah, Max's job. You're the girl from that television show. I didn't recognize you. You look a bit plumper on TV. I'm Oscar." He stuck out his hand, and then, noticing that it was dirty, wiped it on his jeans.

Choosing not to interpret Oscar's comment as an insult, she shook his hand.

"Did you make that beautiful fence around the cemetery?" she asked.

He nodded. "And one day I'll show you how it's done, little fellow."

Mandla jumped up and down with excitement. "I'm gonna hold the fire stick, Sipho," he shouted.

"We'll start with something safer and work up to that when you're, say, fifteen," said Oscar, but Mandla was running around his brother and didn't hear.

Sipho caught him at the waist. "You're going to get dizzy."

Mandla gave him a quick kiss on the cheek and Sipho smiled but still wiped it with his arm.

They said goodbye to Oscar and began the long trek back

to the car. Main Street was a little quieter now, with most people inside the galleries listening to presentations, at the park for the afternoon concert or in the cafés and restaurants getting an early dinner.

The bed-and-breakfast Max had picked out was set on the northeastern edge of town, not far from the hospital. As they passed the cemetery, Mandla shouted, "I'm going to make a fence even bigger than that."

Like most of the buildings in Lady Helen, Abalone House had a tin roof, wood-frame windows, a resident bougain-villea—this one orange—and a wide covered veranda with a polished concrete floor. It felt good to step into the shade at last, and Monica looked longingly at the wicker lounge chairs that were arranged around an old wooden chest. Mandla's attention was piqued, not by a swing with green-and-white-striped cushions, but by some rather rickety-looking rocking chairs.

"Be careful," she told him.

"He'll be fine," said a woman, opening the screen door. "They look ready for the fire, but they're very strong. You must be Monica. I'm Clare, but most people call me Kitty."

Mandla burst into laughter. He loved this magical place where the grown-ups talked his language.

Kitty was tall and slim with high cheekbones, hazel eyes and wisps of short dark hair around her face. She was striking rather than pretty in the conventional sense, and Monica wondered if she had, at one time, been a runway model.

"Let me show you to your room. I'm afraid the main house is full, but as a special favor to Max I've cleared out the Old Dairy."

Mandla gave a whoop. "We're gonna sleep with the cows!"

Kitty laughed. "It was converted into a cottage years ago, but I'd filled it with boxes."

"Have you just moved here?" asked Monica.

"A year ago, from Cape Town. But we've been so busy getting things into shape that I'm afraid there are some things I haven't gotten to yet. Thanks to you, the Old Dairy is no longer one of them."

The whitewashed cottage was behind the main house, across a thick green lawn littered with overripe apricots.

"I'd better make jam before they've all fallen off," said Kitty, opening the barn-door entrance.

The Old Dairy had a living room with a deep green sofa, floral armchair and yellowwood coffee table, a small area with a sink, refrigerator and microwave, a large bathroom with an open shower and a bedroom with a four-poster bed draped in flowing white organza.

"The sofa pulls out into a double bed," explained Kitty. "There are extra sheets and blankets in the cupboard. If you need anything just pick up the phone and dial twenty-nine. You might have to let it ring. The other guests are having dinner in tonight, but I'm sure you're tired and would rather I brought you a tray."

After she'd left, Mandla tore around the place opening cupboards, looking behind the curtains, even investigating the refrigerator. Monica didn't have the energy to stop him.

"There's no TV," he announced dejectedly, when there was nowhere left to search.

She scooped him into her arms. He was tired. "You'll have

fun in that nice big shower. Then we'll eat and play some games. And tomorrow we can go for a walk around the neighborhood."

The next morning Main Street was still closed for the festival, so Monica left the car outside a restaurant and they cut through the park to the newspaper office, which was located in a converted warehouse that had once been full of boxes of ostrich feathers. On one of the exterior walls you could just make out the two-story-high outline of a woman with an elaborate feathered hat. Elegant, Sophisticated, Ahead Of Their Time. That's Parisian Women, said the looping letters underneath.

In its position as the last building before the park, the newspaper office would have been an easy walk from Abalone House, but their long stroll earlier in the morning had worn them out. They'd needed the exercise after the breakfast of muesli, homemade yogurt, fresh fruit, creamy sweet cheese, wholewheat pancakes with walnuts and maple syrup, guava juice and strong red bush tea. No wonder Kitty didn't have time to get everything done.

Watching Mandla eat five chunks of cheese, Kitty had suggested they visit Peg at the local dairy to get some to take home. Any other weekend, she said, Peg would give them a tour, but she would probably be swamped with customers.

They'd walked past the dairy and Mandla had enjoyed talking to the cows, but they didn't go in because it *was* crowded. Behind the farm a green field stretched halfway up a koppie and then stopped abruptly as pale fynbos took over. The farm could not have been more than a mile from the center of town, and on either side of it were regular houses from the same period, which led Monica to believe that it had been planned this way.

When they reached Main Street, Mandla had wandered over to investigate the open irrigation ditch. *Francina and I will have to watch him with those around,* she'd told herself, but then she remembered where Francina was for the weekend and the excitement that had been building inside her fell flat.

Max had agreed to let the boys sit in on the interview, and as they waited in the reception room Monica gave them final instructions on how to behave, or rather, she gave Mandla instructions; Sipho had chosen a novel from Kitty's library and was already engrossed in it. Nobody else was about, but Max had seen them arrive and announced over the public-address system that he would be with them shortly. A ceiling fan clicked overhead. Mandla flipped idly through the books Monica had brought to keep him occupied.

A door opened and an elderly man with tufts of gray hair above each ear appeared. "Miss Brunetti. It's good to meet you," he said, moving slowly toward her using a cane.

She put a hand on Mandla's shoulder to stop him from going over to get a closer look at its ornate handle.

"Come into my office, please. I have some cool drinks for the children."

His cheeks sagged and he had liver spots along his forehead where his hairline used to be, but his clear blue eyes and strong jaw made Monica believe that he had been handsome in his youth.

After they'd followed him into the office, he asked Sipho to shut the door. "Just in case a tourist wanders in," he explained. "The place is like an ants' nest this weekend."

He offered a chair to Monica and directed the boys to a worn orange sofa.

"I'm afraid this doesn't come with the job," he said of the expensive-looking executive chair that he lowered himself into behind his desk. "I bought it when my arthritis got bad, and I'll use it at home when I start writing my memoirs—for my son, not for publication. He bought me a computer. I've never used one before. As you can see I prefer to store my information where I can see it." He waved his arm at the row of metal filing cabinets that lined two walls. "There's fifty years of work in those things—forty in Cape Town, ten here."

He noticed Sipho staring at the framed photographs that almost covered the wall behind him.

"And those are the people I met during that time. How do you take all of this and feed it into a computer?"

Monica sensed that Sipho had the answer on the tip of his tongue, but the question would remain rhetorical because he would not speak unless addressed directly.

"As you may have noticed, we're all on first-name terms in Lady Helen, so please don't call me Mr. Andrews. That's reserved for the taxman and irate readers."

She unzipped her portfolio. "I've brought some of my work to show you," she said.

He waved it away. "That's not necessary. I've seen you on *In-Depth*. You're talented—that's a given. I wanted to meet you in person. I have a knack for sizing people up within seconds. It's what's enabled me to stay in this business when so many have escaped to—" he sniffed "—advertising and public relations."

Monica noticed Sipho's mouth tighten.

"Both of which are essential to a successful economy," said Monica.

Max frowned at the interruption.

"Sipho's mother was a public-relations executive—a brilliant one, I might add," said Monica.

A broad grin spread across Max's wrinkled face. "That's exactly why I wanted to meet you in person. Talent you can see on the screen or on the written page, but character one needs to witness firsthand. The job is yours if you want it."

Monica looked at Sipho, but his face was impassive.

"Thank you. May I take a while to discuss it with my family?"

"Of course," he said. "There's only one thing I require of you, Monica."

"Yes?" she said, expecting a request for a copy of her degree certificate or her driver's license.

"It's respect," he said. "Not for me—you can call me whatever you wish—but for everyone in this town. Some of these city types—like the ones trotting about today—treat us like a country amusement park. Our lives may be simpler here, but that does not mean we are simple people."

Monica felt like telling him that his wonderful skills of judgment had failed him if he thought he needed to warn her about this, but it was too early in their relationship for her to be so bold. It would come later, though; of that she was sure.

They found Dr. Niemand around the back of the clinic staring at the shell of a dismantled generator.

"Monica!" he exclaimed. "Good to see you again. Are you going to take the job?"

How did he know she'd been offered the job when they'd only just left the newspaper office? She'd expected him to be astonished to see her in Lady Helen again.

"I'll have to discuss it with my family," she said, sneaking another peek at Sipho.

"That's wise," said Dr. Niemand, smiling at Sipho.

Why was she surprised that he already knew she was the parent of two young black boys?

"I have to admit I'm stuck," he said, indicating the metal pieces lined up on the grass in front of him. "I thought I'd save money fixing it myself."

He took off his glasses and rubbed his eyes, as he'd done the day she'd first met him. Fatigue was clearly his constant companion. He had allowed his military-style haircut to grow out a little, and whether it was this or the color in his cheeks from today's work outdoors Monica thought he was more attractive than she'd remembered. She glanced at his left hand. He was not wearing a ring.

Mandla picked up a piece that resembled a metal kidney.

"I'll give you five rand if you can tell me where that goes, young man," said Dr. Niemand.

With his jaw set in determination, Mandla began trying to fit the pieces into the nooks and crannies of the machine.

Dr. Niemand turned to Monica. "Don't go thinking we're an inquisitive lot that gets on the phone as soon as something happens here. It was a no-brainer that Max would offer you the job. Everybody here loved the story you did on the hospital."

"How about this?" asked Mandla, pointing to where he had jammed the kidney-shaped metal piece into a hollow.

Dr. Niemand took out his wallet. "A deal is a deal," he told Mandla, handing over a five-rand coin.

"Look, Sipho, money!" shouted Mandla, holding it up. He tugged on Dr. Niemand's trouser leg. "I can do more," he said earnestly.

"I wish I'd known that before, little man," said Dr. Niemand, "but the repair guy should be arriving any minute."

Mandla groaned. "Okay, but we're going to come and live here, so next time don't forget to call me."

"I will," said Dr. Niemand. He nodded knowingly at Monica and she felt excited at the thought of seeing him again.

A car beeped its horn outside the hospital's front entrance.

"I've got to go," he said. "We're picking up my daughter, Yolanda, from a school camp."

"How old is she?" asked Monica, trying hard to hide her disappointment at the news that he was a family man.

"Twelve going on forty. She says she's the boss of me."

"We'll be off then. I just wanted to thank you for sending me the advertisement for the job."

"Max has already done that," he said, smiling. "He called as soon as you left his office."

Mandla joined in on their laughter, but Sipho stood watching warily.

The next day, the sun was still high in the sky when they reached the top of the koppie and took one final look at the town of Lady Helen down below. Even the most jaded of travelers would have paused to admire its cascading bougainvillea, but Monica was sorry that Sipho could not see it late in the afternoon when the vivid colors of sunset reflected gently off the tin roofs, giving it an ephemeral glow.

"What do you think?" she asked finally, when it seemed that he had no intention of offering his opinion.

"My mother's ashes are scattered in the Garden of Remembrance in Johannesburg. That's over nine hundred miles away." His large eyes were a little too shiny.

Monica took her hand off the steering wheel and rested it on his leg. "That's true," she told him. "But her soul is in heaven."

"I can't see her soul, but I can see that the roses in the Garden have grown since we spread her ashes there."

"That's true, too, Sipho. But faith is not seeing, it's knowing, and you *know* your mother watches over you wherever you are."

"You're right," he said, and from the quiver in his voice she knew that he was crying.

She took his hand. "We don't have to go if you don't want to. Think about it, and when you're ready let me know."

"Okay," he said, giving a little shudder of a sob.

A short way ahead a falcon circled high in the sky. Suddenly, it swooped down to the ground in a steep dive, and then reappeared with a wriggling snake gripped in its talons.

"Wow!" exclaimed Sipho. "Did you see that, Mandla?" His cheeks were still wet, but this time his eyes shone with excitement.

"I want to see it again," whined Mandla. It was past his naptime.

Delicate shrubs covered the shale flats in shades of dusty green. Though the art festival in Lady Helen was halfway through, cars were still traveling toward the town, and more than once Monica had to pull onto the verge to allow a tour bus to squeeze past. By the time they got to the main road, Mandla had fallen asleep.

Driving past the giant fish-canning factories on the industrial outskirts of Cape Town—the very factories that had once stolen Lady Helen's men—Monica could not help thinking that if a whole town could reinvent itself, so could she. It wouldn't be easy, but with God's help it could be done. Now she prayed for Him to touch Sipho's heart and make him understand that change could be a wonderful thing, if only he would allow it to happen.

Chapter Eight

Francina did not need a signpost to tell her that she was in her home province of KwaZulu-Natal. Even with her eyes shut she would know when they'd crossed the border. It was a sense of recognition that only grew sharper the longer she lived somewhere else, and, of course, the snake in her stomach helped by coiling restlessly as home grew closer. This time she was not going all the way home, but still she felt a twitch in the pit of her belly.

It was five o'clock when her taxi arrived in Dundee, and, as with all taxi ranks on Friday afternoons, this one was packed. The waiting area under the tin roof had been taken over by women selling plates of hot food, men giving last-minute haircuts to travelers and a few old men in shabby clothes clutching brown paper bags. There were no numbers on any of the concrete pillars, no signs to differentiate between local and long-distance taxis. Hercules should have given her directions to a nearby shop where she could wait for him away from this ants' nest. They'd never find each other now. She closed her eyes and saw herself still here late at night with only the old men and their brown paper bags for company. Was this what her mother had meant when she said it was time for her to find happiness? The driver handed her the small bag she had brought with her for this short visit, and she stepped away from the taxi to avoid being knocked down by people racing to get a seat. Her neck ached from leaning against the window while she'd tried without luck to sleep, and she was disappointed to see that her beautiful new dress had creased rather badly.

"Sorry, sorry," she said as she bumped into someone. Small as these heels were, she was not used to wearing any. Maybe she should have stuck with her comfortable lace-up shoes. She looked down and there stood a young boy holding his cupped hands up to her.

"I'm hungry," he said.

Francina had not been able to finish the sandwich she'd made before leaving Johannesburg, and so she handed this to him and watched as he gobbled it down. His nose ran and his eyes were dull. In a village somewhere a mother lay awake at night crying for the son who had run away. She was tempted to give him money to take a taxi home, but she suspected he would only spend it on glue to sniff. And if she marched him to that policeman buying an orange over there, she would be laughed at and told to stop wasting an official's time.

"Go home to your mother," she said, and the boy looked at her blankly.

What sort of a world is this, she wondered, where a homeless boy can wander through a crowd of people and nobody lifts a finger to help? In the villages, people gossiped, stared and pointed cruel fingers, but they would not let a boy sleep on the street.

A hand clamped down on her shoulder, and she jerked it away with such force that she stumbled through a group of women. They were all wearing trousers and matching jackets.

"Watch it," said one with a briefcase.

"Sorry," said Francina.

"Francina, it's me," called a voice, and there on the other side of the unfriendly women in men's clothing was Hercules.

In a second he was at her side, taking her bag from her, steering her out of the crowd, telling her that it wouldn't be long and she'd be able to freshen up in a clean bathroom at his house. She thought that this was what it must feel like to be a child again. That reminded her—where was the boy? She looked back but he had disappeared, no doubt begging now from another woman who would give him a crust of bread and allow him to go on. "Suffer the little children to come unto me," Jesus had said, but he did not mean we should *let* them suffer if it was within our power to do something. Tonight she would ask God's forgiveness for not having helped a child in need. *You'll never get off your knees,* she told herself, *with all the needy children in Africa.*

In the car on the way to his house Hercules asked after Monica and the boys, and she chose not to tell him that they had gone to the Cape for a job interview. That would only force the conversation in a direction she did not yet feel comfortable to go. If it were up to her, she'd continue to work for Monica in Johannesburg and would see Hercules whenever it could be arranged. Twice a month would be nice. But both Hercules and Monica wanted change, and after years of not making any decisions in her life beyond which fabric to buy and what to prepare for dinner, she would now have to make some.

He pointed out the mountains to her: Indumeni, which means where the thunder rolls; Mpati, place of good waters; and the flat-topped Talana, which means shelf for precious items. On the last peak, he said, the first shot of the Second Anglo-Boer War was fired in 1899.

"I can't get away from being a history teacher," he explained apologetically.

He said history was a hot potato because people saw it differently, depending on the color of their skin. The whites, for example, and especially those in KwaZulu-Natal, thought that the history of their province began in 1824 when British settlers put down roots in Port Natal, now known as Durban. Blacks, he said, knew that before these foreigners Zulu kings like Shaka, Dingane, Mpande and Cetshwayo had ruled the green hills and coastal flats.

"How can we live together today if we don't know how we all got here?" he wanted to know. "Ambiguity sows dissent."

She nodded, even though she wasn't sure what he was talking about.

Hercules's house was on the outskirts of town, where the plots of land were larger. It had a fence around it, the type builders put up when a house is complete but which most people tear down and replace with a wall. At uniform intervals giant cactuses provided a natural version of an electric fence to keep out *ditsotsi*—those men with nothing on their minds but evil. After opening the gate, Hercules got back in the car and drove slowly up the concrete driveway to park under a carport with a yellow corrugated-plastic roof. He opened her door, removed her bag from the trunk, and then pulled a heavy chain across the entrance to the carport and fastened it with a padlock.

"You look very pretty," he said.

"Thank you." She was too shy to look at his face. "I made this dress myself."

"You should have a shop."

From his earnest tone she knew that he was not just trying to flatter her.

"I'm happy with my situation," she said.

A shadow crossed his face and she could have kicked herself for not choosing her words more carefully. The only difference between the educated and people like me, she thought, is that they put their brains in gear before they open their mouths.

The lawn was newly mowed, the edges had been trimmed, but despite its neatness there was a neglected air to the garden. There were no flower beds, no rows of shrubs, no creepers trailing over the fence. It was as though it was kept up as a matter of duty but never enjoyed.

The house was identical to all the others in the street: a square brick block with a tile roof and a small front porch. They had once all belonged to the whites who worked in the coal mines when Dundee was a boomtown, explained Hercules. For an instant Francina allowed herself to wonder what it would be like not to have to go outside in the middle of the night to use the bathroom. When the moment was over she felt guilty. Her bathroom was outside for a practical reason: so the gardener could use it during the day, too. They hadn't had a gardener in ages because they now used a service, but did she really want any of those men to come into her room to use her bathroom? Of course not. Then it was just as well it was outside, icy highveld winter nights or not.

Hercules put a key in the lock, opened the front door and gave a long, loud whistle.

"That's to let my mother know it's me," he explained. "Otherwise she thinks it's a burglar."

In the living room an old but spotless three-piece floral suite was arranged around a dark wood coffee table, on top of which was a crocheted runner and a vase of artificial flowers. Next to the television a bookcase overflowed with music books. A large photograph of Hercules in front of his choir held pride of place above the mock fireplace.

"My mother put that up," he explained.

Above the sofa was one of a large group of people with children: his aunts, uncles, cousins and their families. He did not say anything about the small photo on the mantelpiece of a young bride and groom.

He showed her to the bathroom and when she came out his mother was sitting in the living room with a tray of tea and a plate of freshly baked scones on the table in front of her. She stood up as Francina approached.

"You must be tired, my dear," she said. "We thank you for taking the trouble to come so far." She took both Francina's hands.

"Thank you for inviting me into your home, Mrs. Shabalala," said Francina, wishing that the lady would let go of her hands.

"Call me Mama."

"Yes, Mama," said Francina, but the word did not feel right. It was too soon.

Hercules had told her that his mother was sixty-five, but she appeared older. Her face was lined, her movements slow and deliberate as though she was in pain. Only three things could make a person appear old before their time, thought Francina, and those were a life of backbreaking work, great sorrow or a terrible illness eating the person away from inside. It had to be one of the last two, because Hercules had told her that his mother had not worked outside the home since he was born. Francina decided that she would call the poor woman Mama if that's what she wanted.

There was not much of Hercules in his mother's round face and short, plump build. His father must have been a real string bean, thought Francina.

"What am I doing?" said his mother, finally letting go of Francina. "The tea is getting cold." She sat down with difficulty. Her hand shook as she lifted the teapot.

"Please let me do that, Mama," said Francina.

"Thank you, Daughter."

As Francina took the teapot from her, she noticed Hercules smiling broadly. It was not something this serious man did often, and she had a sudden feeling that she wanted to make it happen again. She, Francina Zuma, one-eyed housekeeper and seamstress, wanted to make this tall, skinny history teacher smile.

* * *

After a dinner of roast lamb, potatoes, spinach and cauliflower, and rice pudding for dessert, Francina carried coffee into the living room and sat down with Hercules's mother while he washed the dishes.

"African men do not do women's work, but my Hercules is different," explained his mother.

Francina did not think this was right, but said nothing. She knew that uncomfortable questions were about to follow.

"Have you passed your time, my daughter?"

Her apprehension had been right on the mark.

"I have, Mama. It came early."

Hercules's mother nodded while she seemed to chew on this. "I have no grandchildren."

Francina hoped that Hercules could not hear this conversation. "I know, Mama. And I am very sorry for this."

What was she supposed to do? Promise that she would not see Hercules again so that he could meet someone younger?

"You know, Francina, the past fifteen years seem like a hundred. First Hercules lost his wife, and then his father." She shook her head. "If you saw my husband and me together you would have said I was the one with sugar sickness. He was like this." She held up a baby finger. "My son is sick, too."

Francina caught her breath. Hercules had the sugar sickness? Why hadn't he told her? Was he testing her attachment? Then he would find out that she, Francina Zuma, was not a flighty young girl who ran from hardship.

"I did not know," she said quietly.

His mother nodded. "It's inside." She patted her chest. "In his heart."

Francina swallowed hard. His heart, too?

"It's hard to tell that he's sick," continued his mother, "but it's clear when he's at home."

Francina thought that she might not have been paying enough attention, because she had not noticed anything. It was probably because she was nervous being here.

"Hercules has not looked at a woman for years. Now he has chosen you. I do not mind that you cannot give me grandchildren because I know you are the one who can make my son better."

Francina wondered if she had heard correctly. Did the woman just say that *she* could make Hercules better? She was not a doctor. Was this a premature touch of old people craziness? But she could not question Hercules's mother because at that moment he walked in, having finished the dishes and taken out the rubbish.

They sat for a while talking, and when it was time for bed Hercules announced that Francina would take his bedroom and he would sleep on the couch in the living room. She followed him down the short passage, past his mother's bedroom and the bathroom, to the closed door at the end.

"I hope you'll be comfortable in here," he said, opening it for her.

There was a double bed with a pale green tasseled bedspread, a padded white headboard and a dressing table with a long skirt like the one in Monica's old room.

"The sheets are clean and there's a fresh towel over there." He pointed to a wooden chest in the corner, upon which lay a hand-embroidered pink towel. "Wake me if you need anything." He smiled tenderly, as one would when tucking in a child for the night.

She grew warm with emotion for this sweet, sick man. She could not do what his mother said, but she could make him smile and sick people sometimes needed that more than anything.

Once he'd closed the door, she went straight to the framed photo on the dressing table. The woman wore the same shy smile as in the photo Hercules carried in his wallet, but he was in this one too, his arm resting loosely around her shoulders and a broad grin on his face such as she'd never seen before. Francina knew then that she did not merely have to make him smile; she had to make him laugh.

Sighing, she slipped out of her new dress. The other clothes she had brought were probably creased like dishrags by now. She unpacked her bag. Yes, the outfit she'd wear tomorrow needed ironing. It was a tent dress, made from a formal navy paisley fabric so that it wouldn't look like something she'd wear around the house. The red jacket and black skirt she'd brought for church simply needed to be hung up. There wasn't a hook on the back of the door. Would Hercules mind if she hung her clothes in his closet? He'd said to ask if she needed anything, but she could hear the water running in the bathroom and didn't want to disturb him for such a small request.

She opened one of the slatted wooden doors of the built-in closet. The rail was tightly packed with shirts and trousers. No wonder his shirt never looked as crisp and fresh as it would if she were taking care of his clothes. She opened the other closet door, and that side, too, was tightly packed—with dresses, blouses, skirts and formal outfits in plastic dry-cleaner bags. At the bottom of the closet was a shoe rack filled with sandals, high-heeled dress shoes, flat slip-ons, a pair of fluffy pink slippers. Francina closed the doors in such a hurry she feared that Hercules would come and investigate the noise. Forgetting everything she knew about respect for another's property, she opened the drawer of the dressing table. There were eye shadows—some cracked into bits, others almost completely used up, lipsticks that had melted, bottles of dried-up nail polish, foundation caked like the earth during a drought. All were from another decade. There were curlers, barrettes, headbands, combs, a hairbrush with black hairs in it. Francina closed the drawer with care as though she were a burglar in the night.

Should she look under the pillow? No, it was pointless; he wouldn't. Or would he? She lifted the bedspread and looked under the pillow on the left. Nothing. She lifted the pillow on the right and there lying neatly folded was a silky slip of peach fabric—a lady's nightgown. She held it to her nose. It smelled of dust. The label was familiar but Francina could not remember where she'd seen it before. Then she remembered; the nightgown was from a women's clothing chain that had gone out of business years ago—probably more than fifteen—when the man in charge skipped the country with the company's money.

His mother—or quite possibly Hercules himself—had put clean sheets on the bed for her, and yet he had not been able to break the fifteen-year-old habit of putting his wife's nightgown under the pillow.

Francina's hands shook as she folded the nightgown neatly and put it back under the pillow.

"Oh, Hercules, Hercules, Hercules," she said under her breath. "Your mother was right. You *are* sick—with sadness."

The room felt too warm and now she was sure she could smell the faint scent of musty perfume. She drew back a curtain and opened the window to let in some cool night air. But still she felt warm. She sat on the bed in her slip, feeling all the time that she was going to be sick. Hercules was in the bathroom. She took deep breaths. How could she sleep on this bed where he slept every night with his dead wife? The toilet flushed. Hurry, please hurry, Hercules, she whispered. She found her dressing gown. The door to the bathroom opened. She waited as long as she thought it would take for him to settle himself in the living room, and then made a dash for the bathroom. Nothing happened, but she felt a lot better knowing that if the nausea returned she wouldn't be caught out. She splashed cold water on her face.

"Look at you, fool," she whispered to her reflection in the mirror. "You thought you were a wise woman. This time you got it all wrong."

"Is everything okay in there, Francina?"

It was Hercules at the door.

"Yes," she said, trying to keep her voice normal.

"I thought I heard talking. Never mind. Sleep tight."

"You, too."

As soon as the light under the door went out, she quietly opened the medicine cabinet. There were no old bottles of moisturizer, ladies' razors or tweezers. Hercules's mother had not allowed the sickness to spread beyond the door of his bedroom. And now she thought that Francina could cure it. Well, it was too big for her to cope with.

She felt pity for this mother who was so desperate that she was willing to forgo grandchildren if her son could be healed, but pity was all she could offer. The tears began to roll down her cheeks. Poor, poor Hercules. It was more than his heart that was broken. But she knew with certainty that she was not the one to make him whole again; the mere thought of having to go back into that room made her shiver. Hercules needed more than what she could give him. He needed a doctor, one that specialized in sicknesses of the head.

She spent an uncomfortable night on the floor with her head resting on her handbag and her gown pulled over her for warmth. She couldn't bear to touch a thing in the bedroom.

The next morning Hercules's mother asked if she had slept well. Francina replied that she had, but her voice or expression must have betrayed her because a look of concern flashed across Mrs. Shabalala's face and she was quiet after that. Francina felt awful because she guessed the woman saw her son's only chance for cure going home to Johannesburg in a minibus taxi.

After breakfast Hercules took Francina for a drive around town. He was full of energy as he showed her the parks, shopping centers and grocery stores.

"You will love the next place I'm taking you to. The sign outside says they have five thousand rolls of fabric—all at discount prices."

She gave a smile.

"You'd have more free time to sew if you—" he took something from his shirt pocket and handed it to her "—if you moved down here to be my wife."

She looked at what he had given her. It was a ring with a small diamond, the band slightly worn on the underside. She remained quiet. He pulled the car into the parking lot outside the House of Fabric and drummed his fingers on the steering wheel. He's an intelligent man, thought Francina. He knows something is up. How truthful should she be about her reasons for not accepting his proposal? She didn't want to hurt him, but a rejection of his proposal without a good reason would do that, too.

"Hercules," she began, turning to face him. "You already have two women in your life. There is no space for me."

She studied his face. There was no change.

When he said nothing, she filled the terrible silence in the car. "I'm very sorry."

"I can't just forget she ever existed," he said, his tone sharp.

"Nobody expects you to. But all her things…"

"I can move them aside to make place for yours." His eyes were earnest. He was like a little boy bargaining with his mother for more time to play outside.

"I wish it were that simple," she said, and his face fell.

She wanted to take him in her arms and rock him, as she did Mandla when he'd fallen down and hurt himself. But Hercules needed more than that. He needed professional help.

"Can I still write to you?" he asked.

She nodded.

Not once on the journey home that afternoon did she find herself digging her nails into the palms of her hands or feeling the urge to sing a hymn, and she barely noticed any of the other passengers. She stared out the window as the land became flatter, the trees more sparse, the towns uglier and the traffic heavier, and she thought about how two people who had suffered could not come together because their pasts got in the way. It was stupid and sad, but as real as a rock in the road.

After walking home from where the taxi dropped her off near the highway, she put her bag in her room and unlocked the back door of the house.

"Oh, it's you, Francina!" said Monica, breathing hard, the phone in her hand. "I heard a noise and was about to call the security company. You weren't supposed to be home till tomorrow night."

"He killed her, didn't he?" said Francina.

"Who?"

"Lady Helen's husband."

Monica looked confused. "Nobody knows, but she was never seen again."

Francina nodded. Her jaw was set. "He killed her. She didn't run far enough away. If this Lady Helen risked her life to settle there, it must be a special place. I'm coming with you."

She didn't wait to see Monica's reaction, as she didn't want to have to explain herself. In a day or so she would tell her the whole story, but for now she needed to be alone in her room to think about how close she had come to opening up her life to a man again, and how the chance of that happening again was more remote than a Zulu woman becoming president.

✤ Chapter Nine ✤

Mandla's squeals echoed through the empty rooms as Monica made a final tour of the house. Every surface gleamed, thanks to Francina and her desire that the new owners should think her an excellent housekeeper. They were a sweet family with two young sons who had been fascinated by Luca's model airplanes. These were now packed away in a box marked Fragile and would remain in storage along with the rest of Monica's, Francina's and the boys' belongings until they'd found a new house.

Without curtains Sipho and Mandla's room was bright with morning light. Francina had filled the holes in the walls where nails had once held pictures of animals, and, before that, Luca's certificates for excellence in sports.

This Christmas had been a strange one. Instead of collecting new things that they'd have to move to Lady Helen, they'd raided the garage to give things away: first Luca's clothes and shoes, then the trophies that had once lined the bookshelves. The airplanes in the room had been spared because Mandla liked looking up at them when he awoke in the morning.

Although Monica had tried to stop her mother from tidying out Luca's closet every spring after his death, she could not understand people who got rid of everything the day after the funeral. Letting go should be done gradually. Now it was time for her to heed her own words to Sipho about leaving the ashes of our loved ones behind. Another set of living boys would fill this room with warm breath, sibling secrets and crazy laughter. This was how it was meant to be.

Francina was outside explaining to the new lady of the house how to take care of potted tomato plants. Inside, it had become quiet—too quiet. Monica ran from room to room looking for the boys and found them in Ella's old room, which had once been hers. Sipho turned his head away, crying.

"I promise I didn't bite him or hit him," said Mandla.

Monica put an arm around Sipho's shoulders, and when he didn't resist she pulled him close.

"It's tough, isn't it?" she said, and he nodded. "Do you remember when you first came here? That wasn't so easy, was it?" He shook his head. "I know you can do it because you've got your mother's strength—" she touched his chest "—deep down inside you."

He wiped his face and gave her a weak smile. "I'll try," he said.

From the closet came muted giggles.

"Your brother wants you to find him."

The giggles grew louder.

"Where on earth can Mandla be?" said Monica in an animated voice. "Is he behind the door? No. Is he…?

"Here he is," yelled Mandla, springing out of the closet.

Sipho took his hand. "Come on, Mandla, we're going on a long trip."

Mandla grinned. "Maybe there'll be cows in the dairy this time," he said.

Monica did not correct him but used his excitement at this prospect to get him into his booster seat. It was comforting to know that there was a familiar little cottage waiting for them on the other end of this two-day journey. Kitty had said that they could rent it for as long as it took to find a new house. With the restrictions on new buildings in the town and few people leaving, that could be some time.

Ebony was already unhappy in her animal carrier, so Monica took her out and put her on the seat between the boys.

As the garage door opened, she wondered if it was the bougainvillea in Lady Helen that had made her believe it would be possible to call the town home. Though burnt and withered now from the drought, the cerise one atop the perimeter wall of her house had always been a cheerful welcome-home banner. On her return from the hospital it had been a voluminous explosion of color, an all-out celebration of her recovery.

"Don't look back," she told Francina and the boys, but one by one they all turned their heads to take a final look at the Greek picture-postcard house on the street with landscaped sidewalks, high walls and illustrated warning signs.

* * *

The next day, after an overnight stop at Colesberg in the Northern Cape, they reached the top of the koppie that overlooked Lady Helen, and it was as though the town had disappeared off the face of the earth. They had been driving along in vivid afternoon sunlight, when all of a sudden there was a crash of thunder. Lightning bolts streaked across the broken terrain, and rain began to strike the windshield with the staccato rhythm of machine-gun fire. Sipho explained calmly that they would be safe in the car because of its rubber tires, but Francina, in the front seat, put her hands over her head and prayed loudly. "Wow!" yelled Mandla every time there was a clap of thunder. Monica had wanted to stop when the storm hit, but they were halfway up the koppie and the road was so narrow she feared somebody might crash into them.

"You never told me we were coming to a swamp," complained Francina as she peered out through the windshield and saw that they were about to descend into an abyss of mud and streaming water.

"This is very strange," said Monica. "The Western Cape is only supposed to get rain in winter. It's the opposite of the rest of South Africa."

"It should have rained like this the day Lord Charles Gray came looking for his wife," said Francina with a wry grin. "He never would have found her."

The open ditches, which Monica had since learned carried springwater for the irrigation of gardens and crops, had overflowed, and Main Street was under three inches of water. Francina kept trying to clear the inside of the windshield with a tissue, while outside the wipers whipped back and forth furiously. Through the sheets of water pouring off the tin overhangs they could see lights on in the galleries and stores. Mandla had tired of the initial excitement of the storm and was feeling trapped.

"We're almost there," Monica told him.

Kitty ran out to meet them with a large golf umbrella.

"Unbelievable, isn't it?" she said, escorting Monica and Mandla while Sipho remained in the car with Francina. "This rain is completely out of season." She left them on the porch and went back for the others.

In the formal living room of the main house a tray set with teacups and a plate of oatmeal squares awaited them.

"I'll go and fill the teapot," Kitty shouted in order to compete with the rain hammering the tin roof.

Monica observed Francina taking in her surroundings: the antiques, the dark wood frame chairs with dense, square cushions, the end tables, the tall bureau, all of it solid, sensible furniture that the early settlers had built when there were more pressing tasks at hand than carving intricate designs and setting inlays of exotic hardwood. An ornate brass bowl filled with smooth yellow gourds occupied the center space of the large, squat coffee table, while in the racks below, magazines on country living and travel in South Africa were arranged in neat stacks. A small sign read Board Games in the Bureau. Ostrich eggs, hand painted with desert scenes and wildflowers, were lined up on top of the bureau—thankfully, out of Mandla's reach. Dust was visible everywhere, and Monica could tell Francina had noticed it because she was pulling her mouth as she would if Mandla walked in the house with muddy shoes, or if Monica left her wet towel on the bed. Monica wanted to explain that Kitty was extremely busy, but at that moment their hostess came in carrying a large china teapot decorated with rambling English roses.

"The Old Dairy is ready for you," she said. "And since there aren't enough beds in there, I've got an en-suite room inside for you, Francina."

Francina shot Monica a look as if to say, "Don't leave me with a stranger."

"Can we take a look at it?" asked Monica, hoping that once Francina saw it her apprehension would fade.

Francina had stayed in hostel dormitories when her choir traveled to competitions, but she'd never stayed in a proper hotel and she couldn't decide which feeling was more overpowering: her fear of doing something that people accustomed to such arrangements never would, or her excitement over the royal bed with its white muslin curtains draped like a wedding dress and the bathroom with the old-fashioned bathtub, tray of little bottles and soaps wrapped like birthday gifts, fluffy white robe hanging behind the door and towels that were so thick they probably took a whole day on the clothesline to dry.

Francina had heard of parents giving their children Zulu names that sounded funny when translated into English. She, personally, had met a Laughter, Goodwill, Pretty, Onward, Brilliant and Blessing, but she'd never heard of anyone naming their baby after a household pet. Like her namesake, Kitty probably spent a lot of time lying in a patch of sunlight, because there was enough dust in this house to fill an entire vacuum bag. What did the woman do all day? And why was she so skinny?

"Pick up the phone and dial twenty-nine if you need anything," Kitty had instructed Francina before they'd all left to make a quick dash to the place they called the Old Dairy. Now, what should she ask for? One of those magazines with pictures of movie stars in ball gowns would be nice, or a sewing magazine. Or what about a box of chocolates, all with toffee centers? Or maybe a foot rub? This was something she could get used to, she decided, the fear disappearing along with the light as the rainy afternoon slipped into evening. But real life knocked at the door in the form of Sipho, who had come to get her to help unload their suitcases from the car.

After the boys had fallen asleep on the sofa bed, the rain slowed and Monica was able to hear the new television that Kitty had bought for the Old Dairy. Sipho had been quieter than usual, no doubt thinking of how far away he was from his mother. Monica hadn't yet told him that they were now closer to his father's family, who lived in the Eastern Cape. Ella had called them "drinkers" and "layabouts" and had been adamant that Monica should take care of the boys, not these relatives whom the boys had never known. One day, when the time was right, Monica would tell Sipho about them. He might insist that she take him to meet them, but she would deal with that issue when and if it arose.

After a quick whispered call to her parents to let them know they'd arrived safely, Monica checked on the boys, climbed into the four-poster bed and pulled the soft down comforter up to her neck. The rain masked the new night sounds she would have to get used to, but one thing she would not hear again here in this little town: the panicky scream of security alarms. Max, Kitty and Dr. Niemand had all assured her that the two new policemen who came to Lady Helen every January always reported, at the end of their one-year stint here, that it had been the most restful they'd ever had. According to Max it was almost as though they were sent here for a sabbatical after working in cities and other areas of the country where the police were over-worked, understaffed and constantly under threat from criminals who wanted their weapons.

Shortly before dawn the rain stopped, and at seven, with Ebony still curled up at the foot of her bed, Monica opened the curtains to a shiny, new world. The dripping branches of the apricot trees glistened in the morning sun as though they'd been hung with a thousand diamonds; the white walls of the main house had been washed clean; and the koppie behind the Old Dairy was starkly etched against a deep blue sky from which all the clouds had disappeared save for a few elegant wisps. From behind the honeysuckle-covered gazebo came the peculiar call of the black-bellied korhaan: a pop that sounded exactly like a champagne cork. Monica won-dered if Francina was awake. It was quite something to move to a place you had never seen before, and Monica hoped that one look out of her window this morning would put any doubts Francina might have to rest.

Francina was awake, but instead of opening the curtains to inspect her new surroundings she was lying in bed flicking through the television channels to find a weather report. Kitty had responded remarkably quickly to her request for coffee and had arrived in her dressing gown with her hair uncombed. Francina did not approve of women who spent hours on their hair and makeup, but this woman thought she was a farmer who could just roll out of bed and into the fields. Francina's father was like that; he wouldn't brush his teeth unless her mother brought him his toothbrush already loaded with toothpaste. And as for the state of this house, it was amazing to her that some women could live with dust, dirt and untidiness for so long that they no longer saw it. Maybe she should point it out to Kitty. She would talk to her at breakfast, but first things first. After years of having to sit on the closed toilet seat when she showered because the showerhead was directly above it, this strange bathtub with bird legs was the closest Francina had ever come to luxury, and, although she didn't like to waste water, this town apparently had enough of it and so a second soak in the space of twelve hours wouldn't burden her conscience.

Mandla's eyes widened at the sight of the breakfast table.

"You don't have to go to all this trouble for us," Monica told Kitty. "We can have cereal in the Old Dairy."

Both Mandla and Francina shot her a look, but Monica was adamant.

"We have to start getting used to everyday life here," she said.

Everyday life entailed preparation, and Monica had made a list. The first item on it was to enroll Sipho in school before the new academic year started in two weeks. Number two was to report to her office so that Max could show her the ropes before he left. Number three was to find a church where they all would feel comfortable, including Francina. And number four was to find a house so that their furniture didn't sit in storage for too long. She'd called the real estate office in town two weeks ago, but except for a few two-bedroom, one-bathroom places, there was nothing on the market.

A couple of days later, Monica and Sipho visited the school, which was four blocks down from Peg's dairy farm. It resembled a green airplane hangar and Monica thought that it was quite possibly the ugliest building she had seen in Lady Helen. Kitty had explained that it was built before the introduction of the strict building codes that now kept the historical town unadulterated by new styles and quirky fads, and nobody had the heart to tear it down as it had been donated to the town by one of its most beloved residents, a spinster artist, who had passed away just last year at the ripe old age of one hundred. A passionate fan of Picasso, Dotty had designed the building with the geometric shapes of his Cubist period in mind, and nobody had dared stop her because at that time the children were squeezed into three rooms at the old school and there was nowhere else for them to go.

Inside Green Block School, as it had come to be known, the classrooms were light and airy with high ceilings and large windows to take in the views of the palm trees and blue-etched koppies. At the time it was built there were ninety pupils ranging in age from six to eighteen, but now there were only forty, a group that would have fit easily into the old school. But most people agreed that although the building jarred with the tin-roofed houses with their lace fil-igrees, shutters and wood frame windows, it was a fitting memorial to a lady who had continued to paint bold, bright pieces when most women her age were resting in front of the television.

What irked some parents about the school would work in Sipho's favor. With only forty children paying tuition, and the government emphatic in its refusal to add to the school's budget because of more pressing needs in underprivileged areas, there was not enough money to hire a teacher for every grade and so two grades were taught in every class-room. If the headmaster agreed to allow Sipho to write the end-of-year exams for both grades each year, he would ef-fectively finish his schooling in half the time. He might not need to jump ahead in the years to come, but right now he was in danger of becoming completely disinterested and disconnected if he didn't.

As Monica shook the headmaster's hand, she decided that there was absolutely nothing about him to suggest the preppy past Kitty had told her about. He had thick, dark hair that was desperately in need of a good cut, a bushy beard, green eyes with dark shadows visible even under his round glasses, and he wore khaki pants, a plaid shirt and the bright-est red velskoens, or handmade leather shoes, Monica had ever seen.

At thirty-four, Lawrence Dell was the youngest headmas-ter ever appointed to a government school in the history of the entire country.

"Let me take you on a little tour before we go to my of-fice," he said.

There was a playground at the back for the younger children, a grassy patch with neat asymmetrical flower beds in the front where the high-school pupils ate their homemade sandwiches at wooden picnic tables, a library with four computers—all donated by the *Lady Helen Herald*—and a central hall for Friday assemblies where students performed their own short plays and poetry after morning prayers. The school didn't have a soccer or hockey field, tennis or netball courts, or a swimming pool, but there were plans over time to raise money for at least one of these. Monica could tell from Sipho's expression that the lack of sporting facilities was not a drawback. The school offered many "cheaper" activities, explained Mr. Dell, like chess, debating, choir, cross-country and the Young Conservationists Club.

"Which one would you be interested in, young man?"

"The Young Conservationists Club, sir," said Sipho, eyes shining.

"Excellent. We're looking for some fresh ideas. And please, don't call me sir. Mr. D. is fine."

Sipho looked to Monica for confirmation, and when she nodded, he said, "Yes, Mr. D."

Mr. D.'s office needed one of Francina's ruthless cleanings. Filing cabinets overflowed, books were piled up on the floor, the notice board was somewhere under a triple layer of loose flyers and government notices, and the desk was invisible under stacks of journals and ring files that wouldn't close because they were so full. The potted fern had been dead for so long that any slight movement in its vicinity sent flakes of black leaves floating down onto the laminated wood floor. The Young Conservationists need to look within the walls of their own establishment, mused Monica as she waited for Mr. D. to clear a box of stationery supplies off one chair and an assortment of jerseys, jackets and raincoats off another.

"Excuse the mess," he said.

Sipho's eyes were wide. He had never seen anything like it in his life.

"I've been meaning to tackle this." Mr. D. cast a hand over the chaos. "But there are so many other more pressing considerations." He opened three bottles of water and passed two to his guests.

Monica had heard of his work with students from underprivileged backgrounds. So intent was he on proving to the Education Department that no child needed to languish long in the gray zone of the learning catch-up, that he would personally go to the homes of those with the worst grades to oversee their homework. He'd give them extra lessons in the subjects that required understanding rather than rote learning, like mathematics and science, and would stick closer to them than their own shadows until they ran home with a report card they were proud of. It was a wonder that he even had time to sleep and comb his hair before work.

"Impressive," said Monica, looking at the framed diploma on the wall, which showed that Mr. D. had graduated magna cum laude.

"Not everyone will agree with you," replied the young headmaster, smiling ruefully. "My father wanted me to study law, not education, so that I could take over the family paper company. Finally, he persuaded himself that it wouldn't be too bad if I joined the staff of my—and his—alma mater. A school in Soweto wasn't even on his radar screen."

"Why did you leave that school?" asked Monica, deliber-
ately steering the conversation away from the topic of his
father's displeasure because she already knew all of this personal information from Kitty.

"The building was declared unsafe, so the children were
squashed into another school fifteen blocks away and the
teachers were retrenched. That's when I got a job in the
Cape teaching prisoners to read and write. It was satisfying because I knew that I was improving the men's odds of
one day gaining honest employment and having a modi-
cum of control over their lives, but I missed the contact
with children."

Sipho nodded emphatically, as though expressing approval of the direction his headmaster's career path had taken.

Mr. D. agreed wholeheartedly with Monica's plan to let
Sipho write the exams of both his own class and the higher
one at the end of the year, and, without any prompting from
Monica, he decided on a let's-see-how-it-goes approach re-
garding Sipho's academic future. Monica was so happy she
grabbed his hand and shook it for so long that she eventually felt embarrassed and sat down mumbling about how
grateful she was.

But she was not the only one to feel the excitement. Sipho
thanked him over and over in an uncharacteristically child-
ish high pitch. It seemed that Mr. D. had the same effect on
both of them. He was just one of those people who made
you want to get up and cheer.

"Right," said Monica as she and Sipho made their way
hand in hand down the street back to Abalone House.

"That's number one on the list. Number two is for me to report to the office."

Sipho squeezed her hand. "I think we did a good thing coming here," he said.

With Sipho and Monica away visiting Green Block School, Francina sat on the veranda swing watching the gardener across the street as he attached a metal grating to a fence that had all but collapsed under the weight of a bright pink bougainvillea. The reinforcement would do for a while, she believed, but it would be much better to replace the fence. Francina didn't approve of patch jobs. If Mandla hadn't been asleep with his head on her lap, she would go over there and politely tell the man to expect the whole fence to come down one day. In the distance she could see the strange rocky koppies that were so unlike the rolling hills near her home but for some reason made her feel safe because they seemed to be guarding the little town.

Four spotted blue butterflies settled on the wisteria, safe—for now—from chubby little fingers that would certainly torment them. In a nearby sweet thorn tree a pair of yellow-throated bokmakieries with pretty, black necklaces began calling to each other. The cicadas would join in with their raucous songs when the sun went down. This occurred much later than in Johannesburg, and Francina wondered if it was because they were so close to the bottom of Africa. It wasn't just big words that she had a problem with; basic ideas that children like Sipho took for granted, such as the seasonal path of the sun, were beyond her. Maybe it wasn't wise to compare herself to a child when that child was a ge-

nius, but it was as though the world had a second floor and
she couldn't reach it because she couldn't even find the stairs.

The gardener saw her watching and waved. Biting her
tongue, she waved back, for that is what people did in these
parts. Sitting on this veranda with a sleeping child in her lap,
she had already greeted three elderly women who were on a
brisk walk, one man with a fluffy poodle, and two young boys
who'd seen Sipho and Mandla about and wanted to know if
they could come back and play tomorrow. She had a growing sense that this town was more like her village than she'd
ever imagined. Her mother and father would be outside their
home right now, her father on his folding chair, her mother
bustling around with little jobs that never seemed to end, and
they, too, would be greeting their neighbors: with an upheld
hand, a few words to those who remarked on the beauty of
the day, coffee and homemade biscuits for those who wished
to lament the disappearing grazing grass. Although it was
hard to believe after the deluge they'd experienced on the day
of their arrival in Lady Helen, the drought had not broken
in the rest of the country.

Mandla stirred. He'd been asleep for more than two hours,
and she'd brought him out here in the hope that the fresh
air would wake him up. Otherwise, he'd never sleep tonight. After cleaning four guest rooms, four bathrooms, the
living room and the dining room, Francina was tired. When
Monica got back with Sipho she thought she might take a
long bath before dinner. Kitty not only responded to her requests for coffee in the morning, she also brought her the
hot chocolate she asked for at night, and Francina wondered
if she'd bring a tray to her room now with something cold.

At the end of the street she could see Monica and Sipho making their way home. They were both talking so much, the visit to the school must have gone well. When Monica first adopted the boys, their relationship had been more like teacher and student, babysitter and child, or maybe distant aunt and nephew, but over time that had changed. Monica no longer appeared bewildered whenever Mandla mixed up his words as young children do, and she anticipated his need for a snack when his favorite television characters ate, a box of juice when everyone drank tea, a cowboy hat when they went outdoors. Almost automatically, she produced cloths to wipe his face, tissues to blow his nose, toys to amuse him in the car, as though she'd been doing it since he was born. And she knew when to leave Sipho alone with his thoughts, when he needed a gentle arm around his shoulders, or when only a wraparound hug would do.

Francina had watched her progress with the patient but critical eye with which a woman watches her new daughter-in-law, and now she had to admit that Monica was the mother—even if the boys would never call her that—and *she* would always be the assistant. It was how it should be, but instead of fulfilling her maternal instincts it left her wanting more.

Monica took charge of Mandla as he stretched and complained about having to leave his comfortable pillow, and Francina left to "prepare herself for dinner."

Cleaning such a large place was tiring for Francina, but Monica knew that Kitty appreciated it, because, until her husband had rewired the house, she had to run things on her own. Monica didn't know if Kitty paid for advertising in the national newspapers, but it seemed that the first hotel tourists tried when they came to town was Abalone House.

"So what do you think of Mr. D.?" asked Kitty, appearing on the veranda with a tray of lemonade and five glasses.

Monica and Sipho looked at each other and grinned.

"Don't even bother to answer," said Kitty, handing out the cold drinks.

"I'll take Francina's to her," said Sipho.

Kitty kicked off her sandals and curled her feet up under her on the swing.

From what Monica had learned yesterday during her late-afternoon chat with Kitty on the veranda, her hostess was a woman of unmatched enthusiasm and puzzling whimsy. All her past undertakings—the flower shop, the ethnic-clothing line, the flea market, the catering company—had been successful beyond expectation, yet she'd abandoned them at that critical stage when it was necessary to expand in order to avoid chaos. Her father, a banker who'd reached the top of his profession after thirty years of punctual drudgery, could not understand his daughter's habitual flight from enterprises where she did not need to bite her tongue, kowtow to loudmouthed fools and punch the clock, and their relationship had soured because he could not let a visit go by without a recriminatory recollection of at least one of them. He was somewhat appeased now that she was running Abalone House.

"You know, I still haven't met your other half," said Monica, brushing a fly away from Mandla's head. After drinking his lemonade, the little boy had gone back to sleep on her lap.

Kitty sighed. "I worry about James doing the electrical rewiring himself. He's an airline pilot, not a licensed electrician."

"How did you two meet?"

"His airline was sponsoring a competition I was judging."

"A model search, right?"

Kitty smiled shyly.

Monica's first impression had been spot on. Kitty had been a runway model, and her career had taken her to Madrid, Paris, Milan and New York, all before the age of twenty-one, when she'd given it up to go to university to study anthropology.

Monica wondered what her mother would have to say about Kitty. At twenty-one, Monica's mother had moved from the small town of Laingsburg to Johannesburg to become a model, but her career had died before it even began when she married Monica's father and, shortly afterward, became pregnant with Luca. The years had not erased Mirinda's sense of loss, and in her mid-fifties she still wore her hair pinned up like royalty, although the comparisons to a Scandinavian princess were more likely to come now from old friends than strangers in stores and restaurants.

Mandla awoke when Sipho returned with Francina's empty glass.

"Look, Monica," said Sipho, pointing at the weeping willow in the corner of the garden, "there's a sickle-winged chat."

Sickle-winged chats, yellow canaries, Cape long-billed larks; they all meant one thing to Mandla—birds to be shooed from the trees with a wild clapping of his chubby hands. Still groggy from sleep, he climbed off Monica's lap to do what he considered to be his duty.

"Come on, it's time to go in," said Monica, heading off an argument between Mandla, who looked thoroughly pleased with himself at the success of his mission, and Sipho, whose face was contorted with disgust. "Thanks for the lemonade, Kitty."

Inside the Old Dairy, there were fresh flowers in the vase on the mantel: bright orange strelitzias this time. Monica was grateful to Kitty for trying to make her family feel at home with little touches like flowers, plates of rusks, the hard sweet bread they dipped in their tea and breakfasts made to order, but she hoped they'd be able to move into a house of their own soon.

Because she'd believed it had been God's plan for them to come to Lady Helen, she'd also believed that everything would work out easily, but her visit to the Realtor's office had proved fruitless and she was beginning to wonder if God wanted to teach her a lesson in compromise, as that was what it would require if they all had to squeeze into a tiny house. Or maybe He wanted to test her patience? In this regard, she was more confident in her abilities. She decided that she would give herself her own test: one of faith.

∽ Chapter Ten ∽

From the layout of the *Lady Helen Herald* it might be assumed that the newspaper was a big-city daily, not a small-town weekly. Above the fold was a main story with a color photograph and a column running down the left-hand side with truncated versions of stories that could be found on the inside pages. Below the fold were two slightly less weighty stories, one of which was accompanied by a small photograph. The main headline this week was, Rain Has Experts Perplexed.

Had she really given up her job at the radio station to work for a paper that gave front-page prominence to the weather? But she found it to be an elegantly written and interesting account of how the unusual weather phenomenon that had brought rain to the West Coast in the middle of summer could not be explained. None of the meteorologists consulted knew why this area had received rain out of season, while the rest of the country, where summer rain was normal, remained parched and dry. Their guess was that it had something to do with the strong winds that accompany the Benguela Current as it flows north from the Southern Ocean off of Antarctica, and along the West Coast of South Africa. Two days before the deluge, these winds had been unusually strong.

When one thought about it, as Monica was able to do while she waited for Max to come out of his office and collect her in the reception room—although why he called it this she did not know, because there was no receptionist, just a closed-circuit camera and intercom—they had really witnessed a remarkable event, and if she'd raised a cynical eyebrow at a weather story making front-page news then she was not the inquiring reporter she thought she was. *It's time to check your big-town elitism at the door,* she told herself. News didn't have to include high-ranking government officials, power struggles, regional conflicts and corruption scandals; it could float in on the wind.

Max's voice on paper was young, authoritative and poetic. It was a shame his arthritis was forcing him to retire, and an even bigger shame that he didn't intend for his memoirs to be published, because she had a feeling that after five decades of observing the changes in life in this country, he had a deep store of wisdom to impart and would do it with prose both beautiful and pragmatic.

"Reading it again, I presume?" said a voice, startling her out of an almost dreamlike state as she read a lyrical description of the rich marine life that fed off the nutrients delivered by the cold upwelling of the Benguela Current.

This was actually the first time she'd had a quiet moment

to read the latest issue, but even the best excuses in the world would look like a lack of commitment on her part, and so she remained quiet about how hard she was working to find a house, getting Sipho ready for school and keeping the family in some type of routine so they'd settle into their new life and not think of it as an extended vacation.

Thankfully, Max didn't press her for any opinions on the rest of the newspaper, because then she would have to admit the truth. Before she had the boys she would have read every word in that newspaper twice, but now she felt as though she were on a treadmill that was going a little too fast for comfort and she just had to keep up the pace or risk an awkward fall.

Leaning heavily on his cane, Max showed her into his office. There were light yellow patches on the wooden floor where the filing cabinets had once stood, and the old orange sofa was gone, too.

"I hope you don't mind," he said, "but when my brain's in a twist over something, or my joints are hurting, that's the only place I can sleep. I've put it in my study next to the computer."

He waved at the wall behind him where the framed photographs had been taken down, leaving dozens of nails exposed.

"I'll have one of the maintenance men remove those."

It was as though his whole career had been erased from this office, and Monica felt a sudden melancholy that was quite inexplicable because she barely knew the man. Here was a mind unwilling to give in to the rigors of the job, but it had no choice because it was trapped in an old man's body that ached for a gentler pace. Though she felt up to the challenge of the position, she decided that she would try to keep Max involved for as long as he was able.

"I've been thinking that I might need some guidance," she told him, hoping that God would forgive this little lie as it was for a good cause. "And I wondered if it would be too big an imposition on you if we were to have a weekly editors' meeting. I know you'll be busy with your memoirs, but I could come to your house."

"That would be no trouble at all," said Max, and Monica was not sure if the laughter in his clear blue eyes was happy gratitude or the recognition of a con job, but no more was said about it as they began work on the next week's issue.

Max had drawn up a list of stories that he wanted included, which irked Monica somewhat as she thought that would be her responsibility, but she pushed her irritation aside.

"At first glance, some of them may appear to be rather dry," said Max.

The local library's purchase of its six thousandth book? A new guide dog for Winnie Fortuin? Monica wanted to reply with an emphatic "They're so dry they'll turn to dust at the slightest touch," but she pulled her mouth into a polite grimace instead.

"There are stories—good stories—everywhere," argued Max without humor. "Just allow yourself to be led."

With effort she managed to maintain a bright and enthusiastic demeanor throughout the rest of their meeting, but when she left with the list of story ideas in her hand she felt so down in the dumps that she took off her shoes and went for a brisk walk along the beach before going home. She hoped that the hot sand underfoot, the breeze in her hair and the sun on her back would lift her spirits, but she returned to Abalone House convinced that she had exchanged her interesting career at the radio station for a merry-go-round of livestock births, art shows, talent contests and obituaries.

The boys were sitting on the veranda with their new friends from down the street, having milk and cookies. Mandla charged up to Monica, and, as she stooped so that he could give her an enthusiastic kiss on the cheek, she noticed Sipho checking the faces of his new friends. But he had nothing to fear because it seemed that a white mother displaying affection toward her little black boy was not as compelling to these twelve-year-olds as the fate of the single remaining cookie.

Francina was packing up her brushes, cloths and floor polish with more noise than was necessary. Something had happened.

"What's the matter?" Monica asked in a soft voice so that the boys would not hear.

"What do you think of this floor?" asked Francina.

It shone so brightly Monica thought she should warn the boys to walk with care.

"It's cleaner than it's ever been," said Francina without waiting for her reply. "Cat got all upset when I told her that. Now she says I'm not needed anymore, that she'll do all the work herself. I don't know what's wrong with that Cat."

"You mean Kitty."

"Cat, Kitty, what's the difference? After today I should call her Catty," said Francina. Then she, too, walked off in a huff.

Please, God, prayed Monica, let us find a house soon.

She found Kitty in the kitchen preparing dinner for the mayor and a group of his friends who were staying at Abalone House before heading north into Namibia for a tour of the Skeleton Coast.

"How did it go at the new job?"

"Great," said Monica, making an instant decision that she would not share her disappointment with anyone.

Apart from her desire to tread carefully in a small town where the grapevine was short, Kitty's red-rimmed eyes and blotchy face told her that her friend's problems were greater.

"Are you okay?"

Kitty wiped away a tear just as it was about to fall into the ground beef she was mixing with chutney, apricot jam, bread, raisins, onion and curry powder for the bobotie.

"It's just too much work."

Monica thought how Kitty's father hoped his son-in-law would prevent her from hopping into another new enterprise. If he only knew that had it not been for the creaking of the attic floorboards and the occasional thud of a dropped tool, Monica might have doubted Kitty's sanity and said that her husband was a product of her imagination.

"When will James be finished with the rewiring so he can help you?"

"Never. He's going to kill himself up there or set the house on fire before he gets it done. Oh, I shouldn't have said that. He *is* trying." As she mixed the eggs to pour on top of the meat, she began to cry softly.

Monica wanted to ask why he didn't call in a professional for the job, but Kitty would have asked him that. She went over to the basin and washed her hands.

"Okay, I'm ready for duty."

Kitty smiled at her. "Thank you, Monica. And after we've finished I've got to apologize to Francina. I threw a bit of a wobbly with her."

"She'll understand," said Monica, crossing her fingers.

While Monica helped prepare dinner for the mayor, Francina gave the boys pasta in the Old Dairy and then turned on the television. The news was on, which disappointed Mandla, but he was nevertheless determined to watch whatever was on the screen.

"Why are those people carrying pictures around?" he wanted to know.

"They're placards," corrected Sipho. "And they're carrying them around because it's a protest."

Mandla laughed. "I want to protest, too."

Francina groaned. He was his mother all over again.

"This one's not fun," explained Sipho. "They're protesting because they want the president to start giving medicine to people with AIDS."

The laughter in Mandla's eyes disappeared. Not yet four, he knew what AIDS was. It was the sickness that had taken his mother from him.

"I want to protest, too," he repeated, banging his fists on his thighs.

Francina switched the channel to a music program and soon Mandla was squirming in his chair in time to the beat. She didn't know whether she was being wise or a coward, but Monica was better at handling this sort of situation.

She felt the crinkle of paper in her pocket as she got up

to make hot chocolate. It was a letter from her mother that she planned to read in the bath later this evening. Going to the postbox this afternoon for Cat, she had allowed herself to remember the flutter of excitement she'd once felt at the possibility of finding one of Hercules's neatly addressed blue envelopes. All of a sudden, the disappointment she'd dragged around with her cleared like the early-morning summer mists that were whisked away by the southeaster, and she was able to think about Hercules in his house of memories without her face growing hot. She wondered if her refusal to marry him had opened his eyes to his sickness.

It was fortunate that she'd never confided in her mother about Hercules. With the drought continuing and four cattle already found stiff-legged, her mother had her own worries. Francina touched her pocket. She hoped that the letter did not hold more bad news.

Monica had still not returned by the time the boys were in their pajamas, so Francina put on a wildlife program for them and curled up on a chair with her letter.

"What are you reading?" Mandla wanted to know.

"News from my mother in the Valley of a Thousand Hills."

His eyes widened. "A thousand hills?"

"It's just an expression," said Sipho.

Francina had been about to tell him that there were indeed a thousand.

Turning back to her letter, she read one more cow had died and the others were so skinny you could count their bones, but her mother had faith that God held the wind in His hands and when they least expected it He would send clouds with enough rain in them to soak the earth through.

Her father spent whole nights out in the kraal watching the cattle's restless sleep, but his spirits had been lifted by the unexpected arrival of twenty bales of hay that Winston's men had carried in on their backs with no explanation whatsoever. Francina's mother had never told him of their visit to the chief and chose to leave it that way.

Just as a young mother tests the bathwater for her baby with an elbow, she had tested the village with small references to Francina at the beading circle, the trading store and at a party for a hundredth birthday, and not once did she notice the smirks and whispers of the past. A few women had even asked after Francina's well-being, and one had wanted to know if she still sewed such beautiful clothes.

Francina had escaped much by living in Johannesburg, but her mother had been forced to live with the false shame for a long time. A hundred bales would not be enough, let alone twenty. But she hoped and prayed that Winston would keep them coming, though prices surged as the drought continued.

She was putting the letter back in her pocket when Monica walked in the door. Her skirt was spattered with brown sauce, her face shone with sweat and her hair had gone frizzy.

"What happened to you?"

"Things got kind of hectic." She bent down to kiss the boys. "I'm sorry I'm late. Thanks for looking after them. Can you believe I met the mayor looking like this? He's big and jolly. I felt like I was serving Father Christmas."

"Maybe it was Father Christmas's brother," said Mandla.

Francina was proud of Sipho for holding back and not setting him straight this time.

As Francina closed the door behind her, she giggled at the sudden realization that she and Monica were now both working at Abalone House. How funny life could be. Would Monica want to join her for Thursday-afternoon cards with the other maids? The thought of Monica sitting on the sidewalk with a mug of tea kept her chuckling all the way out into the moonlit garden.

When she was clear of the apricot trees she stopped to look up at the stars and tried to recall a time when she'd done the same thing in Johannesburg. But she couldn't. She hadn't gone out at night. Hercules would come up with some beautiful words to describe the bright sky, but all she could think of was that it looked as though God had left the lights on up there. The night air was cool but pleasant on her bare arms. From the rafters of the main house she heard the *hoo-hoo* of an owl, and she wondered if it was the spotted-eagle kind Sipho had been telling Mandla to watch for from his window.

Although Durban, the famous seaside town, was close to her village, she'd only been to the beach once—on a school trip after the end-of-year exams. The boys had stripped down to their underwear and dragged each other into the water. The girls had hitched up their dresses and waded in up to their knees, but she'd remained on the beach and watched them run back screaming whenever a large wave approached.

The waves in Lady Helen were smaller, formed much closer to shore, and broke gently. One day she might try walking in up to her knees. She would like to do it at dusk or dawn when nobody was around, but she'd heard Sipho saying that was when sharks attacked. He'd also said that it was dangerous to swim alone, so she'd have to ask Monica to go with her. It would be nice to have a special someone to do things with, but after her experience with Hercules, she knew that it would never happen in her lifetime.

Like a bat on the hunt, Kitty's husband came down from the attic the morning after the mayor's dinner, and sat down at the breakfast table with a triumphant grin.

"It's done," he announced to the strangers at the table, for although they had been living in the Old Dairy for two weeks he had never laid eyes upon them.

"Thank goodness," said Kitty, and she piled his plate so high with pancakes that Mandla stared.

Kitty seemed not to remember that her husband had never met their guests, so Monica introduced herself, Francina and the boys.

"Welcome," said James as though they'd just arrived. "If you need anything during your stay here, give me a shout."

Monica heard Francina take a deep breath of impatience.

"We've been more than comfortable here," said Monica.

James put a hand on the small of his wife's back.

"We work hard to make our guests happy, don't we?"

"Of course," said Kitty, filling the jug with freshly squeezed orange juice. There was nothing in her tone to suggest that she was annoyed with her husband for taking the credit for her effort.

Although James had only just turned forty, his wavy, shoulder-length hair was completely gray. With his faded T-shirt, baggy shorts and strappy sandals, Monica found it difficult to picture him in an airline pilot's uniform.

"I have an announcement," he said, and from the way Kitty stopped halfway to the kitchen with a load of dirty plates, it was clear that whatever it was would be a surprise to her, too.

"I'm opening a new business. Starting tomorrow I will be taking people out on the boat to feed sharks."

"Monica!" said Mandla in a panicky voice. He reached over to grab her wrist.

"That's okay, darling," she said, wrapping her arms around him. "He doesn't mean he's going to feed *people* to the sharks. He's going to give them fish."

James burst into laughter. "You thought I was going to… Oh, that's funny."

He rubbed the top of Mandla's head, but Mandla pulled away and crept onto Monica's lap.

"The cage I ordered came yesterday. It's in the garage," he said.

Monica noticed the astonishment on Kitty's face.

"You boys must come out with me," continued James, oblivious of the effect his words were having on Sipho. "One person goes down in the cage, I throw in a big chunk of bloody tuna, the sharks smell it from miles away and rush at the cage as though they haven't eaten for months." Seeing Sipho's horrified expression, he said, "It's perfectly safe. The diver has a spear with him, which he uses to offer fish to the sharks. Would you like to see the cage?"

Sipho did not answer, his good manners overcome by disgust and fear. Monica realized that the impasse would last forever if she didn't act.

"Sorry, I need him for some research at the library. But thanks for the offer."

James nodded. "Some other time," he said, laying down his knife and fork. "Thanks, Kitty, that was excellent. I'm going to check on the boat. Do *you* want to see the cage?"

If James did not notice the supreme effort it took for his wife to give him a calm reply, Monica did.

"I have to clear this away," she said, pointing at the remains of the breakfast buffet. "And then I've got to get the rooms ready for two couples who arrive at noon from Germany. Maybe later?"

He kissed Kitty on the mouth and ran his fingers through her hair.

Sipho looked at his plate, and Kitty left the room, her face as red as the fresh strawberries she had served for breakfast.

Francina made a circular motion with her finger next to her temple, which Monica was thankful Sipho and Mandla did not see. She sensed that she would have to find out more about this shark-feeding business in order to be able to allay Sipho's fears. Could it be a story for the newspaper? It certainly would make for more vivid copy than a celebration of the library's six thousandth book. Speaking of which, it was time to leave, and she did indeed need Sipho's help. He had agreed to scan the catalog cards so she could mention in her story the type of books favored by the library.

Doreen Olifant was the town's librarian, unofficial historian and weekend emergency dispatch operator. All this kept her busy, but, as a widow whose only child and grandchild lived in Australia, it was how she preferred to be. She could trace her family history to the time her great-great-great-grandmother was brought to the Cape from Malaysia to work as a slave.

Doreen switched back and forth between English and her mother tongue, Afrikaans, until she realized that Sipho could not follow everything she was saying.

"I'm sorry," she said. "I forgot that Afrikaans is no longer compulsory in schools." Looking at Monica, she asked, "Do you know about the Soweto riots?"

Monica nodded. One day she would tell Sipho about the bloody riots of 1976, when schoolchildren took to the streets to protest the use of the language of the oppressor in their classrooms, and how these riots had led to his mother's flight into exile in Zambia in the back of a gardening-supplies truck.

Doreen was in her fifties, yet she had startlingly smooth skin, like that of a young girl. Only later would Monica learn that she never set foot in the sun without her white-tasseled parasol. She wore a sage green linen shift dress with a loose matching jacket, and her hair was scraped back in a roll that seemed to be secured with invisible pins. Everybody in town seemed to wear some sort of handcrafted jewelry and Doreen's was a necklace of large translucent beads with colored centers.

There was no need for Sipho to search through catalog cards as the library was computerized. In ten minutes he had ascertained that Doreen was an enthusiastic supporter of South African fiction, yet looked further afield for her sources of nonfiction.

"It seems to me," said Monica, "that you trust your coun-trymen to make up stories but not to relay facts."

It was an impertinent question, but Doreen looked Monica in the eye and said calmly, "Exactly. I'm accustomed to being lied to. Certain subjects, for example, history, should only be written by those who are geographically removed from the events. Only an outsider can tell the truth."

After the venerable six thousandth book had been brought out, and Sipho had studied all its photographs of colorful South American folk art, they left the library and went to the café downtown for a milk shake.

As they settled themselves into a booth in the corner, Monica kept hearing Doreen say, "Only an outsider can tell the truth." It was as though Max had sent Monica there in the knowledge that Doreen would use these exact words. *She* was an outsider. The stories she would work on now might appear slight, but there was a quiet dignity about these people, and it deserved closer attention. They were not involved in grand-scale schemes to enrich the impoverished, empower the disenfranchised or rewrite laws and policy, yet in the peaceful and gracious way they went about the business of their lives, with respect for their neighbors and a disregard for race and economic standing, they were doing as much for the country as members of Parliament. It was the future Ella had imagined and wished for yet had not lived to see.

By the time she'd finished her milk shake, Monica had decided that never again would she allow her pride to intervene in her career. Truth was not slight or lightweight. It was what kept a community grounded and its members accountable to one another, and her job, as the one to uncover and relay it without adulteration, was more important than she had ever imagined.

❧ *Chapter Eleven* ❧

It seemed natural in this place to go to church with Monica, yet it was something Francina would never have considered in the past. Maids, domestic servants, household assistants—whatever you wanted to call them—just didn't go to church with their employers.

For years she'd had her own church family, and it had existed quite apart from her home life. On weekends her church sisters had converged on the scout hall in their red-and-black uniforms like exotic insects. There they took up where they'd left off the previous week, as though six days of drudgery had not passed, as though they had no other life beyond these walls stuck with diagrams on how to make a fire, tie knots that would keep a tent roof down in a gale and boil water so that it was safe to drink when camping. Their families were never mentioned, not the ones they took care of nor the ones they had left behind in small villages all over the country. Worship was the focus of the day, worship with bone-shaking intensity. Sometimes Francina thought they might lift the roof their singing was so loud, and she wondered how people could come for meetings the next day and not hear the echo of their praise.

The only time that the women allowed conversation about everyday life was when they traveled to choir competitions. Then they would be heard to complain about the son who had dropped out of school to work in a nightclub in Nelspruit, and this after his mother had scrubbed toilets that were not her own to pay for his school fees, or the husband who no longer sent money home to his children. One woman was worried because her mother, who was taking care of the grandchildren in a village in Empangeni, had started to talk to relatives who had been dead since the time of President P. W. Botha. Another woman's son had won a scholarship to study at the University of the Witwatersrand, and she was counting the months until he graduated as a teacher because then she would be able to retire to her village.

One at a time they'd stop singing to relate this story or that, not caring really if their sisters were listening, just happy to be able to talk about something that had been bothering them. But the singing would soon draw them back in, away from their troubles, and the minibus taxi would hurtle along, kept safe by the beautiful voices of fifteen women in black and red.

And now Monica was suggesting that they find a church together. It felt odd, but Francina was willing to give it a try, partly because so much that would have been odd had now become normal for her and Monica, and partly because she had been a member of her previous church for so long she didn't know if she had the strength to start all over again on her own.

So here she was, for the first time since a teenager, going to church without her red-and-black choir uniform, because Monica thought it would not be appropriate.

"We want to blend in," she'd said.

Francina thought there was no chance of this with their unusual family. She chose to wear the dress she'd made to meet Hercules's mother, and as she smoothed down the skirt, she thought of the large woman sitting at home watching her only son live his life in reverse. To be willing to go without grandchildren forever required great sacrifice. For the first time since waving goodbye to Hercules at the taxi rank Francina felt a stab of guilt. Maybe God had sent him her way for a purpose. No, God would not expect her to be a doctor, and that is what Hercules needed. But what if he needed a doctor *and* a friend?

She said nothing, but Francina thought it disrespectful to, as Monica put it, "try out" churches. God's houses were not restaurants to be rated for cleanliness and service, but Monica explained that it was important to find a place where they felt comfortable. The first church they were to attend was Lady Helen's largest, not in building size but by the size of the congregation. They had been warned by Kitty to arrive early or spend the entire hour and a half standing. Francina thought of how her feet would hurt and so she made sure to have the boys dressed long before it was time to depart.

The Little Church of the Lagoon was Lady Helen's first church, and had been built close to the lagoon on the northern edge of town, at a time when the welfare of the thousands of migratory birds who settled there every spring was not taken into consideration. Now there was consensus that it would be impossible to expand the church without upsetting the birds, and there was even a campaign going to demolish the present building. Ten years ago the parking lot was shut down, and now people arrived on Sundays wearing rubber boots for the half-mile trek across the tidal mudflats from the new parking lot. It was not uncommon to see men sitting picking the mud from their boots during the sermon or children drawing fantastic mud creatures on the floor. And it took two ladies all of Monday morning to get the tiled floor clean.

Francina was grateful Kitty had warned them about the walk across the tidal mudflats, but secretly she hoped that Monica would not like this church because it did not seem proper to walk into God's house wearing great big muddy boots. How silly everybody looked in their fine dresses and suits with boots on their feet. Most of the people they met along the way greeted them, as though they knew exactly who they were. More and more Francina was beginning to think that this place was a lot like her village.

"Welcome," said the pastor, standing on the steps outside the church.

Francina had heard that Reverend van Tonder's hair was white in front and black over the rest of his head, yet she still had to remind herself not to stare. It was the strangest hair she had ever seen on a man. Monica behaved as though it were something she saw every day and shook the man's hand warmly. Then she shook the hand of the woman next to him, whom he'd introduced as his wife, Ingrid.

The poor lady can barely move, thought Francina, looking with disbelief at the stiff fabric of her ill-fitting dress. And the color pink makes her big red curls look like burnt pretzels. In her mind she quickly designed an outfit of flowing sage organza that would be far more comfortable—and attractive.

"I love what you're wearing," said the reverend's wife as she shook Francina's hand.

The words were out of Francina's mouth before she even knew it.

"I could make one for you, if you'd like. I'm a seamstress."

And there, standing on those muddy steps surrounded by thousands of birds and a couple hundred humans in their own finery, she had declared herself a woman with a career, a woman ready to take her position in the small economy of this town. She could have said that she was a designer, for that she was, too, but she was not used to building herself up like that. It was something she would have to learn, though. All those outfits she had made for her friends and family in the past had been made with love, but if she was to start charging for her creativity, then she would have to learn this thing they called marketing. Suddenly, she realized that she'd referred to her creativity, and this made her believe that she was off to a good start, because it was not a word she had ever used in reference to herself.

She told Ingrid where they were staying—which was unnecessary because everybody knew anyway—and set up an appointment for her to come to be measured for an outfit that very evening.

"What happened to that man's hair?" asked Mandla as they led him to his Sunday–school class.

"He drew on his brother's books with crayons," said Sipho.

Mandla's eyes widened.

"Sipho, it's not right to fib," said Monica. "Mandla won't be doing that again, will you, Mandla?"

Mandla shook his head solemnly.

"That man is Reverend van Tonder. And that's the way God made him," explained Monica. "He's just different, that's all."

Mandla joined the other young children with a cheery wave and headed straight for the large red fire truck that sat next to a box of toys.

The young woman in charge explained that they let the little ones play for ten minutes and then spent the rest of the hour singing songs and reading a Bible story.

"He'll listen," Francina told her. "Just let him turn the pages for you and he'll sit still for ages."

Sipho joined the ten or so older children in the main Sunday–school hall with less enthusiasm. Francina would have allowed him to come into the church with them, but Monica wanted him to meet other children.

Once she'd persuaded herself not to look at his hair, Francina lost herself in the words of Reverend van Tonder. He was not as passionate as the pastor at her old church, but he spoke as one might to old friends, with warmth and kindness, and a few laughs thrown in for good measure. She wondered if he truly did know everyone here personally, and the more she thought about it the more she realized that it was entirely possible. Nobody offered up an "amen" or a "thank

you, Jesus," or turned around and gave each other backslap-
ping hugs. They looked at each other and nodded when he
said something moving, and when one of the old ladies felt
a bit dizzy the Reverend stopped his sermon and several men
volunteered to carry her out into the fresh air. This church
family cared deeply for each other. She thought that she
might grow to like this place that was so close to the sea you
could taste the salt during the sermon.

The choir, however, was another story. They were not
dressed in uniform, and the five ladies who were supposed
to fill the church with glorious hallelujahs were huddled so
closely Francina wondered if they were trying to hide behind
each other. Not once did they sway in time to the music, or
lift their hands in praise, or click their fingers, because there
was no life in the mournful songs that they sang with such
tiny mouths Francina was sure she wouldn't hear a sound if
she sat at the back. She was convinced that the people standing in the hallway outside the church heard nothing but the
shuffling of their boots and the cries of the birds when the
choir was singing. She wished that she could take them all
to a competition so they'd see how it should be done. Clearly
there was work for her here.

In the short space of an hour and a half, in her smart dress
and ridiculous boots, she had stumbled across not one, but
two jobs, and she had an unusually certain feeling that these
would occupy her for the rest of her life.

After the service, Mandla couldn't wait to set out
across the tidal mudflats.

"I like this church," he pronounced, running toward

Sipho and taking a giant leap to land with both boots to-gether. Mud spattered everywhere.

"Nooooo," said Francina, using her handkerchief to wipe Sipho's shirt. "Don't do that again, Mandla." Her voice was low, but menacing enough to stop the little boy from jog-ging off again.

The disappointment on his face proved that a repeat of the stunt was exactly what he'd had in mind.

Sipho was less concerned about the dirt on his clothes than the attention his family was attracting. Men smiled in amusement and women shook their heads in commiseration.

"The novelty of all this mud will wear off." It was Zak Nie-mand.

Monica had not noticed the doctor during the service. She looked around for his wife and daughter, but he seemed to be on his own.

"I'll take your word for it," she replied.

"This is a coincidence, meeting you here. I was going to phone you at Abalone House. There's something I need to discuss with you. Do you think you could come to the hos-pital today?"

Monica noticed Francina raise her eyebrows.

"Yes, I'm sure I could make it after lunch."

"Thank you," he said. "I'd better hurry back. See you later."

Waving goodbye to Francina and the boys, he picked up the pace and almost ran the rest of the way to the parking lot.

"Men just can't help themselves—not even on Sundays on the steps of God's house," said Francina, shaking her head.

"What?" said Monica. "There's no doubt that it's business he wants to discuss. But what's more important is that he's married."

"I may have only one eye but I see everything," said Francina.

Monica did not pursue the matter with her because it would not be appropriate in front of the boys, and because it was just plain ridiculous.

After lunch, Mandla took a nap and Francina agreed to stay at the Old Dairy to watch him while Monica went to the hospital with Sipho, whose fascination with medicine seemed to be growing.

The nurse Monica had met on her first visit was sitting in the empty waiting room, staring at a piece of paper on the table in front of her. The assortment of chairs was scattered all over the room, a testament to a busy Saturday night. Dr. Niemand had appeared a little tired after church, but then Monica had never seen him any other way.

The nurse looked up as Monica and Sipho entered.

"You could have helped if you'd wanted to," she said, her voice flat. "But it's all over now."

Monica was speechless.

The nurse pushed the piece of paper toward Monica as though she could no longer stand the sight of the words typed on it. "Six weeks is all we have. That's not enough time—even for a miracle."

"I think there's been some mistake," said Monica, finally finding her voice.

The woman shook her head. "The first time you came here, I asked you to meet me after you'd finished your work. You never did."

"Oh, no," said Monica as the memory came to her. "I was so busy with the story on the burn unit that I forgot. I'm really, really sorry. Do you want to talk today?"

"It's too late. Dr. Niemand is through there." The nurse nodded her head at the door off the waiting room.

"Why is she angry with you?" asked Sipho as Monica led him by the hand down a short corridor.

"I forgot to meet her. But I'll try and sort it out." She squeezed his hand.

"In here," said a voice as they passed a small ward that had once been a bedroom in this old farmhouse.

Zak was standing beside a teenage boy who was sitting up in bed eating soup. The boy ignored their entrance, picked up the bowl and drank the last of the soup without using his spoon.

"Okay, Doc, now can I go?" he asked, pulling at the hospital gown.

Zak helped him with the ties at the back. "I hope you'll remember what I told you," he said in a stern voice.

The boy rolled his eyes at Sipho. "One party and they mark you forever. Watch out for the people in this town. They don't let you live."

Monica knew better than to take Sipho's hand again in front of this boy and Zak, but she wished she could gather him up in her arms and never let go. Even in an enchanted place like Lady Helen there were traps for youngsters. How would she fare as the parent of two teenage boys?

The boy pulled on a T-shirt and pair of jeans that reeked of alcohol.

"Your mother will be here in five minutes," Zak told him.

The boy groaned. "You called her?"

"Brian, who do you think brought you in here?"

"No way," said the boy, shaking his head. "She was in Cape Town at her new exhibition."

"I think you and your mother need to talk," said Zak. "Don't move now. She has to sign some papers before you can leave."

"Whatever," mumbled the boy.

As Zak directed Monica and Sipho out of the ward and into his office at the end of the corridor, Sipho took her hand again. The older boy had clearly unnerved him and Monica prayed that things would remain this way.

"Coffee?" said Zak, taking two white cups and saucers out of a cupboard. "These are especially for guests."

"Thanks," said Monica, watching as he filled an electric kettle and added three heaped spoons of instant coffee to a chipped mug for himself. "Only one for me, please. I can't take too much caffeine."

"This stuff is almost pure chicory," he said. "My daughter drinks it, too. Would you like some?" he asked Sipho.

Sipho looked at Monica. She did not give him coffee at home.

"A cold drink would be better," she said.

Zak passed him one and he took it gladly. For now her word held and the temptation had been overcome without effort.

Monica did not know if Zak would talk about one of his staff members, but she decided to ask anyway if he knew what was troubling the nurse in front.

"Daphne and her parents were among those who were forcibly removed from their homes in District Six in the late sixties," he said.

"That's very sad," she said, remembering old photographs she had seen of the once-vibrant neighborhood in Cape Town.

It was likely that this attempt at social engineering by the apartheid government had scarred many young minds. How awful it must have been for them to watch their homes being bulldozed and then to be sent to live in a new area for "Colored" people in the appropriately named Cape Flats.

"It's strange how we've come so far and yet the same thing is happening all over again," said Zak.

She looked at him blankly.

"The golf course extension," he added, to clear her confusion. "Everybody signed the petition against it, but it's still going ahead."

Was she, the new editor of the *Lady Helen Herald,* the only one in town who did not know about this groundbreaking news? Why had Max not told her about it?

Zak explained that the Malaysian businessman who owned the golf resort just north of Lady Helen was planning an additional eighteen-hole course on land that skirted the northern limits of town, land where fifteen families, including the nurse's, lived in modest homes that had been there for fifty years.

The land where the small neighborhood known as Sandpiper Drift stood, and the ninety undeveloped hectares surrounding it, belonged to the government, but when it was determined that there were no diamonds hidden in the sandy shale—as the farmer who'd sold the land to the government had claimed—it was ceded to the town for a period of two hundred years. But if any of the residents were to come across a diamond, they had to turn it in immediately at the Office for Mineral Affairs in Cape Town.

Monica could see from Sipho's expression that he did not understand the irony of Zak's laugh. What a good boy he was.

There were still one hundred and fifty years left on the agreement, but the government had recently sent their man here for a town meeting, and he'd pointed out fine print that stipulated that the land had to be returned if a diamond valuable enough to warrant a permanent mining operation was found. The roar of laughter this produced caused the tin walls of Green Block School, where the meeting was held, to vibrate. Everybody knew that the only shiny things to be found in the sand were soda cans and iron fishing-line sinkers dropped by little boys on their way to the ocean. But the government man insisted that a diamond of considerable value had been found a short distance from the fifteen houses.

A week later he returned with an armed security guard and a pile of eviction orders for the residents of Sandpiper Drift. By then Lady Helen's man up at the resort had brought the news of the golf course expansion, and the people demanded that the government man explain what was going on.

"Do you people think it's cheap to bring in mining equipment?" he wanted to know, and this was met by jeering.

In order to fund the mining operation, some of the land, including the small parcel on which Sandpiper Drift was built, had been sold to the Malaysian businessman. The mining operation itself would be hidden behind trees that were to be trucked in from Cape Town.

Monica felt awful. Some reporter she was. A story had come knocking and she hadn't even answered.

"What do you think of our hospital, Sipho?" asked Zak, and the little boy was caught off guard by the sudden change in the conversation.

"It's great," he stammered.

"For a small town, it's not bad," said Zak. "But there's something we desperately need—a ventilator."

"How does one go about getting one? Do you put in a request to the government?" asked Monica.

Zak nodded. "But we'll have to wait years and we need one now. So I'm going to raise the money to buy one, and that's where you come in."

This time it was clear she was being moved like a chess pawn.

"How much money are we talking about?"

"Less than the burn unit but still a lot."

She half expected him to be apologetic for asking this of her but he wasn't. There was no PR spin or, as Ella had termed it, "the Ella Nkhoma shake and bake" to make it seem more newsworthy. He just stated the facts plainly: Lives would be saved if the hospital had its own ventilator, because patients wouldn't have to be transported one and a half hours away to Cape Town.

Monica admired his honesty and felt a sudden twinge of regret that this earnest and dedicated man was married.

Stop it this minute, she told herself. *There's no room in your life for romance anyway.*

Before he'd even finished speaking she knew that she would give him the publicity he wanted because circumstances had changed and her allegiances were now to this town. Still, she hesitated to give him an answer. This would be the step across the divide between the objective, uninvolved journalist to the...she didn't even know what one would call it.

He was looking at her, waiting for her to speak. He had not said please, she'd noticed, but she sensed that this oversight was not due to a lack of manners but rather to an overwhelming belief in the cause and an inability to comprehend that everyone else might not feel the same way.

"I'll do it," she said, surprised at how right the words felt.

He smiled and for the first time she noticed the laugh lines around his eyes.

"Good. I have about ten minutes before I make my rounds. Is there something I can show you, young man?"

Sipho almost jumped off his seat. "Yes, please. Everything. I want to see everything."

On Monday morning Dudu gave Monica a cup of rooibos tea to "settle her down." Dudu had never worked as a receptionist before, but her cheerful disposition made Monica pleased that her first act as head of the newspaper had been to retire the impersonal camera and public-address system. Dudu's unflappable pragmatism came from years at home with three children, now aged ten, eight and six. Finding an extra staff member had not been easy, and it was only because Dudu's youngest child had just started at Green Block School that the *Lady Helen Herald* had a receptionist. Everybody who needed to work in Lady Helen was employed. Monica wondered if this contributed in any way to the harmonious race relations in town. If people were confident that they could feed, clothe and educate their families, were they less inclined to find fault with people of another race?

Max, who had relocated his office into the meeting room and showed no signs of ever going home to begin his memoirs, listened to her complaint with a smile on his face and did not say a word in his own defense.

"Now you can get started on the story," he told her when she had finished telling him how foolish she had felt the day before at the hospital upon learning the news of the golf course extension from Zak.

"So you're not sorry you never told me?" she asked.

"No. I wanted to see how long it would take you to find out. In your previous job you were probably used to receiving press releases. But it's when a company keeps quiet that there's a real news story brewing."

Monica's instinct was to keep arguing until she had an admission of guilt from him, but she knew that it would never come.

"How long would you have waited before telling me?" she asked.

"You beat your deadline by three days. Congratulations."

It was a strange sort of performance evaluation, yet she could not help feeling pleased that she had passed another of his little tests.

✎ Chapter Twelve ✎

An African hoopoe perched on the postbox, making its loud *hoop-hoop* sound that Mandla loved to mimic. It took off in fright as Francina approached. Mandla had gone down earlier than usual for his nap. A good game of catches in the garden would do that for a little one. What it would do for a forty-year-old woman Francina did not know, but she was sure she'd find out tomorrow morning when she awoke. Sipho was at the new school that he adored, and Monica was at work. Without any problems she had slipped into her job full-time, a fact that Francina noted with pride because she had made it possible.

Only a couple of days had passed since Francina first met Ingrid van Tonder, yet the new dress was already taking shape. It was two dresses really—one navy with discreet darts, the other a delicate organza overlay in the same color. Ingrid looked thirty pounds lighter in it and couldn't wait for Francina to finish so she could show off her new form.

Nervous about satisfying her first paying customer, Francina had worked till the early hours each morning. She would never be able to keep up this pace for the next order. She had felt awkward telling Ingrid the price, but now she realized that she could have charged double and Ingrid would still have ordered three more. If she stayed up two hours later than usual and got up at five instead of six, she would be able to finish a dress a week. Her friends had waited patiently for three weeks at a time for their dresses, but a paying customer could not be kept waiting.

Francina had cut down her soaks in the strange tub with the animal feet from thirty minutes to ten. Cat didn't mind her sewing machine whirring till late at night, but she did say that she would not deliver any hot chocolate past eight o'clock because it was extra work. Extra work! Ha! Who had polished all that ancient wood furniture in the living room till it looked as good as new?

She opened the postbox. No, it could not be. But yes, there, right on top of a pile of letters was the same small blue envelope, the same stamp picturing a heron with a fish in its mouth, the same handwriting, neat but light, as though the owner had been afraid to press too hard, the same Dundee postmark. How had he found her? She turned the letter over in her hands as though it were a weed she'd pulled from her vegetable patch. All of a sudden she saw with certainty that her life would be much simpler if she threw the letter onto the compost heap. But she knew she would never throw this letter away unread. Francina threw away as few things as possible. Everything could be reused, repaired or renovated—everything, that is, except Hercules himself.

This was not a letter that could wait until she had her bath this evening, nor was it one that she would feel comfortable reading in a state of undress. Somehow it would seem improper. She sat down on the step outside the Old Dairy, where inside Mandla lay sleeping on his back as though he were on the beach, and slit the letter open with a sharp stick she'd found at her feet.

The writing covered less than one page. Hercules had always been careful with his words, as though they were precious and not to be wasted. He had been careful, too, not to address her with too much familiarity, and for this she was grateful. A word like *dearest* would have made her face hot—and not in a good way.

She read the letter twice, and then, despite the fact that he had signed off most formally with the words *Kind regards,* she checked the envelope to see if she had missed a page. He wanted nothing from her; not to see her, not permission to write again, nothing. His letter was merely to wish her well in her new home.

That's nice, she thought, stuffing it back into the envelope. But she felt cheated. Reading this letter had been like window-shopping. She'd seen the pretty display that the designer had spent his time on, but not the jam-packed racks, tight spaces and shelves left in a mess from frantic rummaging. Her experience with Hercules had hurt her badly, and now he was offering good wishes in words so light they almost lifted off the page. She had turned down his offer to share his life. By sending this letter, he was merely being the gentleman that he would always be, sickness or no sickness.

There was another letter addressed to Francina in the postbox.

Two for me on one day, she thought. That's a first.

There was no return address and no stamp. Evidently it had been hand delivered. Francina had never seen an envelope like this. The paper was rough and here and there she could see bits of dried flowers that had been set into it. It was a shame to slit it open. Someone should make a fabric like this, she thought. The note read:

The National Mayoral Ball is just over three weeks away, and I can't represent Lady Helen confidently in anything I currently own. I'll come around on Friday so you can take my measurements. Ingrid van Tonder says you're a genius. I need to look at least eight inches taller.

The signature was hard to make out, but it looked like "Evette."

It seemed she was developing a reputation among the Afrikaans ladies of town—one that might be hard to live up to. Shaving off pounds with the clever use of color and texture was easy; making someone look taller was more difficult. But the stakes were high; if she pleased the mayor's wife, her future as a seamstress was set.

The day after her confrontation with Max, Monica phoned Daphne to offer her another—more formal—apology. Daphne didn't really accept it, but she did agree to allow Monica to come out to see the small neighborhood that was under threat.

"It'll be like paying your last respects at a funeral after you failed to offer the person first aid," she told Monica.

Monica found it hard to concentrate as she waited for Thursday—the one day in the week that Daphne would be home in the morning, and when it arrived she went out to Sandpiper Drift earlier than the time she had arranged with the nurse.

The tiny neighborhood was on the eastern edge of the lagoon, a short distance inland from the church. Boots were not needed here since there was no mud, just fine white sand, sparse papery reeds and woody clumps of pincushion protea bushes. The cottages were low, whitewashed stone buildings with brightly colored wooden doors and wood-frame windows, all of which were open to catch the breezes blowing across the lagoon from the ocean. Men's overalls, baby diapers and cheap cotton housedresses fluttered on wash lines hung between the rafters and iron posts. It was the kind of scene that tourists stopped to photograph without a thought for the privacy of the mother watching her children play ball or the grandmother sweeping the yard.

Monica was acutely aware that she was intruding, even before a young man asked her rather brusquely if she had any business there. The people of Sandpiper Drift were about to lose their homes to a businessman from a country thousands of miles away. How ironic that he was from the same country that had once supplied slaves to the Cape when it was a Dutch colony. He might even be distantly related to the people he was about to evict.

The cottage that Daphne shared with her parents was the last on the left, and it was different from the fourteen others only in that it had window boxes filled with red, orange and yellow geraniums.

"They won't grow if you plant them in the ground here," explained Daphne by way of greeting.

Daphne was no longer antagonistic, yet she was still distant. Or was it just weariness?

"I'd like to see them plant fairways and greens in this sand. Come in," she told Monica. "My folks are waiting for you."

The living room was dim after the bright sunshine outside, and it took a while for Monica's eyes to adjust. Daphne's parents stood patiently waiting to greet her, obviously used to their visitors taking time to get their bearings. The light off the ocean really was the starkest Monica had ever seen.

"Mammie, Pappie, this is the lady from the newspaper— the one who's taken Max's place."

"You mean Mr. Andrews," her mother corrected her. "I'll never get used to this first-name business. It's not right. I was taught to call men sir, and women mam. Mr. Andrews is a respected man in this community. I can't call him Max."

Daphne sighed. This was obviously an ongoing argument.

"He's only a few years older than you are, Mammie. Why should you call him Mr. Andrews when everyone calls you Miemps or Tannie?"

"Miemps is my name and Auntie is a sign of respect. But I'm not important like Mr. Andrews."

"You're just as important as he is," snapped Daphne.

"My daughter has some strange ideas," said Miemps.

"Sit, please," said Daphne's father, "or these two will go at it for hours."

Monica lowered herself onto a sofa that was covered with

clear plastic. She was hot after her walk around the neighborhood and her legs stuck to the plastic. A portable television was on in the corner.

"Cricket," explained Daphne's father, who had introduced himself as Reginald. "South Africa's playing India."

"Are we winning?" asked Monica.

For a second his good manners could not disguise the look of disbelief on his face.

"The Indians haven't gone in to bat yet," he explained quietly.

"I don't want to be rude, but my shift starts in an hour," said Daphne.

"Would you mind if I recorded this?" asked Monica. "It will speed things up."

"Go ahead," said Daphne.

Monica did not learn any new facts about the situation, except the price the family had been offered for their house—a paltry sum that would not buy even a one-bedroom house in town. What she did learn was how much more this hurt when it was happening for the second time. When the apartheid government had decided in 1968 to bulldoze the "Colored," or mixed race, area in Cape Town known as District Six to make room for a whites-only suburb, Miemps and Reginald had not received a cent. They were assigned a new two-room concrete blockhouse in a desolate outlying area of the city, and were told that they could take it or be homeless.

A little girl was waiting for Monica when she stepped out of the shade of the house into the bright sunshine. She was about nine or ten and wore a dress the color of egg yolk. It was clear that she had come for a purpose.

Monica got down on her haunches so that she could see the girl's face.

"Zukisa! It's you!" she exclaimed.

The girl smiled shyly. "I came to say thank you. You put me on TV and the boss at my father's work saw it and let him come home for two weeks so he could be with me."

"I'm glad," said Monica. "How are you now?"

The girl lifted her skirt an inch above her knees and Monica saw the scars where the skin grafts had been attached.

"I am much better. I will never be beautiful on the outside, but my mother says that is not important. God sees what is inside us."

Monica thought of the time she'd come across her own mother ruefully examining the stretch-marked folds of her belly in the mirror.

"You are beautiful inside and out," said Miemps, taking the child's hand. "How is your mother, dear?"

"Busy," replied the girl. "I have to go to Mama Dlamini and see if she has any old boxes to spare."

"They're moving to Cape Town," explained Miemps.

"To be with my father," added Zukisa. "Our new house is so close to the fish factory he'll be able to come home for lunch."

Miemps waited until Zukisa had skipped off down the road before allowing her expression to indicate just what she thought of the family's intended home.

"It's in a rough area," she said, wrinkling her nose as though she smelled something offensive. "Zukisa's mother will have to keep her indoors all the time. Bad things happen to little girls down there."

As Monica drove back to her office she kept picturing sweet little Zukisa in her cheerful dress, watching out for her father while predatory figures lurked in the shadows. By the time she'd parked her car she was feeling faintly nauseated. And then she was struck by another thought: Why were Reginald and Miemps not consumed by anger like their daughter?

Mrs. Dube, the old lady who had occupied the bed next to Monica's in the hospital where Monica had been taken after the carjacking, had also seemed resigned to the inequities of life. Her husband had been struck by a car while crossing the street in downtown Johannesburg, yet there was no anger in her heart for the policeman who'd covered his body with a newspaper but not bothered to interview any of the witnesses while waiting for the ambulance. Had a lifetime of apartheid broken the old people's spirit, or were these just gentle folk who did not expect life to be easy? Whatever the answer, Monica knew that she wanted to help Reginald and Miemps retain their home, and she felt prepared to step out of her objective role as a journalist to do so. What would Max have to say about that? she wondered.

Sipho would not hold Francina's hand on the way home from school and neither would Mandla. What am I going to do with two strong-willed boys? she wondered, inserting herself between Mandla and the road so that she could catch him if he strayed. Sipho was explaining to her how he now had twice as much homework because he was completing two grades at once. In her opinion he would do better spending more time outdoors with the children of the neighborhood rather than stuck indoors worrying about finishing school in double time, but she would not say anything to Monica unless she noticed him showing signs of stress. And there were none of those yet. In fact, she had never before seen him so excited about anything. He could barely wait to get home to start his project on solar power.

"Hurry up, Mandla," Sipho said when his brother stopped to watch a snail leaving a shiny trail across the path.

Francina tugged on his hand. She, too, needed to get home as she was expecting a visit from the mysterious Evette.

As they stepped onto the veranda, a white Mercedes pulled up outside Abalone House and a woman slid out from behind the wheel. Francina wondered if she was checking in. Cat had not asked her to get a room ready.

"Are you Francina?" asked the woman. She was not much taller than Sipho.

"Yes," said Francina, curious as to how the woman knew her name.

"I'm Evette."

Francina knew that if she spoke now her surprise might offend the woman, so she remained silent.

"You weren't expecting a black person, were you?" asked the woman, laughing. "My mother named me after the Afrikaans lady she worked for."

Francina did not smile.

"You should see your face," teased Evette. "Come on, it's funny that you thought I was white."

"Your husband is white," said Francina.

Evette shook her head.

"Are you sure?"

"Of course," laughed Evette. "Why on earth would you think he was white?"

"Monica, my employer, served him dinner one night, and she said he looked like Father Christmas."

Evette giggled. "He does have a beard—which I hate. And I've told him he eats too many sweets."

"But Father Christmas is white," interrupted Francina.

"Who said?"

Sipho and Mandla came closer to listen to the conversation that had suddenly become more interesting to them.

"Everybody knows it," said Francina. She looked at Sipho for help, but then realized that it would be better if he didn't say anything with Mandla about.

"My children know he's black," said Evette.

"On Christmas cards he's as white as my sheets," replied Francina.

Mandla's head turned from side to side as though he were at a tennis match.

"He's black," said Evette.

Mandla jumped up and down. "I saw him at the shops and he was red."

"Red?" said Francina, putting a hand on his shoulder so he wouldn't jump on Evette's toes.

"He was," said Sipho. "I think he was sunburned."

The two women looked at each other and burst into laughter.

Francina showed Evette to her room at Abalone House, while the boys sat down at the dining table to eat the lunch she had prepared for them. She could not concentrate on Evette's friendly chatter as she took her measurements. Making Evette look like a woman instead of a child would be her biggest challenge yet. The full floral dress that Evette wore now was obviously from the children's department. It probably saved her money to shop there, but a woman in her forties should not be tying a sash behind her back in a great big bow. Evette was sweet, but Francina wondered how on earth she'd managed to catch a mayor.

"Sipho's angry," announced Mandla when Monica came home from work on Friday afternoon, the day after her visit to Sandpiper Drift.

The boys were watching a television program on sharks, and Francina was in the kitchen preparing dinner and muttering something about women wearing bows.

Sipho did not take his eyes from the screen where a great white was butting its nose against a steel cage that held a diver armed with an electrified stun gun. The shark's jagged teeth appeared luminescent in the photographer's light.

"Sipho says James is a killer."

Sipho glared at his brother.

"Did you?" asked Monica.

He would not look her in the eye.

"I'm sure James doesn't harm the sharks," she said.

"But what if a shark goes for a diver?"

"James will do whatever he can to protect his client."

"If the water's full of blood, a shark does what's natural. And if a stupid person is in the middle he's going to get hurt. And it will serve him right."

Monica was taken aback by his tone and words, which were so out of character for him.

"That's not nice, Sipho."

"People like James make it dangerous for us to swim in the sea, 'cause the sharks start coming closer and closer to the beach to look for their next meal. You should tell him, Monica."

"Sipho, James is our host. It's not my place to tell him what to do."

He turned back to the television, but not before Monica saw the disappointment in his eyes.

"He's still angry," observed Mandla. "Let's tickle him."

He pounced on his brother and worked on the spots that usually elicited the loudest shrieks, but instead of being tickled back he was shoved aside without a word. Mandla looked at Monica in confusion.

"Come on," she said, taking his hand. "Sipho needs some alone time."

As they went into the bedroom to enjoy a raucous game of pillow fighting, she hoped that, left to himself, Sipho would simmer down and forget about James and the sharks.

The next morning, only two days after going to see a family that was about to lose their home, Monica received news of a house that would be perfect for her own family. The couple that lived in it had decided to move into a smaller place, as their boys had both taken jobs in Cape Town. Since it had three bedrooms, two bathrooms and a double garage, Monica was prepared to sign on the dotted line without even looking at it, but Francina told her that would be "one of the stupidest things she had ever done."

The first room the Realtor showed them was the kitchen.

Francina took one look at the brand-new stainless-steel appliances, which were quite out of keeping with the 1920s tin-roofed cottage, and told Monica to make an offer.

"We don't even know if there's a room for you," protested Monica.

"We can convert the garage," said Francina. "Just don't buy a place with an old-fashioned kitchen like Cat's. With all her money I don't know why she doesn't get new stuff. My mother has a better kitchen in the village."

Kitty's wood-fired stove was an antique, worth quite a lot of money, and the kitchen still had its original faucets, sink, cabinets and table. The only new appliance was the refrigerator. When the porcelain sink had started to look shabby, she paid more to have it refinished than she would have to purchase a new one.

Francina's harping on about Kitty was another reason Monica was thankful this house had come onto the market. A move was needed to alleviate the constant friction. Converting the garage was not an outrageous idea. Francina could do with more space than the usual maid's room provided, especially now that she had a dressmaking business. What a coincidence that Ella and her mother had been in the same business while they were in exile in Zambia. Going South they'd called their wedding-dress business because that is what they planned to do as soon as they got the call from the ANC leadership to return to the country of their birth. Ella's mother never set foot on her native soil as a free woman. She died while sewing a slinky wedding dress for a local nightclub singer. Four days later the call came for them to return home.

When the Realtor opened the kitchen door to show them the backyard, Mandla ran out shrieking with joy because he'd spied a jungle gym. Sipho waited for Monica to go out first. The owners of the house were sitting under a tall syringa tree and stood up to greet them. Monica recognized the wife immediately as the woman in the café who'd given them her table when they came to town for the job interview.

"I told you Max would love you, didn't I?" she said. She nudged her husband. "This is the new editor of the *Lady Helen Herald*."

"We're enjoying your reports. I liked the one about the library," he said in a quiet, gentle voice, looking at her over his half-moon spectacles.

His hair was almost entirely gray except for a small strip of black above his collar.

"Oh, David, it was dry as toast," said his wife.

Nervously, the Realtor asked if Monica would like to see the garage while they were outside. Monica was not sure how to take the woman's comment. There was a smile on her face and her tone was playful, but Monica felt as though she ought to defend herself.

"Give her time," said Francina.

Apparently, she agreed with the woman. This was a surprise.

"Please excuse Gift. She says what's on her mind," said David.

"I won't apologize because I mean it," said his wife.

Her afro seemed smaller than before, and she was not wearing the handmade ceramic beads that Monica remembered but rather a choker fashioned from strips of colored leather.

"I'm still learning the ropes," said Monica.

Gift smiled at her. "Humility is so scarce in this world, lovey. I have a feeling we're going to be thankful you chucked in your glamorous television career."

If only she knew, thought Monica. But there was no time to reflect on her past failures. In this tight housing market a move had to be made, and so she said a quick prayer, asking God for His guidance.

"I've got lots of happy memories invested in this house," said Gift. "What could be better than two more little boys growing up here?"

It seemed to be the sign from God that Monica had asked for. Since the owners of the house were both there, Monica's Realtor showed them her offer and they accepted on the spot.

After signing the contract, Monica went in search of Francina and found her in the garage trying to decide how to divide the space between her living quarters and her dressmaking studio.

"David says he knows of a builder," she told Monica. "I think I'd like a bath this time, not a shower."

"I'm sure that won't be a problem," she said.

"But I don't want an old-fashioned one with bird's feet."

"Of course not. Anything else?"

"I'd like to be able to see the television from my bath. And I don't want these ugly garage doors anymore. Do you think we can put some French ones in so that it looks pretty for my clients?"

Aside from any aesthetic reasons, the garage doors needed to go as they wouldn't keep out the cold winter winds people kept warning Monica about.

"Okay, get the builder's number. By the way, we got the house."

"Thanks be to God," said Francina, doing a little shuffle.

It was the first time Monica had ever seen her dance. Mandla joined in by stamping his foot in time to Francina's clapping. Sipho laughed but stayed on the sidelines with Monica.

"Look at those wet rags," said Francina. "Go and get them, Mandla."

Mandla took Monica's and Sipho's hands and tried to drag them toward Francina. When he realized that he was making no progress he started whimpering, and so, feeling bad, Monica began an awkward two-step that was completely out of time with Francina's clapping.

Sipho looked at the three of them and said, "You're all silly. My mother would have loved this."

Monica stopped moving at the mention of Ella, but Francina stepped toward Sipho without interrupting her rhythmic shuffle.

"Well, then, do it for her," she commanded, taking both his hands and moving them as though he were a doll.

He tried to resist, but Mandla bumped up behind him and soon Sipho was giggling and moving his arms and legs like a robot. It was more than five minutes before they realized they had collected an audience.

"Don't stop," said Gift. "The only way I can leave this house without crying buckets is if I know there's going to be a happy little family living here."

What Monica had merely speculated before was now confirmed. Lady Helen was the perfect place for her family. Nobody thought them odd or unconventional; nobody hurt them with careless remarks; everybody just let them be. She never would have guessed how liberating it would feel.

❧ *Chapter Thirteen* ❧

Francina had seen the men in her village decorate themselves on special occasions, but always with paint that washed off. The man erecting a new fence across the road from Abalone House to replace the old one that had collapsed, as Francina predicted it would, had a permanent ink drawing on his arm.

"Medusa," he said when she did not bother to hide the fact that she was staring.

"Why does she have snakes coming out of her head?"

He shrugged. "She was once a beautiful maiden whose hair was her shining glory. But the goddess Athena changed her hair into hissing snakes, and everyone who looked at her turned to stone."

"What part of Africa was she from?" asked Francina.

"It's Greek mythology," said the man.

"What's that?" asked Francina.

She was sick and tired of pretending to understand everything. This man was not a teacher, but a man who built fences, and even *he* knew things that she would have to look up in Sipho's encyclopedia.

"Just a fancy word for old stories," said the man. "When you're out at sea you have a lot of time for reading."

He introduced himself as Oscar, and said he had been named after a famous English playwright but hadn't read any of his plays because he didn't like stories that took place in one room.

"Give me tales about exotic countries, and people who wear bearskins or bark cloth."

Francina thought about this for a while and decided that it was a waste of time when this country alone held more stories than one person could ever know in their entire life. She would be happy just understanding plain, everyday things, like why there was rainfall in winter in Cape Town but in summer in Johannesburg; what people meant when they talked about the country's wonderful new constitution; and the meaning of words like *ironic, frenetic* and *elliptical*—all of which Monica used in conversation. She was tired of nodding as though she knew exactly what everyone meant all the time, and she'd had enough of adding safe comments that meant nothing just to be polite.

"Can a person get a grade nine School Leaver's certificate without going to school?" she asked.

"I don't see why not," said Oscar. "But Mr. D., the principal, would know for sure. Is that something you'd like to do?"

She nodded. "A person without an education is like a tree that doesn't get water. It never grows tall."

Oscar smiled. "I guess you could say that I'm a stubby little tree then."

Francina looked at him in disbelief. "Never. But you talk like a teacher." She stopped herself. "Well, not exactly—I don't mean to insult you but I know a teacher and he sounds a lot cleverer."

Oscar smiled again. "It's not easy to offend me."

"What I mean is that you know lots of things but you don't sound all stiff and professor-like."

"Everything you need to know you can learn on your own from a book."

"I'd still like to have a certificate to hang on my wall so my clients can see it when they walk in."

"If you need any help, just let me know."

Francina decided that this man with the strange drawing on his arm would be exactly the kind of person she'd need if she were to do this. Monica was too busy, she'd never ask Cat, and Sipho had his own schoolwork to do. With the dressmaking business, her work for Monica and now this, life was going to be a whirlwind.

Monica thought that she'd have more chance of finding Mr. Yang, the Malaysian businessman, if she waited till the weekend was over, and so on Monday morning, she headed out to the golf resort to see if she could help save Daphne's home. The construction trailers were lined up behind a ten-foot-high electrified fence, a security measure that would not have looked out of place in Johannesburg yet in this part of the country was cause for suspicion.

Only people with a clear conscience sleep easy, thought Monica as she parked her car next to the gate.

"Can I help you?" asked an armed guard.

"I'm here to see Mr. Yang. I was told he was down here with the construction crew."

"They're in a meeting," said the guard. He looked at his clipboard. "I don't have you on my list."

"You didn't even ask my name."

"Look, lady, I have orders not to let any more women in. Now, I'm going to have to ask you to leave. This is private property."

Monica wondered what he meant by letting any more women in. Could Daphne have been here? She was defiant in front of her parents, but had she been here to beg Mr. Yang to spare her home?

"I'm with the press," said Monica, flashing her Journalists' Association card. "I want to do a piece on the new golf course, on how this is going to become the premier golfing venue in the country."

The guard frowned, but Monica could see that he was weighing the options.

"Okay," he said finally. "But you'll have to wait until their meeting is over."

"Thanks," said Monica.

"It could be an hour or more," he warned.

"I'll go and check out the clubhouse in the meantime."

He tapped his pen on the clipboard. "You're supposed to be with a member, but if you're waiting for Mr. Yang, then technically you're with him." He handed her a visitor's permit to show to the guard at the entrance to the resort. "Just stay out of the bar. Women aren't allowed in there till after dinner."

"Don't worry. I have no intention of spoiling any all-male fun," said Monica, but her sarcasm was lost on him.

The clubhouse was made of natural stone and had soaring windows with panoramic views of the ocean and koppies that surrounded Lady Helen. The town itself, Monica noted with satisfaction, was hidden from view by the dense stand of palm trees that flanked the cemetery in the northern part of town. But there was an unobstructed view of the fifteen whitewashed cottages of Sandpiper Drift and the Little Church of the Lagoon. With a feeling of possessiveness that startled her, she realized that golfers could sit on the patio, cocktails in hand, and watch the migratory birds wading in the mudflats.

No expense had been spared in the clubhouse, which housed the fitness center, spa and restaurant. Limestone floor tiles, which Monica identified as Italian, had been used everywhere except in the restaurant, where there was black slate. In the bathroom, where she touched up her lipstick, the floor was real marble, also Italian, and suddenly it dawned on her that her father might have been Mr. Yang's supplier. No. She could not remember him making a trip to this area.

There was a table of sunburned men in the restaurant, a bride-to-be and her attendants having manicures in the spa, and a couple of elderly men reading newspapers in the lounge. Monica wondered why there was a need for another eighteen holes. Then, while wandering around, she pressed the wrong button in the elevator and found herself in the parking garage. It was full, which meant that the golf course was, too. The hotel itself faced out to sea, and because it was not the focal point of the resort it was covered in sandstone-colored stucco instead of natural stone.

Mr. Yang still had not come out of his meeting when she

checked in with the security guard at the construction trailers fifty minutes later.

"Where exactly is the mine going to be?" asked Monica.

"Over there," said the guard, waving vaguely in the direction of Sandpiper Drift.

"A mine on a golf course," said Monica.

"You know what they say about a diamond in the rough," he replied, sniggering.

"But there's no fence to mark off the area," said Monica. "Shouldn't there be signs saying Government Property. Keep Out?"

Just then the door of the trailer opened and the guard gave an audible sigh of relief. Two Asian men emerged, both dressed in suits, the taller of the two carrying a roll of architect's plans. From the way the guard stood to attention, she gathered that one of them was the Mr. Yang who didn't want any more women around.

"She's a member of the national press, sir," the guard said quickly as the men approached.

The *national* press?

The man holding the plans said something that Monica did not catch, and then got into a waiting car.

"Which newspaper?" asked the man that was left, who Monica was now certain was Mr. Yang.

She thought of the framed pictures on Max's wall, of his unsullied reputation built on fifty years of honest work. Then she thought of the flower baskets Reginald had placed under the windows of their whitewashed cottage.

Please God, forgive me this deception, she prayed.

"The *Sunday National*," she told him.

He could not invite her into his office in the club, he said, because his helicopter would be picking him up in ten minutes for another meeting in Cape Town. When they entered the trailer the men inside converged on him with maps, sheets of figures and computer-rendered drawings. He waved them away and watched, smiling until the last one had left.

Monica had expected an older man, but Mr. Yang was probably only five or six years her senior. He was much shorter than her, and his finely tailored suit did nothing to disguise his thick neck and broad torso. In any other setting he might have passed for a wrestler or weight lifter.

"I believe this is to become the premier golfing resort in Southern Africa," said Monica, predicting that flattery would soften him.

"The premier resort in the whole of the southern hemisphere."

She had underestimated his competitive nature. For five of her allotted ten minutes she listened as he described his plans for the second eighteen-hole golf course, and, as he let slip, a third, but she was not to put that in print because it was still in a sensitive stage of negotiations. Negotiations were only sensitive when one side was unwilling, thought Monica. Whose land was he after next?

"Tell me about the diamonds," she said, feigning an intimate tone. "Off the record—there aren't any, are there?"

For a brief moment he smiled, but then he became businesslike. "Someone from the town found one."

"Who?" she asked, wondering if he would make up a name.

In the distance, she could hear the approaching helicopter.

"Who?" she repeated.

"They asked to remain anonymous," Mr. Yang said. "Do you want a picture of me next to my helicopter?"

The pilot brought it down a hundred yards from the construction trailers, not too far from Monica's car. Although she had just run out of film, she pretended to take Mr. Yang's photograph next to the metallic-blue craft with the Yang Corporation logo emblazoned on its tail.

As the blades sped up again for takeoff she ran for her car, but, just as she grabbed the door handle, a cloud of dust overtook her. Coughing and wheezing, she tried to shield her eyes from the sandstorm, and then, when her lungs felt as though they might burst a question presented itself to her: Where did Mr. Yang get water to keep the fairways of his golf course green in this arid area?

Two weeks after accepting Monica's offer on their house, Gift and David handed over the keys. According to the contract, they didn't have to move out for another two weeks, but their new home was ready and they sensed that Monica and the boys were eager to move out into a home of their own. Monica called the Realtor to make arrangements to pay rent to Gift and David for the extra time in the house, but the Realtor said that they had insisted it was a housewarming present.

Gift and David had been loving owners of the house and it was in tip-top condition despite its age. The man David had recommended to convert the garage into a small cottage for Francina was the one Monica had seen repairing the fence around the statue of Lady Helen. When Oscar arrived to start work the day after they moved in, Mandla recognized him immediately and asked if it was his turn now to use the "fire stick." Francina seemed to have already developed some sort of friendship with him and they spent a couple of hours together after the first day's building was over. Monica did not ask and Francina did not tell her what it was they'd discussed under the syringa tree until it became cool, but she noticed that Oscar had a book with him.

Kitty had been sad to see them go, but Monica felt that it was better if she and her husband had the place to themselves some nights. If they didn't, Monica feared that Kitty might repeat the pattern of her life and run off to something new. Monica knew that she'd miss sitting on the veranda with her friend, drinking coffee and chatting. But there was no reason why she couldn't pop in and do exactly that whenever she had the time.

Until the garage was renovated, Francina would sleep in the third bedroom, which would become Mandla's once she moved out. He'd never had his own room and Monica wondered if he'd like it. His bunk bed had come out of storage, but he'd refused to sleep in it, and she'd given in to his pitiful requests to climb into bed with her. They'd had a lot of change in their lives lately—too much, perhaps, for a three-and-a-half-year-old.

Sipho liked lying in bed with the curtains open so that he could look at the moon and stars above the black outline of the rocky koppies. He couldn't wait for the bunk beds to be separated so he could put up more of his wildlife posters, and he was running an experiment for his biology class that required a lot of space for an assortment of jars containing roots and seeds of various indigenous plants.

Ebony had also taken to her new home, and, unlike at Abalone House, had even ventured outdoors.

On their third night in the house, Monica sat playing board games with the boys in the living room, while Francina again spent time talking to Oscar under the syringa tree. The smell of floor wax hung in the air.

How strange, thought Monica, my mother's caramel leather sofas look more at home here than they did in the modern house in Johannesburg.

The coffee table and television cabinet, both made from old railway sleepers, were almost identical to ones she'd seen in a shop on Main Street. The hand-woven Navajo rug had been retired to a blanket chest in her room because the wooden floors, original but refinished just last year, were far too pretty to cover up.

Monica thought of Daphne, Miemps and Reginald, who were more than likely sitting in their living room now on the sofa covered in plastic. Theirs was the only family that had not yet packed. Every time Miemps started to, Daphne unpacked the box and placed the ornaments back on the shelves of the display cabinet.

"What can I do?" Miemps had asked Monica in real distress.

A crew of government workers had fenced off an area adjacent to Sandpiper Drift and hung signs that threatened prosecution of trespassers. When Miemps washed the dishes now, her view was not of open land but of barbed-wire knots.

With three weeks left before the bulldozers arrived, Monica did not know what Daphne was planning. The eviction notice lay shredded on top of the portable television, and Daphne had forbidden Miemps to tape it together or throw it away.

Three of the families whose children worked in Cape Town were set to move to low-cost housing on the outskirts of the city. "Slums," Daphne called them, "where children use drugs." Zukisa and her mother had moved into a house near the docks in Cape Town; another family had moved to Bloubergstrand; two families had been offered accommodation in the maids' quarters at their places of employment; the caretaker of Green Block School planned to move his family to an unused workshop behind the school; and another six families were ready to go but had no idea where to.

Toward the end of their first week in the house, a package arrived in the mail. Since it was not addressed to anyone, Francina tore off the brown-paper wrapping, taking care to preserve the stamp with the picture of the loggerhead turtle for Sipho, and opened the shoe box inside. At first she thought she had to be dreaming because it contained nothing but a rock. Why on earth would someone send a rock all the way from Johannesburg? With all this talk of diamonds in the town, she wondered for a brief moment if the rock contained one. Sending a rock in the post was silly, but sending a diamond would be even sillier. There was no card, no name, no return address.

But there was no time to think about the strange parcel because Evette would be arriving any minute for a final fitting of her dress and Francina wanted to give it a touch-up with the steam iron. It was an ivory silk, with delicate gold threads running vertically up its entire length, and Francina had made it longer than she normally would have so that it almost touched the floor when Evette wore high heels. Even Sipho agreed that Evette looked about five inches taller. With Evette's lack of curves, the matter of making her look like a woman had been challenging. Francina had paged through magazines in the bookshop before coming up with the idea of creating an indecently low scoop neck, but then inserting a ruffled piece that added fullness and made it completely modest.

"I look like a fairy-tale princess," Evette had exclaimed the first time she'd tried it on. "Don't you dare make one like this for anyone else."

A fairy-tale princess with Father Christmas, thought Francina.

Francina had sent the money Ingrid paid her, including the bonus she'd added because Francina's prices were "ridiculously low," to her mother to put toward the purchase of an electric washing machine. Her mother wrote back to thank her but said she had been washing the family's clothes by hand for more than forty years and nobody could ever say that any of them had ever looked anything but clean and tidy. What she had done with the money was hide it in a plastic bag in the flour tin in case Francina ever needed it. After all, her mother reminded her, she was a woman without a husband or children to take care of her in her old age. Francina did not need to be reminded that she was a battery chicken, keeping another's eggs warm and then being chased off when little beaks started to peck through the flimsy shells.

∻ *Chapter Fourteen* ∻

They'd been in the house a full week before they discovered that S. W. Greeff was their neighbor. After collecting the mail, Sipho came running into the living room waving the famous artist's electricity bill as though it were an item he'd won at auction. Monica slipped the letter into the postbox next door in the middle of the night, in order to give herself time to read up on the man's work before meeting him face-to-face.

The next morning, as she pulled out of the carport Oscar had built next to the old garage, she noticed a new birdbath in Mr. Greeff's garden. A Cape weaverbird perched on its rim. There were always birds in his garden, and Oscar had explained that it was because the plants were all indigenous to the area. Monica looked at the rosebushes in front of her house. David had meant well but they just didn't seem right. Monica's only disappointment with the house was that it was one of only a handful in town that did not have a bougainvillea. But she planned to plant one as soon as she'd put the next issue of the newspaper to bed. How much would her little family have changed by the time the vines crept along the roofline and covered Francina's new cottage?

She could have walked to the hospital from her house, but she wanted to go out and see Miemps and Reg after her meeting with Zak. She wondered why he'd asked to meet her.

When she arrived at the hospital he was waiting for her on the veranda.

"I've got something to show you," he said as she climbed the stairs. He didn't ask after her boys as he usually did—or her new house.

They went through the waiting room, where a mother was trying in vain to keep her toddler from rearranging the chairs. Daphne was nowhere to be seen. He stopped outside one of the doors in the long corridor.

"Try not to stare at the patient." He was almost breathless with exhilaration.

The room was dark. Unlike the other wards, where the windows were bare and most often open, these were closed and covered with heavy green curtains. An overhead fan clicked rhythmically, and there was another sound: of air being sucked in and out. The patient in the corner had a tube in his throat, and it was attached to a machine with a gray screen on which numbers kept blinking.

"How did you do it?" Monica mouthed the words to Zak.

"I'll tell you later," he whispered, his face solemn now.

The woman sitting on the rocking chair next to the bed rose to shake Zak's hand. Feeling like an intruder, Monica turned to leave.

"It's not necessary," said the woman in a weary voice. "My husband's out of danger now, thanks to this marvelous ventilator. He had an epileptic seizure." She started to cry. "He wouldn't have made the ninety-minute trip to Cape Town. What would have happened if the hospital didn't have this new ventilator?"

Zak halted his check of the patient's vital signs to put a hand on her shoulder.

"But, thanks be to God, we do. Now, why don't you go home and get some rest?"

The woman made a weak protest before giving in.

"I thought you had only a fraction of the money you needed," said Monica when they were outside in the corridor again.

"I did," said Zak. "But I just kept badgering the guy that imports these until he let me have one. I still owe him thousands."

"You obviously have a knack for getting people to do what you want," said Monica.

"Not always," he replied dourly.

It was the first time she had seen his professional calm slip. Monica waited for him to continue but he just stared into space and said nothing. Feeling uncomfortable, she changed the conversation to rewriting the story as a plea for donations to help pay off a large debt. People would be less inclined to give now that they had their prize, but one life had already been saved and that made the effort worthwhile. Maybe the patient's wife would be willing to be interviewed.

Soon Zak had shrugged off his bad humor to explain to her how in the past they'd pump air manually into the patient's lungs with a bag until they got him to Cape Town.

When he had finished his explanation, he thanked her. "You always know the right thing to say. You're like a mother hen soothing her agitated chicks."

Monica smiled as politely as she could at the strange compliment.

"No, that came out all wrong. What I mean is that you have a way of making people feel that everything will be okay, that everything happens—"

He stopped when he noticed Daphne arrive.

"He's doing fine," Zak told her. "Just watch his pressure." He turned to Monica. "Now that the ventilator has arrived we officially have an ICU, and Daphne's the only nurse trained to work in one."

"Well, you may be losing me in two weeks," she snapped. "That rich, thieving tycoon isn't going to change his mind."

Monica wished she knew of something to say that would make Daphne feel better, but the condolences of the fortunate so often sounded hollow. It had been the same when she was shot. Behind the concerned smiles there had lurked relief that it hadn't happened to them.

"If there's anything we can do…" said Zak.

It was well meant but sounded just as Monica had feared it would.

"You can persuade Mr. Yang that what he's doing is immoral."

Monica was almost certain now that Daphne had paid the Malaysian businessman a visit and that *she* was the cause of the ban on all female visitors.

"I'll give it a try," said Zak.

Thoughtful as this gesture was, Monica knew it would

amount to nothing because nothing short of the prospect of losing a lot of money would stop Mr. Yang. And what would make an experienced businessman like Mr. Yang lose money? Apart from diamonds, what was the one thing of value in this area? That was it! In this dry area, water was more valuable than anything.

As far as Monica knew, Lady Helen's natural underground spring was the only one for miles, so unless Mr. Yang piped water in from Saldanha Bay—which was possible but unlikely given the distance—he had to be getting his water from Lady Helen. Did the residents of the town know? It seemed reasonable to assume that they did. But why would they tolerate such an agreement when Mr. Yang did his best to keep the resort's guests from frequenting the businesses in town? And, more important, were they happy to supply a second—and, in Monica's opinion, unnecessary— golf course?

A thought had begun to nudge its way into her brain, and at first she tried to push it away, knowing that once it took hold everything would change. The divide she'd crossed when she'd agreed to write a story to help Zak procure donations for the ventilator would seem small in comparison, and she would no longer be able to call herself a journalist in the true sense of the word.

The idea was now fully formed in her head. *What if Mr. Yang were to lose his precious lifeline to Lady Helen's water? Deals went sour all the time,* she told herself, *through poor planning, poor execution or just plain bad luck.* In this situation, somebody had to make this deal go bad, and deep down she knew that this person was her.

"You can come and stay with me if you need a place," Zak told Daphne. "Your parents, too. We have room."

"That won't be necessary," replied Daphne. "We're not leaving our home."

Zak nodded and did not seem offended by her terse response.

Monica found herself wondering about the fortunate woman who shared this compassionate man's life, a woman she'd only ever seen from a distance, dropping her daughter, Yolanda, off at school. Some of the mothers stayed a few minutes after the school bell to chat, but Mrs. Niemand never did. What could have prompted Zak's bad humor earlier? He seemed to have a perfect life.

Miemps and Reg were eating an early lunch in front of the television when Monica arrived at their house. On the drive over, she had decided that she wouldn't share her idea with them—or with anyone, for that matter.

"Why do we watch these silly soaps when we have enough drama in our own lives?" asked Reg.

After insisting that Monica take a plate of food, Miemps turned off the television.

"I'm very worried about Daphne," she said. "She never sleeps. And she won't let me pack a thing." She looked at her collection of miniature teacups in the display cabinet. "I need time to pack all of this properly."

"Where will you go?" asked Monica.

"My sister has a room for us in her house in Paarl," Reg said. "But it's too far for Daphne to travel to work here."

"She can get a job there," said Miemps, and her exasperated tone suggested that this had been the theme of many family arguments.

"Dr. Niemand would really miss her," said Monica.

"I don't know what she's planning, but I know she's not going," said Reg.

"This is what happens when you allow your daughter to go to a university far away from home," said Miemps.

"What did you want her to do? Turn the scholarship down? Clean houses for the rest of her life?"

Miemps sniffed into a lace-edged handkerchief. Half expecting to be rebutted, Monica took her hand. But Miemps held on to it as though it were a perfectly natural thing to do.

"Did you see how the sand is already blowing into the two empty houses?" asked Reg. "The women swept their homes every day, and in a few weeks it's as though nobody ever lived there." He shook his head. "There's even a family of crabs in the front room of DeVilliers's place."

"What does he care? Before the eviction notices had even arrived he'd bought a new house in Bloubergstrand with a turret and a view of Table Mountain." Miemps blew her nose hard.

"DeVilliers's young grandson, Dewald, let the cat out of the bag," explained Reg. "He told me they've got a gate that opens with the push of a button. A six-year-old doesn't know how to keep secrets. And a mechanic shouldn't be able to afford a house like that."

"Where do you think Mr. DeVilliers got the money?" asked Monica.

"Gambling," said Miemps, spitting out the word. "There

were always shady characters dropping by late at night for card games."

Monica doubted that any card games played in modest homes by men who arrived on foot would allow enough to finance a house with a view of Table Mountain. She would jot down a few notes as soon as she got back in her car because one never knew when this sort of information would be useful.

"The new issue comes out tomorrow," she announced to Miemps and Reg. "You're on the front page."

Miemps was ecstatic until Reg reminded her that she would be identified to the nation as a person who was about to become homeless.

"Not to the nation," Monica corrected him. "Only to the people of Lady Helen. But if the story's good enough it might be picked up by the national press."

It was a start, but something far more dramatic was needed. Unfortunately, the short drive over to Miemps and Reg's house hadn't given her enough time to work out a plan. But time was running out. In two weeks, Miemps, Daphne, Reg and all the other families would be thrown out into the street.

"You're our star," said Miemps, squeezing her hand. "We trust in you."

The road outside, where little boys had once played soccer and neighbors had swapped news, was deserted. The families remained indoors where they did not have to see the spiderweb of plastic construction tape that demarcated the places where hills were to be built from the rubble of their houses so that every hole would have a view of the ocean, earning the golf course the coveted status of a links.

Zukisa's mother had removed everything she could from her house. Where once there had been a pretty, brass lantern, cast-iron gates and hand-carved wooden numbers, there were now gaping holes and gouged stucco. The front door had been blown ajar, as had the front door of the DeVillierses' house, and the living rooms were carpeted with fine, white sand. In a month or so it would be impossible to close the doors again, but then nature would not be afforded this time.

Aware that she was being watched through chinks in the curtains, Monica could not help feeling disappointed. These people knew who she was by now, yet still they chose to hide from her in their homes. Would she always be an outsider here, or were these simply people who had given up on the magnanimous yet impotent offers of help that had come their way? She took a few more photographs and then got into her car. As she drove back into town she had the distinct feeling that her plan had better be good or the little houses would end up as they had begun: stones scattered across the sandy flats.

✣ *Chapter Fifteen* ✣

There was nothing in the air to suggest that it was going to be an unusual day, when Francina awoke before five one morning after they'd been in the new house for two weeks. The moon was beginning to fade as the sky lightened; the breeze was cool but slight; and the birds had begun their predawn choir with the same cheerful energy. It promised to be a day like every other in Lady Helen: warm, dry and bright.

The dress she needed the extra time to put the finishing touches to was for an artist who was off to Johannesburg to accept a prize for Most Innovative Use of Mixed Media. Francina had felt like hugging the lady out of pride when she heard that, because she had understood each and every one of her words.

That Oscar is a genius, she thought as she threaded a needle to sew the hem by hand. Hercules could take a page out of his book. Ha! That was good use of an idiom. She really was getting the hang of proper English, which was not easy because it was a rather deceitful language. Look how many words there were that sounded the same but were spelled differently. Yes, English was like a suitor who disguised himself so that he could run around town. Maybe they should think about adding that one to their list of proverbs.

The dress had not been difficult to design because the artist wanted only to look a little less skinny and everybody knew how to do that. Bold prints, bold colors, horizontal stripes.

While she stitched, the sun came up over the koppies and filled the valley with golden light. Francina stopped her work; the view from her window was simply too beautiful to ignore. But instead of the peace this sight would normally have brought to her heart, she started to feel uneasy. *Don't be silly,* she told herself. But as the sun rose higher, and the gentle light turned bright and glaring, she could not shake the sense that something out of the ordinary was about to happen.

At noon, after putting Mandla down for his nap, Francina sat down with a cup of tea. Sipho was at school, Monica at work, and Oscar had taken a break from laying bricks in the garage to meet a friend for lunch. Except for the drip of the kitchen faucet that Oscar had promised to fix, the house was completely quiet.

Suddenly, there was a knock at the door, and Francina was so startled she almost dropped her teacup. Not forgetting the cautious ways of Johannesburg, she lifted the net curtain on the kitchen window to see who it was and let out a gasp. It was Hercules.

She dropped the curtain and flattened herself against the wall. When she was finally over her fright enough that she could think, she realized that she was acting as though he were a criminal who had come to rob them blind. Ah! How could she think in idioms at a time like this? She unlocked the door.

"Francina," he said, taking off a strange hat that made him look like a jazz musician from the fifties. "Thank you for not pretending to be out."

She invited him in and showed him a chair at the kitchen table. He seemed thinner than ever, but once again she was relieved to see him eat with enthusiasm when she put a plate of stew in front of him. He had been traveling since eleven the previous night and had only slept for two or three hours. She did not ask how he had found her address or why he had come. Instead, she tried to conjure up the anger and hurt she had felt the night she stayed at his house in Dundee. But she couldn't. The only feeling she had was guilt for abandoning him when he had so obviously been reaching out to her for help. She had not done the right thing and until now had not even known that she needed to ask forgiveness, both from Hercules and God.

She served him another portion without caring that there wouldn't be enough left for the family for dinner and she would have to start something else from scratch.

"Hercules, I'm sorry," she began, not knowing how she would continue. "I should have—"

"No, I'm sorry," he interrupted. "I understand now why you were frightened. I had no idea that I was clinically depressed. When you left, I finally realized that there was something wrong. My doctor referred me to a psychiatrist, who put me on medication."

"And how do you feel now?" she asked.

"So much better that, before coming here, I was able to take all my late wife's clothes to the church rummage sale."

Francina thought it sad that an entire lifetime's collection of clothes could land up in something that sounded so undignified. All those hands touching and grabbing—it seemed disrespectful. But better that than preventing a man from getting on with his life.

"The bedroom has been redecorated," he continued. "My mother decided that beige was a good color for a man."

Lord, this apology is very late, she prayed, but please forgive me for turning my back on this sweet person.

"I didn't think words on a page would be enough to convince you that I was on the path to being healed," said Hercules. "I'm sorry I surprised you like this, but I presumed you would have told me not to come had I asked your permission beforehand."

Francina could not deny that he was right.

"Don't be afraid," he continued. "I want us to take a giant step back, to where we were before you came to Dundee. Do you think we can do that? Do you think we can be friends again?"

Francina nodded, although she was not sure how they would do this with her down here and him back in Dundee.

"I've resigned from my school," he said.

"Oh, Hercules, you loved it. You loved your students."

He frowned and for the first time she saw some of the anxiety that she remembered in him.

"I wasn't myself the last month I was there, and once students lose respect for you it's impossible to be a good teacher."

Francina wondered what on earth he could have done to

lose their respect, but she did not press him as the memory was clearly painfully fresh.

He said that he had saved enough money to support himself and his mother for nine months, and, since most of his brief relationship with Francina had been through letters, he planned to spend this time getting to know her in person, if she would allow him.

And then what? wondered Francina. She was satisfied with her life in Lady Helen and had no wish to leave it.

When Mandla woke from his nap at one o'clock Francina gave him some juice, and then they walked Hercules over to Abalone House on their way to pick up Sipho from school. She felt proud to be able to help Hercules get a special rate, but she was grateful that Cat did not give him her room. That would have felt improper and inappropriate. She, too, could use big words, but she would wait awhile before showing him.

❧ Chapter Sixteen ❧

Monica tallied the days like a child sharing out toys. I've had two weeks in my new house, you have one week left in yours. In seven days the bulldozers would arrive to knock down the homes of Sandpiper Drift, and Monica still did not have a plan.

Her article had come out and caused a brief stir in Lady Helen, but the people felt powerless to act against the wealthy businessman because he had the backing of the government. "It's a shame that this sort of thing is continuing in the new South Africa" was the opinion most often heard around town. No other newspapers had bothered to pick up the story. It seemed that disputes over land were happening all over the country.

The famous S. W. Greeff was retrieving a rubber duck from his birdbath the first time Monica laid eyes on him. Not sure whether he would be angry with her because her children had trespassed on his property, she hid behind the trash cans with the bag she had been about to dump. He leaned heavily on a gnarled stick as he studied the new visitor to his garden.

"It's a rather rare species," he said loudly.

Monica wondered if he was deaf, because people didn't usually speak that loudly when talking to themselves. But he was an artist, and they did things others wouldn't.

"You're going to get a crick in your back crouched down like that," he said, looking in her direction.

With her face burning, Monica stood up and gave a feeble wave.

"I'm sorry my boys climbed in your rockery. In future I'll make sure they stay on this side of the boundary."

"Nonsense. This boy's got a sense of humor. I like that. He can run wherever he pleases."

"Thank you, Mr. Greeff," said Monica.

"S.W.," he said. "And in case you're wondering, it stands for Stephen Walter. My Afrikaans parents thought that if they gave me an English name, I'd end up in a dignified profession like law." He gave a little snicker. "Is Max still going in to the office every day?"

Monica nodded.

"Old coots like us can't let go. I'll paint until they put me in the ground. I've already made my tombstone. Come over sometime to see it."

"Thanks," said Monica.

S.W. had grown silent, but he was staring at her as though he expected something.

"I've been told that everything in your garden is indigenous," she said in an attempt to continue the conversation.

"It uses less water. Lady Helen has its own natural spring, but nobody knows if that's going to last forever."

As the person credited with rediscovering Lady Helen, he might be able to confirm her suspicion that the golf resort was using the town's water.

S.W. struck the base of the birdbath with his stick in answer to her question.

Oh, Monica, she thought, *why couldn't you keep it nice and neighborly instead of being a nosy reporter?*

"That was the biggest mistake we ever made," he said, frowning. "We needed money to bring the town back to life—money to repair the roads, overhaul the sewage system, restore the public buildings, build the park. But we were just a small group of artists then with no money. So when they came asking if they could strike a deal to buy our water, we took it. We were so naive we didn't even get a lawyer to check the contract. By today's standards, they're getting the water practically for nothing."

"What will happen when the second golf course is built?" asked Monica.

"That was one thing we did right," said S.W. "The town council has to vote on any increase in consumption."

"I haven't heard anything about a vote coming up."

"That's my concern. If our newspaper editor doesn't know about it, nobody does. It's tomorrow night. I know that because I watch over Lady Helen as though she were the child I never had. Like all parents, I'm plagued by feelings of guilt. In this case because I let Lady Helen down when I signed that contract with the golfers all those years ago. I feel as though I have to make it up to her."

Monica smiled, knowing full well what he meant about parenthood. Even with the best intentions, your words and actions might return later in life to spoil your contentment.

"Thank you for telling me," she said.

"There's more you should know. As far as I'm concerned, we're about to find out if our mayor can resist the temptation of foreign money. If he wants to he can slip it in with a vote on something else. The majority of the townsfolk weren't around when this deal was made, so most have no idea that their water is being diverted. If our mayor so wishes, his constituents might only find out about tomorrow's vote after it's signed and sealed. But now if a reporter were to hear about this…"

He gave her a broad grin, and Monica realized that it had not been coincidence that he'd come outside to look at his birdbath at the exact time she always took out the trash.

Monica could see value in Doreen Olifant's philosophy that only an outsider could tell the truth, because as an outsider she saw things people who had lived here for decades did not. But was an outsider supposed to create the news? There was no reason why not. Was a journalist supposed to create the news? Definitely not. This thought—and others, such as how what she was about to do could go horribly wrong—ran through her head after lunch as she walked to Mayor Oupa Sithole's office.

"Monica, I was wondering when you'd come to visit," said the mayor, opening the door personally.

He did not seem to have an assistant at his office, which was in a building that used to be a hardware store, sandwiched between Lady Helen's house and a photography studio.

"Welcome. Sit down and I'll make us a cup of tea."

She was struck once again by his resemblance to the Father Christmas she knew from films and cards.

"My wife cannot stop praising the skills of Francina," he said, switching on the electric kettle. "I was so proud of her at the mayoral ball in Cape Town. She was as confident as a queen. Sugar and milk?"

"Yes, please, Mayor Sithole."

"Just Oupa, please."

She nodded politely but did not address him by name. Oupa meant grandfather in Afrikaans, and, although he looked like one with his gray beard and hair, she felt uncomfortable calling him this.

He handed her a mug of tea and then took a box of chocolate cookies from his desk drawer. Before he shut the drawer again, Monica glimpsed a stockpile of cookie boxes and chocolate bars.

"Thanks to the dress Francina made, it was the most relaxing time we've had in years. Normally, my wife tries to hide behind me and disappears to the bathroom a million times, but she was like a new person."

Monica took a sip of her tea, and he took the opportunity to launch into an ode to Lady Helen. Much of it sounded like a travel brochure he had memorized, but his face was alive with real feeling for the place he had called home for six years.

If Monica were back in Johannesburg she would have cut him off by now with a question about the real reason she had come, but things moved slower in Lady Helen. People inquired after your health and family before they got down to business—and they were interested in your replies. And if they wanted to tell you a long story about the problem they were having with ants in the house, you listened until they had no more to say and the conversation made a natural turn in your direction.

"I have a feeling this is not a social call," said the mayor, taking his sixth chocolate cookie out of the box.

Monica felt chastised. She thought she had small-town etiquette down pat, but obviously he had noticed her distraction.

"I'm sorry. I'm being rude," she said.

He looked puzzled, and then pointed at her digital tape machine.

"You've brought your weaponry. You must need a sound bite from me." He cleared his throat loudly. "Let me take another sip of tea. There, that's better. Shoot."

He was so disarmingly nice that Monica was reluctant to begin the line of questioning she had rehearsed in her office before coming over here. Father Christmas wouldn't be on the take. Father Christmas wouldn't tack an important vote like this onto the coattails of something contentious, or make a town council meeting drag into the wee hours so that the delegates would pass anything just to be able to go home. Underneath the stash of cookies there was probably a flyer ready to put up in store windows to let people know about the upcoming vote. And he had more than likely already notified council members of the issue so that they had time to ponder it before the next meeting, which, as S.W. had told her, was tomorrow.

Mr. Yang was wealthy beyond the comprehension of most ordinary people, including a small-town mayor whose office was downright shabby and who could not afford a gleaming conference table or a secretary. The mayor's wife drove a Mercedes, but it was as old as their youngest child and he was about to complete high school. And then there were university fees for their eldest, who was doing his master's at Stellenbosch. Mayor Sithole needed money.

"Give me a minute to put my jacket on," he said.

She looked at him blankly.

"I don't want to look scruffy in your photograph."

Monica snapped a photo of him sitting at his desk, pen in hand, as though about to sign a ceasefire.

As he took off his jacket again she had a sudden feeling that first instincts were not always the best ones. It was not her place to create news, but if she were to give it a little push in the right direction, then people could make their own choices according to their conscience. And maybe, she would save them from doing something they would regret.

"I came to find out your feelings on how the vote will go tomorrow," she said.

He blinked. "What vote?"

She paused, weighing her options. It was not too late to go in for the kill like a hard-nosed, battle-scarred Johannesburg reporter. It wasn't possible for the mayor not to know about an upcoming vote. Her suspicions about him, she felt, were correct. He would be rewarded by Mr. Yang if the vote passed.

"You know, the vote on allowing those golfers to use more of our water for another eighteen holes?"

He nodded emphatically—too emphatically, thought Monica.

"I heard you were worried about getting the word out to everyone. It's bad timing for the *Lady Helen Herald* because it comes out in only three days—" a look of relief passed over his face "—but I have an idea how to get the job done."

"Yes, yes," he said rather tersely. "I'm glad you got my message to come."

There had been no such message.

"We'll do this the old-fashioned way," she told him. "I'll take a statement from you, run off copies and post them around town."

He smiled, but it was clearly an effort.

She turned on her recorder.

"Honorable citizens," he began, "your city council is about to vote on whether Lady Helen should supply water to the new golf course that is to be built on our land."

Monica noted that he did not mention the homes of his constituents that would be destroyed in the process.

"If you wish to make your voices heard, catch your council members around town in their places of business or at Mama Dlamini's Eating Establishment. Or you can come down to my office before the meeting tomorrow night."

He made a circle in the air with his hand to warn her that he was about to wrap it up.

"I, Mayor Oupa, have always cared about your opinions and will continue to do so for as long as you give me the privilege." He drew his finger across his throat to indicate that he was finished.

"Thanks, Mayor Oupa, I mean Oupa. Well done."

He shook her hand firmly. "Thank *you* for coming."

Outside his office two elderly tourists were reading the

brochures they'd just picked up at Lady Helen's house. Monica was almost certain that inside, Mayor Oupa was picking up the telephone.

Back at her own office, Monica had never written an article so quickly and with such little effort. She opened by quoting the mayor, then went on to describe in detail—again—how fifteen families were about to lose their homes, and finally, she mentioned how the town of Lady Helen could one day be forced to pipe in municipal water if its own natural spring ran dry.

"Thank you, Lord," she whispered as she sat reading the finished copy, for she was certain she had felt His hand while writing it.

She found the number for the largest newspaper in Cape Town and faxed off the article with a cover page marked Urgent. Then she quickly designed a flyer with the eye-catching heading Town Emergency, and put it up in every store window and on every second lamppost.

By the time the crowd gathered outside the mayor's office late the next afternoon, Monica's article had run on the third page of the largest newspaper in Cape Town. The editor had chopped the part about fifteen families losing their homes to concentrate instead on how the town of Lady Helen could one day be forced to pipe in municipal water. Monica did not know whether it was this mutilated story or her flyers that had motivated the townsfolk to appear in droves, but the result was the one she'd wanted. The council voted to deny any increase in water supply to the golf resort, and by ten o'clock the next morning Mr. Yang had been forced to put on hold his plans for the second eighteen-hole course.

Soon after Mr. Yang's announcement she was on the phone to Reg when Max came into her office.

"I did nothing more than report the news," she replied to Reg's warm words of gratitude.

Max wagged a finger at her.

"What?" she asked after saying goodbye to Reg.

"I thought I had you on a short leash, but I was obviously wrong."

"If you have a complaint about my work, please tell me," said Monica.

Lately, she'd begun to wonder if Max would ever allow her to run the newspaper.

"On the contrary," he said. "I feel that I should be congratulating you for something you've done, but the problem is I don't know what."

It was the first time she'd ever heard him use the words *I don't know*. The mentor who had made her jittery just learning font types was now admitting that he'd lost control. She thought of her parents the day she had taken them to the airport. It had been one of those milestones people don't usually take note of: the daughter becoming a parent to her parents. She'd looked in her rearview mirror at the two of them buckled up for safety in the back seat, and suddenly realized that if her parents visited once a year and, God willing, lived to be eighty, she would only see them another twenty times in her life. Twenty times fourteen days makes two hundred and eighty. The thought had made her cry silently behind her sunglasses.

"Oh, Max, don't pretend. You're on top of everything, as always," she said in a teasing voice, hoping to make up for her earlier impatience.

"Not that computer, I'm not. Last night I plugged it in for the first time, but that's about all I can do. I wish there was someone who had time to teach me."

Monica knew of the perfect person, but she didn't know if Max would take offense at being offered the services of a ten-year-old tutor.

"Sipho could help you," she said nervously.

"That would be marvelous," said Max. "I'll pay him for his time."

Monica's initial reaction was to decline this arrangement, but why shouldn't Sipho earn some pocket money? He would find something sensible to spend it on. Her own hope was that Sipho would get more than a few rand out of it; she hoped that regular contact with Max would fulfill his need for the presence of an older male in his life.

Max stopped in the doorway of her office on his way out. "Just remember that Mr. Yang has merely put the eviction on hold," he said.

Max still had the power to send Monica sliding down into her old position as apprentice. He was right; the victory was only temporary.

⸙ Chapter Seventeen ⸙

Hercules had been in town a little over a week when he and Francina had their first disagreement, and Francina's only question was why it had taken that long. It was Sunday evening, and the atmosphere in town was still electric after the victory over Mr. Yang the previous week. In the afternoon, Francina had baked banana bread for Sipho to take to school the next day for a cake-and-candy sale that would raise money for new computer software. As this was a most worthy cause in Sipho's eyes, he had wanted her to make a dozen loaves, but they wouldn't have fit in the oven and so she'd settled on six—and one small extra. And now, as Hercules sat sipping hot rooibos tea and eating the cake Francina had saved for him, he was telling her that he didn't understand why she did not want his help to get her grade nine School Leaver's certificate.

"That's what I do for a living. And that man who's helping you is a handyman."

"I know that you are a great teacher," she told him, trying her best to keep a balance between stroking his ego and defending Oscar. "But Oscar is wise, too. Does a person have to wear a necktie to have knowledge?"

"Of course not. But what I'm talking about is method. Does he know the right method to teach?"

"Is eighty percent not proof?"

Francina had done a mock version of the grade eight English exam and scored eighty percent.

She busied herself clearing away his cake plate and would not allow him to speak another word about Oscar. Sipho might be completing two years at a time, but she'd just jumped ahead by four.

Oscar would probably not mind if she switched teachers, but she was reluctant to break up a partnership that was working. She knew he enjoyed teaching her, but sometimes she wondered if he was just doing it to impress Monica. The man sure asked a lot of questions about her.

While Francina was at work during the day, Hercules walked the streets of Lady Helen. He talked to the neighbors—and even some dogs—and browsed the galleries where the abstract works both disturbed and fascinated him. Not wanting to risk appearing ignorant, he took to spending hours in the library where he read every book Doreen Olifant had ever bought on art and art history.

"Art is a powerful way to say something," he told Francina.

"Why don't you give it a try," she urged. "I'll ask Gift if she'll let you use her studio."

But he refused to even consider it.

In the evenings, after she had finished her schoolwork with Oscar, Hercules would join her in her room and they'd talk over the noise of her electric sewing machine. She found it amusing to watch him bite his tongue when she mentioned her studies. He never complained about how little time she could give him, and this made her appreciate him even more.

At the end of Hercules's first month in Lady Helen, another anonymous package arrived, this time a small piece of rubber tire. As with the rock, it was not addressed to anyone in particular.

"Ask the old owners of the house if they know anything about this," suggested Hercules, but Francina decided she would rather wait and see. Maybe it was all a big joke and the joker would make himself known.

Hercules said she should throw away the rock and the piece of tire, but she disagreed and hid them under a pile of building supplies behind the cottage that would be hers in less than two weeks. She hoped that Mandla wouldn't find the box and tell Monica. Every day he begged Francina to take him outside to watch Oscar work. It kept her from her housework, as she had to make sure he stayed out of harm's way, but Oscar would fire study questions at her and so she felt as though she was killing two birds with one stone. Honestly, some of these English expressions were so gruesome.

Mandla had a toy building set, which Oscar had bought for him, and he'd lay plastic bricks and hammer imaginary nails into blocks of wood. While he played at building he was constantly watching to see if Oscar would leave one of his tools unattended. Francina couldn't let him out of her sight.

* * *

The following Saturday afternoon, emboldened by her new status as the town's genius dressmaker, Francina marched into the church choir's practice like a rebel going to war. She had learned to accept the muddy boots in God's house, but there was one thing she never would, and that was the sick-little-bird singing of the choir. If she didn't do something about this choir nobody would. Her people sang with feeling even when they were at a funeral—or maybe because they were at a funeral. This bunch would make the dead glad they were departing.

Ingrid had worried that she might upset the ladies.

"They've been in the choir for as long as I can remember," she'd said.

But Francina would not listen. And once she was standing in front of the choir, not a single voice was raised in protest. Instead, she was made to suffer a long sullen silence, which did not dissolve into laughter as she expected when she showed them her side-to-side shuffle and accompanying hand roll. As the stares continued, she began to wish that she had an argument to contend with. After thirty minutes she put Hercules's lucky baton back in her bag and closed her hymnbook. Her coup d'état had failed miserably. Nobody tried to stop her from leaving, and as she exited the church she found herself crying.

"It'll be all right," said a voice in the shadows, and there was Hercules, waiting to accompany her home.

She had never cried in a man's arms, and pathetic as it was, it felt strangely good—almost like being a child again with someone strong to look after her. She pulled away as the choir members came out of the church, but Hercules did not take his arm from around her shoulders.

As they listened to the squelch of five pairs of boots receding into the distance, Hercules said, "Francina, I love you," and without hesitating she answered, "I love you, too."

They didn't say another word on the way back home, and Francina was glad because she didn't want anything to distract from the feel of his warm, smooth fingers entwined with hers.

The third package arrived a week later, on the day Francina moved into her new home and studio. Because Monica was around helping to move her furniture out of the main house, Francina hid the unopened package under her bed.

She had tried to think of a clever name for her cottage that would let people know that a seamstress lived under this roof, but they all sounded rather silly. Who wanted to live in a place called Hemming House or Dressmaker's Domicile? In the end she'd settled on the name of her village, Jabulani, because it was Zulu for happiness and she wanted her mother to know that she had finally found some of her own.

Later that night, after Monica and the boys had gone to sleep, and Oscar and Hercules were still hanging around, each waiting for the other to be the first to leave, Francina removed the package from its hiding place under her bed and ripped off the brown paper.

"It's a book of matches," she said, looking directly at Hercules.

Oscar laughed. "That's a strange sort of housewarming gift."

"It's not funny," snapped Hercules. "This is the third such package we've received."

Francina noted his use of the word *we,* which, if her over-crowded brain was correct, was the first person plural, and as far as she could see only one person lived here. But she didn't set him straight because what was the point of embarrassing him in front of Oscar? Men were such competitive creatures. It started right from day one. When Mandla played with the train set in the children's area of the bookstore, he tried to collect as many locomotives and carriages as he could, in order to make the longest train possible. The little girls, however, were content with one carriage each.

Hercules seemed to be talking to her, yet she didn't hear a word because all she could think about was having a little girl of her own whom she'd teach to stand up to the boys when they tried to take her train away. She would have Hercules's height, but hopefully not his build, because it wasn't good for a girl to be too skinny.

"You should call the police," said Oscar. "We don't need trouble from outsiders in Lady Helen."

Francina saw Hercules raise his eyebrows. He was not used to Oscar's straightforward way of talking and had taken this as a reference to himself. It was a stretch, even by Francina's standards, and she was known for her sensitive nature. But one of the things that Francina admired about Hercules was his perfect manners, and for this reason she was confident that the prickly conversation between the two men would go no further. She was wrong.

"If you are referring to me, we are faced with a grave predicament," he said in a stern tone that Francina had never heard before.

"Come on, now," said Oscar. "Don't use big words. I'm aware that you're the teacher and I'm the bricklayer."

"And you've done an admirable job with the bricks, but the job is over now," replied Hercules.

"Hey, listen, buddy. Francina asked me to help her with her studies."

They've forgotten all about the matches, thought Francina, and are at each other's throats like village mongrels.

"Stop it," she shouted.

They both turned to look at her, Hercules rather sheepishly and Oscar with an expression of anguish that took her off guard.

"I'd better go," he said, grabbing his pile of books.

"What time tomorrow?" called Francina as he opened the door.

If he replied, it was lost to the brisk wind that whistled through the cottage before he slammed the door shut.

"It's good he knows where he stands now," said Hercules matter-of-factly.

"What on earth do you mean?" she asked.

"Francina, the man is in love with you," said Hercules in a tone of voice he might have used for the slowest student in class.

Francina shook her head emphatically. "No, he's not. He's in love with Monica."

"You're wrong. I could see it a mile off. It took all my patience to go off to the art galleries and leave you alone with him every afternoon."

Not a word of this had been uttered, and yet the men had gone at each other anyway like dogs defending their territory. If she thought too hard about it she might be insulted, so she chose instead to admire the vigor that she had not realized Hercules possessed and the graciousness that had made Oscar go out into the night alone. If she'd had any idea of his feelings for her she would have… Exactly what *would* she have done? Would she have given up a teacher who made learning easy and a grade nine certificate seem within reach? Probably not, but she would have told him that his affections were wasted on her. Hopefully this was a minor wound in comparison to the one a woman had inflicted on him in the past, because Francina couldn't bear to think of him suffering.

Hercules put on his sweater and held out hers.

"Where are we going?" she asked.

"To visit the previous owners of this house, Gift and David. I want to find out what they know about these packages."

She had almost forgotten about the matches.

"But they'll be in bed now."

"Francina, this is serious. It could even be dangerous."

She wasn't convinced, but Gift was so nice she'd understand that sometimes it was impossible to stop a man on a mission.

Gift was furious when they explained why they were knocking on her back door at a time when most people were asleep. Her words were surprisingly harsh, making Francina wonder if they were motivated by something other than irritation. She was right. When Gift saw what was in the box she had to sit down to compose herself.

With David standing behind her, his hand on her shoulder, Gift admitted that the packages had been arriving for more than four months now—usually every two weeks. At first they thought it was one of their sons' friends playing a joke on them, but when they could not find the joker, Gift started to believe in something more sinister.

"Like what?" Francina asked.

"A hex," she whispered. An evil spell.

Many people believed in such things, and, while Francina did not, she respected their fear for it was as real as any of her own.

"Then you must get down on your knees and pray," she told them.

Hercules murmured in agreement.

"I am not a believer," said Gift.

"Well, then, I will pray for God to touch your heart," replied Francina. "For only through Him will you find the strength to face the pitfalls of life."

Hercules quietly said, "Amen."

⚭ Chapter Eighteen ⚭

Autumn came to Lady Helen without fuss. The bougainvillea continued to bloom, and since most of the trees, including the palms, were evergreen, there were not many outward signs of a change of season. Instead, they were more subtle. Francina no longer leaped out of bed to run the water in her very own bathtub but stayed warm as long as she could under the thick eiderdown Monica had bought in preparation for the winter. It was not yet cold enough to warrant its use, but Francina had put it on the bed because it was too pretty to leave in its bag.

With dawn coming later now she would spend the first hour of the day sewing with the light on in Jabulani Cottage, and the sun would creep over the koppies just as she was leaving to go and wake Monica and the boys. It was only a short walk to the back door of their house, but if she didn't have a scarf on her head, as was so often now the case, she could feel the chill right in the center of her brain. Good, she'd think to herself, wake up all those sleepy gray cells so they'll remember everything I study today. The grade nine class at Green Block School would be writing exams in just over six months and Mr. D. had obtained permission from the Department of Education for her to join them. On mornings when she looked at her growing list of dress orders she truly believed that she was crazy to take on so much. Her solution was to look at her list in the evenings when the stress could get lost in the labyrinth of her dreams.

One morning she opened the door and could not see her hand in front of her face because a thick fog had settled over the town during the night. Making her way through it, she decided that if Monica would not tell the principal it was time for the boys to wear their long pants for winter, she would do it herself.

Last night Hercules had asked if she would come sit with him one evening in front of the fire in his room. It was just as well she had so much to do because it was a tempting proposal. Young women nowadays seemed to have no problem being in a man's bedroom without another adult present, but not Francina, and not even with a man she'd confessed her love to. She had no idea of his long-term plans, nor how long he could afford to stay at Abalone House, yet she had promised herself that she would not be the one to bring it up.

"Psst," said a voice in the fog.

Francina turned and ran blindly toward her cottage, ready to put her key in the lock or in the eye of her would-be attacker.

"Don't be afraid," said the voice. "It's me, Hercules."

"I could have run into a tree and hurt myself." She could feel her heart racing.

"I'm sorry." He sounded closer. His hand reached out and touched her arm. "I just had to see you."

"So early?"

"I know. I'm not myself this morning."

"Come in, it's cold out. I have to go and wake Monica and the boys in a few minutes." She closed the door and turned on the light.

"Come back afterward," he said.

"I have to make breakfast for them."

"Can't Monica do that?"

She gave him an impatient look. "Yes, but I do it better. They're my family and they need me."

"I need you, too," he said quietly.

"You have Cat to make you a fancy buffet breakfast."

He took her hand. "Francina, this is no joking matter." He pulled away and began to pace the room. "Why did I not stick with my plan?" he muttered.

"Hercules, if it was important enough to bring you out in this weather then you'd better say it."

"Okay," he said, coming closer again. "I know I messed this up last time, and I'd planned to take you out to dinner and do it properly, but I'm so afraid something, or someone, is going to come between us that I can't wait. Francina, will you marry me?" He produced a little box wrapped in silver paper.

She tore it off and recognized the name of the jeweler on Main Street.

"It's white gold," he said, "and it's new." To an outsider this last word might have seemed trite and unnecessary, but to Francina it meant everything.

"Yes," she said, taking his cold face between her even

colder hands and looking into his eyes. "My answer is yes. But where…"

"I knew I should have done this in the right order. I'm on my way now to see Mr. D. about a job teaching at the school."

"And your mother?"

"If I get the job she'll move down here."

Francina was glad that he had thought of his mother. Any man who did not was not good husband material.

He pulled her close. "Even if I don't get the job at the school, I'll find another one here. I'll dig ditches to be near you."

"You'll get it," she told him. "Sipho thinks Mr. D. is the cleverest man in the world. If that's so, he'll give you a job on the spot."

A long time ago she had decided that more than anything in the world she wanted to make this tall, skinny history teacher smile. Seeing his face lit up now, she thought that it had been a most worthy goal after all. Laughter, surely, was just around the corner.

Monica opened one eye to look at the red numbers on her alarm clock and sat up in haste. Sipho was going to be late for school. Why had Francina not woken her? Mandla lay stretched out beside her, his hands cold to the touch, sleeping peacefully. No matter the temperature in the house, he always kicked off his covers. Pulling them back up, she decided that she wouldn't disturb him as he didn't have to go to school. Sipho, however, might get his first demerit for being late if they didn't hurry.

His room seemed much larger without the second bunk bed, and he'd already put up more wildlife posters and spread his books around to assert control over the space. He was burrowed under the covers like a little mole. The first time she ever saw him sleeping she panicked because she thought he wouldn't get enough air to breathe, but no matter how many times she turned down the covers he'd always retreat back under them.

"Time to get up," she said, shaking him gently until the top of his head appeared.

As soon as he was out of bed she would go to Jabulani Cottage and make sure that Francina wasn't ill. She heard a key turn in the back door and then the *slick-slack* of Francina's house slippers on the polished wood floors.

"Sorry I'm late," said Francina, coming into Sipho's room. "Something happened…"

"Are you all right?"

"Don't worry, it's nothing bad." She held out her left hand. "Hercules proposed and I said yes. I said yes, yes, yes, yes." She did a little dance and stamped her feet.

"Hey, you're waking me up." Mandla stood in the doorway cradling his slippers. "What are you doing?"

"Francina's getting married, Baba," she sang, scooping him up into her arms.

"To Oscar?" he asked, struggling, and succeeding, to free himself.

"No, silly, to Hercules."

"Francina's getting married, Francina's getting married," sang Mandla, running circles around her.

"His parents made a mistake with his name," said Sipho.

"I know, my little prince," said Francina. "He looks like a giraffe but he has a bigger heart than any man I know."

"Well, then he's sick and needs to go to hospital," said Sipho.

"Congratulations," said Monica, giving Francina a warm hug. She did not know what had got into Sipho. He wasn't normally this petulant and she didn't want him to spoil Francina's moment.

"Thank you," said Francina. "And don't worry, we won't be leaving because I just know he's going to get a job at Green Block School."

"What is he going to teach?" asked Sipho, and from his suddenly happy tone Monica realized that he had been afraid Francina would go away.

"History," said Francina proudly. "I can't believe that I'm going to be a schoolteacher's wife."

"It's lucky for him that we decided to convert the garage," said Monica.

Francina's face fell. "That's the only bad thing. I'm going to have to leave beautiful Jabulani Cottage."

"No," said Sipho in a panicked voice.

"It would be perfect for two, but his mother will be coming to live with us."

"Can you buy the house next door?" asked Sipho.

"I don't think S.W. has any plans to sell," said Monica gently, "but I'm sure they'll find something close by."

He was only slightly appeased.

"So who's going to live in Jabulani Cottage?" Mandla wanted to know.

Though premature, it was a good question, but not one they could discuss because there was a knock at the door.

Monica wondered who on earth would be calling so early in the morning.

The stained-glass inset in the front door was beautiful, but not much use for screening visitors as only their dark silhouettes could be seen. There appeared to be more than one person outside, so Monica went into Mandla's room to look out the window. Immediately, she ducked down so that they would not see her. There were six young men on her veranda, none of whom she had ever laid eyes on before.

Staying low, she crept back to Sipho's room, although this precaution was unnecessary because nobody could see in with the net curtains Francina had made for the whole house.

"I don't think those men are from Lady Helen," she told Francina. "Go and see if you know them."

"No, no, no. I don't know any men." Francina grabbed Mandla and Sipho.

"It could be your brothers and some friends."

Francina shook her head vehemently. "They wouldn't come here without telling me."

Monica stood up straight. "This is silly. Bad things don't happen here." She turned to leave Sipho's room.

"Don't open the door," Francina begged her.

"Who is it?" she called through the glass.

"We need to speak to David," said a voice.

Of course. It was a case of a mistaken address.

"He's moved. He now lives—" She saw Francina mouthing the word *no*.

"Give us his address or we'll kick this door in," said the voice belligerently.

"He didn't leave it," said Monica. It sounded lame, but she didn't have time to think of a better excuse.

"I know the address," said Mandla proudly, and before Francina or Monica could stop him he'd shouted out the correct street name and number.

As Francina watched the men leave, Monica picked up the phone and dialed Gift's number. It was busy.

"The police," shouted Francina. "Phone them."

The policeman on the other end said he and his partner would come on foot.

"No, no," said Monica. "You need to get there quickly."

But the department's two vehicles were both in the garage, and with Mr. DeVilliers gone there was only one mechanic left in town to do the job.

Monica tried Gift's number again, wondering who had made the decision to put both police vehicles out of action at the same time. The number was still busy.

"I'll go in my car," she told Francina. "Keep the boys inside."

"What about school?" moaned Sipho.

"I'll explain it all to Mr. D. later," she said, grabbing her keys.

"Be careful, Monica," Francina called after her, and then she locked the front door and put on the latch.

Something awful was about to happen to Gift and David but if Monica got there before the men—who did not seem to have a vehicle with them—she could warn them not to open their front door.

She was too late. Gift's screams reached her ears before she'd even rounded the corner. The men had surrounded David, who was barefoot and wearing striped pajamas, and they were throwing stones at him.

"Leave him alone," shrieked Gift. She wore a clingy lounge suit in blue velour. Monica had never seen her in anything but a caftan and was surprised to see how plump she was. Her face did not give any clues.

"Didn't you know what was coming when we sent you the rock?" shouted one of the men, hurling a broken piece of brick at David.

"Where are the matches we sent you?" barked another.

Monica grabbed Gift.

"The police are on their way," she whispered. "Where are your neighbors?"

"Left for work already," sobbed Gift.

"I don't have them," cried David.

"What's he talking about?" asked Monica.

"Didn't Francina tell you?"

"Tell me what?" asked Monica, but Gift was in no mood to explain. "The police are on their way," she screamed at the men.

The man who appeared to be the leader gave a slow, triumphant smile. "We saw their cars up on lifts in the garage. We know we have time."

Giving Monica a treacherous look, Gift broke out of her hold and ran toward the men.

"I'll give you my jewelry and money. Take our car. Just leave my husband alone."

The men laughed in unison.

"We're not common criminals," said the leader. "We're cleanup men. We get rid of vermin."

He spat at David, who could do nothing to wipe the slick globule from his forehead.

"You pig!" screamed Gift, rushing at the man and knocking him off balance.

As he steadied himself he took out a knife. "If you don't

shut up, woman, you'll get it, too." He turned back to David, who was kneeling on the floor while one of the men held his hands together behind his back.

"Don't worry if you've lost the matches we sent you. We've brought more."

Another man held out a book of matches as though he were an assistant at a magic show.

"And we've decided to forget the tire," said the leader. "The smoke stinks too much. Go on, my man, sprinkle him with perfume."

They all laughed as the youngest member of their group soaked David's hair with lighter fluid.

"What has he done?" screamed Gift.

"Oh, he's vermin of the worst kind. Worse than a cockroach, worse than a mouse. He's a stinking rat, aren't you, David?" He gave David a kick in the ribs. "Tell your wife how you spied on us during the Struggle and then told the apartheid pigs where to find us."

"It's not true," moaned David.

The leader kicked him over and over, shouting, "You're a sellout, a police spy."

"No," said David, and the word came out as a gurgle, as though he were underwater.

Blood seeped through his lips and dropped onto his pajamas.

"You've got the wrong man," shouted Gift.

She tried to ram her way through their tight circle to get to David, but they blocked her with jabs of their elbows.

"Drop the knife!" shouted a voice.

It was the police, whose lack of a vehicle had enabled them to approach in complete silence.

The leader took one look at the pistols pointed at his head and did as he was told. Within five minutes the men had all been restrained.

There was no room in the ambulance for Gift, so she rode with Monica.

"Let's pray together," Monica shouted over the shriek of the siren.

"No, no, I can't," sobbed Gift. "Not to your God."

"What do you mean?"

"How can I pray to a God who gives whites special treatment? The apartheid government prided itself on Christian principles, didn't it?"

Monica hesitated. It was true. And the church to which most of the government officials belonged during that time had claimed to have biblical justification for the separation of races.

"You are right," she told Gift. "But that church has apologized."

Gift continued to sob but did not argue.

Monica began to pray aloud for God to save David's life. Although Gift did not join in, she stopped crying and seemed to be listening.

Zak met the ambulance outside the hospital and gave Gift and Monica a pained smile before disappearing inside with the stretcher. Gift was trembling so much Monica had to help her up the steps. As soon as she had her settled, she'd phone Francina to let her know what had happened, and then she'd stay with Gift until David was out of danger. She wouldn't allow any thoughts of the other possibility to enter her head, preferring to crowd them out with prayers for Zak to be able to do his work without mishap.

Francina was silent when Monica asked her what Gift had meant when she'd said, "Didn't Francina tell you?"

"Never mind," said Monica. "We'll discuss it when I get home."

David was hooked up to the ventilator that had yet to be paid for. He had six broken ribs, one of which had perforated his left lung. While Zak and Daphne worked on him, Gift remained in the front waiting room sobbing silently into her hands. Adelaide's bracelets made a soft tinkling noise as she stroked Gift's back.

Monica sat down next to her and said the only thing that came to mind. "He's in good hands now."

"You're right," said Adelaide in her calm, gentle voice.

Monica hoped she would never again be a patient in the hospital, but if she was she wanted Adelaide to be her nurse. Adelaide was one of those people whose mere presence soothed and calmed you.

Daphne stuck her head through the door and said, "You can come in."

Here was someone who should be calmer, now that her eviction order had been put on hold, yet she was not. Miemps had told Monica that Daphne was convinced the bulldozers were still coming, and that, frankly, she was starting to worry about her daughter's sanity.

Monica tried to prepare Gift for the sight of her husband with a breathing tube down his throat, but Gift still gasped in shock. Zak was at her side in an instant.

"He's aware of what's going on around him, so try not to be distressed," he told her.

Gift nodded meekly. The couple's sons had just arrived from Cape Town in record time. As the family huddled around David's bed, Monica slipped out of the ICU and ran into Zak, who was about to go back in and give his prognosis. She knew he wouldn't be able to share it with her, but his relaxed expression said it all and she silently thanked God for answering her prayers.

"Nice shoes," he said, looking at her fluffy blue slippers.

She smiled. "I always try to look my best."

"My daughter says Sipho's in the Young Conservationists Club with her. Apparently he's quite distressed by Lady Helen's shark-feeding operations."

Monica nodded.

"He has a point," said Zak. "But whether or not anything can be done about it, I don't know. If you ever want to talk— you know, about parenting stuff—give me a call. Sometimes I think it's harder being a parent than a doctor."

Monica found it strange that a married man should tell a single woman to give him a call, even if it was to talk about their children.

Don't be ridiculous, she told herself. *It's just Zak being interminably kind again.*

The door of the ICU opened and Gift and David's eldest son stuck his head out.

"I'll be right there," Zak told him. Then he turned to Monica. "I'll speak to you another time—when you're more suitably attired."

He could never have guessed the effect his impish smile

would have on Monica, and her face showed no trace of the sudden decision she had made to keep her distance from this man who was so appealing, yet also so completely unavailable.

If Monica was angry with her for not saying anything about the packages, so be it. She could just huff and puff until she was red in the face, but Francina was not going to apologize—not for trying to spare her the worry.

After Monica had left for Gift's house, Francina had gone around the house closing all the windows. When she was sure there was no way for anyone to get in, she went back into Sipho's room and found him trembling like a leaf in a storm and Mandla crying for Monica. She turned on the television, made pancakes with cinnamon and brown sugar for breakfast, and phoned Sipho's school to let them know that he was a bit under the weather. Sometimes these silly English expressions allowed one to escape a long explanation.

When she heard Monica's car pull up in the driveway just after lunch, she put the kettle on. Nothing went better with an interrogation than a strong cup of hot tea.

Monica gave the boys hugs that lasted longer than usual. Mandla hopped into her lap as she sat down at the kitchen table and refused to move, even when he heard his favorite TV show in the living room. Francina was grateful because there'd be a lot less huffing and puffing with the children nearby.

"I'm sure you have your reasons for not telling me what was going on," said Monica in a falsely happy voice.

"Of course," said Francina, matching her tone.

"Would you mind sharing them with me?" asked Monica, continuing the farce.

"No, of course not."

Sipho looked at them with an expression of bewildered disdain. "Mandla and I are going to watch TV now," he said, lifting his brother from Monica's lap.

"How many packages were there?" Monica asked.

"Three. But you must understand that I spoke to Gift because I didn't want you to worry. She admitted they'd received a few packages before moving from this house. I think she should have warned us."

Monica nodded in agreement. "I am a worrier, aren't I?"

"Yes," said Francina, "but only because you care."

Monica held up Francina's left hand. "That ring really is beautiful."

"It's not right, is it, to spend so much money on a piece of jewelry?"

"He loves you and wants to make you happy."

"It would make me happy if he'd sell it and give the money to my father. I know he doesn't have to pay my father lebola because it's not my first marriage, but it still doesn't feel right to me to walk around with a diamond on my finger when my parents need money."

Francina didn't know why she was discussing this with Monica, who did not know a thing about lebola or the ways of her people. It would take a long time to explain to her that Hercules would have to pay lebola to Winston if she really had cheated on him.

"He seems like a man who respects parents. Just be honest."

Maybe Monica was right. She might not know anything about their ways, but respect for a person's parents was universal.

✀ *Chapter Nineteen* ✀

Winter did not officially begin in Lady Helen until the last of the birds had left the lagoon for the arduous journey north to warmer climes. The curlews, bartailed godwits and greenshanks had already been gone for over a month, but the long-billed whimbrels seemed intent on enjoying the rich shallow waters of the West Coast a while longer. Sipho worried that if they left too late they'd fly into bad weather or wouldn't be able to find any food along the way.

One Sunday, as Monica sat in church between Sipho and Francina, she saw the remaining flock of whimbrels taking flight and then landing again, as though they'd had second thoughts about leaving.

A latecomer slipped into the space next to Sipho; it was Kitty—alone as usual. James said business was too good on a Sunday morning for him to go to church. She smiled at them and then sat back and closed her eyes. Sipho looked up at Monica for an explanation, but it had been a week since she'd visited Kitty and she was ashamed to say that she had no idea what was going on.

As they sang the final words of the closing hymn, there was a loud squawking and urgent flapping outside. Sipho rushed to the window.

"They're really going now," he shouted excitedly.

Monica and Francina joined him and watched as the flock of whimbrels took off, heading upward, and then leveling off somewhat to allow the stragglers to catch up. By the time they'd reached the golf resort they were flying in perfect unison.

"God speed," said Sipho, who'd recently watched the takeoff of the space shuttle on television. "Come back safely to us in the spring."

They watched as the birds receded into the distance, following the coastline that would take them north through Namibia, and then Angola, Congo, Gabon, all the way up to Cameroon, where they would leave the coast and fly over Nigeria, Niger and Libya, before making a brave crossing of the Mediterranean to arrive in Europe for a second summer.

The lagoon was empty at last, and Sipho was convinced he could hear the frogs and crickets rejoicing now that they were safe from the snapping bills of thousands of hungry birds. Monica heard only the rustle of the ocean wind in the reeds that fringed the lagoon and the regimented sucking sounds of two hundred pairs of boots squelching through the mud on their way back to dry land.

"So winter's begun," said Kitty, putting a hand on Sipho's shoulder. "Now I can get some rest."

Monica indicated for Francina to go on ahead with Sipho so that she could stay behind with Kitty.

"Are you okay?" she asked her friend when they were alone.

"I look awful, don't I? James and I aren't getting on. Actually, we might get on if we saw each other, but he's never home. If I didn't have proof that he was on his boat all the time, I'd think he had another woman."

"Oh, Kitty, I'm sorry."

She sighed. "In the past I would have been out of here already. But marriage is not a business I can ditch. When I said those vows I meant them."

"Do you need the money from the shark diving?" asked Monica.

Kitty shook her head. "Absolutely not. Abalone House did well this season. He's just fond of danger and risk. He was a fighter pilot in the air force before he started flying commercial."

"The water's become so cold he's soon not going to have any clients," said Monica, smiling encouragingly.

"Oh, there'll always be a crazy foreigner with a dry suit."

Reverend van Tonder had come back into the church to fetch his boots; he wore regular shoes during the service, a habit for which Francina was most grateful. He saw Monica hugging Kitty and came over to see if anything was the matter. Monica could tell that Kitty wanted to talk to him, so she said goodbye and promised that she would come and visit her soon.

Francina and Sipho had collected Mandla but had chosen not to begin the walk back to the car without her, and were waiting at a spot where the level of the mud dropped off and the water was knee deep. Sipho was crouched over a hole, waiting for a hermit crab to come out.

"Is she all right?" asked Francina.

Monica knew that Francina and Kitty had their differences, but Francina could not bear to see anyone in pain, especially not if it was caused by a man.

"They should probably go for counseling," said Monica. "Reverend van Tonder is talking to her now."

"Ooh, all these people with relationship problems. Do you think I'm doing the right thing getting married? I've done okay on my own so far."

Monica had too, but the truth was, she was jealous of Francina who had a man willing to move all the way across the country to be with her.

"He's a good man," Monica told her. "If you feel that this is what God wants for you, relax and enjoy it."

Francina nodded, and the four of them began the long walk back to their car.

Winter was a tease. It would start out so cold Francina could see her breath as she walked from Jabulani Cottage to the main house every morning, but by lunchtime it was warm enough to take Mandla outside—so long as they found a sheltered spot in the sun where the wind could not reach them. No matter how cold it got there was never any frost, which explained why the bougainvillea thrived without attention, when in Johannesburg they had to be covered with sacking whenever the temperature dipped below freezing.

Hercules had been offered the teaching job, as Francina predicted, and had accepted it on the spot. He wanted to get married as soon as possible, but Francina had convinced him that they should wait until after her exams at the end of the school year. He would understand if she spent all her free time studying, but when she became his wife she wanted to cook for him every evening and this would be impossible if her nose was always in her books. Secretly, she also wanted to have more time in her beautiful cottage with the sweeping views of the koppies. It was the first real home she'd had of her own, because you could not count that poky little room in the backyard of Monica's house in Johannesburg. She had never been unhappy there, but she certainly had not been able to lie in a bathtub and watch television.

The exams were just over three months away, and in a way she wished that Oscar would come back to help her prepare for them. Hercules was without a doubt better educated, and he knew how to organize the learning material into manageable chunks, each with a theme and a handy acronym to aid memorization, but he'd set up a chalkboard in Jabulani Cottage, and every afternoon before they read the text he'd write the date on the board, the number of days she had left before the exams, and, alongside little dots he called bullets, the objectives for the lesson. With Oscar the learning had seemed like a storytelling session similar to the ones her family had enjoyed around the fire back in the Valley of a Thousand Hills. And she never thought first before asking Oscar a question. Sometimes he'd laugh but never in a cruel way. And once he'd pointed out her error, she'd laugh at herself, too.

Hercules never laughed at her because she never gave him the opportunity; she never asked questions, and when he asked her something directly she kept her answers as brief as possible. Maybe it was better this way, she thought, because after he'd left for the night she'd spend the time they'd saved reading. Against his advice she insisted on continuing to take orders for dresses; however, her customers were told that they'd have to wait a bit longer than usual. After dinner she'd rise from the little dining room table Monica had bought her, and, ignoring Hercules's look of forced patience, sit down behind her sewing machine to work while he lectured. She'd look up when he wrote new phrases next to his bullets, but for the most part she'd listen and sew and wonder how his students could sit there without anything to occupy their hands.

Sipho was on his winter holidays, which pleased Mandla because at last he had someone to play with. He was to start nursery school the following January; Monica felt that he needed the company of other children.

The boys were eating their lunch one Wednesday when the phone rang. At first Francina did not recognize her youngest brother's voice, as they had never before spoken on the telephone, and when he identified himself, her hands began to tremble.

"Tell me quickly, Brother," she said.

"Don't worry, Sissie," he replied. "Our parents are healthy. Father is actually happy."

Francina watched the weather report every night for news of rain in the rest of the country, but so far she had heard nothing.

"Did Winston send more food for the cattle?"

"Every month," said her brother. "Francina, we need you to come home."

Hadn't he just said that their parents were healthy and happy? Why else would they need her?

Dingane explained that the village was in the middle of a week-long celebration because the government had given them two thousand hectares as part of the country's land-redistribution program. Three years back the village had filed a claim for land that was taken from them by white settlers in the late nineteenth century, and the farmer who owned the land had finally agreed to take the government's offer.

Winston had decided that the village would set up a game reserve and that Dingane should run it as he had experience in this field. Just this once Dingane did not mind being dictated to by his ex-brother-in-law because it was a dream come true. There wasn't any big game on it yet, but Winston had applied for a loan from the government's fund for black empowerment.

"God has truly blessed us," he told Francina. "And we want you here to share in our blessing."

Francina would be in charge of housekeeping for the fifteen rondavels, or round houses, that the men of the village planned to build. She wouldn't have to clean, he assured her, as there were many young girls who could do that, but she would have to order the furnishings, supervise the staff and, ultimately, make sure that the guests were happy with their accommodations.

"You won't have to take care of that woman anymore," he told her.

"That woman's name is Monica," said Francina, "and it's not just for her that I cook and clean. It's for my boys, too."

"Come on, Francina, this is what the new South Africa is all about."

He was right. And she was happy for her people. But she had found what she was looking for.

"I'm going to write the exams for the grade nine School Leaver's certificate," she told him, because she didn't know what else to say.

"That's wonderful. And when you pass I'll promote you to manager of Guest Services."

"What does my mother say about it?"

"You know Mother—she wants her beloved daughter to be happy."

Francina knew that he was not being sarcastic because her brother would never be unkind to her. For so long she had dreamed of going back to the Valley of a Thousand Hills. Now there was work for her and yet she was reluctant to go. Why was it that people in this country were always leaving one place for another? Men left the villages to seek work in the cities, women left their children at home with their mothers to go and raise the children of strangers, poor families were forced out of their homes by rich foreigners, and even Monica, with all her money, faced constant nagging by her parents to move to Italy. Francina's ancestors had been evicted from their land and now a farmer had to give it up, too. Was it at all possible to put down roots in this country and not have them ripped out from under you?

Oscar had told her to look at things from a different angle. Maybe land ownership was one of the things that would benefit from this tactic. Right now everybody was like those greedy little boys who tried to collect as many trains as they could, only to have to leave them behind for the next group of children when it was time to go home.

She smiled as she thought of this because suddenly it became clear what she ought to do. There was no doubt that it would be lovely to return home to the village where she was born, but there was also no reason Lady Helen couldn't be her home for the remaining years of her life. For the twenty-three years she had lived in Johannesburg she had never thought of it as home. A quarter of her life had gone by, disappeared, with her feeling like a visitor. Monica would cringe at the definition, but Francina had been a migrant laborer. It was time now to change that way of thinking. She would not be an outsider in this place for another twenty years. Even if she never owned any land of her own, this place would be home from now on, and she would only return to the Valley of a Thousand Hills if her parents needed her to look after them.

Her brother was bitterly disappointed. "One day you will be an old woman on your own, my sister," he told her. "Come back so I can take care of you."

She wanted to tell him that she had taken care of herself for many years, but not wishing to insult him she chose instead to tell him the news that she had almost finished putting in a letter to her mother.

"I am engaged to be married."

"Ah," said Dingane. "That explains it. And this man, can *he* take care of you?"

"Yes, Brother, he is a teacher."

Her brother was impressed. She would have liked to explain that she was marrying Hercules because she loved him and not because she needed someone to look after her, but unlike beds some points were best left unmade.

"Please don't tell our mother," she said.

"But she will be very happy. She has never stopped worrying about you since Winston..."

"Beat me," she wanted to say, "since he beat my face in." But her family had never spoken about what her husband had done to her, not since the day she'd gone home to try and convince her father that she was not running around with other men as Winston claimed. And now that her brother had alluded to it, he was clearly upset.

"Let's think rather about the future," he said, trying to sound positive but failing miserably.

"It's okay, brother," said Francina. "God has taught me how to forgive."

"You are a good woman, sister."

And I have forgiven you your silence, she wanted to say, but chose to keep silent herself.

Clouds hung low over Table Mountain, covering its level top like fly netting on a buffet lunch. It was a blustery day on the flat land across the bay, and save for a few cawing gulls fighting greedily over the discarded remains of a boxed fish lunch, the wide beach was empty. There were no pleasure boats or windsurfers out on the choppy water, and as the wind strengthened, two old men who had been fishing off the pier packed up and drove off in a rusted van.

Monica finished her fish and chips and got out of the car to throw away the disposable container, but as she did the wind whipped it out of her hand and into the air, where it flapped around like a giant white moth before coming to rest on the gravel parking lot next to the takeaway stand. While she was retrieving it she noticed a young boy approach her car and cup his hands against the back window.

"Hello," she called.

The boy turned but did not run away. He was probably no older than Sipho, but boys younger than that were breaking into cars nowadays to get money to buy "tik-tik," the local name for crystal methamphetamine.

"Ek love sokker," he said, mixing Afrikaans and English and pointing at the ball Mandla had left in her car.

His sweatshirt was so small on him his belly button was exposed to the wind, and his toes stuck out of slits cut in the front of his canvas tennis shoes.

"Are you cold?" she asked.

He shrugged. "I run to get warm."

She opened the trunk where she kept extra sweaters and blankets in case her car broke down during winter.

"Put this on," she said, holding out a blue sweater that her mother had knitted for Sipho.

An adult might have protested out of politeness, but the little boy did not.

"It's soft," he said, running his fingers down the sleeve.

"Have you seen a house around here with a turret?" asked Monica.

He gave her a blank look.

"Like in a fairy story."

"Fairy?"

Monica's first reaction was pity for the child who had never been read a fairy story, but Ella had taught her to step out of her precious little life and broaden her worldview. What good were fairies, princesses, enchanted forests and unicorns when you didn't have a pair of shoes that fit or a diphtheria vaccination or food with nutritious value?

"I'm looking for a house that has a tall tower."

His face lit up. "That way," he said, pointing to a road that was blocked off by a security boom. "I saw it one day when the guard fell asleep."

He was not asleep now, and Monica wondered what excuse she might give to gain access to the closed neighborhood.

"What do they keep in that tower?" asked the boy. "Is it gold? My mother says all white people hide gold in their houses."

"These people aren't white," said Monica. "And I'll find out what they keep in that tower and let you know—if you're still around when I return."

"I always come here to look for leftover fish and chips," he said. "I live up there, past the shops, in Eshowe Settlement."

Monica had passed the squatter camp on her way here. It was behind a small strip mall. The tin shacks all leaned on one another like fallen dominoes, and chickens ran freely up and down the dusty alleys.

"Take this," she said, handing him Mandla's soccer ball. "You can scratch off my boy's name and put your own."

"I can't write," he said, taking the ball from her with a huge grin on his face. He was too young to realize the tragedy of his admission. "Thank you," he said. "One day I'm going to play for Bafana Bafana."

It was Mandla's dream, too, to play for the national side. Monica did not like the way sportsmen were rewarded when teachers, firefighters and nurses had to struggle to make ends meet. But, sadly, sport was sometimes the only way for a child to lift himself out of poverty. As she watched him run off, kicking the ball in front of him, she prayed that he would have talent in his feet.

The guard at the checkpoint returned her wave and lifted the boom without a single question. Now, here's security that's worth every penny, she thought in amazement.

She had driven all the way from Lady Helen because her reporter's instincts told her that it was suspicious that the DeVilliers family had moved out of Sandpiper Drift right before the eviction notices were issued.

The house was simple to find amid the Spanish villas, New Orleans–style mansions and thatched English cottages. She parked under an ornate street lamp that was already on, though it was only midafternoon, and rang the buzzer next to the gate. For a long while there was no answer, and she was just about to climb back into her car to get warm when a woman's voice said, *"Ja?"*

Monica identified herself and the tall metal gate began to slide across the driveway. That was easy, she thought, but when the gate had slid all the way across, two men blocked her path.

"What do you want?" asked the elder of the two.

"Dad, it's that reporter woman from Lady Helen," said the other man, presumably talkative little Dewald's father.

"Monica Brunetti," said Monica, sticking out her hand, but neither of the men made a move to take it. "I wanted to speak to you about your old neighborhood."

"What's going on?" said a woman's voice behind them.

Monica presumed that the lady with long gray hair scraped into a bun at the nape of her neck was Mrs. DeVilliers.

Seizing her chance, Monica called out, "Where did your husband get the money for this house?"

"Go back inside," Mr. DeVilliers instructed his wife. "This has nothing to do with you."

"What's she talking about?" cried Mrs. DeVillliers, but her son pushed her inside and stood with his back to the door so that she could not come out again.

"Go away, Miss Brunetti," commanded Mr. DeVilliers Senior. "We have nothing to say."

Before Monica could speak another word the gate began to close, and she had to scramble backward to avoid being crushed.

"The neighborhood's not going to be demolished," she shouted over the high gate.

There was urgent whispering behind the gate and she could just make out the words *cash,* and *take it away.*

"But they're going to mine there." It was Mr. DeVilliers Senior's voice.

"There weren't any diamonds after all," she shouted back.

The whispering reached a feverish pitch, and she hoped they might open the gate again in order to find out more. But they didn't.

"Go away and leave us alone. We have nothing to say."

Monica waited awhile before getting into her car. For a long journey it had been a very brief conversation, but it was a beginning. Nature was filled with the unexpected. The mighty African river, the Zambezi, flows south toward the Okavango Swamp in Botswana, but turns east at the border of Zambia and Namibia and finally empties into the Indian Ocean. If the Zambezi could change course, so could a man, who while trying to improve life for his family, had given in to a moment of weakness.

⨳ *Chapter Twenty* ⨳

After a winter of average rainfall, the countryside around Lady Helen erupted into color almost overnight. Swirls of mauve, pale pink and bright purple-red vygies climbed the rocky koppies, the green fields behind the dairy were blanketed with orange Cape dandelions, and everywhere you looked, yellow daisies spread like a contagion, jealously coveting every inch of coarse-grained soil. It was as though this hidden world of color and sweet vanilla smells had been waiting for nature's conductor to give the sign for the spring symphony to commence.

Francina sat on the steps outside the Little Church of the Lagoon, enjoying the warmth of the sun on her bare arms. The wind that had roared across the mudflats all winter long had been tamed by the change of season, and she watched with amusement as it tried in vain to turn the page of the science textbook she held in her lap.

"I need help to get past this chapter," she said out loud, laughing.

Science was not her strongest subject, and it was the only one that made her appreciate Hercules's keywords and bullets.

White-breasted gulls fought angrily over the rotting remains of a large crab that lay half covered in mud. If the calendar were anything to go by, they would have already been forced to give up their cheeky ownership of the lagoon and nearby beach, but the migrating birds seemed reluctant to return this year. All spring activities at church and Green Block School were on hold until the first bird touched down in the now-warm waters of the lagoon.

Francina was sure that inside the church Hercules was getting a wintry response. She'd warned him that this choir was a tough group, but he'd still wanted to give it a try.

The exams were two months away, their wedding two and a half. Good sense told her to get the bulk of her studying done before making her wedding dress, but she'd already sketched a few designs. She couldn't help herself because Lady Helen's most popular dressmaker had to have a spectacular dress.

Hercules, being the kind, sweet man that he was, had not complained when she'd asked if they could sell the ring and give the money to her parents, but her mother had begged her not to do it because every person in the village would be getting a monthly check for their share of the profits of the game lodge. Although he never said it, Francina knew that Hercules was glad she'd kept the ring. He'd almost glow with pleasure when someone complimented her on it.

When he came out of these double doors he wanted to

take her back into town to show her something. She imagined that a new art book had arrived at the library or his mother had sent him a textbook. He could go on about books forever.

What was that? The noise of the gulls made it hard to hear anything coming from inside the church, but she was sure that she heard laughter. Never. There it was again. It was laughter, and this time it went on and on. She had warned him of a chilly reception but she hadn't thought to warn him that they might laugh at him. Poor Hercules. She stood up in order to be able to take his arm as he left the church. The laughter grew louder and then the door opened and Hercules came out surrounded by the women of the choir—and they were all laughing, Hercules included.

"You've met my fiancée," he said, stopping to take her hand.

It was a statement, not a question, and the women stopped laughing to look at their feet, their watches, their hymnbooks—everywhere except at Francina's face. It was the plainest expression of guilt she had ever seen.

She could have told them how they had hurt her, she could have ignored them and walked away, but she chose to forgive them.

"I'm looking forward to hearing your Spring Program," she said.

There were a few nervous smiles.

"There's no sign of the birds yet, so there's still time to learn the songs if you'd like to join us," said a lady who had been particularly hostile to Francina the last time.

"Thank you. I'd like that," said Francina, and in her mind she was already designing some striking blue-and-white tunics for the women. She wondered if they'd be up to wearing headdresses.

Walking with Hercules across the mudflats toward town, Francina felt so proud of him she wanted to shout it out loud until echoes bounced off the koppies up ahead. He had succeeded where she had failed, and although she might have sulked she was pleasantly surprised to discover that there was not one grain of resentment within her. It's funny what true love will do to you, she thought.

Hercules would not tell her what his secret was, only that it was to be found on Main Street.

Well, if it wasn't a new book in the library, maybe it was one in the bookstore. Maybe there was a painting he wanted to show her. In his imagination he had gathered a collection of more than twenty paintings, all of them realistic landscapes. Hercules was not one for modern art. He called it egotistic and frivolous.

They did not go into any of the galleries but stopped instead in front of the watchmaker's store that had been closed ever since old Richard Kumalo passed away in his sleep three months ago.

"What do you think?" Hercules asked.

"Of what?" she replied. Then she noticed the For Sale sign that had not been there the day before.

"The son has decided not to continue in his father's footsteps after all," explained Hercules.

Francina remembered the thin young man who'd sold her a new strap for her watch, and she hoped that he had waited until after his father's death before revealing his lack of interest in the family business. Hercules explained that there was a two-bedroom flat above the shop that would be perfect for the two of them and his mother.

"And we can rent out the shop," she said excitedly.

"I was thinking we'd get someone to erase the watch-maker sign and put up a new one. How do you think Jabulani Dressmakers would look in large gold letters?"

Francina gave a little screech of excitement, causing a mother and child who were walking past to stop in their tracks. After making sure that she wasn't in distress, they moved on, smiling in amusement.

On their return to Jabulani Cottage, Francina told Hercules that it would have to be an after-hours sort of business because she couldn't possibly leave Mandla and Sipho.

"But you will need to make twice the number of dresses you're making now for us to afford the mortgage payments," he said.

"If it's going to be a problem, we may as well live in my cottage after our marriage," replied Francina.

"What about my mother?"

"Hmm, your mother," said Francina as an idea came into her head. "Can she sew?"

"Yes, but she's never made anything fancy like you."

"Do you think she would want to help? She could lay out the pattern pieces, cut the fabric, pin the pieces together, take measurements, write invoices. Maybe do some hems. They are so time consuming."

It was such a cheeky idea that Francina did not dare look at him. Hercules was silent, and she was sure she'd over-stepped her mark. You did not ask your mother-in-law to work, especially when you weren't even married to her son yet.

"I think she'd like to be involved," said Hercules. "She's been cooped up at home worrying about me for so long, she might enjoy being in a shop on Main Street with people coming in and out." He took her hand. "You see how we work things out."

Until Mandla started nursery school in January, Francina would only work in the shop on weekends. Once Mandla was settled—and if Hercules's mother agreed to the plan— Francina would be in charge until one-thirty when Mandla and Sipho finished school, and then Mrs. Shabalala would take over until five. On Saturdays, Francina would work in the shop all day and it would be up to Mrs. Shabalala to decide whether she wanted to join her or not. The only duty of Francina's that would suffer was the cleaning, but she'd talk to Monica and they'd work something out.

The rest of the country had marked the beginning of spring, but the residents of Lady Helen were still watching for the dark cloud that would herald the return of the first migratory birds. Sipho was not one to question nature, but the delay in their return irked him because his long winter school pants were starting to feel too warm in the mild weather.

It was lunchtime, and Monica was eating her sandwiches on a bench next to the statue of Lady Helen in the park. A little way down the beach she could see James launching his boat from a trailer, while a man in a shiny black wet suit stood by, watching. On board was a large rectangular steel cage. Out at sea an oil tanker inched across the horizon like a shiny slug, presumably on its way to the West Coast, where international companies were finding rich new reserves.

Monica hoped that the leaders of these countries would learn from the mistakes of the past and share the wealth with their countrymen.

"Don't you think that's a good idea?" she said, addressing the statue of Lady Helen.

"It depends what you're talking about," came the reply.

Monica almost choked on her lunch.

"Hey, you okay?"

It was Oscar. She hadn't seen him crouched down on the other side, where he was touching up the paint on the fence.

"I'm fine," she said, still coughing.

He handed her a bottle of water and she took a sip.

"Thanks." She nodded at the statue. "You take good care of her, don't you?"

"I'll let you in on a little secret. She's somewhere here in town. Her husband never took her back to Cape Town and kept her prisoner in the cellar."

"He killed her here?"

Oscar shrugged. "Maybe. Or maybe she escaped and lived here on her own until death took her naturally. There are some old unmarked graves in the cemetery that nobody knows anything about."

"But if all the slaves were marched back to Cape Town, who do the other unmarked graves belong to?"

"There were nomadic tribes—San—in the area. Who knows what happened?"

Monica wondered if there was any way to find out, but Oscar said he wanted to talk about another of the town's strong, independent women.

"She's going to lead a happy life," said Monica, gently trying to head off any plea for her to make Francina change her mind about marrying Hercules.

"No, she won't," said Oscar. "Disappointment is worse the second time around."

Monica looked at the water, wondering how to reply without revealing too many details of Francina and Hercules's relationship. James's boat had stopped about a half mile out to sea, near the site of a wreck that was known to be a breeding ground for ragged-tooth sharks.

Finally, she turned back to Oscar and said, "He's sorted himself out now."

"It's easy to do that when you have millions at your disposal," said Oscar, emphasizing the first letter in millions and making it sound like a provocation.

"Hercules is rich?"

"Of course not. I'm talking about Mr. Yang."

He explained that the Malaysian businessman had just broken ground on a desalination plant that could supply enough water for four golf courses, if needed, and a new hotel. As soon as it was operational, work on the second eighteen holes would go ahead. Oscar had heard it from a land surveyor he'd met while out looking for ancient San art, and it was his guess that the residents of Sandpiper Drift would be getting new eviction orders within a day or so.

He was correct; the disappointment *was* going to be worse the second time around.

"What's that fool doing?" said Oscar, and Monica followed the line of his gaze to where James's boat was coming in far too fast. "He's going to crack the hull if he doesn't slow down."

They watched as the boat hit the beach in front of them with such force that the cage fell forward and barely missed the back of James's skull. The man in the wet suit jumped out, shouting and gesticulating at James, but Monica and Oscar could not hear what he was saying over the noise of the screeching engine. Sand flew everywhere as the propeller dug a deep hole in the beach. The man went to retrieve a stick from inside the boat and then appeared to be waiting for James to climb out.

James switched off the engine and they heard him say, "It's not my fault. I checked it last night."

"You should have checked it again before we went out," screamed the man. "I could have been killed." He lunged forward with the stick, but James was wise and stayed in the boat.

"I'm going down there," said Oscar.

Monica knew that he would protest if she said she was coming, too, so she waited until he had met up with them before following, and got the tail end of the story when she arrived.

James and his client had been expecting to encounter ragged-tooth sharks, but the blood of the dead tuna James had thrown into the water from the boat had also attracted a great white, and in its hurry to snatch the chunks of fish away from the smaller sharks, it had bumped the cage with enormous force.

Ordinarily, tourists were thrilled with a visit from one of the larger sharks. From above, James saw that this man did not take out his camera. In addition to the long diving spear he had used to offer dead fish to the small ragged-tooth sharks, he had another weapon attached to his weight belt: a rod rigged with enough electricity to knock a grown man out for twenty minutes but not enough to do more than irritate a fifteen-foot great white. Crazed by the blood in the water and the annoying sporadic pain in its nose, the shark rammed the cage again and again until the door flew open. By this time James had activated the motor to hoist the cage back up, and as it ascended slowly he watched in terror as the shark tried to insert its head into the cage. There was nothing he could do to speed up the motor, and so he said a prayer out loud, asking God to save the man's life.

"It's a miracle he didn't fall out of the cage and get eaten," said James, looking paler than Monica had ever seen him.

"It'll be a miracle if I don't have you prosecuted for criminal negligence," shouted the man.

"Would you like me to drive you to the hospital, sir?" said Oscar.

"There's nothing wrong with me," snapped the man.

"I'm sure James will refund your money," said Oscar.

James nodded wildly and fished in his pocket for his wallet. "Here, take a hundred extra," he said.

"You can't buy me," said the man, but took it anyway.

"I'll give you a ride back to your car," said Oscar.

The man had calmed down and was starting to shiver. "I could have died," he said as Oscar led him away.

"I'm so sorry," called James. "I promise I checked the cage door."

"Did anyone else have access to it this morning?" asked Monica.

James shook his head. She helped him push the boat back into the water so he could return to where he had parked his trailer, and as she waded back to shore he said, "Thanks, Monica. I appreciate your help."

As he opened the throttle to launch his boat through the waves, Monica realized that this was the first time he'd ever addressed her by name.

The light crept slowly down the sides of the koppie, like a stray cat slinking into a henhouse. Though dawn came earlier now, Francina had already been up for an hour with her English literature book. Once she was used to the overly polite way in which the characters addressed each other, she enjoyed the story and especially liked the beautiful heroine who was trying to find a husband for her poor friend. From the accompanying notes she knew that she was supposed to find this meddling distasteful, but secretly she wondered how her life would have turned out if one of her friends, and not her parents, had chosen a husband for her.

On the cover, the heroine strolled across a neat lawn, parasol in one hand, a book in the other, her dress more feminine than any Francina had ever seen. This was it! Francina had found her wedding dress. She took care tracing the empire waist, sheer long sleeves gathered daintily at the shoulders, and flowing skirt. This wedding dress would be her best creation yet.

Her life was filled almost to the brim with blessings: marriage, exams, the dress shop. There was only one other thing she wanted, but God had decided that it was not to be and she would have to learn to live with His decision.

The day after Oscar told her about the desalination plant, Monica drove out to see Miemps and Reg. They'd just received the news.

"That man is determined," said Reg, shaking his head.

"And he's never even been here," said Miemps, her voice quavering. "He doesn't have the courage to tell us himself." She waved an envelope at Monica. "He sent this with a security guard. Look at it—full of official stamps like it came from the president himself." She began to cry softly into a lace handkerchief.

"What did Daphne say?" asked Monica.

Reg put an arm around his wife's shaking shoulders. "She tore off in her car. I hope she doesn't do something foolish."

"I'll do another story," said Monica, aware of how feeble it sounded.

Miemps lowered her handkerchief. "Oh, thank you, Monica. You are so kind to us."

Her words only made Monica feel worse. Through some careful maneuvering she had managed to help them once, but Mr. Yang was more formidable than any of them had presumed.

"Shall we take a walk so you can take pictures?" asked Miemps.

Monica took her arm and Reg went inside to prepare lunch for when they returned.

The sand had reached the lower edge of the window in the living room of the DeVillierses' old house, and it was now impossible to close the front door.

"It didn't surprise us that they never came back when Mr. Yang put the eviction on hold," said Miemps. "Do you know that Lizbet left the lace curtains hanging in the window? Of course, they've disappeared now, but can you imagine leaving something you once spent weeks making?"

Monica watched a green lizard creep up the smooth surface of an interior wall. From the black-and-white droppings on the windowsill it was obvious that the seagulls had also stopped by.

"If someone else chooses to get ahead in life through shady shenanigans," continued Miemps, "that's between them and God. God hasn't called me to be one of His judges on this earth, only to take care of my family and anyone else who needs me."

There was neither resentment nor suspicion in her voice, only hurt; her friend had left quickly, with only a hurried goodbye and no explanation of how they had managed to afford a big new house.

Everybody in town believed, as Miemps did, that Mr. DeVilliers had won a large sum of money, and Monica wondered how they would react when they discovered the truth. Would Miemps choose then to judge the man whose actions had had a direct impact on her beloved family, and would she no longer consider Lizbet a friend?

Monica took a photograph of the living room, and then they moved on to the next house, where the wife of the caretaker of Green Block School was standing on a ladder outside her front door.

"All this stuff—" she pointed to a pile of door handles, curtain rods, kitchen drawers and lightbulbs "—will take up so much space in the maintenance shed that there'll hardly be enough room for us. But it's worth good money and if we can ever afford to build again…"

With tears in her eyes she flashed a courageous smile for Monica's camera. Monica used a whole roll of film photographing the houses that were about to be abandoned. As they returned to Miemps's home, Daphne arrived from work and insisted on posing for Monica. With her hands on her hips, she stood outside the front door and glared into the camera, as though daring anyone to come and take her home. In her white button-down nurse's uniform, she might have cut a pitiable figure, but instead she looked coolly official and formidable.

Later that afternoon Monica put the photographs in a brown envelope, addressed it to Mrs. DeVilliers and dropped it in the postbox outside her office. Usually, she would have given it to Dudu to mail, but she did not want anyone to know where the photographs were going. If she was wrong about her suspicions it was better that nobody knew about them. As she was going back inside, she saw Kitty hurrying toward her.

"What? No guests?" joked Monica when Kitty had caught up with her.

"We're full, but James is taking care of things this afternoon and I'm off to get my hair cut. Yes, you heard correctly," she said in response to Monica's raised eyebrows, "he hasn't been out feeding sharks today. He's agreed to come with me for couples counseling at church, and you'll even see him there on Sunday. He truly believes it was a miracle the man wasn't injured or killed."

"I'm so happy for you," said Monica. "Come inside and have some tea."

But Kitty was expected at the hairdresser's in ten minutes. "I'll come back later. Actually, there's something serious I need to discuss with you. There's probably a logical explanation, but we thought you'd want to know that James found this outside the boat garage."

She handed Monica a tin pencil box. On top, in fat, neat letters were the words Property of Sipho Nkhoma.

"The boys were over at Abalone House with Francina the other day to see Hercules," said Monica. "It's a coincidence."

Kitty would not meet her gaze. "James found it yesterday afternoon, right after the accident. And he said it wasn't there the night before when he checked the equipment. I'm sorry, Monica. I really wish we weren't having this conversation."

"It's one that you started," said Monica icily.

"Please don't let this come between us."

"I've got to get back to work. Enjoy your free afternoon."

As Monica opened the door to the newspaper office she was aware that Kitty was staring after her, but she could not find it in herself to turn around and say goodbye as though nothing had happened.

✧ Chapter Twenty-One ✧

The next morning, Monica got out of bed and resigned herself to a day of yawning. Twice during the night she'd taken Sipho's pencil box from the drawer next to her bed, as though a closer study of it might reveal some clues to the mystery of his alleged involvement, and when it didn't, she lay awake for hours on end, praying at first, then trying to shut her mind down. She could not believe that the child who had written his name on the lid in such precise letters could do what Kitty was insinuating he'd done, and she wondered how she'd ever be able to bring up the subject with him. As the milky light that comes before dawn filled the sky, she'd felt God telling her that there was no formula for dealing with a child—she should follow her heart.

Mandla woke first and came running to her bedroom and jumped onto her bed. Since Francina's move to Jabulani

Cottage, he'd only slept in his own room a few nights but was gradually becoming more enthusiastic about the idea.

"Can we go to the beach this morning, *pleaaase?*" he asked, flopping down onto her pillow.

"It's Friday—a school day, sweetie. Sipho has to hand in his science experiment and I've got to go to work."

She planned to go up to the golf resort and, much as Mandla would enjoy it, she might actually find Mr. Yang and it would not be wise to have a little boy along if that were to happen.

"Tomorrow we'll go to the beach," she told him.

Mandla needed more interaction with other children. January, the time when he started nursery school, was just over three months away. Where would Daphne, Miemps and Reg be then?

Later that morning, after checking in at the office, she drove up to the golf course and parked her car in the underground lot. It wasn't much of a hiding place because her car did not fit in here among the luxury German sedans, but it was preferable to parking it outside the clubhouse, where it might attract the attention of the security guard if he decided to wander over for an early lunch. She'd told the armed guard in the slate-roofed gatehouse at the main entrance that she wanted to find out about rates for wedding receptions at the club, and he'd called to see if the event manager was in. The lady had said that Monica should come straight to her office.

Now, as she got in the elevator, she hoped that she wouldn't make the mistake of walking past the event planner's office or she'd have to waste time listening to menu options.

The clubhouse was fuller than the previous time she was there, and for this Monica was grateful, as the crowd enabled her to move around without raising suspicion. She had tried contacting Mr. Yang from her office but was told that he would be in meetings all day. His "no female visitors" ban had been extended to include female telephone callers, too. Her only hope was to find him herself.

She wondered if the golf course was the best place to begin her search. But the prospect of walking eighteen holes put her off. She peeked her head in the restaurant, where a breakfast buffet was laid out around a large ice sculpture of a sunflower. A waiter asked politely if he could seat her, but she said she wouldn't be eating. Neither, apparently, was Mr. Yang. Looking for him among the resort guests was useless.

Walking down the quieter corridors of the administrative wing, she saw a sign that said Event Planner on a door that was ajar.

That's all I need now, she thought, wondering how to make her escape. As she approached, it was clear that the lady inside was on the telephone.

"No, he's not here at the moment," she was saying. "But I'll speak to him when he gets back from the gym."

Monica made a quick U-turn. If the lady hadn't been talking about Mr. Yang, she would just have to return and waste time listening to wedding packages in order to find out his exact location.

"Good morning," said the receptionist at the spa. "What type of service are you interested in today?" She looked at Monica's hands. "A manicure?"

"No, thanks, I'm looking for the gym."

Monica would have preferred to find it on her own, but a sign told her that she had to walk past the spa's reception area.

A frown appeared briefly on the lady's face as she took in Monica's capri pants and loose, Indian-print top.

"Just to take a look for next time," added Monica.

"Oh, I see. Through those double doors then."

Monica peered through the little square window in the doors and was disappointed to discover that the gym was empty. Feeling thirsty, she decided to go in anyway to get a drink of water. And then she saw him. He was standing in an alcove at the watercooler with his back to her.

"Mr. Yang," she called, and he spun around, his face ready with a wide smile for his paying guests. It quickly disappeared when he saw her.

"Who let you in?" he snarled. "I'll fire him immediately."

"One of your guests brought me in." She did not like to lie, but she thought God would forgive her if it was to save a man's job. "I want to talk to you about your new plans."

He came closer. She hadn't before noticed the peculiar way he held his arms when he walked, as though he were holding something large in each of them. Dressed in gym attire, he didn't look as short and thickset as he did in a business suit. His shorts and T-shirt were wet with sweat.

"I haven't found out what your role was in the town council voting against me, but I know you had something to do with it." He dried himself with a towel as he spoke.

He was lying. Mayor Oupa would have told him exactly what her involvement had been. He was protecting Mayor

Oupa, but he was also protecting his own reputation as it wouldn't be wise for him to admit a secret friendship with an elected official.

"I'd like to invite you to visit the families in the homes you want to demolish," she said.

In appealing to his sense of compassion, she wanted to give him a chance to redeem himself, but he just continued his workout.

"Just imagine yourself out on the fairways of the new golf course," she insisted. "Won't you feel guilty when you think of the families you've displaced?"

"I don't play golf," he muttered as he lifted the weight above his shoulders.

Monica felt so angry with him that she wanted to scream. It wouldn't have made a difference to Daphne, Miemps and Reg if he did play golf, but to her, his simple statement epitomized his ambition and greed.

"I'm planning a trip to the Department of Mineral Affairs," she said.

He dropped the weight with a clang. "That's nice," he said, but his fake smile and measured voice could not hide what his actions had revealed.

She pressed on, hoping to discover why he was so rattled by her plan to look into his land deal with the government. "I'm sure the great diamond discovery is documented. Everybody is keen to know exactly where it was found, and by whom."

As far as Monica knew, she was the only one who suspected that it was Mr. DeVilliers. The rest of the town believed the story that he'd won money.

"I can save you a trip," Yang said. "The official who did all the paperwork will be here on Monday." He noted her raised eyebrows. "To finalize some details."

The coincidence seemed far too fortuitous to be above suspicion. Did he not want her poking her nose in at the government office, where she might tip off any of his connection's colleagues who were not in on the scam? Because a scam it was, one way or the other.

"I'll be back on Monday then," she said. "And I trust I won't have a problem getting in."

"No, of course not. And on your way out now, stop at the restaurant and have breakfast on me."

With renewed vigor he lifted an even heavier stack of weights. When his arms were straight over his head, he exhaled loudly and then slowly lowered the weights. He did this nine more times before reaching for his towel.

"I'm serious about my invitation for you to visit the families of Sandpiper Drift," she said.

He seemed surprised that she was still there. "I fly over them in my helicopter on my way to Cape Town every evening. That's enough."

Monica pushed through the double doors without even saying goodbye to him.

From the living-room window Francina could see the tops of the koppies above the row of stores and galleries on the opposite side of Main Street, and if she went out onto the balcony she could see the park and beyond that the ocean. A glimpse of that shimmering ribbon of water would be an acceptable trade for the loss of her unobstructed views of the koppies at sunrise, and, of course, the view of the television from the bathtub.

It was Saturday, and Francina had left Jabulani Cottage early to give Hercules's flat one final cleaning before the arrival of his mother. Just before noon, she took a final tour.

The wooden floors were so shiny they looked new. Before Hercules had moved in, Francina had gone down on her hands and knees and scrubbed layers of old polish from the yellowwood planks until they were practically naked. Then she'd given them a light coat of polish and a hard buffing. Hercules had painted all the walls white, and against his advice she'd made new curtains. Yes, her time would have been better spent studying, but under no circumstances would she have any of the old curtains from Hercules's house in Dundee in her new home.

She'd cleaned every surface in the bathroom this morning with bleach, and the window was open to allow the strong smell to escape. The tub, unfortunately, was not long enough for her to stretch out in, but she was thankful that there was one. Hercules had said that his mother was a light sleeper and should take the back bedroom that overlooked the quiet side street, and he would take the bedroom with the balcony above Main Street. Monica had told Francina to pick roses whenever she needed them, and now a vase full of peach buds stood on the floor in Mrs. Shabalala's room.

In the tiny kitchen, where the smell of vinegar still lingered an hour after Francina had used it to shine the faucets, she filled a jam jar with water and walked out onto the balcony to check her potted tomato plants. The dry air and warm sunshine suited them, and it wouldn't be long before she'd have to transplant them to Monica's garden. Thankfully, there were no water restrictions here. She went back into the kitchen, filled a pitcher of water and placed it in the fridge next to the chicken stew she'd made yesterday in her kitchen at Jabulani Cottage. Travelers were always hungry when they reached their destination.

The breeze pushed gently at the net curtains she'd made to prevent the neighbors across the street from being able to look into the living room. There was nothing left to do but wait for the arrival of Hercules and his mother. It was kind of Mrs. Shabalala to agree to come. Many mothers would have refused and reeled their son back in. This was the thing about Zulu people that whites did not understand. You were not just marrying the man, you were marrying the whole family. It was enough to make some young wives cry into their pillows at night, but even the worst mother-in-laws were a big help when children came. Francina could not believe that there were white grandmothers who would only help take care of their grandchildren when it didn't interfere with their tennis lessons, lunches or trips overseas. Not once had she ever heard a Zulu woman complain that her mother or mother-in-law did not help. And when the mother-in-law got old, it was the daughter-in-law's turn to take care of her. In this case, sad to say, there were daughters-in-law who did not do their duty and they were a disgrace to the Zulu nation. How anyone could dump an old person at a hospital and never return to fetch them, Francina did not know.

She heard the bell on the downstairs door tinkle, and a few seconds later the thud of footsteps on the stairs that led from the shop up to the flat. Quickly she took the stew out and put it onto the stove to heat. Then she smoothed her dress and waited for the arrival of the woman who would share her home for as many years as God would still allow them both to walk this earth.

"Welcome, Mama," she said when Mrs. Shabalala had reached the top of the stairs.

The older lady was breathless after the climb and couldn't speak. Francina took her hands, kissed her on both cheeks and poured her a glass of water, which she accepted gratefully.

While Hercules went downstairs to start unloading the furniture from the trailer, Francina conducted a tour of the flat.

"It's so clean," said her mother-in-law. "I'll try my best to keep it that way."

Francina smiled at her. It was natural that she would be nervous after leaving her home of many years, but if they all kept a flexible attitude and a sense of humor everything would be fine.

⤝ Chapter Twenty-Two ⤞

The children heard them first and came rushing out of Sunday school, flapping their arms and squawking in a noisy welcome.

Reverend van Tonder paused in his sermon. "I wonder if that's what I think it is."

Sipho, who was sitting next to Monica on the aisle, stood up and looked out the window. He whispered in a loud voice, "They're back!"

Monica motioned for him to sit down, and everyone looked at Reverend van Tonder to see whether he would continue his sermon.

He smiled at his congregation. "I think that's a sign from the Lord to give thanks for a new season."

"Amen," said Francina loudly, and all eyes turned their gaze to her.

This was a place where people spoke in turn, not whenever they felt the urge.

"Amen," said Reverend van Tonder, "and thank you, Francina, for the enthusiasm of which God's blessings are so worthy."

There were murmurs up and down the rows.

"I see we have a visitor. Would you like to introduce your friend, Francina?"

Francina rose and said, "May I present to you Mrs. Ntombi Shabalala, my friend and soon-to-be honorable mother-in-law."

Everybody clapped and Francina sat down with a huge grin on her face. Then she stood up again and announced to tumultuous applause, "And you're all invited to the wedding."

Monica looked across to where Hercules was sitting in the front row waiting to be introduced as the new leader of the choir. His eyes were wide. Oh dear, Francina had succumbed to the allure of the spotlight and overstated her intentions.

Reverend van Tonder led them in a prayer of thanks for the return of Lady Helen's little travelers, and said that he would not discuss church business this morning as it was all in the bulletin anyway and a welcome-home party had to be held on time or it wouldn't be a welcome-home party at all.

"But before you go," he said, "I would like to introduce to you Hercules Shabalala. Some of you already know him as a fine history teacher, but now you will know him as the man with the baton. I know his debut was meant to be at the Spring Program, which will take place next Sunday now that our feathered friends have returned, but I wonder if we might persuade him to lead the choir in a song of praise on this exciting day."

Hercules stood up and bowed his head in response to the applause. He removed something that looked like a pen from his top pocket and extended it until everyone could see that it was a baton. The ladies of the choir smiled in expectation. He raised the baton. Everyone was quiet.

As Hercules dropped the baton, the organ sounded the opening bars of "Amazing Grace," but it was soon clear that this was not the traditional arrangement but an up-tempo jazzier version.

The choir started to sing, and the reedy voices that had sometimes been eclipsed by the whir of the electric fan took on a new confidence that translated into a mellow, mature sound. They had been trying to sing an octave higher than what suited their voices, and now that they had found their pitch, the tone, rhythm and volume followed. They began to sway from side to side, and Monica watched as one by one, members of the congregation followed suit. Hercules clicked his fingers in time to the music and his ladies joined in. Monica could see that Francina was just itching to scramble out from the middle of the row and join them one week ahead of her debut at the Spring Program.

From the back of the church came the sound of someone clapping in time to the music. Monica turned around to see who it was and there was Gift, on her feet, clapping her hands above her head and wearing a look of rapt worship. Beside her, a little thinner than before but otherwise none the worse for wear, was David. Then Monica too got on her feet and began to clap. Then Francina was up, and everybody else in their row, including Sipho. And one by one, starting from the back and rolling forward like the tide, every row stood up until the whole congregation had joined in.

Some clapped in the right place; others were too early or too late. But that didn't matter. What mattered was that everybody was participating and enjoying it without feeling self-conscious. Would Hercules have received the same reaction if the birds hadn't returned in the middle of the Sunday service? They would never know, but everybody would remember the first day of this year's spring as the day the Little Church of the Lagoon found a way to express the joy they'd always felt but never knew how to let out.

Reverend van Tonder told them to go in peace, and Sipho bolted ahead of Monica, bounded down the steps and ran straight into a strong wind coming off the ocean.

"Hurray!" he shouted, breathing in the salt air, his arms outstretched.

The birds formed a massive dark cloud that blocked the sun. Monica hung back, wondering how she could broach the topic that she needed to on a day such as this. The arrangements had all been made. Francina, Hercules and Mrs. Shabalala would fetch Mandla from Sunday school, and she would wait until everybody had cleared out to talk to Sipho. Now it seemed that the people would never leave. They were all clustered around the church, scanning the sky and marveling at the birds' different landing techniques. On and on the birds kept coming, until the dark cloud in the sky thinned out, and then disappeared altogether.

"Look at the seagulls," said Sipho.

Huddled in a tight group with their backs to each other, they eyed the territory they had ruled for a season with impotent anger. As the hungry invaders noisily rediscovered old fishing spots, the gulls took off toward the beach with a synchronized screech in a last-ditch show of bravado.

The members of the congregation began to think of their empty stomachs, too, and soon Monica and Sipho were the only people left in the company of thousands of birds.

"Where's Mandla?" he asked, suddenly aware of the world outside the small ecosystem of the lagoon.

"Gone with Francina to Hercules's new home. We're joining them for lunch in a while."

She took a deep breath. The time had come.

"Sipho," she began. "Have you lost a pencil box?"

He looked down at his feet, but not before she saw that the excitement in his eyes had been replaced with panic.

"No," he mumbled.

Sipho hadn't ever lied to her, and it hurt that he thought it was acceptable to start doing so now. But lying wasn't the same as criminal mischief, and she refused to believe that he'd tampered with the shark cage, as Kitty had implied. Only if words of confession came from his mouth would Monica believe it, and then she'd wonder if he had been coerced into doing it. There was nothing to do but find out if those words would come.

She held out the pencil box Kitty had given her.

"I think you lost this."

"Where did you get it?" He sounded breathless.

"James found it outside his boat shed the day he had the accident with the shark cage."

Sipho began to cry, and Monica felt as though her heart might stop.

"I didn't mean…" he sobbed. "I was just talking."

"The man could have died," said Monica, fighting back tears herself.

"He asked me what it would take to stop them and I…oh, Monica, I didn't know he'd do it."

He grabbed her around the waist and she felt his little body shaking with sobs.

"Who's *he?*" asked Monica. She took his shoulders and held him away from her so that she could see his face. "Sipho, who is *he?*"

"Brian. You saw him at the hospital."

Monica remembered the teenage boy who'd been admitted for alcohol poisoning. At the time, Sipho was clearly intimidated by him. She had no idea they were friends.

"He's in the Young Conservationists Club. On Tuesday he took away my pencil box and said he would give it back if I told him where James kept the shark cage. I told him, but he still didn't give it back. The next day I asked him for it again, and he was really angry when he couldn't find it in his backpack. He said some very bad words. He must have gone to James's boathouse before school, and the pencil box probably dropped out of his backpack while he was fiddling with the cage."

"What does he have against shark feeding?"

Sipho gave a little involuntary shudder. "In our meetings

I explained to them all why it was so bad. But, Monica, I didn't ever say we should do anything about it. I wouldn't have talked about it if I'd known one of them would do something like this. Please believe me."

What she wanted to do was hug him in relief, but she knew that she ought to scold him for lying to her.

He listened to her, eyes downcast, and when she was finished he said, "I'm sorry I lied about my pencil box. I thought you'd be cross I let someone take it."

"Sipho, there are all sorts of people in this world," she explained. "Some have physical power—like the big boy who took away your pencil box, others—like you—have a very special sort of power."

"Me?" he said.

"You are like your mother, Sipho. She was clever and people took notice of what she said."

He nodded, his head suddenly full of the idea that he was like his mother. Before this he had always heard Mandla referred to as the image of his mother.

Monica hugged him tightly. "Thank you, God," she whispered, "for my good boy."

"What's going to happen to Brian?" he asked once she'd let him go.

"I think I'd better tell Mr. D."

Sipho nodded. "He'll know what to do."

As the two of them walked hand in hand across the mud-flats, the squelch of their boots was inaudible over the choir of the birds.

Monica telephoned Mr. D. the next morning and he said he could see her at five that afternoon, which suited her because she had to go out to the golf resort to meet the government official. She was irritated with herself for forgetting to ask what time the man would be visiting, as all her calls to Mr. Yang's office this morning had been fruitless. If she had to go out there and wait all day she would, but there were other stories that needed her attention, too, such as the afternoon arrival of an American television-commercial director. A Cape Town–based advertising firm had approached Mayor Oupa with a request to film a car commercial on Main Street, and would you believe it, the man had held a public debate about the issue and called for an informal vote. Since the money the town would be paid for providing the location was to go toward paying for the ventilator, everybody had raised a hand in support of the proposal. Political transparency had come late to South Africa, but it had come even later to Lady Helen.

By midmorning, Mr. Yang's secretary begged Monica to stop calling.

"I have to do what he says," she argued, "and he doesn't want to take any calls from you."

"Can you just tell me when he's meeting with the government official?"

There was silence as the secretary checked her daily planner.

"I don't have him down for any meeting with a government official, but—" her voice dropped to a whisper "—he's with someone now. Normally, I make his appointments, but this man just showed up and Mr. Yang still hasn't told me who he is. They've gone off somewhere together."

Monica quickly phoned Kitty to tell her that she would

be at Abalone House later than expected to interview the American. The animosity between the two women had ended yesterday as soon as Monica reported that Sipho was not the one who'd tampered with the cage.

"I was about to call you," said Kitty. "He's gone to his room for a nap and asked not to be disturbed. Nineteen hours in an airplane from Atlanta to Cape Town is no joke."

"I'll come tomorrow morning instead."

"He might even sleep from now until then, or—" Kitty groaned "—he'll appear at midnight and want me to cook him a meal. Why are you in such a rush to meet him? He's booked his room for a week."

"I'd like to point out to him the virtues of our local workforce. We have people of many talents here. There's no need to bring in a whole busload from Cape Town."

She heard Kitty laughing softly on the other end of the line.

"What's so funny?"

"I think I just had a vision of the future. And you were sitting in Mayor Oupa's office—on his side of the desk."

"Don't be silly," chided Monica.

"I'm not. In a year his term will be over and we'll have an election."

After saying goodbye to Kitty, Monica drove up to the golf resort. True to his word, Mr. Yang had instructed the guard at the gate to let her in.

She found Mr. Yang in the place she least wanted to. All heads turned in her direction as she pushed open the door of the bar. Although it was barely eleven in the morning, the lights in the ornate wrought-iron fittings were on and the room was filled with smoke. More than twenty pairs of eyes went to the clock above the long burnished bar. On her first visit to the resort, the security guard had warned her not to enter this bar as it was for men only until after dinner. The eyes returned to rest on the intruder, challenging her to step over the threshold.

Pretend they're unfriendly neighborhood dogs, she told herself. *The trick is not to let on that you're nervous, because then they will bite.*

She took not one, but three steps into the crowd. Two men who had been about to exit the bar blocked her way and made no effort to move. As she walked forward they lifted their drinks to their lips, blocking her way even further with their raised elbows.

If only she could see Mr. Yang. Negotiating this hostile crowd was going to be difficult enough, but her dignity depended on not having to zigzag up and down the room in search of him.

She dodged the elbows of the men blocking her path by ducking down and squeezing past, and then did the same with the next unrelenting knot of men.

"Wrong place, girlie," said a hefty man with a nasty-looking sunburn—or was it the flush of alcohol?

"Yes," chipped in his friend. "Manicures are down that way."

Both of them thought this was hilarious and howled like a pair of hyenas.

"Are you lost?" asked the barman, an elderly man who wore a white apron.

"No," she said.

"Well, I'm sorry I can't serve you until after dinner." He seemed genuinely apologetic. "The rules are printed in the members' handbook."

It was remarkable, thought Monica, how even the most ridiculous of rules gained credence if they were just put in writing. Take, for example, the petty rules of apartheid, which interfered in every aspect of normal, everyday life. They had all been conscientiously tabled in parliament. Black people could only live, shop, eat and play in places designated for them. If they went into white residential areas, it was only to work in supportive or menial roles, and they could not, under any circumstances, date or marry a white person. Monica could not imagine how it would have felt to tell Sipho and Mandla that they couldn't join the children in the playground because their skin was the wrong color.

She was about to tell the barman what she thought of the rules, when Mr. Yang appeared, arms extended in an affected welcome and a big smile on his face.

"Let's go somewhere else before we have an incident on our hands," he whispered in her ear.

A small man with a briefcase stood one pace behind him: the government man.

Mr. Yang led them into the administrative wing and past his secretary, who quickly busied herself and did not make eye contact with Monica.

"Three coffees," Mr. Yang told her before closing his office door.

He sat down behind a modern metal-and-glass desk and began sifting through a pile of messages. Monica wondered if any were from Daphne. She noticed that the government man sat down on the stiff black leather sofa without waiting for permission, as though it was his regular place.

"Sit please," Mr. Yang told her. "I'd like you to meet Pieter van Jaarsveld of the government's mining division."

The government man stood up, but did not offer her his hand. He was of the old school—the one in which only men shook hands and women were merely nodded at when introduced.

He had a trim mustache and hair combed neatly into a side part. His suit was expensive but lacking in style, and it reeked of smoke.

"Do you mind?" he asked, taking out a pack of cigarettes.

She was about to answer that she did, when Mr. Yang interrupted.

"You know I do, Pieter."

Instead of looking embarrassed, the government man looked frustrated. There was something odd about the status quo between these two men, decided Monica. It was decidedly weighted in Mr. Yang's favor, when it should have been the other way around. But maybe she was being naive; wealthy men all over the world had special relationships with public officials.

Monica sat down in one of the single leather chairs opposite Mr. Yang's desk and moved it a little so that she could see both men. An enormous piece of colorful abstract art dominated one wall, and an enlarged aerial photograph of the resort another. The homes of Sandpiper Drift crouched on the very edge of the photograph.

She was taking out her notepad, when the secretary came in with the coffee.

"No, no, no," barked the government man, waving his cigarette box.

The secretary was so startled she almost dropped the tray. "But Mr. Yang said—"

"He's talking to Monica," said Mr. Yang, indicating for his secretary to put the coffee down on his desk.

The government man's voice was still harsh. "This is all off the record."

Monica looked at Mr. Yang. He was nodding. This meeting had taken an odd turn.

"Everything you want to know is in here," said the government man, removing a folder from his maroon briefcase and then handing it to her.

She fanned through the pages. There were copies of the original agreement between the government and the town of Lady Helen, the old contract drawn up between Mr. Yang and the group of artists who had rebuilt Lady Helen—she noticed S.W.'s youthful signature, and a sworn statement by the discoverer of the diamond that had set the ball rolling on Sandpiper Drift's demise. The signature and name had been blacked out.

"That's to protect his identity," said the government man, noticing her raised eyebrows. "He doesn't want the media hounding him." He quickly added, "I didn't mean you. I meant those guys with flashbulbs who dig out all the personal details."

Monica gave a forced smile at the backhanded compliment that had placed her above gutter journalism. It wasn't inconceivable that a person might wish to keep his identity a secret; lottery winners did it all the time to save themselves from long-lost relatives and friends who might appear on their doorstep with a number of pressing needs. A man who had been paid a substantial sum of money for finding a diamond might have the same need for privacy.

According to the original agreement between the town and the government, anyone who discovered a diamond and turned it in was not to be compensated, for they were merely fulfilling their civic duty. This was a piece of information that she would need to store.

Monica was disappointed that the sworn statement had not confirmed her suspicion that the man who had discovered the diamond was Mr. DeVilliers, because now it meant she would have to hear the words from his mouth, and her previous encounter with him had been anything but promising.

"May I make some copies?" she asked the government man.

He hesitated. Although Monica was looking away from Mr. Yang, she could see his reflection in his giant flat-screen television. He was nodding.

"No problem," said the government man, smiling magnanimously.

Mr. Yang pressed a button on his desk and the secretary appeared within seconds. "Our visitor needs some copies."

The secretary disappeared with the folder.

Mr. Yang rose to his feet. "You can get those copies on the way out."

The government man rose, too. "It was a pleasure," he said.

"I have one more question," said Monica.

The men looked at each other.

"How much longer do the residents have in their homes?"

"I don't need to take occupation for another two months or so."

Monica was astonished that Mr. Yang would use real estate terminology, as though he would be coming around to
do a walk-through and exchange of keys, when in reality he
would be giving orders to a wrecking crew.

"Can you give me a date?"

"A date? Okay, let's say December the seventh."

With his breezy tone, he made it sound as though he
were making an appointment to have his teeth cleaned. But
at least she still had two months to try and save Sandpiper
Drift. December the seventh was exactly one week after
Francina's wedding.

"This way I'll have the land cleared well before my crew
goes on their Christmas holidays," said Mr. Yang, sounding
pleased with his decision, "and we can go ahead with the
construction when they return on January the fifteenth."

Monica could not believe her ears. He planned to evict the
residents right before Christmas, when he only needed the
land in January. Was there no end to the man's cruelty?

There were other questions she wanted to ask, but from
the way these two men were ready to usher her out the
door, it was clear that her time was up.

On her way out, she thanked the secretary for the coffee
and the copies.

"Have they all found new homes?" the lady whispered,
keeping a constant eye on her boss's closed door.

"No," replied Monica, "but thanks for asking. Mr. Yang
never did. The problem is that the money he's offering is not
enough to buy a house in town."

The secretary nodded. "I feel bad about—" She stopped
immediately as the door to Mr. Yang's office opened and the
government man stepped out.

Sensing her fear, Monica said, "Thanks for the copies."

"You're welcome," said the secretary with a fixed smile on her face.

Monica waved at the government man before walking toward the public space in the resort. Her visit might not have brought the definitive answers she had sought, but she had discovered a sympathetic ear—even an ally—right in the heart of enemy territory.

That afternoon, after spending three hours editing stories she had already written, selecting letters for the Dear Editor page and mulling over the details of the morning's meeting at the resort, Monica left work fifteen minutes early and went home to ask Francina if she could stay a little later than usual with the boys while she dealt with some rather serious business. Sipho caught her eye and nodded solemnly. Francina said she could stay an hour, but that was all, as she had *couture* waiting for her at Jabulani Cottage. Monica hid a smile. Not only had Francina's English become more complex; she was starting to throw in French words, too.

As Monica set off on foot for the short walk to the school, clouds began to roll in, and by the time she'd arrived, they covered the koppies like a bridal veil. While she waited outside for Mr. D., she watched a father pushing his young son past on a tricycle with a long handle. Mandla could pedal by himself now, but that nifty handle would have saved *her* a lot of backache.

The maintenance shed was empty right now, but come December the seventh when the school caretaker and his family moved in, any late-afternoon visitor to Green Block

School would see wisps of smoke curling into the air from behind the main building. The caretaker's wife would be stoking yet another fire to cook for her husband and children, who would soon have grown tired of stepping over one another in the tiny space.

Fuchsia geraniums in mismatched pots lined both sides of the walkway. Sipho had informed Monica that the common geranium, which could be found in pots and window boxes all over the world, was not only a plant native to South Africa but it was actually part of the genus Pelargonium and not, as everybody thought, the genus Geranium. She smiled at the recollection. Someday, whether in a research lab, a rural clinic or a classroom, he was going to do his part to make the world a better place.

A crispness had crept into the spring afternoon, and Monica was just putting on her sweater, when the door to the administrative offices opened.

"I'm sorry, I didn't know you were here already. Why didn't you come in?" said Mr. D.

Monica shrugged. "I was enjoying the fresh air."

Mr. D. nodded. "It makes you wonder how you ever lived in a city. Come in, or would you prefer to take a walk?" He looked up at the clouds.

"I think they're just being dramatic," she said. "It's too late in the year for rain. Let's walk."

She could not help smiling to herself. In less than a year she had become an expert on the West Coast's weather patterns. Or so she thought—the clouds had suddenly darkened. She noted with relief that he chose to walk in the direction of her home—and that he made sure he was between her and the road. Her high-school guidance teacher had taught the class that this was where a gentleman walked when accompanying a lady, but she didn't know of any men who actually did it.

"Is Sipho doing okay?" she asked after they'd walked half a block without talking.

"Okay? He's doing fantastically."

"Good," said Monica.

They neared the end of the block and two little boys called out in greeting from their garden.

Mr. D. waved at the boys and yelled, "See you tomorrow morning."

The boys looked at each other and giggled.

"I like nothing better than my students getting excited about their studies."

"I have something rather unpleasant to tell you," she said.

"What is it?" he asked, his face full of concern. "Please don't say you're taking Sipho out of my school and sending him to boarding school."

She shook her head vigorously. "I would never do that. But this does concern Sipho, in a roundabout way."

As she told him of the incident with Brian and the shark cage, his brow grew more and more creased, and when she had finished, his eyes were narrow slits.

"I didn't want to go to the police," she said. "That's why I asked to see you."

He stroked his beard. The clouds were almost black now, and she felt bad for having chosen to walk. He would get soaked on the way back—unless she invited him in.

Finally, he spoke. "Brian will have to be punished. His actions had serious consequences, and he will now have to take responsibility. Have you told James about this?"

"Yes. But he promised not to do anything until I'd spoken to you."

"I'll speak to Brian. If he confesses and shows remorse, I'll try to persuade James to leave the police out of this. If Brian is defiant, I won't try to stop James from calling the police—if that's what he wants to do."

They'd reached the beginning of her road.

"Thanks for handling this so rationally," he said. "You're a good mother."

"Thank you." He would never know how much those words meant to her. "Would you like to come in to wait out the storm?"

"No, you were right. This is just nature posturing."

Watching him turn and walk back in the direction of Green Block School, she could not help smiling at his bright red velskoens.

She should have stuck with her earlier conviction; a wind came up and blew the clouds back to sea without letting a single drop of rain fall.

↣ Chapter Twenty-Three ↢

By the time summer had taken a firm grip of the Western Cape, Monica had sent a total of six letters—marked private and confidential—to Mrs. DeVilliers, and not a single reply had come.

It was Wednesday morning, and Monica left the office on foot to interview an Italian painter, who was in Lady Helen for a month to try his hand at capturing the little West Coast town he had seen in a painting hanging in a private home at Lake Como—a piece Gift had sold at last year's summer art festival. Gift had made sure that everyone she came into contact with appreciated the irony of a picture of Lady Helen being displayed in a place whose own homes and idyllic views graced the walls of millions of houses all over the world.

Although Monica had made an appointment to see the painter, there was no answer when she pressed the buzzer for the tiny studio flat he'd rented above the post office on

Main Street. There were many tasks waiting for her at the newspaper office, most of them tedious administrative duties that she had been putting off for days, but she did not feel like returning to tackle them. In six weeks, Daphne, Miemps and Reg would have to be settled in their new home—wherever that might be—unless she could do something to stop Mr. Yang's plans. Once had been fortunate, but twice would be astonishing. Her effort, however, was not off to a good start: The letter campaign to Mrs. DeVilliers was obviously not working.

While she waited for the Italian artist to return, she would take a walk in the park.

She strolled around the top edge of the amphitheater, where just last weekend Mandla had screeched with laughter at the antics of Bob the baboon and his fellow cast of pantomime safari animals. Sipho had managed a few chuckles, mostly at his brother's uninhibited display of delight, but he was a good sport and had not nagged to go home.

A child's turquoise sweater lay on the grass at the top of the stairs. Monica picked it up so that she could hand it in at the post office, where the town kept its lost-and-found box.

She walked in the direction of the statue of Lady Helen, half hoping that Oscar would be working there, as he had been on the day of the shark-cage incident. The fate of Sandpiper Drift was becoming a heavy burden for just one person to shoulder, and Oscar would make a good confidant. Francina had told her about how little formal education he'd had, but that might be the reason his wisdom seemed so profound—it came unfettered by academic reasoning and trite phrases that did little except add unnecessary polish to an argument.

Yes, Oscar would be the perfect person to confide in. But he was not there. Monica sat down on the bench and looked up at the sculpted face of Lady Helen. In the last years of her life, she had probably never worn the serene expression that the artist had created. If her husband had killed her, Monica hoped that he'd been quick, so that she had not suffered. But maybe Oscar was right; maybe she had lived here until she'd died a natural death.

One day she might investigate the story, but right now, while pelicans soared low over the strip of bright ocean and the leaves of the palm trees rustled in the gentle breeze, Miemps was carefully packing the ornaments and collectibles that were a history of her life, and Monica had made no progress in her effort to remove the necessity for the move.

Apart from the sculpted Lady Helen and the reticent Mrs. DeVilliers, one other person was remaining silent: Mr. Yang. Each time Monica called, he was in a meeting and could not be disturbed. Monica had tried without success to entice the secretary into a conversation. Either Mr. Yang was standing nearby or the secretary regretted having ever dropped her guard.

The government official had given Monica his card, and just as she'd presumed, he came from the Cape Town office. It might be a good idea to make an appointment to talk to him without the hulking presence of Mr. Yang, but what she would ask him, she did not know; the documents he had given her had all been deemed legal and straightforward by a Cape Town lawyer she had consulted. Still, something about the government man bothered her. It wasn't his groomed but unstylish appearance, but rather the unbalanced relationship with Mr. Yang. It was as though he had been waiting for Mr. Yang to provide the words he would speak. The most obvious explanation was that the government man was on the take and Mr. Yang certainly had enough to keep a middle-level official as obedient as a well-schooled dog.

Mayor Oupa had seen the error of his ways with only a mere prodding on her part, but she sensed that the government man would not be as easy to convince and her steps would have to be careful. She had no evidence, and if he interpreted her prodding as a threat to expose him—which it would be—he might do something rash, even violent.

Mrs. DeVilliers, however, was a different case. When Monica had asked her if she knew how they were able to afford that house, she was so distressed that Monica could not believe she knew of any diamond. The fact that she was not answering Monica's letters might mean that she had since been told.

There was only one thing Monica could do, and that was to go and see Mrs. DeVilliers herself.

A week went by before Monica could leave Lady Helen for a trip to Cape Town. Since she was not only the newspaper's editor and sole reporter but also the layout designer and production liaison, she could not go haring off whenever she felt the need, as there was a schedule to be followed. She knew of small-town newspapers that came out sporadically, but Max had never been late with an issue and she was not about to change that.

There was a different security guard this time at the gate to the DeVillierses' neighborhood, and he did not let her in with a wave.

"Who are you coming to see?" he wanted to know.

"The DeVilliers family," she said. Would he ask for her name and call Mr. DeVilliers?

The guard checked a list on his clipboard.

"I see them," he said.

Then the boom lifted and he waved her through. Ridiculous as it seemed, a visitor just needed to give the name of a legitimate resident and they were in.

She would not be as fortunate if she rang the buzzer on the DeVillierses' gate. Mr. DeVilliers would probably call the security company and have her escorted out. There was no choice but to wait outside until one of two things happened: Mr. DeVilliers left or a neighbor grew suspicious of the woman sitting outside in her car and called the security company. Either way, it looked as though she had an unpleasant day ahead of her, and it all had to be over by three-thirty so that she could make it home by five when Francina left.

As she approached the house, she was disappointed to see that there was a gardener tidying the flower beds on the landscaped sidewalk. He would certainly alert his employer to the presence of a woman outside. She would just have to drive around until he was finished, unless…

"Good morning," she said, and the gardener paused in his trimming of the edges with a large pair of shears. He did not stand up.

"Is Mr. DeVilliers in?"

The gardener studied her for a moment, and then seemed to decide that she was not a threat. "No, he and the young Mr. DeVilliers have gone fishing."

"And Mrs. DeVilliers?"

"Inside."

Monica felt like whooping with joy. "Thank you," she told him, and he grunted in reply.

She parked her car in the driveway and got out to ring the buzzer.

A minute went by before a voice came through the speaker. "Yes?"

"Mrs. DeVilliers, it's Monica Brunetti from Lady Helen. I'm the one who sent you those photographs of Sandpiper Drift."

Silence.

"Did you look at them?"

The intercom gave off a strange whining sound. It took a while for Monica to realize that it was not a mechanical malfunction but the sound of Mrs. DeVilliers crying.

"Please don't cry," she told her. "We can work everything out. Just let me in so we can talk."

Curious because his employer had not opened the gate, the gardener inched closer to listen. Monica knew that if Mrs. DeVilliers did not open up in less than a minute she would have to leave, because a security car was approaching, presumably on its regular patrol, and the gardener might flag it down if he heard his employer crying.

Please, please open the gate, Monica begged silently. She heard a click and the gate began to slide across just as the security car went by.

Mrs. DeVilliers was waiting for her at the open front door in a blue cotton print housecoat. A few wisps of her long straight gray hair had fallen from her bun. A mop and bucket sat in the middle of the entrance hall.

"This is a big place to clean," said Monica.

Mrs. DeVilliers shook her head and sniffed. "Too big. I used to finish cleaning the old place by lunch. This place—" she waved her hand dismissively at the sunken living room and dining room with its wide archways "—takes me all day."

"I saw your old house, Mrs. DeVilliers."

Her eyes filled with tears again. "My son was born in the front bedroom. It's hard for women to walk away from a house where they've birthed a child."

The unusual turn of phrase, which might have come from the wife of a farmer not a mechanic, hit Monica like a punch in the stomach. Until this very moment in Mrs. DeVilliers's spotless entrance hall, she hadn't realized how strongly she felt about one day having a baby of her own.

"Where are my manners? Come in and have some tea," said Mrs. DeVilliers, wiping her eyes on the corner of her housecoat.

Monica looked at her watch.

"Don't worry, they won't be back until this evening. Come with me."

Monica followed her into the kitchen, a bright rectangular room with a central island, light-wood cabinets and melamine countertops. Two pots simmered on the stove that was built into the central island, and Mrs. DeVilliers lifted the lids of these and gave the contents a quick stir.

"I have to make dinner while I clean," she explained, "because if I only start cooking when I've finished my housework, we'll eat at ten o'clock at night."

She put the kettle on and got out two mugs. Monica appreciated that she didn't haul out cups and saucers and didn't disappear to take off her housecoat and tidy her hair. Here was a woman to whom people were more important than appearances. There were far too few like her around.

"Have a seat—and please don't call me Mrs. DeVilliers. I may have left Lady Helen, but I'm still the same old Lizbet."

Monica sat down at the round wooden table and took a sip of the tea. It was rooibos. "Did you get the photographs?"

Lizbet nodded. "I locked myself in the bathroom to look at them and when I came out my husband asked me why I'd been crying. I told him I had hay fever. It was the first time in thirty-five years that I lied to my husband." She sniffed loudly. "It didn't feel good."

Since Monica could not come right out and ask Lizbet if her husband had discovered the diamond, she continued to talk about Sandpiper Drift, in the hope that with time she would find a more subtle way to approach the subject.

"Miemps and Reg are still in their house."

Lizbet smiled. "I miss my old friend. After lunch I'd knock on her door and the two of us would sit in the shade for a while with a cup of tea. You can't do that in this neighborhood with all the security."

Monica knew that her next question would have to be carefully worded because it would either open or close the door to a meaningful discussion of Mr. DeVilliers's dealings. "Miemps said you worried about your husband."

Lizbet looked at her for a second, trying, Monica thought, to guess how much Miemps would have told an outsider.

"He gambles," she said quietly, as though the walls might be listening.

"I see," said Monica. The pretense that it was news to her was necessary to preserve Miemps's high standing in her friend's estimation. "He must have won a lot of money to be able to afford this house."

Lizbet hung her head. The words were barely a whisper. "He went to a big game in Cape Town."

Poor Lizbet. Not only was her faith in her friend's loyalty misplaced, but her husband had misled her, too, because this was not how he had come into money—Monica was sure of it. He would not have been given a reward by the government for finding the diamond so it must have come from Mr. Yang in an arrangement Monica had not yet figured out. The time to plant the seed of doubt in Lizbet's mind was now, because Monica might never have the opportunity to see her alone again.

"I know it must have been hard for you to tell me," she said.

Lizbet nodded. "I couldn't bear to face Miemps with the truth. I felt terrible about our quick goodbye, but my husband came home one afternoon and said we were leaving the next morning. I didn't even have time to take down my lace curtains."

"Have you ever considered that your husband might have been the one to discover the diamond?" asked Monica, watching carefully for a reaction to her words.

A light seemed to come into Lizbet's eyes as she realized

that her house might not have been purchased with the spoils of gambling. "Do you think he could be the one?"

Monica nodded.

"But why would he hide it from me?" Lizbet shook her head, and this time her eyes showed anger. "You're wrong. If he'd found a diamond he would have come straight home, dancing and singing."

"I don't think so," said Monica. "If you recall, the agreement between the government and the town stated that any diamonds discovered on the land were to be handed over immediately to the government."

"Yes. And the government gave him a lot of money for the diamond."

Monica shook her head. "They are not legally required to give him anything. If they did give him a reward, it would have been a token amount—definitely not enough to pay for this house."

"Oh," said Lizbet, sounding deflated. She had been hoping to find out that her husband had gained the money in a moral way. Now it seemed as though her husband was a thief as well as a gambler; he had stolen what was rightfully government property and sold it on the black market. No wonder he hadn't told her anything.

"I know what you're thinking and it's wrong," said Monica. "The government has the diamond—that's why they're taking the land back. But Mr. Yang somehow managed to persuade them to sell him most of the land."

"So where did my husband get the money?"

"I was hoping you would help me find that out. Your husband is hiding something, but I don't know what."

"You don't know?" Lizbet stood up from the table. "You're accusing my husband of underhanded business, yet you don't exactly know what?"

This had not gone the way Monica had intended. "I'm trying to get to the truth," she said quietly.

"Well, you should consider the feelings of others while you're trying," said Lizbet. "Now, if you'll excuse me, this large house, bought with money from who knows where, has to be cleaned."

"Your friends are about to lose their homes." Monica hoped that this last appeal to Lizbet's conscience might set the conversation on a gentler path.

But Lizbet opened the front door without another word, pressed a button on a remote control to slide the gate across and closed the front door again before Monica was even halfway down the driveway.

As she drove north toward Lady Helen, all Monica could think about was Lizbet's angry face. Her efforts to be subtle had failed and instead of recruiting Lizbet as an ally, she had pushed her further away.

Although Lizbet's reaction was far from what Monica had hoped for, it was understandable; the man was her husband after all. But Monica prayed that the anger would soon pass and Lizbet would start to think about what Monica had said. Since Mr. DeVilliers would not speak to Monica, she would have to rely on Lizbet to do her investigating for her. If Lizbet shut her mind to the possibilities and chose instead to console herself with the belief that her husband had a gambling problem, then this was the end of the road for Monica's investigation and the only hope for Sandpiper Drift was that her newspaper stories would generate enough of an outcry to stop Mr. Yang's plans.

As Monica neared Lady Helen, she thought of her position in the town. Miemps had chosen to divulge Lizbet's secrets to her. Did that mean that Monica was no longer an outsider and Lizbet, in her abandonment of Sandpiper Drift, had become one?

✦ Chapter Twenty-Four ✦

The day after her visit to Lizbet, with just over three weeks till Francina's wedding and four till the bulldozers arrived, Monica typed a press release to send to her successor at *In-Depth*. Although the content was serious, she could not help smiling as she thought of what Ella might have said about her enlisting the help of a competitor to get the story out.

Monica's photographs in the *Lady Helen Herald* were disturbing, but obviously not disturbing enough, because not a single member of the government's opposition, or even a nonpartisan civic leader, had issued so much as a comment, and nobody had marched on the government offices in Cape Town to demand an end to this injustice. Much as Monica hated to admit it, television cameras were needed to show the real heartbreak of the story.

She would have liked to do the piece herself, but since

that was no longer possible, the rising star of *In-Depth* would have to do it.

When she had faxed off the release, she sat down in front of her computer again and composed a letter to Pieter van Jaarsveld, the government representative she had met at the golf resort, requesting a meeting at his office in Cape Town.

Her final order of business for the day was to call Mayor Oupa and get him to organize a town meeting. The residents of Lady Helen were far too passive in the face of Mr. Yang's onslaught, and this had to change.

Mayor Oupa's mouth was full when he answered his telephone. "Ah, Moonca," he said, and she waited one full minute for him to finish chewing.

"There, that's better," he said. "You got me in the middle of my morning tea. Have you tried Mama Dlamini's lemon meringue pie?"

Monica said that she had and a few minutes went by as they discussed the merits of the various items on the dessert menu at the café. When she tried to bring the conversation back to business, he wanted to tell her about a restaurant he had visited in Cape Town, and she had a feeling that he was being inspired by more than a love of food. Her last discussion with him had pushed him into an uncomfortable situation with Mr. Yang, and so now he wished to avoid discussing anything of importance with her—just in case. Monica was disappointed, as she'd hoped that he'd cut his ties with the golfing magnate, but this evasive chatter now made it clear that he had not. Maybe she was being too harsh. He might have freed himself from the influence of Mr. Yang, but now, like most politicians, was doing his best not to be caught in a sandstorm, which a call from the local newspaper editor almost always heralded.

"I'd like your help in calling a town meeting," she said.

There was silence on the other end. Then he said, "What for?"

She explained how important it was to galvanize the support of the residents if Sandpiper Drift was to be saved.

"I don't know, Monica," he said. "My people are a law-abiding bunch, and the government has sanctioned this deal. Haven't you seen the government signs on the fence that demarcates the area to be mined?"

She was losing patience. "I'll have to call a meeting myself then," she said. "But I wouldn't want it to look like a vote of no confidence in our mayor."

"Yes, yes, yes," he said tersely. "I'll check the calendar and get back to you."

A day later she had not heard from the government man and so she dialed his office. After inquiring who was calling, his secretary put her on hold and then came back on the line to tell her that Mr. van Jaarsveld was in a meeting and would be all day.

Monica dialed the switchboard again and asked to be put through to Mr. van Jaarsveld's deputy.

The voice that came on the line was young and confident.

"Yes," he told Monica. "Mr. van Jaarsveld is handling the Lady Helen case."

"Can you tell me why the government agreed to sell the majority of the land to the golf resort?" asked Monica.

"This is off the record," said the young man.

"Well…"

"I'm not asking you, I'm telling you." His tone was assertive for a young employee, and Monica guessed he had risen quickly in the ranks.

"Fine," said Monica.

"The Department of Mineral Affairs doesn't have as much money as it used to," he explained. "Cuts have been made. Other departments have needs that are considered more urgent." From his derisive tone it was obvious that he disagreed with this policy. "The bottom line is that it costs money to mine and so we chose the area where the diamond was discovered and sold off the rest."

"And what about the people who are losing their homes?"

"They're to be compensated by the owner of the golf resort. That's a better deal than our people received in the past. They were forced off their land by whites and received nothing. The people of your community should be grateful. They won't have to go through the laborious task of filing a land claim."

Monica thanked him for his time and put down the telephone feeling depressed. Indifference seemed to be spreading in the world like an infection.

A week later she had not heard from Nomsa at *In-Depth* or Mayor Oupa, and only three weeks remained before the bulldozers came.

Three days went by and she decided that she would give the mayor a reminder before calling the meeting herself. He answered the phone with a bright hello, but quickly lost his cheerfulness when he heard her voice.

"No, I haven't forgotten," he told her. "You must remember that mayors have a lot of work to do."

"I see," said Monica, when, really, she didn't. "Should I do it for you then?"

"No, no, no. Don't do that. I'll let you know tomorrow."

Monica waited at her office the whole of the next day, but he did not call. On Thursday morning she was just about to march over to his office, when he called her to let her know that he'd booked the hall at Green Block School for the following evening. Since it was too late for Monica to advertise the meeting in the newspaper, she went around town sticking notices to lampposts, notice boards and store windows.

On Friday night, two weeks before the bulldozers were to arrive, she entered Green Block School and was dismayed to find it only half-full. Gift and David were sitting in the front row.

"Where is everybody?" she asked.

Gift shrugged. "People don't believe they can fight the government. I don't know why. We fought the old government, so there's no reason we can't fight the new one."

David looked upset. "I'm sorry, Monica. But we'll help you."

"Thanks, David. Well, I don't see the mayor, so I'd better do a jig or something to keep the crowd in their seats."

She climbed onto the stage and greeted the small group. It was not necessary to introduce herself, and this would have given her satisfaction if the hall had been full. But not now.

Ten minutes went by and she was torn between starting without Mayor Oupa and risking his bruised ego or waiting and risking the crowd walking out.

Another five minutes went by and she decided that it

was more important to keep the crowd. As she launched into an explanation of how important it was to save Sandpiper Drift, she noticed Mayor Oupa slip in and take a seat at the back.

When she had finished her passionate plea to the residents of Lady Helen to unite against Mr. Yang and, if need be, stage a protest outside the government offices in Cape Town, she asked Mayor Oupa if he had anything to add.

"Thank you," he said, and made his way toward the stage.

What followed was a meandering speech extolling the virtues of small-town life and the peace it afforded everyone. Monica noticed people shifting in their seats and looking at their watches. Mayor Oupa was saying nothing of significance to the issue at hand but was, in short, being a politician.

Monica took pity on the residents of Lady Helen, who were a polite bunch and would not walk out while their mayor was speaking, and she edged closer to the podium until Mayor Oupa became puzzled by her physical proximity and lost his train of thought. She seized the opportunity immediately and thanked him profusely for his eloquent comments on the matter. The crowd clapped politely and then dispersed.

When she got home, Monica wished she had someone to talk to and was tempted to knock on Francina's door. But it was exam time and Francina would be studying.

She lay on her bed and tried not to think uncharitable thoughts about all those who had not turned up for the meeting. Why did they not have any fight in them? Were the people of South Africa sick of fighting? They'd certainly had more than their fair share of it.

* * *

Despite her worries, Monica was so exhausted she slept soundly and woke the next morning feeling refreshed. If the people of Lady Helen were too worn out to fight, she would do it on her own, and the first item of action on her agenda when she got to the office on Monday would be to telephone Nomsa at the *In-Depth* studio.

Saturday started out like most summer mornings, sunny yet cool, but by lunchtime the temperature had soared. Monica switched on fans all around the house and for the rest of the day the boys stayed on the front porch in the shade.

Francina came into the house in the afternoon to ask if there were any extra fans as one did not seem to be enough to cool her studio. Her face shone with sweat. Monica gave her the fan from her own bedroom.

"Thank you," said Francina. "I'm trying to finish the dress my mother is going to wear to the wedding. Oh, Monica, I wish now that I hadn't read all those old English books. If I take the long sleeves off my wedding dress it will be ruined, but who wants to see the bride glowing with anything but happiness?"

"This heat won't last," said Monica, trying to sound confident.

"I hope you're right. Only one more exam—English literature. Hercules is firing questions at me while I work."

"Let me know if you need anything."

"You can pray for the heat to go away."

"I will," said Monica.

On Monday morning, when Mandla found out that Francina had another exam to write, he sulked.

"I want to go to work with you," he said. He was not fond of Trudy, the replacement Francina had gotten to look after him while she was at Green Block School writing her exams.

"Oh, Mandla, you know you can't," said Monica.

He began to cry. "Please," he begged, hanging on to her leg. "I'll be very quiet. I'll sit and draw."

She knew that she should resist, but since it was the final day of Francina's exams and Trudy's service she decided not to.

Mandla was delighted. "Thank you. I promise I'll be good."

She hoped her negotiations with Nomsa wouldn't be as ineffectual.

Once she'd explained to Trudy that Mandla was feeling a little unsettled but that there was nothing wrong with her work, Monica dropped Sipho at school and drove to the office with Mandla. True to his word, he sat down with his crayons and paper and began drawing.

After half an hour of trying to reach Nomsa, she tracked her down on her cell phone.

"It's too similar to a story I'm doing on an illegal occupation of land by a group of squatters," explained Nomsa.

"You'll get great footage," Monica persisted. "And the people are willing to go on camera."

But Nomsa would not be persuaded. "You're talking about fifteen families. There are four hundred families here. You were a journalist. You tell me which will give the best footage."

You *were* a journalist. Monica was sorely tempted to tell this confident young woman that the only reason she had the job at *In-Depth* was because of her family's connection, but then she might already know that and not care. This had been the way people got their jobs in the old South Africa; why should it be any different in the new one?

To reward Mandla for his good behavior, Monica took him to lunch at Mama Dlamini's. It was late morning, and although he would have preferred to go during the lunchtime crush when there'd be lots of people around, he was still excited.

"Let's sit here," he said, selecting a table in the middle of the room.

Monica would rather have sat in one of the booths, but he always wanted to be in on the action—if there was any.

A couple from their church was sitting at the counter drinking milk shakes, and when they finished they came over to greet Monica and Mandla. Mandla stuck out his hand as though he were a businessman welcoming clients to his table.

There was fresh snoek on the menu, and since it had been awhile since Monica had eaten the flat salty fish, which Mama Dlamini cooked West Coast style over an open fire with a marinade of apricot jam and lemon juice, she ordered it for both of them.

Only two other tables were occupied, one by a group of elderly ladies who would all come over and squeeze Mandla's cheeks on the way out, and one by a man Monica had never seen before. As was the custom when encountering strangers in Lady Helen—who were all most likely patrons of the arts—she nodded and smiled at him, but a few uncomfortable seconds passed before he gave a forced smile back.

A big-city type, she thought. It seemed like years since she had lived in Johannesburg and yet it was only eleven months.

Mama Dlamini brought their snoek out herself.

"I heard my best boy was in," she said. "What have you been doing today, sunshine?"

"Working," Mandla replied.

He beamed at her and did not complain when she gave him a kiss on the cheek.

"Ah, well, then you need your strength, so eat up. I've removed all the bones for you and if you clear your plate there's baked custard for dessert."

Mandla did not want to leave after they'd finished their meal, as the restaurant was beginning to fill up, but Monica had to get back to the office. She noticed that the man who had struggled to return her greeting left when they did, even though he had finished eating long before.

Outside the restaurant he lingered at the window of a gallery. Monica took Mandla's hand—against his will—and crossed the street. Before opening her office's front door, she looked back and saw that the man was still there, although now he wasn't staring into the display window at the paintings but straight at her. She quickly ushered Mandla into the office and closed the door behind them.

By one o'clock Mandla was tired of "working" and wanted to go home. Monica's usual route was not up Main Street, but today she felt compelled to take it. The man was still there, although now he was sitting on a bench outside the Lady Helen General Store. If he'd had a large flat brown paper parcel with him, she would not have been at all alarmed; people from Cape Town came here all the time to buy art and take photographs of the bougainvillea. But something about this man made her uneasy.

Mandla was not perturbed about going back to Trudy, as

he was just in time to accompany her for the walk to school to collect Sipho. There was nothing the little boy enjoyed more than a stroll through his neighborhood at the end of the school day. Francina was always complaining that it took them ages to get home because Mandla had to stop and greet everyone.

The man was not around the next morning, but Monica had the camera reinstalled outside the newspaper office just in case. A little before noon she checked the monitor and saw a different stranger loitering on the sidewalk directly across the street. He was tall and gaunt, and his hair was so short he might have been in the military. When his cigarette was finished, he lit another.

Before venturing out for lunch, she checked the monitor again to make sure that he was not still there. When she was sure he was not, she went outside and found ten cigarette butts on the white line in the middle of the street. The man had good aim.

He was sitting at the counter when she walked into Mama Dlamini's, and although he did not turn around, she was aware that he could see her reflection in the glass doors of the refrigerator.

For a man so obviously addicted to nicotine, he lingered quite awhile in the smoke-free restaurant. From time to time he'd turn around to scan the room, and his eyes would come to rest on her for a few seconds longer than was considered polite.

Monica wondered if she should go to the police station. What would she report? A stranger in town who had looked at her? Although she had no proof, she felt sure that this man and the one yesterday were connected to Mr. Yang. She knew that the businessman would not allow them to hurt her because she would immediately point a finger at him. But just the same, she would go back into Johannesburg mode and triple-check the locks on all her doors and windows.

She reconsidered this thinking when she arrived at work the next morning and found Dudu in tears and Max hyperventilating. The rear door had been forced open with a crowbar and peeled back as though it were the lid of a sardine can.

"Nothing's missing," said Dudu after Max had tried to speak but failed. "I called the police anyway. Whoever it was searched your filing cabinet."

All four drawers of the single metal cabinet, which stood on the light patches on the wooden floor where Max's legion of filing cabinets had once stood, were open, and cuttings, photographs and documents were strewn across the room.

The police searched for fingerprints but found none because the intruder or intruders had been careful to wear gloves.

"You'd better have that door repaired right away," said the policeman. He was the one who had shouted, "Drop the knife!" when David was being beaten by the thugs. "And we need you to come to the police station so you can give a description over the phone to the composite artist in Cape Town of the stranger you saw yesterday."

After a one-hour telephone conversation and the exchange of four faxes, the composite artist had sketched a reasonable likeness of the stranger, and Monica was free to leave the police station. She went back to the office to make arrangements to have the rear door repaired, and then she did what she had decided to do when she first saw the damaged door: she drove up to the golf resort.

This time the guard at the gate refused to let her in.

"You're not on Mr. Yang's list of visitors today," he told her.

"Did Mr. Yang specifically tell you not to let me in today?"

From the way that he hesitated, she knew that she was correct. Mr. Yang had been expecting her, and this meant only one thing: he had ordered the break-in at her office.

"I'm not going to leave until you let me in."

The guard glanced nervously at a camera mounted above the gatehouse. "You're blocking the road," he told her.

"Then let me in."

He scanned a list on his clipboard again, as though hoping that her name would miraculously appear and then he could be rid of this nuisance.

Monica switched off the engine, took out a magazine and pretended to read. Before long a car pulled up behind her.

"Madam, you have to move your car," said the guard, sounding flustered.

Monica turned the page of her magazine and continued reading.

The guard got out of his chair and walked to the other car. In her rearview mirror, Monica could see him talking to the driver and pointing at her. Then he walked back to the gatehouse and picked up the telephone. When he became aware that she was trying to eavesdrop on his conversation, he closed the window and turned his back on her.

Monica pretended not to notice when he opened the window again.

"Mr. Yang said you can't come in," he said with a satisfied note of vehemence. "He doesn't want you causing trouble."

The driver of the car behind leaned on his horn.

"You'd better go and deal with him," said Monica, thumbing backward, "because I'm still not moving."

The guard scowled at her. "Mr. Yang says he will meet you on the beach. Park your car over there—" he pointed at a small paved circle, presumably where cars that were refused turned around "—and walk down there." There was a footpath leading through the fynbos toward the dunes.

The driver of the other car was more than happy to back up so that she could remove her car, and gave her a jaunty wave as he drove through the open gate for his day of golf. She parked her car where the guard had indicated but did not get out. The path appeared to be well used—and might even have been the route taken by fishermen from Sandpiper Drift—but now it was deserted. Would Mr. Yang be there on his own or would he have one of his men with him? For the first time since moving to Lady Helen, she felt fear. Although she assumed that he would not harm her, the faces of her two boys flashed before her, and in that second she had decided.

She got out of her car and approached the guard on foot.

"Please telephone Mr. Yang's office and tell him to meet me here, outside the gate."

The guard looked at her as though she'd asked him to turn somersaults.

"Do it now, please. Before he leaves."

Shaking his head, he picked up the telephone and again closed the window so that she could not hear. From the wild gesturing, she knew that Mr. Yang's secretary was being difficult. He replaced the receiver and opened the window again.

"Wait in your car," he barked, and then he shut the window again and turned on a portable television.

She went back to her car.

An hour later Mr. Yang drove out of the resort in an imported sport-utility vehicle and parked next to her car.

"Thank you, God," whispered Monica when she saw that he was alone.

He lowered his passenger window and shouted, "Get in."

There was no way she would put herself in a vulnerable position like that. She shouted back, "You get in."

Shaking his head, he switched off his vehicle and got into the passenger seat next to her.

"Miss Brunetti, you've written some terrible things about me in the newspaper. You stirred up trouble with the council so that they voted against me. I've been patient with you, but my patience is beginning to wear thin."

Thin enough that he would want to get rid of her? she wondered.

"I don't want you on my property. If you cause a scene and upset my guests, I could become very angry."

Was that a threat?

He picked up an action figure at his feet and smiled.

"How are Sipho and Mandla?"

Monica felt an icy grip on her heart. She had not told him that she had two boys. That stranger in town, however, had seen her with Mandla at Mama Dlamini's and may even have been lurking outside her house when Trudy walked Sipho home from school. But who had told *him* their names?

She ignored his question and launched straight into the business she had come to discuss. "My office was broken into," she said.

He frowned. "I'm sorry to hear that."

"Nothing was taken, but I think you're aware of that."

"You think I had something to do with it?"

She nodded.

"Miss Brunetti, I am a businessman not a thug. Even if I had the time, why would I break into your office?"

"Not you," she said, "one of your men. You want to scare me off so that your precious new golf course can go ahead."

He forced a chuckle. "Oh, Miss Brunetti, you overestimate your power. Don't forget that I made the deal with the government. It's all aboveboard. And now that I can produce my own water, nothing will stop me from building the extra eighteen holes."

He got out of the car and leaned in the window. His suit looked uncomfortably snug on his thick forearms.

"I want you to listen carefully to me. This is the end of the story. Understand? Go back to your sweet little town and write about the six thousand and first book in the library."

Laughing, he got into his car and sped up to the gate, which the guard managed to open just before the large SUV crashed into it. Monica had a feeling that Mr. Yang enjoyed taking risks like that and that his merriment would continue all the way up to the clubhouse.

She felt so angry with his callous attitude toward the people of Sandpiper Drift that she slammed her fists on the steering wheel, accidentally beeping the horn.

"What do you want?" shouted the guard at the gate.

Monica ignored him and started her car. In exactly ten days, Daphne, Miemps and Reg would lose their home, yet Mr. Yang believed the story was over. Like so many developers all over the world he had no difficulty seeing numbers on balance sheets, but when it came to seeing the home owners displaced, or the trees cut down, or the birds and animals chased away, his vision became mysteriously cloudy.

Chapter Twenty-Five

The next morning Monica woke with a hollow feeling in the pit of her stomach. She hadn't slept well, partly because of the unrelenting heat, but mostly because she felt as though she had not made any headway. Her dreams, when she had finally fallen asleep, had been filled with giant yellow earthmoving machines that had flattened Sandpiper Drift and then set to work on the town of Lady Helen.

The heat wave couldn't have come at a more inconvenient time. Not only was it threatening to spoil Francina's wedding, but after the break-in at her office yesterday and Mr. Yang's mention of the boys by name, she had felt it necessary to close all the windows last night. With wide eyes the boys had listened to her excuse that there had been a spate of thefts of food by a troop of roving monkeys.

She and the boys had taken a cold shower before bed and slept under the new ceiling fans that Oscar had installed in all the rooms of the house, but it had still been like trying to get comfortable in a kitchen after the oven had been in use all day. Close to midnight, she had resorted to spraying Sipho's sheets with the bottle of water Francina used for ironing. Mandla never slept under the covers, but Sipho could not sleep without anything over him.

Since Francina's family was arriving tomorrow, the day before her wedding, Monica had taken today off from work to give her a wedding shower at Abalone House. It had been out of the question while Francina was writing exams, but these were now over, her dress was finished, and her mother's dress only needed to be hemmed. Everything had slipped into place, everything, that is, except the weather.

For a woman who had lived in Lady Helen less than a year, Francina had gathered quite a crowd of friends. There was Monica and, of course, Kitty, the members of her choir, Gift, Reverend van Tonder's wife, Ingrid, Mayor Oupa's wife, Evette, five other clients who had become friends and a few of the ladies from church, who were all hoping to audition for the choir at the beginning of the new year.

While Kitty was putting the final touches to the buffet table, Monica welcomed everybody and asked Francina to say a few words.

Francina stood up and waved at her friends. "I want to thank you all for coming today, but more than that I want to thank you for opening your town and your hearts to me and—" she smiled at Monica "—my family. God works in mysterious ways. I'm a girl from the Valley of a Thousand Hills. Who would have thought I'd end up in the Cape next to the Atlantic Ocean? But I am very happy here with all of you, my lovely friends, and I feel blessed to have been given this opportunity to start a new life. Enjoy yourselves, and if you don't wish to see a sweaty bride, please keep praying for cooler weather."

Since Ingrid was the reverend's wife, Monica asked if she would say grace.

"Before I start," said Ingrid, getting to her feet, "I just want to say, on behalf of all Francina's clients, thank you for our new looks. You may think that all you're doing is making new dresses, but you are so positive and enthusiastic that I look forward to my fittings like a young girl looks forward to a party. After an hour with you, I walk out feeling on top of the world. I can't tell you how many times I've thanked God for bringing you to us."

Monica had never seen Francina at a loss for words. She sat with a wide smile on her face, but Monica sensed that if Ingrid didn't get on with the grace, she would cry.

"Thank you, Lord, for everyone assembled here," began Ingrid.

Francina squeezed her eyes shut and a tear rolled down her cheek.

"Amen," said Ingrid when she had finished.

"Amen," added the ladies.

And at that point, Monica's cell phone rang. Thinking that it might be the school or David, who was looking after Mandla for the duration of the lunch, she ran outside to answer it. It was Nomsa.

"The squatter story's moving too slowly to make my Tuesday deadline. You say I'd get good footage down there?"

"Yes," said Monica, wondering how Nomsa could have

expected a land-distribution problem that had persisted for hundreds of years to be neatly solved in time for her show.

"There's a flight at 8:00 a.m. tomorrow morning that arrives in Cape Town at ten. I can stay for the weekend."

Monica thought of Francina's wedding. Everybody Nomsa would need to interview would be at the wedding on Saturday.

"I'll need you to pick me up at the airport."

"I'll be there," said Monica.

"This better not be another lame story like the one you did on the burn unit at the hospital."

God give me patience, prayed Monica.

"I promise you it's not."

That night the boys begged Monica to open the windows, but she said she could not. Although she preferred them to know the world as it really was and not as a parent wished it to be, this was something that she felt bound not to share as it would only frighten them. If the heat continued past this weekend—and for Francina's sake she prayed it wouldn't—she would ask Oscar to put burglar bars on their windows so that they could sleep with them open. That would truly be a sad day.

"Let's put fruit outside so the monkeys won't need to come in," said Mandla.

"Nobody at school today mentioned any monkeys," said Sipho warily.

"Yes," chimed in Mandla. "We know everyone in town and nobody else sleeps with their windows closed."

"We don't know everyone in town," Sipho corrected him.

"What do you mean?" asked Monica.

"On the way home from school the other day, a strange man in a car asked us for directions to the hospital. He said he was going to visit his sick mother. Trudy told him how to get there."

"Yes," interrupted Mandla, "and I had my sword and brave knight's helmet and he said, 'You look like a warrior. I bet your name is Prince.' And I said, 'No, I'm just Mandla and this is just Sipho.'"

Sipho rolled his eyes. "Francina would have given him the directions and moved us on. She's scared of strangers. He was a little older than most soldiers, but I thought he might be in the army."

"Why do you say that?" asked Monica, although she had a dreadful premonition that she knew what his answer would be.

"Because his hair was so short."

She felt a tightening in her chest and was sure that her face had drained of color.

"Well, I hope he managed to find his sick mother," she said in as airy a voice as she could muster. "It's bedtime now, boys. And I'm sorry, but the windows will have to stay closed until the monkeys decide to move on to another area."

As she tucked Sipho in under the covers, he whispered, "There aren't any monkeys, are there?"

She kissed him on the cheek. "No, Sipho, there aren't."

"Are we in danger?"

Asked directly, she could not lie to him. "I'm not sure, so we need to take precautions." She put her hand against his cheek. "After Wednesday night, it will all be over."

"What's happening on Wednesday night?"

"*In-Depth*. When the whole country sees what Mr. Yang is doing to Sandpiper Drift, there'll be an outcry and he will be forced to back down."

His eyes brightened. "Are you going to be on TV again?"

"No, sweetie. Nomsa is doing the report."

"Oh," he said, sounding deflated. "You'd do a better job."

"Thank you, sweetie." She kissed the top of his head. "Now go to sleep. Are you sure you want a sheet over you?"

He nodded and closed his eyes.

After she'd closed up the house for the night, she lay in bed under the strong blast from the ceiling fan trying not to think of the latest turn of events as a personal failure. If Sandpiper Drift was saved after the story aired on *In-Depth*, it would be because television always triumphed over the printed word in a modern world. But in the solitary darkness of her bedroom she found herself wishing that she could be the one to save Sandpiper Drift. And then, as though it were a pocket handkerchief she could hide, she tucked her ego away and drifted off to sleep thinking of how happy Daphne, Miemps and Reg would be once they knew that nobody was about to destroy their home.

The temperature had already climbed well beyond a comfortable level when Monica dropped Sipho off at school the next morning and headed toward Cape Town. Although Francina was not supposed to be working the day before her wedding, she had not minded at all when Monica had nervously asked if Mandla could spend the day with her.

"Don't be silly," Francina had scolded. "He won't be in the way. My parents will love him."

"I'll try to be back by five."

"Do what you have to do," said Francina. "I'll pick Sipho up from school and he can meet my family. My nephews are a lot older than him, but you know our Sipho, he's way beyond his years."

Coming from anyone else, the word *our* might have angered Monica, but she had to admit that she and Francina were a team. And now the other half of the team was about to go off and get married. A team of one wasn't a team at all. Even if she didn't feel guilty about thinking such thoughts, there was no time for them now.

"Don't let the boys out of your sight," she told Francina, and before she'd finished her sentence she knew that it was unnecessary and insulting.

Francina's look said it all.

With the air-conditioning in her car on high, she sat ramrod straight in her seat, concentrating on the road ahead and not even noticing that the delicate vegetation had begun to turn yellow in the prolonged heat.

Nomsa's flight was late and by the time she and her cameraman had loaded all their equipment into Monica's car, the air was stiflingly hot.

"Where are the breezes Cape Town is famous for?" complained Nomsa. "I hope it's cooler up in Lady Frances."

"Lady Helen," Monica corrected her.

"Whatever. They're both Eurocentric anyway. The name should be changed to something more African. All the other small towns in South Africa have done it."

Monica kept her uncharitable thoughts on the Eurocentric education Nomsa had received abroad to herself. Right
now it was important to get to Lady Helen quickly so that
Nomsa could obtain footage of Sandpiper Drift and interview the residents who were about to be displaced. A sudden thought crossed Monica's mind. What about the
residents who had already been displaced—those living
right here in Cape Town? She quickly switched over into the
left lane and took the turnoff for the harbor. The car that
had been following directly behind them did exactly the
same thing.

"What are you doing?" asked Nomsa, hanging on to the
door handle as though at any moment she might fly out.

"I'd like you to interview a very young resident of Sandpiper Drift. She and her parents now live near the docks."

Nomsa checked the lock on her door.

"There are three of us. It'll be okay," said Monica reassur-
ingly, trying to convince herself as much as her traveling
companions.

Miemps was not wrong; the area *was* rough. Most of the
houses had probably once been neat cottages, where fishermen's wives kept the yards tidy while scanning the sea for a returning boat. There were windows missing in many of the
houses, but although they looked abandoned there were signs
of human inhabitation: piles of dirty bedding left out in the
sunshine to air, newspapers covering the remaining window-
panes, upturned paint tins grouped together in the dusty
yards around the remains of cooking fires. Outside one of these
houses, which had obviously passed into the hands of illegal
squatters who had nothing to do with the fishing industry,

Monica saw a row of graying cloth diapers hanging on a fence to dry.

Monica reached into the glove compartment and gave Nomsa a map. "Give me directions, please, to Orange Street." She looked in the rearview mirror. The car that had followed them off the highway was keeping up. It was a white sedan and appeared to have only one occupant.

Nomsa threw the map into the back seat. "You do it," she told the cameraman. "I hate maps."

With the cameraman's help, Monica found Zukisa's street quite easily, and as she turned into it she gave an audible sigh of relief; the houses in this street were in good condition. There weren't any people about—which was understandable, given the neighborhood—but as they passed each house a curtain moved and then was opened wider when the observer realized that two of the passengers in this unfamiliar car were women. The car that Monica had thought might be following them was nowhere in sight, and she was forced to admit that she had jumped to an incorrect conclusion.

They found Zukisa's house at the end of the dead-end street and parked outside her gate.

"Your car won't be here when we get back," said Nomsa.

"I'll ask Zukisa's mother if I can park inside the gate," replied Monica.

As the cameraman unloaded his equipment, the residents of the street appeared on their driveways. There was no movement from inside Zukisa's house.

She knocked on the door. When there was no response after thirty seconds, Nomsa pushed her aside and banged on the door with her fist.

"You'll scare them," said Monica.

"That's if there's anybody here." Nomsa shook her head. "Surprise visits, uh-huh."

"Shh," said Monica. "I hear something."

There was a scuffling sound on the other side of the door.

"Zukisa," called Monica. "It's Monica, the lady who took your picture for TV."

A couple of seconds later the curtain of the front room lifted and there was Zukisa, wearing another cheerful dress, this one printed with bright red cherries.

She dropped the curtain and they heard the sound of three locks being undone.

"You look wonderful," she told Zukisa when the little girl finally stood before her. "You've grown so much." She noticed Zukisa staring at the television camera. "We're still trying to save Sandpiper Drift," she explained. "These people are from the same program I used to work on—" she noticed Nomsa rolling her eyes "—and they'd like to interview you and your parents."

Zukisa cast her eyes downward. "My mother is sick. And my father is late."

"I'm sorry to hear that," said Monica. "Do you think she'd mind if we waited for your father?"

She felt an elbow in her ribs and Nomsa whispered fiercely in her ear, "Late means dead."

"Oh, Zukisa, I'm so sorry," said Monica.

The little girl tried to smile, but it was clear that she was upset, and Monica was furious with herself.

"Can we interview your mother?" asked Nomsa. Then she turned to Monica and whispered again, "I'm glad you asked me to come. You don't get much better footage than a mother on her deathbed."

"She's not going to die," said Zukisa, her eyes flashing.

She did not say what disease her mother was suffering from, but Monica, Nomsa and the cameraman had already guessed. The ordinariness of this disease had become heartbreaking.

"Sweetie, is there anything I can do for you?" asked Monica.

Zukisa thought for a while and then shook her head. "No, we'll be okay. I don't go to school anymore, so I have time to take care of Mammie. She told me I make better pap than she does."

"Where are you getting money from to buy food?" Monica asked.

"My Mammie has nobody left, but my Daddy has a sister who brings us money every week. She gets a pension from the government." She said this proudly, as though she were a parent sharing the news with friends that her child had won a scholarship.

Monica took out her business card and quickly wrote her home phone number on the back. "If you ever need anything, just phone me reverse charges."

Zukisa nodded. "There's no phone around here, but sometimes the one in the kaffie is working."

Monica hoped that Zukisa would never have to walk through the neighborhood to the café they'd seen near the main road. She slipped a few rolled-up notes into Zukisa's fist and whispered, "Find a good place to hide this."

"Can we go in and talk to your mother?" asked Nomsa.

Zukisa looked at Monica with confusion in her eyes.

Monica drew the reporter aside. "Her mother is sick. You can't do the interview."

Nomsa sighed. "I don't want to interview the mother, silly. I just want to get her permission to interview this little girl. She's a natural."

Monica shook her head. "No, I won't allow it. She has gone through enough."

"Come on, you've filmed her once before yourself. And when we go inside to ask the mother, we won't let them know that the camera is on. That way we'll get great footage of the sick mother and the interior of this sad little house."

"Forget it. We're going," snapped Monica. She was so disgusted she felt like shaking Nomsa.

But Nomsa did not see why she had to listen to Monica, who was, after all, only their driver on this trip.

"You have no idea what makes good journalism, do you, Monica?" She made no effort to keep her voice down. "That's why I got the job and you didn't."

"If that's what it takes to be a good journalist, then I'd rather be a typist," hissed Monica.

"If you won't ask her, I will."

"Excuse me," said a voice behind them. It was Zukisa. "I'll do the interview."

Monica put her hand on the girl's shoulder. "You don't have to do anything you don't want to do, sweetie."

Zukisa nodded. "Will this help save the homes of all my aunties in Sandpiper Drift?"

"Of course," said Nomsa, seeing things about to go her way.

Zukisa looked to Monica for confirmation.

"We hope so," she said.

"Then I'll go and ask Mammie's permission."

Nomsa beckoned for the cameraman to follow the child into the house, but Monica put out her hand to stop him.

"Don't," she said.

The cameraman lowered the camera and said, "You're right."

"Come on, fool," said Nomsa. "We might not get another chance."

"I'm not moving," said the cameraman.

"Well, there's no point in me going in if I don't get footage," said Nomsa, unwrapping a stick of gum.

When Zukisa came out she had changed into a white dress edged with lace.

"You look like an angel," said Monica.

Zukisa smiled. "That's what my mother always calls me."

On the way home, Monica thought she spotted the white car tailing them again, but it turned off the road at Saldanha Bay. When they got back to Lady Helen, she dropped Nomsa and the cameraman off at Abalone House and promised to return in thirty minutes to take them to Sandpiper Drift.

"Make it an hour and a half," said Nomsa. "I want to have a nap."

"But it's already four-thirty," said Monica. "Aren't you worried about getting everything done before the light goes? I won't have much time to take you around tomorrow with the wedding on."

"Oh, relax," Nomsa told her. "You're such a worrier."

Monica found Francina, Mandla and Sipho sitting in the shade in the garden when she arrived home.

"Did your family arrive safely?" she asked.

Francina nodded. "They've taken a walk to stretch their legs. They won't be long."

"Francina, I'm really sorry, but I have to go back to work. Nomsa needed to rest for a while."

Francina shook her head. "That one. I don't know why they chose her over you."

"Thanks," said Monica. She'd tried to push that thought aside the whole day she was with Nomsa.

"But it's a good thing they did or we wouldn't be here."

"You're right. It's a good thing."

Francina got up and motioned for Monica to move away from the boys. When they were a few feet away she said, "I invited him to the wedding today."

"Who?" asked Monica.

"The doctor. I told him you were not bringing a date."

Monica felt her face grow hot. "Are you crazy?"

Francina chuckled.

"It's not funny, Francina. He's a married man."

"While you were in Cape Town this morning the word came out. He's getting a divorce. His wife has been running around with another man. Apparently, the doctor was willing to work on their marriage. But she wants out. She's moving to Cape Town to be with the other man." Francina looked at Monica expectantly.

Monica's head reeled. Poor Zak. All this time he had been suffering and yet he'd found the strength to go beyond the call of duty with his patients. He always looked tired, but not once had Monica seen him try to cut a patient short or avoid a particularly talkative member of a patient's family. And she had never seen him looking despondent.

"What do you think of that?" Francina asked.

"I don't know."

"I tell you the news of the year and that's all you can say, I don't know?"

"I'm shocked."

"I'm not. I told you I see everything. That day outside the church I was right."

Monica smiled and then, feeling guilty, composed her face into a more appropriate look of concern. It was not right for her to be feeling this flicker of hope for herself when Zak was mourning the end of his marriage.

"He can't come. He has to work," said Francina. "But that's something you'll have to get used to when you're married to a doctor."

"Francina!" Monica looked to see if her raised voice had attracted the interest of the boys. But they seemed too tired and lethargic in the heat to do anything but sit and doze on the blanket Francina had laid down next to the tree. "Wedding jitters are making you crazy."

"And you're crazy if you can't see what I can," replied Francina. "Now let me get these boys into a cool bath or they'll fall into a deep sleep and wake up at eight tonight and want to play."

Monica returned to Abalone House at five-thirty. The cameraman was ready but Nomsa was taking a shower. Since it was summer, they still had more than three hours till dark, but Monica knew how things worked: Hitches and holdups were normal, and before you knew it the light was fading and you didn't have enough on tape to fill your time slot. She hoped that thinking of details like these would clear her mind of Zak. It didn't.

As Monica and the cameraman chatted to Kitty, who was clearly itching to discuss Zak but couldn't because of the presence of a stranger, a white car slowed down outside Abalone House. When the driver noticed that there were people on the porch, he quickly moved on and turned the corner.

Monica excused herself and made a quick call on her cell phone to the police to ask them to keep a lookout for the white car, as it could be related to the break-in at the *Lady Helen Herald*. The police officer Monica was so fond of assured her that he would do it himself. Since theirs was a department of just two, and his partner was off for the afternoon, Monica felt uncomfortable taking Lady Helen's only on-duty policeman away from his post, but she would not do it if she didn't think it necessary.

Miemps and Reg were dressed in their church clothes when Monica, Nomsa and the cameraman arrived.

Daphne, who had elected to remain in her nurse's uniform, poured the tea. Her hand shook so much that Monica looked away to spare her any embarrassment. Miemps had told her that Daphne no longer slept for more than three hours at a time, and she would often find her in the kitchen with her head in her hands or outside in the garden looking up at the stars.

The house was filled with brown boxes, some of them still open, but most taped shut. Monica noticed that there was no delivery address on any of them. There was one week left before the bulldozers came.

The cameraman set up his equipment and began shooting without warning. Miemps and Reg looked at each other in fright, but Nomsa acted as though nothing was different and continued the conversation, asking questions casually, as though they were old friends catching up. Soon Miemps and Reg lost their frozen expressions and were answering with real emotion. Miemps pulled out a handkerchief and began to cry. Reg put an arm around his wife and spoke directly to the camera.

"They threw us out of our house once to make room for a white suburb, and now we're being thrown out so that men can chase a little white ball around." He shook his head.

Monica had to admit that Nomsa was a true professional. In no time at all, Miemps and Reg had opened up to her as though she were a trusted confidante.

Up until this point, Daphne had not offered more than her name, but now all the anger and frustration she had been feeling spilled out.

"My parents are good people. Everything they've ever done has been to help others. They deserve a bit more respect. A man who forces the elderly or people with young children from their homes has no conscience. Did you know that one of the families will be moving into the maintenance shed at the school? Only dogs should bring up their young in a shed." She leaned closer to Nomsa. "That man, up there—" she pointed in the direction of the golf course "—will tell you that he's offering us a fair price for our houses, but I'm telling you now that all we can afford with the money is a home in a bad neighborhood in Cape Town or a patch of land in the middle of nowhere."

Monica deeply regretted that she had not done this same

interview on her first visit to Lady Helen. But nothing could be done to change the past, and at least Daphne was finally getting her moment in front of the camera, even if it was only one week before the arrival of the bulldozers.

Moving at breathtaking speed, Nomsa arranged the other families in clusters outside their front doors and interviewed each and every member. The women cried openly, but it was the men's attempts at stoicism that Monica found most heartbreaking. As with Miemps and Reginald, they all relaxed in Nomsa's skilled hands and talked as though they'd known her since birth.

Finally, after a continuous sixty-minute take, she called, "Cut!"

She did not shake the hands of all those who wished to thank her, and everybody thought it was because the light was going and she still had work to do, but Monica knew that this was her way. The people of Sandpiper Drift had served her purpose.

The cameraman loaded his equipment into the trunk of Monica's car, and as she drove away, the children ran after them, calling to Nomsa and waving. But Nomsa was on her cell phone and did not offer so much as a smile.

As the sun slipped into the ocean, Monica parked a little distance from the gate of the golf resort, and like an army reconnaissance team, the three of them crept through the bushes and onto the beach, from where the cameraman filmed the golf resort with a powerful zoom lens.

When it was finally too dark to get decent footage, they started back up the path to Monica's car. None of them had thought to bring a flashlight, and although the moon was doing its best to light the sky, it was not enough for them to know for sure that they were retracing their exact route. At one point the cameraman stumbled over a large rock and almost dropped the camera.

"I don't remember any rocks in the path on the way down," he said.

Monica didn't either and she was beginning to worry. It was the night before Francina's wedding and she really had to fetch the boys so that the bride-to-be could get her beauty sleep.

Although the twilight had been still and airless, a wind had picked up while they were down on the beach, and now Monica had to hold on to the hat she had stupidly forgotten to remove when the sun went down.

"I'm chilly," complained Nomsa.

"Me, too," said Monica without thinking, and then it hit her. The night was no longer sweltering, but cool and breezy. She had been so wrapped up in their mission that she hadn't even noticed.

"Thank you, God," she whispered. Francina would be so relieved.

Up ahead she could just make out the shape of a car.

"We're almost there," she called to Nomsa and the cameraman, who had both fallen behind, he with his heavy load and she with her strappy sandals that were unsuitable for tramping through the brush.

Fishing her keys out of her pocket, she stepped onto the road and froze. It was not her car, but a small white sedan and there was a man sitting on the hood smoking a cigarette.

"Nice night for a walk," he said.

She nodded. The man got off the hood and reached into his car to turn on the headlights, and it was then that Monica saw his military-style short hair. This was the stranger she had seen loitering outside her office and later inside Mama Dlamini's Eating Establishment. Her gut feeling that he was the man who had broken into her office would not be admissible in a court of law, but she felt certain that she was right. The sound of Nomsa's heavy breathing announced her arrival.

"Hi," said the stranger as Nomsa stepped into the powerful beam from his headlights. He flicked his cigarette onto the road and stamped it out with his shoe. "I'm a real fan of yours."

Monica noted that he said this without the few seconds of recognition required by most people—and the lighting was far from ideal. It was almost as though he had been expecting her.

Nomsa patted her shining face with a tissue. "Thank you."

"And this must be your colleague," he said as the cameraman stepped onto the road.

The cameraman looked to Monica for an introduction and she tried to send a warning with her eyes, but he did not catch it.

"Let me get rid of this heavy equipment," he said, putting his hand out for Monica's keys.

"Are you doing something about golf for *In-Depth?*" asked the stranger. "Or is it an artsy piece about the galleries?"

Monica sensed that he knew it was neither, but Nomsa, through no fault of her own, did not realize that she was being baited.

"It's a piece about the town actually," she explained, "and how that resort up there is trying to take their land."

"Let's go," said Monica, giving her a nudge. "We've got to find my car."

"You only missed it by a hundred yards," said the stranger. He moved toward Nomsa and put out his hand. "I've never met a celebrity before."

With a fixed smile, she touched his fingertips lightly in a semblance of a handshake.

"When can I expect to see this story on TV?" he asked.

"On Wednesday at eight-thirty sharp," Nomsa said. "I'm always on first."

Another dig, thought Monica, who had only once had the lead story. But this was not the time or place to reexamine old wounds.

"That soon?" said the stranger. "I'll make a note of it. Good night." Waving, he climbed into his car and drove off in the direction of the golf resort.

"He could have offered us a lift to your car," grumbled Nomsa as she stopped to remove yet another stone from her sandals.

Monica was grateful that the stranger had left without incident, but she felt an ominous certainty that the man had gone to report every word to Mr. Yang. One week. So much could happen in one week.

❧ Chapter Twenty-Six ❧

The smell of a yesterday, today and tomorrow shrub drifted into Jabulani Cottage, where Francina sat in front of the mirror while her mother piled her head with the full, looping curls of the extensions she'd decided on at the last minute. Monica had planted the shrub to remind herself of the smell of her childhood home, and it had taken at once to Lady Helen's dry air and soil. Not all plants were faring well in the heat wave; the roses David had planted looked like dried beetles. But the tomatoes were thriving.

Tourists were a hardy bunch, too, and last weekend's summer art festival had enjoyed the best attendance ever. Most of them had come to see S.W.'s *Face of a Woman,* which was fresh off an airplane from Paris, where it had hung in a fancy gallery for six months. Francina didn't know what all the fuss was about; Mandla had done paintings that looked more like a real woman.

Up until last night, when strong, gusty winds blew in from the ocean to break the heat wave, Francina had despaired of making it through her wedding without soaking her dress with sweat. When she awoke this morning and felt the cooler air coming through her window, she said a prayer of thanks out loud.

"You look beautiful," said her mother, putting in the final pin.

For the first time in her life, Francina was wearing makeup.

"Thanks to you, Mama," said Francina shyly. "But you better go take your place in the church. And please remind my brothers to tell people to take off their boots. Nobody is to wear muddy boots to my wedding."

Her mother kissed her on the cheek, picked up the beaded turquoise bag that she had bought to match the dress Francina had somehow managed to find time to make for her and hurried outside to where her eldest son was waiting with the engine running.

"Are they comfortable at Abalone House?" asked Monica, waving at the departing car.

"Yes, very," replied Francina.

Monica had arrived to accompany Francina to the church. Reverend van Tonder had kindly loaned the bride his cloakroom so that she wouldn't have to traipse across the mud in her beautiful wedding dress. She and Monica were supposed to be the first ones at the church, but Mandla's stomach had been upset this morning and Francina had insisted on making him her special tea for such complaints. "I want him to enjoy my happy day," she'd said.

Now they would have to risk making the long walk across

the mudflats in the company of the wedding guests. Thanks to Francina's burst of generosity, the entire congregation of the Little Church of the Lagoon was coming, as well as thirty others, including Francina's family, who'd made the long journey from KwaZulu-Natal. Francina knew their group would have been smaller if Kitty had not offered them free accommodation. Nobody had received money from the game lodge yet, as the rondavels were taking longer to build than anticipated.

"The boys are ready," said Monica. "Is there anything I can do for you before we go?"

"Carry my dress, please. I'm so nervous I'll drop it in the mud."

Monica hung the garment bag over her arm as Francina went around Jabulani Cottage saying goodbye to her bathtub, her television, her bed, her view.

"I told you you could take the furniture with you," said Monica.

Francina shook her head. "Thank you, but Hercules has enough."

Francina did not know if she could explain to Monica what she felt. She was saying goodbye to the part of herself that had coped alone for so long and was now going to take a well-earned rest. With one last look around she closed the door, and, if the boys had not been there in their new suits to distract her, she might have ruined her makeup by crying.

"Look at my handsome fellows," she said, and Mandla gave the first smile she had ever seen that might be described as shy.

Francina had wanted them to dress at the church, too,

but Monica thought there wouldn't be enough space and had extracted a promise from Mandla to walk calmly and not splatter his brother with mud by jumping with two feet together. Their navy blue trouser pants were tucked into their rubber boots, and Monica had their shiny new black shoes in her bag.

"An added precaution," said Francina, fishing two disposable plastic rain ponchos from her bag of wedding paraphernalia.

The boys slipped them on and then they all climbed into Monica's car for the trip to the edge of the mudflats.

After an initial moment of panic when she saw the guests already making their way to the church, Francina joked with everyone that she'd had to go back because she'd left the iron on.

Ingrid had stocked her husband's cloakroom with bottles of water, a plate of oatmeal cookies, a selection of makeup, hairsprays, brushes and combs, and a good-luck note. She had been a good sport when Francina told her that she couldn't make her dress for the wedding. Until that time nobody but Monica, Hercules and Oscar had known that she was writing her grade nine exams, but after telling Ingrid the whole town knew. If the pressure had been bad before, it was a whole lot worse with everyone rooting for her.

After the first exam she'd declared that not only had she failed, but she'd also provided enough stupid answers to be made examples of for years to come. Hercules assured her that this would never happen because all the answers were confidential, and she turned around and accused him of not believing in her. It was a stressful time. A man could not hope to say the right thing when a woman was facing important exams, and a short while later her wedding.

Monica was just fastening the final hook and eye on Francina's dress, when there was a soft tapping at the door. It was the bride's father.

"Don't be nervous, Baba," Francina told him. She could tell that he was unsure of his role in this wedding that was unlike any he had attended in his village. "Reverend van Tonder will tell everyone that you're giving me away, but it's only an expression. These people don't believe a man should pay lebola to his father-in-law to make up for the loss of a hardworking daughter."

Her father bowed his head in greeting to Monica. He was clearly uncomfortable with his daughter talking about such private matters in front of her employer.

"You can say whatever you want around Monica," Francina assured him.

But he would not speak until Monica had considerately excused herself to check if the boys were ready to walk down the aisle carrying the rings on velvet pillows. Sipho thought it a silly idea and Mandla had tried to toss one of the rings to the birds, so Monica was keeping them till the very last minute. They were silver, not white gold like the engagement ring, but Francina had not allowed Hercules to spend any more money on jewelry for her humble finger, especially when nobody would be able to tell the difference anyway.

As Francina came out of the cloakroom on her father's arm, Monica placed the rings on the pillows and signaled to the organist to begin. Everyone stood up on the first note, and the boys began their slow, practiced walk down the aisle, with Francina and her father following four paces behind.

Monica slipped into her place behind Francina's family and watched the boys walk toward Reverend van Tonder. Sipho looked straight ahead, but Mandla greeted everyone he passed with a smile or stage whisper. Ella would have laughed.

The cameraman had kindly offered to film the wedding for Francina free of charge. Nomsa had been invited but had declined because she said she needed her rest.

With the windows on both sides of the church open, there was no need for the giant electric fan that had provided relief last Sunday, and the bride would be happy to know that there was not a hint of a shine on her face. The sun was almost overhead, making it difficult to look out the windows on the left of the church, to where the white sand met the ocean. It was a good thing the photographs were to be taken under the trees at Abalone House, or they would be flat and devoid of detail in this unforgiving light. Kitty sat three rows back with James. Because Francina had invited more people than initially planned, she'd decided to forgo the meal at Abalone House in favor of cake and a glass of punch. The immediate families would have dinner together that evening in Hercules and Francina's flat.

The boys stepped forward when Reverend van Tonder asked for the rings, and then slipped into the places Monica had reserved for them beside her.

"Good job," she whispered, and they both smiled.

Francina and Hercules said their vows in strong, clear voices that even the people in the back could hear.

"I now pronounce you man and wife," said Reverend van Tonder. "You may kiss the bride."

Monica knew Hercules had been dreading this public display of affection, but now he leaned in toward Francina with purpose. Just as he'd closed his eyes, ready to make contact, the back doors of the church flew open.

"The bulldozers are here a week early!" shouted Miemps. "And Daphne is on the roof and won't come down!"

As though one body, everybody rose and made a dash for the overflow hall, which was full of muddy boots. Not used to leaving their boots behind, nobody had thought to put them in any sort of order for purposes of identification, and now there was a mad trying-on until people found a pair, any pair, that fit. Then one by one, like triathletes in a changeover, they took off inland across the mudflats toward the little settlement of Sandpiper Drift with the cameraman filming their every step.

Monica rushed immediately to Francina, but there was no need to console her.

"It's okay, we have plenty of time for kissing now that we're married. Go and help Daphne. I'll keep the boys."

Leaving the bride's family to find a way to get the newly married couple across the mud to have their photographs taken at Abalone House, Monica took the last boots left—a pair that was two sizes too small—and raced to join the rest of the town.

One of the bulldozers had already rammed the DeVilli- erses' house, causing a crack to open up in the front wall. Monica watched as the driver reversed and tried again. It seemed that he was not prepared for the resistance the strong stone walls offered, and he had to stop and rub his neck before trying a third time. The other bulldozer had rammed the front door of Daphne's house once, but it could not try again because Miemps was blocking its path.

"Don't hurt my daughter," she screamed at the driver.

He looked in the direction of a pickup truck that had accompanied them on this mission, and eventually a man got out. It was the guard Monica had met at the golf resort.

"Mr. Yang is paying good money for these properties, Mam," he said.

"No, he isn't," shouted Daphne from on top of the roof.

The guard looked at the papers in his hand.

Please, God, prayed Monica, don't let anyone do anything rash. And please save these people's homes.

There was a crash as the front wall of the DeVillierses' house gave way, and then a splintering sound as the rafters that had held up the zinc roof followed suit. In another three maneuvers the house was a pile of stones, whitewashed stucco and warped metal.

"You'll have to kill me before you do that to my home," screamed Daphne.

The guard looked at his papers again, as though searching for a subclause that would lay out his course of action if there happened to be a person on top of one of the houses.

"Get down, Daphne," begged Miemps. "A house is not worth it."

"It's not just the house they want to crush, Ma. It's our rights as human beings."

"Daphne, listen to your mother and come down," commanded Reg, but his attempt at sternness failed.

Content with his victory over the Devillierses' house, the driver moved to the one that belonged to the caretaker of Green Block School.

"No," shouted the caretaker's wife. She disappeared around the back and returned with a ladder. Then she, too, climbed onto the roof of her home.

The driver of the bulldozer looked at the guard in consternation.

"Get down, lady," shouted the guard.

The caretaker's wife shook her head and sat down.

"Congratulations, Sissie," shouted Daphne.

A small titter of approval ran through the crowd. The guard said something into his walkie-talkie.

"Just you wait," he said, wagging his finger, first at Daphne and then at the caretaker's wife.

He looked about wildly as the crowd started to roar, and what he saw made him scream into his walkie-talkie for backup. One by one, the women of the neighborhood were climbing onto their husbands' shoulders and then onto the roofs of their homes. It was a good old-fashioned sit-in—at a slightly higher elevation than usual.

Nomsa arrived on foot, wearing a sheen of sweat and a thunderous look because she'd missed the action.

A troop of security guards from the golf resort turned up in a company truck and taunted the women with threats of arrest and bodily harm. But they held their tongues when the only response they got was laughter. The cameraman never stopped filming and Monica took pictures with the camera she'd taken along to the wedding.

The guards retreated to their vehicle but did not leave, and eventually the crowd heard the *thwack-thwack* of an approaching helicopter. The whirring blades churned up a sandstorm that stung their eyes and left them coughing and choking. Mr. Yang jumped out before it had even touched down.

"Get down or I will be forced to report this to the government," he yelled, waving a sheaf of papers at the women. He turned toward Nomsa's microphone. "A deal is a deal. A diamond was found on the land, so it reverts to the government. And it's the government's business if they choose to sell it to me. I don't have to give these people anything if I don't want to. They should be grateful for my generosity."

"There are no diamonds here," said the caretaker of Green Block School.

"That's where you're wrong, my friend. One of your own neighbors found one not too far from here."

Everybody started to talk at once. Please, God, prayed Monica, don't let him name names.

"Now, get down and let my men get on with their work."

Mr. Yang flinched as something hit him on the back. It was a lady's shoe. Then another one hit him on the arm, and soon all the women were removing their shoes and flinging them at him. Instead of running, he shielded his head with his arms and allowed himself to be pelted. When the women had no shoes left to throw, he lowered his arms and addressed them in a firm voice.

"Tomorrow I will be back with the police."

Everybody found a space to hide in the houses as his helicopter took off. For some this was the first time they'd ever set foot in Sandpiper Drift, and now here they were, squeezed between a toilet and a shower, trying to escape a sandstorm.

After the air had cleared, the townsfolk went to work setting up a roster to cook meals for the women, and Monica
dashed to the one-hour photo shop. While her film was
being developed she drove to Abalone House, where Francina, Hercules and their families had just finished their session with the photographer, and the punch was growing
warm and the icing on the cake was beginning to melt.
Monica was explaining what had happened, when the wind-
blown and dusty guests began to arrive.

"I have to go somewhere," she whispered to Francina.
"I'm really sorry. And I don't want to make the boys miss
the reception, too, so I'll ask Kitty to keep them until I
get back."

"They'll stay with me—I mean us," said Francina.

"I may be back late."

"Never mind."

Monica kissed her on the cheek, and Francina flapped her
hand at her, just as Ella had always done.

Luckily, the road was quiet and she made it to Bloubergstrand in an hour. This time the guard did not want to let
her in.

"I've been given orders," he told her.

She didn't know whether to go away and wait until he fell
asleep, as the little boy she'd met had done, or to ask him
to pass the envelope of photographs on to Lizbet. Somehow
she felt God telling her to trust this man.

"Fine, I'll give them to her when she comes home this evening," he said.

"Don't give them to her husband," Monica reminded him.

When she returned to Lady Helen, Kitty was serving dinner to two tables of French tourists, and there was no sign that a wedding reception had taken place at Abalone House that afternoon.

"They've gone back to Hercules's flat," said Kitty. "I mean Hercules and Francina's flat."

Hearing these words, Monica felt a pang of sadness. She and Francina had been together for twenty-two years. And now Francina had left and would never again be mere steps away.

Monica found them all eating the beef stew and ratatouille Mrs. Shabalala had prepared the day before in anticipation of the celebratory gathering. Mandla and Sipho looked up and waved when she walked in the door, but then went back to listening to a story that was being told by one of Francina's nephews.

"Sit down," said Francina, and Hercules gave her his chair and fetched a stool for himself from the kitchen.

Francina's mother and father smiled at her politely, and her brother, the game ranger, shook her hand, while the other brother gave a cheery wave.

"How are your accommodations?" asked Monica. It sounded formal and she was acutely aware of having broken up a happy party.

"Beautiful," said Francina's sister-in-law. "We're taking tips for our game lodge."

"My wife will be in charge of the restaurant," explained Dingane. "The women are still arguing over who will be in charge of housekeeping. I offered it to my sister but she turned me down—for a good reason, I'm glad to say."

He slapped his new brother-in-law on the back and they all laughed, Sipho and Mandla included.

Monica looked at her boys, so at ease with this family, and for the first time since her arrival she realized that she was the only white person present. Was she depriving Sipho and Mandla of their own culture? She'd promised their father, Themba, as he lay dying, that they'd keep up their language, but they hardly ever spoke it now. And they were always subjected to her taste in music, food, books and television. Would they one day resent her for this? Maybe it was time for her to take Sotho lessons.

People took turns to climb up onto the roofs and watch over the women as they slept. A fall from that height would break an ankle at the very least. They built a fire in the middle of the road where the driver of one of the bulldozers had dug a hole just for spite, and throughout the night people arrived with blankets, guitars, cookies and flasks of hot tea.

In the morning, the women brushed their teeth and washed their faces in buckets, and called across to each other as they enjoyed a breakfast of pancakes, homemade muesli, muffins and freshly squeezed juice—made by who else but Kitty and delivered by James in the back of his truck. As he was walking back with the empty trays, James became aware of someone following him and turned around. Monica watched Sipho trying to do as he had been told. After a few excruciating minutes Monica was relieved to see James shake his hand. It was the perfect response; Sipho would have endured a hug as though it were penance, instead of the beginnings, hopefully, of a friendship.

Lady Helen's two policemen arrived as the ten o'clock

tea mugs were being cleared away. They shuffled and conferred in whispers and were clearly most uncomfortable with the situation.

"Unless Mr. Yang calls off his theft of our properties," Daphne told them, "you'll have to climb up here and carry us down yourselves."

But they clearly had no intention of doing that and hurriedly left to interview Mr. Yang.

For the rest of the day the women sat up on the roofs holding umbrellas to shade themselves from the harsh summer sun, and singing protest songs from the apartheid era. Nomsa climbed up to interview Daphne, but the height clearly bothered her and she didn't interview anybody else.

At around five o'clock Daphne complained of feeling dizzy.

"Get down this minute," her father commanded her, and when she would not budge he ran to the hospital to get Zak.

It was heatstroke, Zak said after examining her, and she needed to take in more fluids and try to keep cool.

"You hear that, girl?" said Reg. "He says come down."

"It'll cool down when the sun sets," said Daphne.

Monica searched Zak's face for a sign of any change but there was none. He noticed her staring and smiled. Mortified at being caught out and even more so by the blush she felt spreading over her face, she quickly busied herself taking water up to one of the other women.

After promising to check on Daphne later, Zak went back to the hospital.

Daphne went to sleep and Monica climbed onto the roof to watch over her. Reg and Miemps had taken turns the night before, but at their age it was not wise to be scaling any heights.

Max arrived at eight and asked Monica if she realized that by climbing the ladder she had become part of the news.

"Yes, Max," she told him.

It hurt his neck to talk to her up there, so he left shortly afterward. Monica could not tell if he was pleased or not, but for the first time since meeting him she was not concerned. She knew that what she was doing was right.

At nine Zak climbed onto the roof and checked Daphne's vital signs. She did not wake up and he said that she was doing better and should not be disturbed.

"There's something I've been meaning to tell you," he whispered to Monica.

Someone at the fire picked up a guitar and the women on the roof began to sing softly. It was so perfect Monica wanted to laugh.

She looked at Daphne, who lay with her head on the pillow her mother had brought up onto the roof. It was the first time she'd ever seen her looking peaceful.

"I'm glad you came to Lady Helen—we all are," said Zak. "I would say that you fit in well, but you do more than fit in. You make things better."

"I'm glad we came, too. Thanks for sending me the advertisement for the job."

"Your bosses in Johannesburg made a huge mistake."

Monica was taken aback. She had not told him, or anyone in town, that she hadn't been offered a permanent job on *In-Depth* because the editors and producers hadn't liked her story on the burn unit. Maybe it was her turn now to reveal her knowledge of *his* secret.

"What a perfect night," he said.

He was right: too perfect to ruin with talk of infidelity and divorce.

"Have you ever walked past the resort?" he asked.

"No, I've always been wary of going onto their stretch of the beach."

"It's not theirs. Never will be. The beach belongs to everybody. A mile past the resort there's a shipwreck very close to shore. At low tide you can walk out to it."

She wondered if he was about to ask her to go with him one day and tried to compose herself for a calm reply. But it was not necessary.

"Take care tonight," he told her in a gentle voice as he stood up to go.

"I will."

She watched him climb down the ladder and jump off the last rung. He said a few words to the guitar player and then was gone.

It was too soon. She realized that now. But one day it would not be.

The neighbors kept the fire burning the whole night, not because the women needed warmth but as a sign of solidarity. Monica lay down between Daphne and the edge of the roof and looked up at the stars. At around midnight an owl started a low, mournful cry. There were no trees nearby, and after looking around, Monica decided that it had to be perched alongside one of the sleeping women.

She prayed that the guard had managed to give the photographs to Lizbet and that they would touch her heart. When she started to feel sleepy, she sat up and took deep breaths of the salty breeze coming off the ocean. She hoped that Mandla and Sipho were sleeping soundly on the sofa in Francina and Hercules's flat.

As the sky over the koppies started to lighten, she noticed a dark car speeding down the winding road toward Lady Helen. Please, God, let that be who I think it is, she prayed.

Ten minutes later the car pulled up in front of the fire.

"It's Lizbet," called Miemps, who had been cooking porridge in a large three-legged pot over the fire.

There were sleepy calls of greeting from the women on the rooftops.

"Thank you," said Lizbet, accepting a mug of coffee from her old friend.

The men and children of the neighborhood came out of their houses to see who the visitor was. From her vantage point on the roof, Monica could see Reverend van Tonder leading a procession toward them for a sunrise service.

Lizbet deflected the questions about her new house in Bloubergstrand and asked, instead, for an update on what was happening here. When she'd heard it, she walked over to where her house had once stood and bent down to pick up a handful of broken stucco. There were tears in her eyes when she stood up.

"My friends," she said, "I am here to make a confession."

Reverend van Tonder and the townsfolk reached the campfire. Nomsa, who had accompanied them, hurried to the front.

For an instant it seemed as though Lizbet might not speak another word with Nomsa's microphone six inches from her face, but then she looked past it, at the expectant faces of her friends, and continued in a faltering voice:

"I thought my husband had won the money for our new

house. I know that gambling is a sin, but God tells us to love the sinner and hate the sin. And I love my husband. But I should not have taken a house bought with money won at cards." She started to cry and Miemps made a move to hug her, but Lizbet held her at arm's length. "But last night I got the truth from my husband, and it's much worse."

For a while she could not speak because she was sobbing so much. In silence, everybody waited for her to explain what she had meant. Finally, she blew her nose.

"Mr. Yang gave my husband a diamond and paid him a lot of money to say he'd discovered it here in the sand."

There was a sharp, collective intake of breath from the crowd. Monica scrambled down from the roof and went to stand at Lizbet's side.

"Please forgive my husband," pleaded Lizbet. "He's not a bad man. He just had a moment of weakness."

"He was prepared to watch us lose our homes," shouted one of the men.

If Lizbet had an answer she was too distraught to give it. Monica put an arm around her shoulders.

"You're a brave woman," she whispered.

Miemps put an arm around Lizbet's waist and she and Monica both held on until Lizbet's sobs had subsided.

"Can a person be sent to prison for lying to a government official?" whispered Lizbet.

Monica did not know how much she should say at this point. The answer was yes, because in this case it was more than lying; it was fraud.

Instead of answering the question, Monica asked if Lizbet needed a place to stay for a while. But Lizbet wanted to go home to try and persuade her husband that she had done the right thing. People patted Lizbet on the back and said thank-you as she climbed into her car, but there was no triumph or relief on her face, just misery.

After everybody had watched Lizbet's car disappear over the koppies, Reverend van Tonder began his service. He said a prayer of thanks to the Lord for saving the houses and asked that God open Mr. DeVilliers's heart to what his wife would tell him. Then he started to sing:

"God is good…"

The man with the guitar joined in, and soon everybody else had, too. And then, one by one, the women climbed down from the rooftops into the waiting arms of their families.

"Enough hugging," announced Daphne. "We have unfinished business with someone up there." She thumbed in the direction of the golf course.

"No, Daphne, please," begged Miemps. "It could be dangerous."

Daphne put an arm around her mother. "What's he going to do, Ma? Order his thugs to shoot us?" She raised her voice. "You're all coming with me, aren't you?"

A chorus of assent went up around her.

"And it will be on tape, won't it?" Daphne looked at Nomsa, who was already nodding wildly.

"We're not staying behind," said Reg, grabbing hold of his wife's hand.

Miemps looked up at him with admiration and gave a stoic nod.

"Well, let's go then," shouted Daphne, and the crowd cheered.

With her limp Monica found it hard to keep up with Daphne in the front and kept pace instead with Miemps and Reg.

When the golf resort was in sight, Daphne turned around and put her finger to her lips.

"Keep quiet," she instructed everybody.

"How are we going to get past that guard?" asked Monica. "I've had problems with him before."

"Follow me," commanded Daphne and she led the crowd away from the main entrance, in the opposite direction from the beach.

They walked in the shadow of the high wall, not talking, even though Nomsa was trying her best to get someone to describe the situation on tape. Daphne had become their leader and she had told them to remain quiet.

They followed the wall until it made a curve northward. By then the older people had begun to show signs of fatigue and everybody was thirsty. But when Daphne told them that they still had a distance to go, nobody complained.

Twenty minutes later, Daphne stopped.

"This is the place," she said. "We have to surprise Mr. Yang or he'll fly out of here in his helicopter like the pathetic vulture that he is."

She retrieved an old wooden crate from behind a large boulder, placed it next to the wall and used it to give herself a leg up.

Monica's suspicions were confirmed; Daphne had been Mr. Yang's unwelcome visitor all along.

As Daphne straddled the top of the wall, she whispered loudly, "We're in line with the administrative wing of the golf resort. If you follow me, we can go in the back way and nobody will see us until it's too late."

Some of the men climbed over first to check for danger, while others stayed behind to help the women over. Miemps, who had not uttered a word of protest up till then, told her husband that this was as far as she would go. Two other older women agreed that it would be impossible for them to scale the wall and so they decided that they would stay on the outside to watch for Mr. Yang's men.

"Go and keep an eye on our daughter," Miemps instructed her husband when he said he would stay behind with her. "I've never seen her like this."

Inside the golf resort, Daphne led the crowd of residents from Sandpiper Drift toward a grove of palm trees that had been planted to hide a tangle of electrical boxes and air-conditioning units.

"Our next target is the staff quarters up ahead," she said, pointing at a two-story building with balconies. "A few of the workers' wives will be about, but they won't interfere with us. They're on our side."

Daphne was absolutely correct. A woman hanging bright white diapers on a clothesline waved at them, and another, who was teaching a toddler to ride a tricycle, gave them the thumbs-up.

Thirty yards ahead of them, Daphne and the crowd saw the back entrance of the administration building.

"Let's keep going, friends," said Daphne, her voice unusually high pitched.

When she reached the building, she waited until Nomsa

and the cameraman had caught up with her. And then she threw open the glass door and marched in.

Everybody squeezed through the doorway and crowded the hallway.

Up ahead, they heard Daphne shout, "There he is! Stop him!" and they surged forward to encircle Mr. Yang, who was trying to make his getaway into the main club.

The cameraman zoomed in on Mr. Yang's bewildered expression and Nomsa stuck a microphone in his face.

Mr. Yang looked around in desperation.

"We know all about your diamond," Daphne told him gleefully. "It's on tape."

"Call security," Mr. Yang yelled to his secretary, who was cowering behind her desk.

The woman caught Monica's eye.

"Call them!" screamed Mr. Yang.

Although her face showed fear, the secretary shook her head.

"You may as well give yourself up to the police," Daphne shouted at Mr. Yang. "Tomorrow night the whole country is going to know that you tried to steal our land."

Mr. Yang attempted to push his way through the crowd, but everyone closed ranks, and even with his broad shoulders and muscular arms he made no progress against the determination of the people whose anger gave them a strength they had not known they possessed.

At the back of the crowd came yelps of outrage and pain and Monica turned to see Mr. Yang's security guards using batons to clear a path to their employer.

"Stop!" she screamed at them, and the cameraman swung around to capture the scene.

Mr. Yang used the diversion to try and make his escape out the back door, but Daphne blocked his way.

"You'll have to kill me with your bare hands before I let you go," she snarled.

Mr. Yang made a motion toward her, but she clung to the door handle as though her life depended on it.

The hallway was suddenly filled with the familiar sound of an approaching helicopter. Emboldened by the arrival of his means of escape, Mr. Yang gave Daphne an almighty push that sent her crashing to the floor.

She scrambled to her feet, but by the time she was out the door he was swinging himself up into the helicopter.

"Fly away," she shouted, shaking her fist at him. "But on Wednesday night, when *In-Depth* airs, everyone will know the truth."

❧ Chapter Twenty-Seven ❧

Francina's unobstructed view of the koppies might have gone, but the breeze that the second-floor flat caught when the windows on both sides were open was a worthy consolation, as was the small triangle of ocean she saw at the end of the street when she went out onto the balcony to water her tomato plants.

A full week had not passed since the wedding, and yet the new little family had already found a natural rhythm that made each of them happy to return home from work. Whenever Francina came across Mrs. Shabalala stirring a pot on the stove, she would be reminded of her childhood and her mother's constant company that she had missed for too many years. It was easy and comfortable with her mother-in-law, and Hercules seemed pleased that the two women in his life got on so well.

But despite being a wonderful cook and keeping everything cleaner than even Francina herself could, Mrs. Shabalala's talents downstairs were not as obvious. Francina never said anything, but she often had to unpick the hems her mother-in-law had sewed because they were too untidy to present to a client, and sometimes she would be ready to stitch together an outfit her mother-in-law had cut out, only to find that she had two fronts and no back, or a flared skirt when the client wanted a fitted one. At present she was not saving Francina any time, and on the occasions when Francina had to buy additional fabric because of an error in the pattern layout, she was costing her money.

Monica was taking the boys to see her parents in Italy over Christmas, and Francina planned to use those three weeks to teach her mother-in-law the correct way to put a dress together. It wasn't her fault that she made mistakes; she'd never made a formal dress in her life. You can't put a person in a new job and expect them to master it overnight. Look how long it was taking the new government to get to work fighting the AIDS epidemic.

Francina's clients had all commented on Mrs. Shabalala's friendly nature. Yes, the measurements she took weren't always accurate, but keeping people happy was more than half the battle and she would learn quickly when taught.

On this specific morning Francina found cause for dissatisfaction with her own work. There was no uniformity in her hemstitches, which were either overzealous and showed on the right side of the garment or too tight and made the fabric pucker. Her fingers felt like fat bananas and her mind would not stay on the job, which was a black silk and chiffon dress for Doreen Olifant, who was being awarded a medal at the National Librarians' Association ball in Cape

Town for the best library in the small-town category. Francina did not usually like to work with black, but the clear, bright natural light in Lady Helen not only helped artists, it enabled a one-eyed seamstress to expand her color palette to include jet black, night-sky black, and her own personal favorite, blacker than black.

It was the last day of the school year, and Monica had taken Mandla to work with her so that Francina could have the day off, as Mr. D. would be putting the list of exam results up outside his office at noon. Hercules planned to meet her there shortly beforehand—for moral support, he'd said. The aroma of the surprise lunch her mother-in-law was preparing had been drifting downstairs all morning. There was no mistaking beef simmering in a sauce spiced with cardamom, turmeric, red pepper, coriander, cumin and cloves. It was the dish she and Hercules had eaten on their first date in the tiny restaurant in Pongola. Francina wondered if her mother-in-law would also add turmeric to the rice to make it yellow.

Unlike Monica, who never gave herself a break for not being perfect, Francina was not afraid of failure. She had often wondered what made them different in this respect, and her latest conclusion was that it was ego. Monica's was big and majestic like an elephant, but if it fell, it fell hard. Hers was small, common and hardy like an impala. Who would have thought that she, the daughter of a subsistence farmer, would have compassion for a rich white woman with a university education?

Tucked away under the cash register was a beautiful pewter frame she'd bought at the church market. Much as she pretended to be calm about the whole thing, she couldn't help thinking how good the certificate would look in that frame on the shop wall for all her clients to see. Maybe her ego wasn't a puny little impala after all.

Whether she passed or not, today was a day for celebration and thanksgiving to God. Early this morning, at a time when farmers, truck drivers and raggedy newspaper boys were the only ones awake, rain had begun to fall, not over the Western Cape, where it only rained in winter, but over the rest of the entire country.

Francina put down Doreen's dress, tidied up the shop and called upstairs to her mother-in-law to tell her that she was leaving to meet Hercules. Before setting off, she looked up at the letters the sign writer had outlined in masking tape on the display window. They were straight and solid—like herself—with a wavy line underneath to add a touch of elegance. Elsewhere in the world there were businessmen who could call towering skyscrapers their own, but she did not believe that their feelings of satisfaction could be any greater than her own. The Lord had truly blessed her.

Nothing would change if she had not passed, but Hercules and Oscar would feel as though they had failed her, and that was not true. In their own different ways, both of them had taught her more than she had ever thought possible.

Hercules was talking to a group of students when she arrived, and she noted with pride and pleasure the respectful way they looked at him. The bright children had already figured out that he was a steady, wise man, who was worthy of their trust. The rest of them would learn that there were more important attributes in a teacher than dramatics and entertaining high jinks. When Hercules became aware of her presence, he excused himself and walked over to where she stood. Francina was conscious of the students' stares as he took her arm. She didn't mean to grin like a crazed donkey, but somehow she just couldn't help herself.

There was a crowd waiting outside the office. When Mr. D. came out at noon on the dot, it fell silent.

"It's not that bad, people," he said.

There were nervous giggles from the fifteen-year-olds, none of whom would be leaving school, even though they were entitled to if they had passed.

Francinca and Hercules waited until they had all checked the list before stepping forward.

"You look," said Francina.

Hercules shook his head. "You did all the work."

Francina found her name and ran her finger across to see the marks for each of the six subjects. Next to every one of them was a pass mark, not a spectacular one, but a sound pass. She felt Hercules slip his arm around her waist and squeeze.

"Congratulations," he said. "I knew you'd do it."

For a reason that was still not clear to her, Francina looked back over her shoulder when they were some distance away from the school. A solitary man stood at the notice board. She couldn't see his face, but from his height and clothing she could tell it was Oscar. This afternoon, after the celebratory lunch, she would go to his house and thank him. It might not put things right between them, but it would be a start.

It was Sipho's final day of school before the summer vacation. Cup in hand, Monica paced up and down outside the meeting room where Max had been working for almost a year. On her way over to show him her copy, Dudu had asked if she wanted tea, and Monica had accepted gratefully.

After Nomsa's report for *In-Depth* aired on Wednesday night, Mr. Yang and Mr. DeVilliers were arrested by Cape Town police. Three hours into their interrogation the police went out and picked up Pieter van Jaarsveld, the government man, as well. From the scant information Monica had been able to glean from the Lady Helen policemen, Pieter van Jaarsveld had taken a bribe from Mr. Yang to sell him as much land as he wanted for his new golf course. Although it would not come out until the trial, Monica thought it likely that Mr. Yang had not been the only manipulator in this deal and that Pieter van Jaarsveld had taken his own cut from the price Mr. Yang had paid the government for the land.

"Stop walking, you're making me nervous," called Max. "Come in and sit down."

How quickly they could revert to the old status quo. He might as well take his old office back, too. Her story lay on his desk.

"You have an interesting approach to work," he said.

"By interesting you mean flawed?"

"You broke an important rule of journalism—the one that says we should always be objective."

"So you do mean flawed?" Now she wished she had not told him about her trips to Bloubergstrand.

"Monica, let's face the truth here."

Was it possible for him to fire her now, after he had supposedly retired?

Max inched forward in his chair and then used his cane to pull himself up. Monica watched and waited. She had learned that he would not accept any help. When he had steadied himself he walked over to the window and looked out at the lunchtime activity on Main Street. The tables outside Mama Dlamini's Eating Establishment were already full.

"This is not Johannesburg or Cape Town—thank goodness for that. The rules you learned in your journalism class at university can be bent here. It's the people who count, and frankly, my dear, I don't know what would have happened had you not intervened."

Monica could think of nothing to say except, "So you're not firing me?"

Max laughed. "How could I fire you? You're the boss. And you've been most patient with an old man who can't seem to let go."

She felt a lump in her throat. "I need you, Max."

He smiled. "No, you don't. And it's high time I retired for real. Sipho is a masterful teacher. I'm ready to tackle my memoirs on that computer."

"You don't have to leave."

"You're a good person, Monica, but I need to. I'm confident that I'm leaving the paper in competent hands."

"Can I come and see you if I need advice?"

"You will never stop trying to make an old man feel useful, will you? Now get out of here and go and spend the afternoon with your boys. It's my final piece of advice."

Monica picked up her story and paused at Max's side. "Thanks, Max, for everything."

"We're fortunate to have you here in Lady Helen, Monica. I mean that."

* * *

It was hot on the beach, so they sat on the grass in the small circular shade of a palm tree and ate the sandwiches Monica had packed that morning. Sipho's school day had ended at noon; he had a month off before the new school year started in January. Mandla got up and cheered as a solitary windsurfer raced across the water close to shore. It was hard to believe that they would soon be bundled up in winter coats. Her parents had sent them plane tickets and they would be spending Christmas and New Year's together. Sipho and Mandla were praying for snow.

Other families had had the same idea to come down to the park for an end-of-year picnic, and soon Mandla was going from group to group to say hello and check what was on the menu for lunch.

"Come back," called Monica, but the mothers, all of whom she knew from school or church, waved and said, "He's fine."

When he had completed his investigation he returned to announce that he, too, was ready for big school.

"I'm glad to hear that because you'll be starting nursery school when we get back from Italy."

"Can Nonno and Nonna come home with us?"

It was the innocent sort of remark four-year-olds made all the time, yet it was a brilliant idea. Jabulani Cottage was empty. If they could be persuaded to come for a few months—and that wouldn't be too difficult to accomplish—they might never leave. What was it that Gift said on the day they first met? "Once you've discovered Lady Helen you always come back."

Another person would be coming back, although not entirely willingly. Mr. DeVilliers was being forced to give up his mansion in Bloubergstrand and rebuild his old house. He was escaping prison by agreeing to be a witness for the state, but the residents of Sandpiper Drift would monitor all his actions now and no late-night visitors would be allowed.

Understandably, Zukisa's family had not come back. Before going to Italy, Monica would drive down to Cape Town to check on them.

"We'll see what Nonno and Nonna say about coming home with us."

As she and the boys walked back into town for ice cream, they stopped at Jabulani Dressmakers and found Francina directing Hercules where to hammer in the nail that would hang her grade nine certificate.

"Right there," suggested Mandla, pointing to the spot next to a photo of her family standing before the newly finished rondavels at Jabulani Safari Lodge.

"I don't think there's enough space, my baby," said Francina, slipping him one of the wrapped chocolates reserved for clients.

"How about there, next to the fitting room?" said Sipho. "Then, when people go in to get their measurements taken, they'll know they're in good hands."

Hercules held the framed certificate next to the fitting-room door.

"Perfect," said Francina.

"We're off to get ice cream," said Monica. "Would you like to join us?"

Francina looked at the half-finished dress in her hands and then at Mandla's expectant face.

"What a great idea," she said, putting down the dress. "Mama!" she called up the stairs. "Come and get ice cream with us."

As the group walked to the ice-cream store, Monica caught a glimpse of their reflection in a gallery window. God truly worked in mysterious ways. One news story had cost her a job and led to an increase in the population of Lady Helen by six people. In a small town six people could make a real difference over a lifetime. She watched Francina and Hercules swing Mandla between them, and Sipho take Mrs. Shabalala's arm as they crossed the street. Her expedition to find a better life for the boys had taken on new traveling partners. They'd all left their beloved homes to be with each other. Under any other circumstances they might not have shared more than a greeting or a comment on the weather, but now they were connected, and because of this they would support each other in the routine of everyday life as well as in trying times. This is what families did. And the boys would be far better off because of it.

In the distance, the koppies were pink with a covering of trumpet-lilies that seemed to have appeared overnight. A car towing a silver trailer down the winding road had stopped so its occupants could admire the view. Monica remembered the stormy day they'd made the same journey, when Francina had wondered what sort of hole in the mud she was bringing her to. They'd looked out from the same place where that car was now and had seen nothing. Her future had once been like that. But now she saw where she was going, and sometimes she, too, liked to stop and admire the view.

* * * * *

QUESTIONS FOR DISCUSSION

1. The strong underlying force of this novel is the relationship between Monica and Francina. Discuss their relationship. Is it a true friendship? Is it based on equality? For those who have read *The Road to Home,* how has this relationship evolved since Monica's carjacking?

2. From the opening of the book, Monica is drawn to the beauty of the town of Lady Helen. "With the sun reflecting off the green, blue and deep red tin roofs, the whole town had a bright glow, almost like a halo." Monica is experiencing unexpected pitfalls in her new role as adoptive mother and in her career, and she believes that the solution lies in moving to Lady Helen. If you had been Monica's friend, would you have advised her to make the move or to try and solve her problems at home?

3. One of the major themes of the story is transformation. "Driving past the giant fish-canning factories on the industrial outskirts of Cape Town—the very factories that had once stolen Lady Helen's men—Monica could not help thinking that if a whole town could reinvent itself, so then could she. It wouldn't be easy, but with God's help it could be done. Now she prayed for Him to touch Sipho's heart and make him understand that change could be a wonderful thing, if only he would allow it to happen." Monica buys a new house and takes on a new career. To what extent does the theme of transformation go beyond these tangible developments? Discuss the ways in which you think Monica is transformed in terms of her relationship with her children, with Francina, her openness to a new romantic relationship, her attitude toward figures of authority and the people of Lady Helen. How is Francina transformed?

4. Another of the major themes is that of belonging. Doreen the librarian tells Monica that "only an outsider can tell the truth." Later on, when a book of matches arrives in the mail, Oscar tells Francina, "We don't need trouble from outsiders in Lady Helen." When Francina's brother asks her to return to the Valley of a Thousand Hills to work on the village's game lodge, she decides that "she would not be an outsider

in this place for another twenty years. Even if she never owned any land of her own, this place would be home from now on..." Discuss this theme as it relates to Monica and Francina. After a visit to Lizbet in Bloubergstrand, Monica suspects that she is no longer an outsider in Lady Helen. What leads to this change in her position in the town?

5. The town of Lady Helen is "squeezed between the koppies and the Atlantic Ocean." Francina sits on the veranda swing watching the gardener across the street. "In the distance she could see the strange rocky koppies that were so unlike the rolling hills near her home, but for some reason made her feel safe because they seemed to be guarding the little town." Lady Helen seems secure and idyllic, and so it is shocking when a group of men attacks David. What do you think the author's intention is with this scene? What is the significance of malevolent outsiders entering the town?

6. The new government of South Africa seems to be making progress in improving the lives of impoverished citizens. List the developments and events in this book that exemplify this.

7. Of Lady Helen and its residents, Monica says, "It was the future Ella had imagined and wished for, yet had not lived to see." What does she mean by this? Later on she wonders, "If people were confident that they could feed, clothe and educate their families, were they less inclined to find fault with the differences they saw in people of another race?" Do you think that this is the key to the harmonious race relations in Lady Helen? Is it valid for any town or place?

8. Going home for a visit, Francina "began to feel the familiar snake in her stomach that couldn't get comfortable. This was her land, these were her people, but it seemed that Winston had changed that forever with a mouth full of poisonous lies." Discuss the inequitable relationship between Francina and her ex-husband. Do you get a sense that it is typical of the relationships between men and women in the village? Why has her family never spoken about what her husband did to her? How does Francina go about changing the status quo and restoring her dignity? How is her relationship with Hercules different?

9. During her first visit to Lady Helen, Monica is impressed with Zak when, although overworked and tired, he stays on to wash and dress newborn twins. "She sensed that although his caring attitude seemed special to her, it was actually typical for Lady Helen, where every patient or customer or person waiting in line behind you was someone you knew and would meet again tomorrow or the next day." Discuss the relevance of this line to the entire story. Do you think that it is possible for people to have the same caring attitude in a large city?

10. Throughout the story, we are constantly reminded of Sipho and Mandla's biological mother, Ella. Discuss the different ways in which Monica, Sipho, Mandla and Francina deal with her absence.

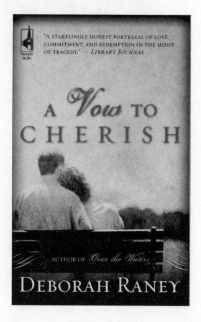

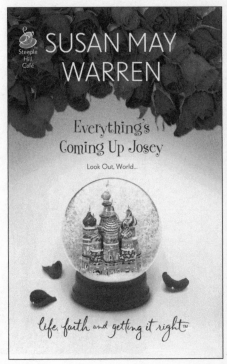